ALIEN MOBSTER

Jozeph Picasso's Alien Trilogy
Act 3
Filmmaking Adventures

Karl J. Niemiec

ALIEN MOBSTER

Find Jozeph Picasso's Alien Trilogy apparel and gear at: LapTopPublishing.com

Alien Trilogy
LapTopPublishing.com

LapTopPublishing.com
Carmel, Indiana 46033

ISBN 978-0-9833663-2-4

FOR THOSE WHO DIDN'T MAKE IT OUT

Based on real Hollywood adventures

When face to face with yourself,
the trick is in which life you live

Jozeph Picasso

PROLOGUE

Given the gravity of the moment, I hope this isn't my final confession for the horrible things they make me do on their behalf. For I, Jozeph Picasso, Alien Mobster, do humbly admit that my violent and despicable actions are being controlled by Aliens.

Only, it's not working out so well.

The scent of burning Java-Logs from designer Frazer Park Mountain log cabins stifles the air. I'm covered to my eyelids in frozen snow-slush, staring up at foreboding night clouds above the trees. Their rims glow wild from a fool's moon.

Mother Nature is freeze-drying me with her steady icy flake onslaught, kindly mummifying me before I'm eaten by an Alien enhanced werewolf. Yes, I hear the words rattle around in my skull. It's a true Humanimalia crime study unfolding before me.

You bastard, Mook. How could you leave me in these mountains alone to kill a cold-bloodedly monster-strong, hairy, wolf-like man-thing? With a set of gnarly white teeth and claws so full of razor sharp nails, that they allow him to scale anything at will, bounding like a cartoon villain from tree to tree. A real Alien werewolf! Just thinking it congregates images of my childhood watching old Universal B Movies. Me shivering in endless back-lake hotel rooms waiting for Pop to come off the ice so we could trade what he caught for other foods. But this is no movie. This is as real as a horror-able life gets. I'm fighting for my life in immense bloodletting pain. Hiding from a thing so supernatural and scary I actually soiled myself.

Add freezing to my misery since my ski jacket is half torn away. I'm freezing to death because I missed it. I missed with the only Alien enhanced laser guided silver bullet shot I took before he bit my arm in two and took the gun from me. Missed slightly I should say, because I hit the bastard good. I just missed his heart by that much.

Not a bad shot considering I was on the run, slipping and sliding, nearly shooting over my shoulder. The bullet passed right through him without hitting his heart and killing him. Hit or miss, it's a matter of inches that can make or take one's career in this town. In my case, it's my newfound fandangle showbiz life.

This werewolf has me dead to right. I've lost this round fair and square. I'm a lunar eclipse as we humans go. I'm about to pass into never-happeness. Because the unfortunate part is that Dr. James Elwartowski, aka Alien Werewolf from another solar system, has already bitten me. It grabbed a great big chunk out of my right arm, breaking the bone just above the elbow. Now the shattered arm is pinned behind me completely useless in my moment of needing to flap my arms and flee. The only two chances I've got of not bleeding to death are if I freeze to death first, or if the good doctor finds me in time to finish the deadly deed by eating me alive.

One thing for sure, I won't underestimate anyone again and won't run if I miss. I'll stand my ground next time and take what I've got coming. Especially, if I'm still in the middle of directing my first Hollywood movie with the Hollywood starlet I think I'm in love with. Next time, I won't allow my clone to get all the glory of spending New Years Eve with her in a romantic Connecticut rental home, all alone, accept for her two lesbian coworkers and my cuddly dog.

I won't let what's happening to me happen to me silently again if given the chance. I won't become one of their button men hidden from the human world. What I take from this moment is simple. If I live long enough for them to ever call upon me again. And I'm talking about the Alien Mob. I'll end it quickly by killing myself publicly. Instead of living the secret lies they make for me. This is the last time I'll ever let this happen to me. From now on, nobody lives my life but me. Even if it is my own Alien enhanced identical clone.

Damn, I'm dying again. I can feel it coming on now, creeping up from my toes.

"Mook, where are you? Caw, help me!" Nothing....then....

1

LAST NIGHT - CHRISTMAS EVE

Three more squeaky dog gifts to go and I'm done wrapping. Sometimes it pays off being unmarried, unattached, and an only child with a Great Lakes fisherman pop who neither sends nor expects anything but a funny Christmas card. But here I am the new/old kid on the block, directing my first Hollywood motion picture. Yet, I've been alone all day in my apartment with my dog, Bubba, once again on Christmas Eve, awaiting platonic dinner guests. Some things never change. Even if Bubba is the greatest snow white show-poodle on earth, he's not much at holiday conversation.

Bubba looks up at me with his unblinking eyes. "Speak for yourself, Dogman. At least I don't talk to myself."Canine actors, they're all bark.

I was invited to several local studio Christmas events over this upcoming weekend. Now that everyone wants to hang with Jozeph Picasso. I'm still the apartment manager who seemingly has gotten away with murder. But unraveling it all somehow helped twist me into a bankable Hollywood filmmaker. Thanks to my all powerful agent. So now I'm penciled in, magically worth posting on Holiday Twitter and Facebook invitee lists. I now have four thousand Twitter followers and my Facebook account is jammed with requests I stopped friending months ago. Actually, I have yet to Tweet. The agency has someone handling all my social media.

The ever desirable Claire Davis even extended a personal invite. It's just that she is traveling today on a private jet to a rental house in Connecticut. She's leaving much too early in our holiday hiatus for me to get away. She's traveling with two other people from her crowd. One of those people, a particular lesbian production assistant from her TV show, somehow still hates me, even though I'm lovable now. And there's still a chance she might be an Alien.

So I begged off, knowing I had a shitload of work to do once we ramped up production after the New Year. However, I readily agreed to catch up with them two days before the end of the year by rail car, in hope of that one special New Years kiss. Of course, I'm to bring Bubba with. Knowing lover-poodle, he'll end up in her arms just in the Saint Nick of time. And get all the licking and smooching come the turn of the year. The little bugger.

Bubba looks up at me again like he knows I'm calling him names. I smile, and he just lowers his head, "Hurry up, Dogman, bring on the chicks. I'm hungry and need more worthy entertainment than your babbling nonsense."

Yes, we await four of my neighbors. Three are due to knock on our apartment door, 308, any second. Erin, the young ringleader, and her roomy Janet from apartment 104 are bringing wine. Our new found drinking buddy, Patty Stable, from apartment 103 is bringing side dishes. I haven't heard from J.J., our actor that lives in my garden apartment. Hopefully he'll bless us before dinner is served.

I have prepared a traditional Christmas Goose. Of which I've never cooked before. Every good tradition needs a first. And since my childhood memories were filled with none. Why not start one with a baked goose on this Southern California Christmas Eve? I even plucked the feathers to show how manly I've become. Something I don't plan to ever manhandle again because it was messy and disgusting. I'm sure we'll all end up tasting at least one feather before all is said and digested. But there's a first and last time for all parts of traditions.

Bubba lifts his head like I'm talking to myself again. He puts his paws over his ears, so I guess I am. I have been talking to myself a lot lately. I'm not sure why. I'm even getting images of being somewhere else at times, as though it's not really daydreaming. It's more like the ability to separate my awareness from my physical body, a being there, an astral projection.

I haven't seen anyone for it yet. Mook said it might just be one of many aftereffects of the surgery on my leg and butt that I could encounter for awhile. He told me not to think about being up there, using my Alien health insurance and it would go away quicker.

Sometimes it happens when I look off into the distance. I'll see myself standing there looking back. It's kind of freaky because it's so real. I feel as though I'm studying myself. So I stopped gazing, and started just focusing on things at hand.

So far I'm staying in the moment on the set. Only Claire Davis has noticed I'm somewhere else at times. She takes those moments to privately draw me back with a simple butter touch of her fingers. Or just by saying my name in that salty whisper of hers, "Jozeph, come back to us." Everything just seems to refocus, racking back to reality, panning to the here and now, allowing my life to move forward again in real time. It often leaves me feeling blue and missing something I once had. Maybe it's my missing leg looking for me. I don't know. That's a creepy thought on Christmas Eve. Because as weird as it sounds, it's possible considering all I've gone through.

Caw, my Alien trained Japanese Jungle Crow hasn't been around for a while. He was at the first day of shooting but when the assistant director, Tim from apartment 101 started yelling through his megaphone, "Shut the hell up on the set. And that means the stupid crow, too."Caw stopped shitting on the cast and crew alike while dive bombing the craft tables. He headed north to points I'm not sure of, to shit somewhere else. He'll be back. He does this often, traveling to points unknown, with never a wish-you-were-here postcard.

I've got to admit, directing my first film isn't that hard so far. Crazy Kind Of Love is based on the pains of an ex-girlfriend. So having had a hand in casting it, along with the Burnstein Burnouts, I feel I am in complete control of where this story is going. From what I've heard back from The Burn Post the footage looks great. We have barely a week of exteriors left to shoot before we move into the studio to catch a few interiors and wrap the film by March.

The sound is nearly perfect. No reshoots are stacked on my desk. All the money people are keeping out of my hair. Even most of my original dialogue is working and being used. This is surprising, though scary to me the writer. Because in the first preproduction meeting it was clearly stated that the least important part of my script was the dialogue, when all is said and edited.

Of course I'm still the infamous filmmaker who seemingly got away with murdering four of my pig-tenants. May their carcasses rot in swill. I'll always be that writer-director who somehow had the biggest comeback in Hollywood lore. Since all that was really left of my career to cremate was a waterlogged leg and boot. So it's not completely surprising that other non-creative people on the set are keeping their distance and letting me do my thing.

What's really nice, is that not one person has disparagingly questioned that out of nowhere I magically made it all the way back from the Tujunga Wash to a greenlit studio film starring the hottest young starlet in town. Being signed by one of the most powerful and oldest agents in the Universe, yes it's Jerry, or I should say one of the humans Jerry inhabits, Gerald Zeiger, has opened all the doors to success. I think this is the case anyway, because Jerry has yet to revel himself to me through Gerald. I don't mean flash his privates. I mean, admit that it is he, Jerry, inhabiting my agent.

I've actually brought it up a couple of times over a glass of Scotch and Zeiger just looked at me like I was having a moment of insanity. So I've stopped caring whether Alien Jerry is in there or not. Let him have his fantasy of being human. As long as I am free to shoot my film the way I see fit.

Zeiger's a randy old guy. He's extraordinarily likeable. He knows everyone and everyone loves him because he constantly goes out of his way in making deals where everyone wins. Even if the project tanks in the end.

He's practically harmless if you don't mind being goosed once in a while. His spin put on who I am, and who I was, has seemed to only benefit me. I'm guessing the truth of having survived the unemployable stigma of a shallow grave still tends to make people step aside when I walk down the hall. They at least pretend to be glad I made it all the way back to Paycheck-Ville when they first meet me.

At this point of the shoot, we all know the whole film production is moving exceptionally smooth, that we're doing good work. But truth be told, none of us, including me, are expecting any kind of nomination. Other than hoping our names aren't called to give a speech in tomorrow's unemployment line.

Bubba barks and jumps up on me for scrubs. He's probably trying to keep me from thinking too much.

"I love you, too, Bubba."

Bubba licks my hand. He's such a good loving dog. I give him scrubs behind his ears. I dig my fingers into his snowy white, poodle hair. Today, life is good. I'm looking forward to a Marry Christmas.

2

Finally, a soft tap-tap on our door draws me out of my champagne-grape thoughts. Bubba springs into action. The four legged doorbell. I assume the proper holiday attitude. I put a festive smile on my face and close the oven. Having just removed the golden goose, yelling to them as I turn off the heat, "It's open. Bubba, stop, sit." Bubba stops and sits with anticipation of all the licking, petting, and hugging that may ensue at any moment. I don't feel so lucky. Yet, all three girls pile into my foyer, slipping out of their slip-ons, happy and hungry, laden with gifts for me and Bubba.

It's a heartwarming sight, indeed. Removing the shoes is a custom all my best of human friends understand. Mooky hasn't quite caught onto my clean carpet fetish yet. Maybe he doesn't because he never uses the door. Usually, he Blips in as an Alien induced hologram. He no longer trusts me after being moed in the eyes twice and shot in the chest once by a fed up me.

Erin comes into the kitchen first, "Marry Christmas, Jozeph," she plants a sloppy kiss on the side of my face, squeezing my cheeks as though she were my grandmother, making me speak with a pucker.

"Thank you. I see we started the wine on the way up."

"Of course. Your spooky elevator is slow."

"I think it's haunted," Janet adds. "Something goosed me."

"I didn't do it this time," Erin says defending herself.

"Don't look at me, I was hanging on for dear life," Patty adds.

I ignore them because there's a truth to it, something is going on in there, and I haven't been using the elevator for months. "What do you think?" I ask proudly displaying my Christmas goose.

"Smells delish. How close are we?"

"I was just checking, yep my goose is cooked. Where's J.J.?"

"He ran across the street for smokes," Janet answers, coming into the kitchen to give me a hug. "What's with his tan? Talk about your cooked Christmas gooses."

"It's what you do on vacation. Try to kill yourself. I thought he quit smoking?"

"Cigars, for all of us. I brought brandy and I thought it would enhance the moment," Patty says, holding Bubba in her arms, getting licked.

"Here, let me take that," I said, reaching out for the bottle. "Wow, this is the good stuff."

"As the natives of Charente-Maritime say, "All cognac is brandy, but not all brandy is cognac. My daddy sends me a bottle from Connecticut every Christmas."

"Don't mention Connecticut. Jozeph is pining over the actress who left him behind to play with her two lesbian coworkers in the snow."

I shoot Erin a 'bite me' look.

"What?" Erin pushes her long dark hair out of her face as she smiles.

"Who wants wine?"Janet interjects.

"Me," we all add in.

Janet pinches me on the butt as I drill the corkscrew into a nice lively bottle of California Cabernet. "She's just jealous. Why don't you corkscrew her tonight and get it over with?"

"Why don't you?"

"Who says I haven't?"

"Not me."

"Watch it, you jokesters. He can spend New Year's Eve with whomever he wants and wherever he wants. I couldn't care less," Erin says.

"Gee, thanks for giving Bubba and me permission to have a life beyond Mystery Towers Magical Tour."

"It's only mysterious because you own it," Janet says.

"None of us will be home anyway," Erin says.

"Then it's settled. Bubba, we're flying to Connecticut for New Years."

Bubba looks at me like I'm very nuts. "You fly, Dogman. I'm a traveling show bus kind of dog."

Bubba squirms down out of Patty's arms and runs over to the closed terrace doors where just outside the double glass panel sits

Caw. "Caw-Caw-Caw," he announces himself and goes into something very close to human speech.

"See," says Erin, even Caw couldn't give a shit." Just then Caw lets out a great big white glob into the poop-tray suspended below the baker's rake shelf. Apparently he could, and often.

"Uggh, why do you let that disgusting dinosaur throwback hang around here?"Janet asks.

"He adopted me, I didn't adopt him. Besides, he's been highly trained by Aliens to protect me."

"Who?"Patty asks.

"Don't ask," Erin tells her, shooting me the angry-mother-look to watch my mouth.

"Jozeph thinks he's been probed by Aliens," Janet explains.

"Does that explain his two different sizes of feet?"Patty asks, pointing at my socks.

"Don't get him going on that cockamamie story. Do something about Caw. He wants you," Erin says shooing me towards the terrace. "You promised not to include us," she adds.

"May I be cloned if I ever mention it again."

"I'm warning you."

"Give me a break. I never once claimed any of that was true. So back off, Mom, before I pinch you."

"I won't visit you in the loony bin."

"I won't invite you."I turn to the terrace doors and open one, reaching out my elbow for Caw to step on. I bring him in to place him on his indoor perch just inside the dining room. It's where he stalks road kill out the window, or scrutinizes my game on the purple felt pool table.

"Do you think he'll mind," Patty asks?

"What, the goose?"

"Well yeah, it's almost cannibalism, isn't it?"

"Please, he eats solar cooked squab off the street."I cut him a piece of the goose and give it to him. Caw takes it and shakes his head quickly back and forth about ten times, splashing the goose juice across the table cloth covered the pool table and onto the wall.

"That's even more disgusting," Patty says.

"He gets worse," Janet adds, as Caw steps on the meat and tears it apart like some living Cretaceous raptor.

"He does eat like a dinosaur," Patty says.

"Maybe he'd be more comfortable outside," Erin says.

Bubba barks in agreement. "Throw the uncouth bum out into the night before he interferes with my scrubs and kisses."

"Sorry, forgot. Come on, back outside, Caw. You're too uncivilized for these classy drunks." He looks at me, and flies up onto my head and grips my hair without scaring my scalp. "Would one of you three lovelies mind serving goose while I remove this bird from my head?"

"I'll do it."Erin picks up the carving set and starts cutting the goose as I go out onto the terrace to open a bag of monkey chow.

"Hey, Jozeph, Patty is going sledding with her family tomorrow up in Frazer Park. Why don't you go with her so you won't have to be alone on Christmas?"

"Sledding? On Christmas? Why?"I call back from outside.

"My niece has her boyfriend over for the holidays. They don't want to just hang around the house. I agreed to chaperone so their parents would let them go. Young love. But now they're stuck taking all the younger kids to keep them from just necking in the car."

I slide the door closed, leaving Caw to feed on his own. I look back and he's watching me with those weird knowing bird-eyes. It's almost as though he's waiting for my answer. He's in on this snow job. I definitely don't want to go. I'll have to tread lightly so the girls don't gang up on me, as they often do while drinking. "Ah, so we're talking teens?"I glance back at them. All three are laying in wait for my answer. Shit, this won't be easy.

"Just a couple, my niece and her boyfriend, but the others are ten and under. It'll be fun."

"Yeah, I'm gonna have to pass. I've got my whole day planned."

"Oh come on, Jozeph. You can't let Patty drive up there by herself with all those kids to keep an eye on."

"Watch me. The snow I can deal with. Bubba and I would much rather sit back and watch football on TV in the calm of our own home than keep young love from petting each other. Besides, I've got work to do. And Bubba is due for a bath if he plans on sleeping in my bed anytime soon."

Bubba barks. "You don't smell so good at night either, Dogman."

"It's Christmas. You don't want to be alone."

"I won't, I'll be with Bubba and Caw. And it's Sunday. I'm back to directing a film come Monday."

"Listen to mister big shot director," Janet says. "Six months ago he was a dead boot literally washing down the Tujunga Wash. Now he's too alive to be seen with the likes of us."

"Look who's talking about dying, with all the screaming coming from your room."

"Low blow," Erin says.

"Quit standing outside my windows, pervert," Janet says.

"People think this place is haunted enough without you playing Jacob Marley."

"Joseph. It's A Christmas Carol," Erin says, a total deadpan.

"At least I've got an afterlife. You two should try it sometime."

"Cheers to getting laid." Patty raises her glass. "I'm all for it."

Bubba jumps up on her. "Relax, lover boy." Bubba jumps off, running over to attack his teddy bear. He flops, spread eagle on the floor watching us, waiting for someone to play with him. I don't think he gets his TV show being on hiatus. He knows that he does special things and is paid in treats. Then he watches himself on TV snuggling with lead actress, Claire Davis, as her best friend. I'm sure he misses all the primping and pampering he gets at least twice a week. Being stuck with me, his real life best friend, watching me get all the special attention pales in comparison to having his own paid groomer. So I bring him to my movie set to get his hair brushed and his eye-boogers cleaned. He hangs out in Claire's dressing room when we shoot days.

"Come here." Bubba rolls over and sprints to me, jumping into my arms. "We don't want the snow for Christmas, do we, Bubba."

Bubba licks my face. "I'm with ya, Dogman. It's skinny chicks, sunshine, and dog bones for me."

"Everyone else in Hollywood is taking the week off. Even humbugs who don't believe in Santa." I cover Bubba's ears. "So you can afford time to help our neighbor take a station wagon full of kids up into the snow and make sure they get back alright on Christmas."

"When did you become my stage mother, Erin?"

"When you started acting like a big shot Hollywood baby."

"Yeah, it's bad enough getting attitude from your furry pet."

"Bite her, Bubba."

Bubba growls and yaps at Janet, jumping down.

Patty takes her plate and sits down at the makeshift dining room table on top of my pool table. She picks up her wine, sipping it with a hand that slightly shakes as it moves the glass up to her lips. "It's okay, I'll manage."

Janet and Erin glare at me.

"What?"

9

They glare at me even more.

"Will you two stop it?"

"Really, I agreed to take them. I'll be fine."

Janet takes her plate to the table and sits. Erin takes hers and sits across from Patty on the bar stools standing in for dining room chairs. I'm not too insensitive to notice I didn't get served. I look down and Bubba is eating away at the plate that was meant for me. He looks up at me with goose grease on his goatee. "What up, Dogman? You should try some. This bird is phat."

"This isn't funny." The three girls look across at each other and giggle amongst themselves.

"Nice try."They're ganging up on me as usual. I look at Bubba. We dogs need to stick together. "Sorry, you're on your own with this one, Dogman. I've got dibs on humping the couch pillows." I serve myself, making sure I get my share of Patty's sweet potatoes and Erin's classic green bean casserole. I sit down as far from them as I can.

As I sit, J.J., the actor, just freshly back yesterday without a word of explanation from planet Milicalazarra enters the unlocked front door. Oddly, he came back alone, his shattered arm all healed, without Stacey Carson. She is the natural redheaded woman who stole Bubba and tried to kill me over Alien healing stones. She and her killer partners thought they were facet cuts of the actual Hope Diamond. J.J. has yet to explain her absence or describe his adventure. Or admit to anything ever happening to him beyond spending time on a remote island contemplating his career while being pampered by real island natives. He just showed up again suddenly.

He lives downstairs in my garage studio apartment, outback where I let him stay for free. He helps me around the building with odd jobs, like dealing with cannibalistic Space Travelers and other pissed off human types who try to kill me. He's also tax deductable as part of my security system. He was asleep when I walked in on him. I left without talking to him much, other than to ask where he went and where Stacey was. He just said, "She stayed," and rolled over to go back to sleep. So I haven't pressed yet.

He shows up now with the stogies, broken bones completely healed from his mob-beating. I take my first holiday bite and just watch him look back at us. He acts like he never left for another planet. Except his out of this world tan is borderline comical in a freaky-George Hamilton-mocking sort of way. J.J. gets a load of the seating arrangements and the long faces.

"Who died? He asks.

"Picasso's chivalry," Erin says. "How's the wine, Patty?"

"Perfect. Thanks."

"Take J.J., he loves the snow. He's even from Alaska."

"Note the word from. I'm into beach bumming and pose-surfing now. What gives?"

"Jozeph won't help Patty take kids to Frazer Park."

"What kind of kids?"

"Kid-kids. Her kissing cousins that I've never met."

"Oh, sounds like fun. I'd go, but I've got a party in the hills and I'm taking this young honey of a dish I met on Milicalazarra."

"See, everyone's got somewhere else to be but you," Erin says.

"Where's Milicalazarra," asks Patty?

"A small remote island," J.J. answers.

"In the South Pacific," Erin clarifies.

"I've never heard of it."

"It's very private, Patty. But while pose-surfing there I pitched your surfer-detective series, Jozeph, Consider It Done, Matt Dunn."

"That old thing? I couldn't get anyone to even read it."

"I know, but I think I sold it. These guys saw me learning to surf with the broken arm and thought it was a good vehicle for me to pitch to the networks. Turns out they were development guys at NBC."

"J.J., you don't just walk off the beach and get offered TV deals."

"It had your name attached to it. Once they heard I lived here in Mystery Towers and hung out with you, they couldn't stop buying me drinks. Our agent is working on it now."

I swallow hard at the mentioning of my agent being our agent and start to choke. Seriously, I point to Erin and my throat and she comes and strikes me on the back. I spit up a piece of goose meat.

Bubba just looks at it and turns up his nose.

"Stop playing around, you too."

"Zeiger?"

"I didn't know who else to tell them to contact. I met Gerald out front once, and it was your concept, but it's all falling into place."

"Why wasn't I told about this?"

"I was just told myself a few minutes ago while crossing the street. Where do you think I've been?"

"Buying cigars."

"Here, look," he takes out his BlackBerry and shows us a text message. "Things look good so far, we'll know more in a week. Picasso will get over it when he sees the first check. Gerald."

"That is so crazy, remote islands, surfing on vacation," Erin says. She shoots both of us a look she gets when mentioning any of the nonsense that's been going on. "Isn't it, J.J.?"

"Yeah, sure, we showbiz types are all nuts. So...."

"Patty, do you really need me to go?" I ask, changing the subject to something back on this planet.

"It would be safer if you drove, in case it snowed. My niece's boyfriend said he'd drive, but he's seventeen. I'm not sure he's even driven in the snow."

"Crap. You see what I go through, Bubba? With friends like these, who wants a driver's licenses?"

Bubba barks. "Go already, Dogman, I could use some peace and quiet while I chew my new doggy toys."

"What time?"

"Ten a.m., right out front."

"Fine, but if I hear any crying or complaining about my driving I'm turning the car around and heading back."

"They're not babies, Joseph," Erin reminds me.

"They're good kids. You'll have a great time, and love my family," Patty assures me.

Bubba looks. "Do it, Dogman. Just leave me out."

"Okay, it will be fun. I haven't gone sledding in years."

"On purpose, I'm sure," J.J. adds. "It's friggin' cold up in them there hills, bro. Give me the burn of the surf and turf any day."

"Easy for you to say with that tan, goose-boy," I answer.

"You like? The sun is intense on the Islands."

"J.J., you look fine," Erin tells him.

"You might want to tone it down a little. Melanoma is a killer," Patty says."

"Let's not go this way, we're eating."

"So let's celebrate. You have a series together,' Janet adds.

"Last one drunk sleeps alone," Patty throws into the air.

We pick up our drinks before realizing that if anyone were to get laid tonight it would be amongst ourselves. Awkward silence follows.

Bubba jumps on my lap, hopeful. "Which one you want, Dogman?"

"Bubba doesn't count," Patty clarifies.

Bubba growls at her again. He's disappointed.

3

At ten sharp the next morning, I'm waiting out front in seventy-five degree weather. I'm trying to hide from the Southern California glare by lurking in what little shade I can get this time of day under the pines out front of Mystery Towers. I must look like an idiot in my moon boots and dark blue ski jacket concealed amongst the branches. Joggers in short-shorts and hundred dollar running shoes prance by, giving me the once over, panting "Happy Holidays," as they flee from Yukon Jack-me.

I haven't skied in years but the jacket still fits, though snugger. I have a matching blue wool hat still in one pocket and blue ski gloves crammed in the other. Ten-fifteen, still no Patty or station wagon full of kids, so I head back up the stairs. Just as I dig out my keys to unlock the door, hoping beyond hope they've left me behind, a horn blares at me. Making me nearly jump out of my moon boots. And that's how my day starts.

Behind the wheel of the surprisingly well maintained 1973 wood paneled green station wagon, I push the big V-8 up the 101 and hit the 405 heading north. The young couple sitting up front with me, Jed and Nance, cling to each other like spider monkeys and as far away from me as their seatbelts will allow. Young love, with bad taste in music, my favorite pastime. Jed brought his own 90's grunge rock selection to annoy me with. He must be hard of hearing from listening to it, because he's not listening to me. So I have to keep turning it down every time he preselects a song and cranks up the aftermarket CD player's volume again.

"Chill dude. This is killer."

"So am I, Jethro. Read my resume. Don't touch the knob again."

"The name is Jed. And I can't hear it."

"Aunt Patty, your boyfriend just threatened us."

"It's okay, Nance, turn the music down a little so we can talk."

Within seconds the rest of the kids jammed in the back bring the laughing and screaming to the unbearable stage. So I reached over and crank the music as high as I can take it. This makes both Jed and Nance love crabby big-brother-man Picasso. Like that we converge onto the Five North, zooming past Magic Mountain up towards Castac Lake on our way past Santa Clarita to winter wonderland, in Frazer Park. As we near the park, snow capped mountains are plainly visible. In driving north we quickly climb 4,639 feet out of the San Fernando Valley and into the San Gabriel Mountains. We've got a ways to go before we reach Frazier Park, an unincorporated community in Kern County, just west of Lebec.

Come to think of it, the last time I was up this way, I was nearly killed by Aliens and left blindfolded and shackled to rot in a very deep hole. A non-Kodak memory I can survive without ever reliving. The thought hits me so hard that I almost stop the car.

"What's the matter, Jozeph?"Patty asks.

"I was remembering something I had almost forgotten."

"Everything copacetic?"

"Yeah sure, we're good."I take the Frazer Mountain Park Road exit and hang a left on Cerro Noroest Road, back under the Five.

Just up the road we come to Lebec Road and I hang a right and head towards two small gas stations, laden with shopping corners. The first one with a convenience store appears to be a trustworthy rest stop. So I pull over. "Who has to tinkle?"

Nobody answers. So I get out. Who wants water? "I do, I do," all the little ones chime in. "I'll take a coke, dude," Jed informs me.

"Good, here's a twenty. Get two six packs of cold water, and get you and Nance sodas. Anything else?"

"Can we go to McDonald's?"Eight year-old Mindy asks.

The whole station wagon burst out in an annoyingly loud chant of "We want McDonald's."

"Quiet!"I yell. "Everyone, get out of this car. And get in line for the bathroom, right now. You first, Patty."

"I'm okay."

"Trust me on this. We'll be ten miles from here, if not farther. I'm not coming back until we all come back. So everyone, get in line behind Aunt Patty or we squat behind trees. Jed, you go for drinks and two large bags of chips."

"I need smokes."

"Buy smokes with my money and I'll make you eat them."

"Harsh, dude."

"What a butt wad."

"He's just old. And his life is almost over, so he's bitter."

"I'm barely past thirty. Still young enough to beat your butt. And I've had more lives than your cat. Now move your ass onward before I crush all of your tapes."

"I would have to murder you, dude. It's the grunge oath."

"Let's not find out."

Jed and Nance take off for the convenience shopping. I go into the gas station, get the keys for the restrooms, and get in the back of the little boys' line. By the time it was my turn, five little boys and three little girls plus Patty had gone in and out, making me severely wish I had gone first. I let Jed stand behind me. Moments later we were all flushed, washed, and back into the station wagon, pulling back onto the mountain road.

"That wasted over a half hour," Nance informs me.

"You'll thank me later while you're not looking for a tree to pee behind."

"Mr. Picasso?"Mindy asks.

"Yes."

"Are we eating McDonald's now?"

"No."

The whole car breaks out in another, yet even more annoying McDonald's chant. I adjust the mirror to catch the look on Patty's face and she is chanting right along with the kids. My day is getting better. Patty catches my eyes and sticks her tongue out at me. Some kids never grow up.

Like this, up the mountain we climb. We follow the unavoidable odor of poorly tuned car emissions, all the way up Frazer Mountain Park Road, past Frazer Park itself. At least it shuts them up. Finally we're able to hang a left at a fork in the road onto to Lockwood Valley Road. We make this turn only because the piece of shit car in front of us stays right onto Cuddy Valley Road. Without recycled air in this old station wagon we are all looking forward to an exhaust-free place to sled.

4

It does smell of winter up here. And I like it. Up until now, the day was no different from what I expected. The kids are yelling and screaming. Getting cold and wet without much crying from bumps and fears. They tumble into the once fluffy snow turned to slippery slush. It zooms them towards the bottom of the ravine, strait at the parking alongside the road, lined with Frazer Pine. Only to capture them just in time behind plowed snow piled in the ditch.

The one thing I didn't expect is that ten year-old Billy Boy Smith would lace on flat bottom leather sole boots. They are made for little more than marching on high school football fields. Making it impossible for the bulky kid to walk up a slushy snow covered hillside. I do my best not to laugh. Bump, there he goes again, right on his belly, sloshing back down to the very bottom. I turn so he can't see me chuckling at his expense. It makes me feel like a dickhead. But I haven't laughed in weeks, so I can't stop it, knowing I'll pay for it with bad karma.

All the other kids in proper snow boots are able to climb up the ravine and race down the steep slope to eventually bottom out in the ditch. It's about a five minute process on each trip.

But they are getting wetter and wetter from the mounting slush. The sun has crested the peeks above and it is now filtering down through the pine trees upon this portion of the mountain slope. No one seems to care because they are still warm. I figure, in half an hour we'd hit the road, wet, tired and happy to go home.

I walk over and offer to help Billy up the hill, so he could get at least one trip down. He takes my arm while I do my best to steady him but it's no use. The kid cannot stand up in the melting snow to save his life. Not on this steep of an incline. Five minutes of trying and we are still at the base of the hill. I'm as winded from holding him up as if I had sprinted up the hill myself. I put my hands on my knees. "Hold on. Gees, kid, you ever been in the snow before?"

"No. These are my dad's boots."

"Tell your dad they suck."

"Yeah, I think he used these for a Halloween costume. Got them at the army surplus store. He didn't like them and gave them to me."

"Your dad sucks, too."

"Yeah, these are lame. I'll go sit in the car and figure out how to get even with him later. I'm sopped."

I look back at the car, about a hundred cars had come in behind us since we arrived and picked their own ravine to play in. We're not blocked in but there are a lot of cars for such a cramped mountain area. Most of the cars are beat up, or fixed up versions of once nice cars. We are probably one of the few non Hispanic groups in this part of the mountain.

I check the phone Mooky gave me. It is almost three-thirty. How'd that happen? I hadn't gone down the hill once. I look up when a chilling wind hits me. I can see a quick moving monstrously-dark cloud formation rolling up over the mountain peaks, heading straight to gobble up the sun. Crap! Ten seconds later the sun is eaten alive, gone completely from the sky, almost a total eclipse.

I look over at Billy Boy and he takes one step and sprawls out on the snow and starts sliding down. The slush has instantly turned to solid ice. Up above me the screams and laughter heighten as suddenly the sled and saucer bound kids come racing down the hill faster than any of them anticipated, or wanted. Those who weren't lucky enough to get stopped by the mounds of snow jet out amongst the cars.

"Damn."I look up to find Patty clinging to a pine tree.

"What's happening, Jozeph?"

"Cold front is blowing in. A sudden drop in temp. The freeze is hitting us fast. Hurry up. Get the kids back in the car. We've got to beat this crowd out of here."

"Everyone, to the car. Right now," Patty yells. But the kids are scattered up and down the hill.

"We don't want to go," Josh, pushing nine, yelled from bellow. "We just got here."

"Right now." I yell. "Quietly. Move it."

Jed comes down with Nancy between his legs, both screaming their head off. "Stop us!"

I grab Jed by the hoodie as he goes by and both he and Nance drag me down the hill. Their sled careens into the parked cars.

"Holy crap, dude. What the hell is going on?"

"Everything is turning to ice."

"Ice? You mean…?"

"Yes, a mini glacier is upon us, our own little ice age. Quick, get the kids in the car. Or we'll never get out of here before morning."

Jed and Nance grab a hold of the nearest two kids and start them down what is left of the slope. All of them falling and taking the last twenty yards on their butts."

"What's happening?"Billy Boy yells.

"Get those two in the car. Hurry!"

Billy stands up, clinging to the stations wagon."It's locked."

I take off my gloves, the temp dropping fast, stinging already, and fish into my pocket, counting the kids. "Shit. We're short two girls." I throw the keys to Billy Boy, while looking up the hill, into the tree line. Sure enough, halfway up are two kids clinging for their lives.

Patty makes it to the station wagon. "Look, there they are. It's Mindy and Judy."

"I see them."

"Oh, my god, get us down from here," Judy yells.

I look around, thinking of what to do first. Off in the neighboring ravines where other groups had claimed their private sledding, we can hear the screams and yelling. Much like our own, but most of them are in Spanish. There is no mistaking it. Panic and terror sound very much alike in any language. Cars start up and pull out into the road, sliding as they fight to gain traction on the frozen road.

Then the snow hits. Or should I say icy-rain. And lots of it.

"Get everyone in the car, start it up, turn on the defrost, quickly. I'll go up. Turn the heat on full blast to keep the windows from icing up." My moon boots are not affected by the freezing snow, partly due to my weight pushing fresh foot prints into the emerging ice. Finally gaining all this weight after quitting smoking pays off. Still, it takes me nearly eight minutes to make it up the fifty yards to where the two young girls cling to the trunk of a virgin Frazer Pine. When I get to them I am winded, needing a break. But in looking down from this elevation I see what I feared most, a tangle of cars getting ahead of us down Lockwood Valley heading back into Frazer Park. My second wind leaps back into action. "Come on, jump on. We're going down."

"Are you nuts?"

"We were doing a thousand miles an hour by ourselves."

"I'll drag my boots."

"But...."

"Look at the roads, they're already packed. We'll be up here all night if we don't move now. And you won't be home for Christmas dinner. Jump on top."

The two girls jump on top of me. Down we go on the saucer. Me dragging my boots the best I can. Even with that amount of drag, we are careening down the hill, straight for the cars. We hit the up slope of the plowed snow and flip right over backwards like stacked ragdolls. We roll down into the frozen drainage ditch, arms and legs tangled in a pile of mittens and boots. That was my one turn down, and I admit, it was kinda fun. Despite the terror of possibly hitting a car door face first.

"Son of a...."

"Oh, my god, that was sooo cool!"

"Can we do it again?"

"Get in the car, we're going to McDonalds."

"Yay!"

"He's lying."

"Booooo."

5

We all make it back into the station wagon and I get behind the wheel. Lockwood Valley Road is already jammed with cars leaving for the same reason we are. The Iceman Comith, Eugene O'Neill, and we wanna go home. But the other cars are still moving forward. Luckily, this part of the road had been recently plowed so it still had patchy pavement and the oncoming ice storm hasn't taken full effect yet. So we are able to make it across the first plateau unscathed. I hope to hit the main road out of here before anything stupid happens. Three taps on wood and I cross my fingers, but fat chance, Picasso, is what I'm really thinking.

I remember when coming up the mountain that every plateau ended at a slope taking us further into the mountain. So I figure I better slow to a near stop at the end of the first plateau. Good thing I do. Because in carefully cresting the first one we can see the small valley below us is completely hidden from the sun. It probably had been for most of the day. The menagerie of cars with unchained tires that were not able to make it all the way down in a civilized manner are littered across the darken side of the slope. Their lights point in all directions, as the ice storm laminates them into a frozen untamed fatter-chance of me getting my carload of children home in time for Christmas bird.

We look over the carnage of this great car catastrophe. It's still evolving into a slow motion mess. Gravity has a hold of them now and is drawing them leisurely down the hill, a giant octopus, fatally sinking ships by pulling them down into the icy sea.

Oddly, all the cars and trucks have been sugar coated into a magical setting. So that no one could possibly be injured beyond dented fenders and bent egos. I take a quick estimate that almost forty cars are piled to either side of the road. Some remain still while others slip profanely downwards, as they lose their grip of the ice. Most gently slide off the road or into each other, depending on what portion of the road they ended up on, and what kind of natural slope it possesses. It's very surreal, yet very creepy. Because behind the luminous clouds rises a big shinny full moon. It casts a hoary evil-glow on all that shifts and tangles below us.

Below them, from my guess, about twenty local cars with proper snow chains are stranded by the tangle of uninformed day tourist. There is no driving off road to get around anyone. The deep ditches filled with plowed snow, make sure of that.

"Crap, holiday traffic is already trying to come up."I check my Mooky phone. It's 4:17 p.m. There could be hundreds more wanting to get up here. Hopefully, someone has the road from the Five closed off and are making sure everyone has chains on before attempting the climb. Not that they'll get past this even with them. Looking back at the tangle of cars and trucks behind me I figure I'm probably somewhere in the middle of all this excitement. "Remind me to turn off Erin's hot water while she's in the shower when I get home."

"Who's Erin? Your giiiiiirlfriend?"

"What? No, Erin is my troublemaking, bossy neighbor who goaded me into this mess."

"Why isn't Erin your girlfriend?"Patty asks.

"Since when are you my love guru, Patty?"

"Just stating the obvious, Mister Manager."

"Erin and I are best of friends."

"Butt buddies?"

"Mindy!"

"That's what my uncle calls his best friend."

"Well, that's not nice talk."

"Your uncle's best friend is named Ulysses and lives in West Hollywood and sings in a cabaret club," Billy says.

"Ulysses? That's a funny girl's name."

"Mindy, never mind. And watch your mouth, Billy."

"Just stating the obvious."

"Sorry, Joseph. We'll be fine."

"We'll be fine if I can get past these cars before we run out of the gas keeping us warm all night."

"I can't stay up after nine. It's past my bedtime. I'll get grounded."

"Relax. We'll get home. Who has wet clothes?"

Everyone does. "Okay. Patty, pick one and start drying their jackets or if you have to, pants on the heater up here, just in case."

"I'm not taking off my pants in front of you, pervo."

"Patty. Get it done."

"Don't worry. We've got a blanket to cover up with while changing. Wendy, you first. Off with the boots and let me have your pants."

"No. I'm fine. Pick one of them."

"I'll go," Jed said. "I don't want to be sitting around in wet pants and underwear when the heat shuts off." He starts undoing his pants.

"Hand me the blanket, Aunt Patty, and don't you dare tell my mother Jed took off his pants while I was in the car."

"Twenty bucks will keep my mouth shut," Billy says.

"And my eyes," Josh adds.

"Creeps."

Everything is coming to an unnatural standstill. People emerge from their cars to look down the hill at everyone else blocking their way. With us, my band of not so merry young wet children stranded at the top of the slope. Crud, nightfall will be here any moment with the clouds and wind pushing it down the hills. All I can selfishly think of is that every one of these cars is in the way of me getting these kids home. And I back to my loving dog, Bubba, for leftover goose and gravy. "I could use some Alien help right about now if anyone is listening."

"Aliens?"

"Did I say that out loud?"

"My mom says you're weird. And your building gives her chills."

"I am weird and live in a spooky place, so do as I say."

"How weird?" Jose asks.

"Disobey me and find out,"

"He's a good weird," Patty says. "Let him think. What will we do, Jozeph? And stop scaring the kids."

"I'm thinking."

"I'm thinking I got to pee again."

"Hold it as long as you can. I'll be right back." I pull the station wagon over and park to keep anyone from accidently rear ending us. Someone has to take control or we'll all end up freezing through the night when we, one by one, run out of gas to keep warm. Damn.

So I make the choice. It's gonna be me. I know how to drive down hills in the snow. Ice not so much, but snow you pump your brake, never locking them and turn into the skid if it occurs. Armed with this info I run and slide down to the first group of cars and do my best to pick a car that would do the most good to get it out of everyone's way.

A 1966 Pontiac sea green LeMans is my first selection. First, because I used to own one just like it in high school. Secondly, it's filled with scared Spanish kids and a father who looks like he hasn't a clue as to how to get his car out of the way. He must have come to a panicked sliding-stop sideways after cresting the hill. Realizing too late that he had no ability to stop on his way down so he locked his brakes and his car took off from under him.

This is where it stopped dead duck, sideways in the middle of the road, completely unable to move in any direction. I can only imagine the terror from within, a sitting wreck, waiting while car load after frantic car load did their best not to T-bone them into oblivion. Just another hundred yards and the driver would be at the plateau just south of Frazer Park where the road forks east and west and where he could drive safely for awhile, if he listens to me.

So, I tap on his window. He looks at me like I'm an Alien Clone. "Hello, do you speak English?"I ask him. He winds down his window helping it with his hand to stay in line. It doesn't help much and the window sticks halfway.

"I do," says a pretty young teen in the passenger seat.

"I know how to drive in the snow. Allow me to drive your car down to the flat area so you can get out of everyone's way."

She translates this to the rest of the car and the man driving nods his head, "Si," he answers, and slides to the front passenger seat so that I can get behind the wheel. The young teen piles into a male teen's lap in the back. I'm now that teen's best friend. Right away I know why the guy couldn't handle slowing down in the snow. His power brakes go right to the floor. He had driven his family for an outing in the snowy mountains without properly working brakes. He was so used to the brake working this poorly he didn't even think of how they would respond going back down the hills, never mind in the snow. I look at him, pointing to the brake.

"You don't have brakes."

"Si. No work so good."

"Leaky master cylinder," the teen loaning his lap says.

No shit. "You need to pump your brakes. I'll show you how, and don't turn the wheel, keep it as straight as you can. You understand?"

"Si. Turning no work so good."

Great. I put the car in gear. Tap the brakes. I push down on the accelerator to move the car forward. I bring the frontend to point back down the hill. That is the easy part. The hard part begins once we point down the hill. The car takes a mind of its own and starts moving as fast as gravity wants it to go. I pump like mad and I am probably getting about ten percent stopping power from what is left of the braking system, but only on the left front.

Having forced my way into their car and now placing them all in harm's way, I drive explaining the best I can of what I'm doing as we experiment. This isn't taken lightly by my inner panic. I nearly run the car into the embankment at the bottom of the hill. But we finally make it down and out of the way, despite the Pontiac's windshield wipers nearly being useless in keeping the ice from freezing. This makes me crank the heater up full blast and keep the windows closed. All the while I peak through a slight hole in the ice to see where we're all going. This sucks with a carload of scared-shitless Spanish kids and their confused parents praying that this crazy gringo doesn't kill them all.

The three or four cars we were immediately blocking zoom buy us. I stick my head out the opening door for a breath of fresh air. "Thanks, Buddy," I hear from one of them. The other two cars honk politely. The crowded LeMans erupts into happy glee as we stop. The young Spanish girl leans over and touches my hand. "Thank you, mister. God blesses."

"You're welcome. Okay, you understand enough of what I just did to explain it to him and make sure he tries it?"

"Yes, don't lock the brakes. Pump very fast. Keep the wheel straight. Turn into the skid to regain control."

"Smart girl. And get those brakes fixed. I'm going back up there to get the other cars down and out of my way. So keep moving. You will come to a few of these hills after each plateau. Slow down before going over the ridge. Pump as fast as you can on the way down. Keeping your wheels pointed straight down the road. Your right front break isn't working at all, from what I could tell."

"Good luck."

Luck has nothing to do with it. I walk over to the cars and trucks with chains that had pulled over to the side of the road and explain to them what I was about to do. They were all for whatever got them to their destination the quickest.

I yell into the oncoming night. "Everyone without chains or snow tires on your cars or trucks, get your vehicles to the side of the road. As far as you can. Let these cars headed up the hill get out of our way."Oddly enough, I am taken seriously. Without much help from me they push their cars sideways out of the center of the road. Within fifteen minutes there is enough room for the uphill bound vehicles to pass us by and climb up the hill.

"Okay," I yell again. "Any vehicles that have chains or snow tires heading down the hill, please pull back onto the road and make your way down. Pump your brakes and turn into skids as you go."

I look at the headlights moving around. The frozen rain has now turned into very small snowflakes, thick and fast, making it hard to see beyond what was right in front of me.

Another half hour goes by and there are only about ten cars crammed alongside the road. There is a clear one lane path for cars coming down from above to make it past. As I'm walking back up to our station wagon, smartly on the shoulder of the road, a car load of teens crests the hill going way too fast. Somehow they make it all the way down the slop and onto the next plateau. I yell, "Slow down." But they don't, and off they go into the night.

I walk to all the remaining vehicles one by one as I make my way up. I explain to them what to do when they come to the hills and how to use their brakes to get down the hill. I even drive four of the vehicles down for them to show them how to do it when I sensed they were too frightened to do it themselves.

An hour and a half later I have all the cars out of our way and we are ready to pull back onto the road. By the time I sit back behind the wheel, I am both wiped out and jazzed because I have accomplished helping all those families out of our way, maybe even back home. But it's already after six. The temp is dropping fast. The night has rolled further upon us. So I put the station wagon into gear and ease it back onto the road, heeding my own advice to get us down safely to the next plateau.

6

At the end of the next plateau I slow the station wagon in anticipation of what I was about to find. Damn. Ninety percent of the cars I just untangled were in the same knot that I had just untied. Only, this time there's a young cop involved trying to figure things out.

I pull the station wagon over again. There is no getting down. "I'll be right back."

"Wait. Let the police handle this one."

"I don't think he knows how from the look on his face."

So I get out and make my way through the cars. I nod and say hello to those I just drove down the last slope. I make sure the cop sees this to give him some kind of assurance that I know what I'm talking about.

"What's going on?"I ask a guy in a Chevy.

"He's not letting us through. He says that a snowplow is waiting downhill to come up and he wants us all to wait here until it passes."

"He give you a time frame?"

"Said he wasn't sure."

"Okay. Come with me. You, too." I point to a young husband I had driven down and explained how it works.

"Okay."

The four of us make our way to the local cop. He's maybe in his late twenties at best, nice looking guy, all bundled up for the holiday night shift. So I figure he's probably not the best this area has to offer, experience wise. He's standing there listening to his phone trying to hear what the person on the other side is saying to him. He does not like it much. This gives me hope he'll listen to reason when he sees I've got a posse of stranded motorist on my side.

"Just a minute, Sam. Yes, Sir?"

"My name is Jozeph Picasso. I got most of these people out of the upper section of the mountain. If you let me take control here with those I've already worked with, we'll get this taken care of as quickly as we can. Then you can get your snowplow up here to do its thing."

"He won't drop the salt coming up. He's telling me there are too many cars that could get damaged. He won't take responsibility."

"Fine, how far down is he?"

"He's stuck on the downside of two other slopes just like this as you get out of Frazer Park, back on the main road out. He said he's gotten word that they are as jammed with cars as we are here."

"Tell him if he can make his way up here beyond us, he can start dropping salt on his way back down as we clear the cars."

The cop looks me over, thinking about it. "What'd you say your name was?"

"Jozeph Picasso."

"The Jozeph Picasso? You're the writer-director with the leg and boot that came back to life?"

The others around me look closer at me moving slightly closer to each other and away from me. "Yes, that's me. The slash-sometimes filmmaker."

"Aren't you supposed to be directing a movie?"

"Yes. We're halfway done. On a Christmas break. I'm here with a car full of kids up there trying to get them back home."

"Shit. And you can get these people down?"

"He got us all down that last slope. Nearly every one of us."

The young cop looks around him, at both the down and up moving traffic. He knows if he says yes that he's probably breaking every rule of road safety that he can think of. But I can see that he's over his head and just wants to move on.

"What you should do," I tell him, "is lead those with chains and snow tires up the mountain to see if there's any stragglers up above who can't make it this far. Make sure they're going to make it out of the snow truck's way so he can drop his salt up there. If you pull up just a little we can get that car out of your way. You can pretty much lead the rest of these cars up the hill once we get the others without chains to the side of the road."

"Yeah, I guess that's probably what I should do. You sure you can handle this?"

"We've got it covered. Right, guys?"

"We got it."

"Okay, good luck."And with that he gets back into his patrol truck as we push a light pickup out from in front of him. He puts on his lights, and gets on his PA system announcing that he is leading the cars with snow tires and chains up the hill. Those without them would have to remain at the side of the road and wait until after the snow truck drops its salt. Only those standing around me knew that the truck wasn't dropping its salt on the way up the hill.

"What do you want us to do first?"

"Let's get everyone without snow tires or chains to the side of the road and let those with them get by. Just like we did up there."

So we worked our way up the hill together pushing and shoving and got everyone without proper traction out of the way. Except those at the bottom. We just drove them to the next plateau and set them free. By the time we get back to our own vehicles it is pushing 9:30.

"How are we doing on gas?"

"Less than a quarter tank left."

"Is everyone okay in here?"

"We peed in the snow."

"You're famous. I wrote your name. Even dotted the i."

"Congratulations to me. Seatbelts. Here we go."

We make it down with no problem. The snow that is now falling is starting to cover the ice, so this slope isn't as nearly as treacherous as the last one. We get up to thirty miles an hour moving along the plateau. Car lights up ahead are keeping a good distance between each other.

"The next slope proved to be even easier to get down and all but one car made it all the way. Two cars behind us stopped to help them, so they either knew them or felt for them. It makes me smile thinking that my helping the others is catching on and people are actually stopping to help the next guy get out of this frozen mousetrap.

7

Unfortunately, luck runs out at the top of the next hill. I look down to check the gas gage, turning down the music once again, and it blindsides us. The plateau suddenly ends and we are still going thirty miles an hour over the ridge. We're heading down the steepest slope of our plunge back into civilization. Screams fill the car with me being the loudest amongst them.

"Holy crap! Hold on to something."I pump the brakes the best I can. But we sail down the hill as though I am stepping on the gas. In front of us we all see a camper. Yes, a new white camper truck turned sideways is right in our way. We are still about fifty yards from it but we are moving in real fast.

The guy driving it is already out of its cab standing looking down the hill. When he turns to see us his eyes light up. All he can do is step back out of the way and let the anticipated destruction happen.

I wish I can take credit for this last bit of action. But I really have no control of what is taking place, because suddenly, the wagon's rear end swings out into the middle of the road. This puts us into a full sideways slide. We're now angling towards the oncoming traffic side.

Somehow this manages to slow us down at the same time. The closer we get to the camper the slower we get until just before we broadside it at barely a crawl, Jed rolls down his window, sticks out his hand, and pushes on the camper. This causes the camper to slide another two feet down the hill, and us to completely and safely stop.

That's right, he simply pushes the camper away to allow us to come to a complete unscathed stop. You can't make these kinds of miracles up. I look into the back of our car and everyone's teeth are still clenched for a collision. When it doesn't happen it takes a moment for them all to melt out of their collision ready positions.

Patty looks through her fingers, letting go of Billy Boy. She smiles warily, "What happened?"

I look back out my windshield and the driver of the camper is now standing right in front the station wagon in the same place he had left his camper truck. He opens his eyes and is as amazed as we all are that there was no collision.

"Are you shitting me?!" he says. "What happened?"

"Good going, Jed."

"You saved us."

"Nah."

"Jed, that was brilliant. What made you think to push on the camper?"

"Didn't you tell me to?"

"Me? I don't think so."

"Sure, you said, 'Jed, roll down your window and push the camper away with your hand.' Didn't you?"

"No he didn't. He was screaming like a little girl."

"Jed, you did that all on your own," Patty said.

Nance throws her arms around him and plants a big wet kiss on his face.

"Gross. Get a cabin."

"Come on, Jed. Let's go see what's going on down below."

Jed and I get out of the station wagon this time, new best friends and move around the camper. All the way down the road are about seventy cars. Just then the snow truck, with his plow raised, comes zooming up the hill, making its way through the cars, not dropping his salt. The guys who helped me earlier come running up.

"None of use saw this hill coming. Shit. And that damn truck had the bottom jammed. He was sitting there waiting to come up."

"He can't drop his salt."

"There's too many cars. It's okay. Come on, we're almost back to civilization. We're almost there."

A female voice comes out of the dark from up above the embankment. "Is anyone hurt down there?" I can't see her but she must have a home not too far off the road. This means we're probably close to neighborhoods of Frazer Park.

"I think we're good. Do you have a shovel?"

"Yes, a couple. I'll be right back."

I look around at all the faces I'd seen before. Most of them get out of their cars with determined looks to get their loved ones home.

My mind races to put all the elements together. I'm still warm, but the snow is continuing to cover the ice with a nice thick blanket of soft cover.

"It's too bad that son-of-a-bitch couldn't drop salt on this hill. Shit we'd be out of here."

Then it hits me. "Listen up. The way out of here is at the side of the road. Just under the new snow is gravel and salt from other salt drops. Use whatever you have, even your hands, and start throwing the sand, gravel, and salt onto the snow."

"Look out below, here come some shovels."Out of the dark come four shovels. I give one to Jed. The other two to my other new found friends. "Throw as much of the sand and salt as far into the road as you can. Work your way up to your cars. Then hand the shovel onto someone else."

"Thank you," I yell into the dark.

"You're welcome, Jozeph."

I look up into the darkness. "Hello. Jerry?"But the voice is gone. So I run down to the bottom of the hill with the others and start digging under the snow, throwing as much sand and salt as I can. Those around me catch on quick and before they know it their own vehicles are free to make it down the hill. The thank yous roll down the hill as fast as the cars and trucks that carry them. We work at a frenzy pace and before I realize it Jed and I are all the way back up at our station wagon. I take the shovel from Jed, "Nice work, Jed."

"Thanks. You're amazing, for a really weird old guy."

"It's the Aliens."

"Yeah, okay. But thanks for watching out for us. All of us. I'll never forget this night. None of us will."

"We're not home yet. Get in."I turn to the nearest guys and hand them the shovels. "Work your way up to your cars and pass it on." The guys take the shovels without a word, just a knowing smile and set off to work. It's amazing what humans can accomplish when put under pressure and given a clear direction. I move to the station wagon, looking up at the team of men, women, and kids working their way up the slope. "I did this."

"Move it, white boy."

I look around, but no one's there. "Mooky?" Nothing.

8

That was the headcheese Mook talking to us from inside our heads. He told me to move it and Jed to stick out his arm and push the camper. I'm sure of it.

Who that person was up in the hills lending us shovels, is debatable. Perhaps she heard me say my name to the cop. I don't know. Could it be the lovable yet ugly, pure energy, not seeable first Alien here on earth, oddly named Jerry, with two butts? Neither of which I've seen. Has he taken over some gorgeous woman's body again, because he hates being himself?

Why he would be up here at this time, placing himself to be helpful by conveniently handing out shovels worries me, if it was him. Because all of this could mean more than it appears in person. Was the idea of using shovels mine, or his?

With this sort of doubt in my head, I'll never be free of them in anything I do. Including women, writing, or directing. Even if they have nothing to do with it, there will always be that doubt. Even if I do my best to forget them as much as my mind will allow. They are here with us right now. At least Mooky is. That fact I'm sure of. Is it because I asked for their help? Did I bring this upon myself again by conquering up my need to have them help me get out of this icy mess? If I did, what will those sick bastards want in return?

Trust me; I do have moments where I'm free of them from my thoughts. But it's not easy to forget the unfortunate displeasure of being buried and left moribund with Jerry's decapitated Magical Man's body in his magic portmanteau. Yes, a human body of which he cloned thousands of years ago, during the reign of the Greeks. So that he could walk amongst men and women as a beloved Adonis to which he eventually became known in modern times as Gray McGuiness, The Magical Man, throughout Europe. Only to end up beheaded in my apartment building, aptly named Mystery Towers for reasons that are more apparent than I'd like. He had eventually turned himself into a unique form of a human clone-vampire from carrying Alien enriched healing stones.

Jerry says he didn't know what the effects would be at first. I'm sure he's lying, and did it on purpose so that Jerry could be Gray just long enough to screw up my turn here on Earth. Though I'm also sure that I'm just overly sensitive, and have no real proof that he changed my life's direction on purpose. Somehow, in moments late at night when I can't get them, those controlling us, out of my droll thoughts, it helps to blame all this Alien bullshit on him. I wish, beyond hope, that I could someday flip Jerry's power grid switch and turn his butts off forevermore. Like all the other space travelers who fear him want. The ones who have sucked me into their other worldly dirty work.

For Jerry's McGuiness, the overall side effect of human clone with Alien healing stones, of course, was the sucking of blood from young innocent women assistants and runaway kids. Ultimately his grim actions left me holding a bag full of the vampire-clone's body parts. All of this happened to me because of the Alien Council's concerns of Jerry making their presence known worldwide by resurrecting Gray McGuiness, and using our human mass media to prove it really happened before our very eyes.

Thus, literally making me run around LA with an arm and nearly get washed out to sea with his head. Somehow I became the Alien Mob's bagman. I had to make sure Gray's body parts remained separated from healing stones long enough for them all to decay beyond putting them back together in a civilized picture of respectable health. Just so that Jerry could finally let his alter ego go. Ironically, somehow just being touched by Gray changed the way Hollywood looked at me and my life, if not forever, at least for now.

Why Jozeph Picasso was chosen to be involved in this Alien mayhem is still in question. But it has brought me here tonight, a hot, not so new writer-slash-director of my first Hollywood film. I'm currently stupidly-stuck in Frazer Park Christmas snow with a station wagon full of other people's kids, trying to get back home to my loveable TV star poodle. Knowing anything Alien could happen to me at any human moment, is probably the worst of my fears.

So I deal with it, hoping the memory will soon fade fast enough to save me. Because explaining all of this is way too confusing. Even to me, button man to the Alien Council, who wants only to get on with my private life. All I want is to sit in front of my computer, tapping away at make-believe. I want to leave all this bigger than what life is meant to be behind for my imagination to conjure up.

But that's not gonna happen. Suddenly, I'm now standing outside the gas station, where all this mountaintop adventure began. I'm actually watching another Jozeph Picasso being hugged and kissed with added heartfelt handshakes until the real me standing out here wants to scream, "Cut, you're all overacting!" But it's true. I'm watching myself. Inside the glass wall that houses all the goodies sold to travelers heading into and out of the Frazer Park Mountains, stands me, the Jozeph Picasso, brave mountain man, hero snow driver, slash writer sometimes director.

Yet, it's not me. Even though people are actually taking pictures with me, right now, it's still not me. To them, that is me. He is the infamous writer-slash-murderer and now working director. He just rescued well over two hundred men, women and children, many not speaking English. He even took over for the local police, and taught them all how to get out of the mountain safely on Christmas night. I'm the man. And if I am that man inside, who the hell is this dumbfounded man standing all alone out here in the snow in my moonboots? Who is this reflection watching that me being so gracious. Who is this guy seemingly handling all the cheerful gratitude much better than the real me could?

Blip. "Pretty cool, huh?"

"You shithead, Mook."

"What, you think you drove all those cars up and down those hills all by yourself?"

"I didn't?"

"Hell no. You and your cracker head clone did."

"Clone? You cloned me?"

"Consider him spare parts if it helps. I do mine."

I swing at Mook. Swishing right through his face. "Stinking Alain hologram! What have you done?"

"You ungrateful puss. You want to spend all night in these cold mountains with dumb-asses, we can arrange it."

"He's getting all the credit. Look at him eating it up."

"Don't worry. Let him deal with that bullshit. We improved on your ungrateful bad manners and propensity to being an irritating asshole. We even grew your original leg back with two alike feet.

How do you like that? He's more you than you are him at this point, so what are you bitching about?"

"He's got...."

"Relax, when all this is done, we'll give your life back to you as a gift for helping us one last time."

"When what is all done?"

"That's why you're here, white boy."

"You brought me here? Made me go through all this?"

"We brought you here. Mother Nature made you go through this. We're just using the confusion to cover what's really going down."

I look at the station wagon and Patty is gathering the kids back in after water and bathroom breaks. She turns to us and smiles. "Thank you, Jozeph. Good luck. I hope you make it back."She waves.

I wave back. "Patty is one of you?"

"I told you to watch who you rent to."

"You son-of-a-bitch. What the hell do you want now?"

"We've got another little problem. And we need your help."

"You? The Alien Council? Or your stinking Alien Travelers Advisory Board?"

"All three. Feel better?"

"Crap. Look, forget about me, I'm in the middle of directing my first film. I can't just run off into one of your Alien induced adventures again." I walk toward the station wagon and suddenly come face to face with myself. Now I know what identical twins must feel like. My clone just looks at me, blankly as I look at him.

"Hello," I say.

"Hi."My clone moves on, not recognizing himself. He looks back at us like I'm weird for getting into his face and acting so awkward.

I look at Mook.

Mook turns and walks towards the back of the gas station. "Relax, he's programmed not to recognize you if you two are to meet."

I go after Mook. What else can I do? "Wait. Mook, what if I don't make it back?"

"The show must go on. We've transferred all of your data into him that we could so far with you still alive, and added some good character qualities you lack. To make sure your life goes on and your dog has a Dogman to clean his eye boogers. Jerry actually had them add piano man and some other talents. So you can sing at night in bars to him in case your filmmaking career takes a dump on this film."

"Data? Wait, I play piano and sing? Mooky, don't do this to me."

"People are coming out. The moon is full, we got to go."

I look at myself. I look at me. "Don't screw my movie up."

"What?" New me says back to old me.

"Merry Christmas and a happy New Year."

I smile and wave sadly at myself. My new self gets back into the station wagon eyeing me wearily.

"Wait! Mook, he'll get to be with Claire for New Year's Eve?"

"Only if you don't make it back in time. Come on."

I swing at Mook, passing right through his hologram face again. "Stinking hologram!"

9

Mook puts his hand on my shoulder. Just like that I'm standing in front of a majestic six thousand square foot log cabin perched high up on the side of a mountain overlooking the little town of Fraser Park.

"What am I doing here, Mook?"

"Wait for it."

"Wait for what?"

"Ooowwowooooooooooooo!"

"That."

"Holy crap, what in hell is it?"

"Dr. James Elwartowski."

"Sounded like a werewolf."

"He is."

"Please."

"Take this. Use it. One laser enhanced silver bullet to the heart. There's only one shot because you won't get a second."

I inspect the normal looking 9 millimeter. "Is this a joke?"

"Let him bite you and find out."

"Bite me? Mooky, I'm not shooting anyone or anything."

"You've got to do it tonight or you'll be here all month waiting for the full moon, Picasso. If you live that long. Your clone will spend New Years with Claire."

"Take this. I'm out of here."

"Ooowwowooooooooooooo!"

"Shit, that was even closer. Mook? Mook? MOOK?!"

"Shhhhhhhh," Mooky's voice comes from the dark. But he's not there. "He already knows why you're here. Don't worry, if you live through the night, I'll come get you. This is the first step in getting your life back."

"Don't do this."

"Ooowwowoooooooooooo!"

I turn around and over the crest of the nearest hill bounds a hairy, scary werewolf. His clothes are completely ripped away. Blood drips from his mouth. He stops to eye me, standing on all fours, naked as a jaybird. His eyes are aglow, nearly a florescent green in the moonlight. He looks away and up to the moon. Then back to me with every intention of adding me to his midnight snack.

I point the gun. What can I do? I have no intentions of being eaten by a werewolf tonight or any other night. He leaps into the air, Christ he's fast. I fall back over snow covered brush. I'm involuntarily on the run. But he's on me, ripping my arm in two. Zing-bam, goes the gun, point blank into his chest. The laser enhanced silver bullet flips him off me. Blood is everywhere. Most of it is mine. I can smell it.

I pick myself up, wanting to grab up the gun but it's impossible. The werewolf is wounded badly, not dying. He rolls over exposing the hole the bullet and laser blasted out of his back. I turn and run again seeing a black Ford F250 pickup truck with a snowplow passing by on the road below. I wave my good hand at the driver wearing a black cowboy hat. I don't have the wind to use my voice. He doesn't see me, and only pays attention to scraping the road.

So I pull off my belt the best I can. I descend the hillside, gravity picking up my pace. The smell of my own blood fills my lungs. Crap, I'm gonna have to tie this off on the run. My moonboots keep me from falling on my face. It takes ten seconds before the adrenalin of shock wears off. I start feeling light headed and the reality of the moment starts running its course as my blood empties out of me.

A freshly plowed snow mound looms in front of me at the side of the road, reflecting the full moon that lights my futile attempt to escape. So I lunge into the snow as I tighten the belt around my arm. My torn ski jacket sleeve is barely keeping my severed arm from falling behind. I get the noose up above my elbow and pull with all my might. I start piling snow down over me, covering myself up. I hope to bring my temperature down as low as I can to stem the flow of my blood. It's the only chance I have of not bleeding to death before I can find my Mooky phone.

That's how I got here. I should've seen this damn train wreck coming. Sure see it going. Damn, I'm dying again. Mook, where are you? Caw!

"Ooowwowoooooooooooo!"

Crap, even with a laser guided silver bullet in him and blasting out his back, he's still coming for me. He's coming for me, Mook. He's coming for me! He's right here. He's digging in the snow. I can feel his footsteps above me. Where's my phone. I can't move. I can't move anything but my eyes!

"Caw, caw, caw!" I hear over head. The smell of my own blood mingles with the smoke of countless cabins. No one ever mentioned that you can smell yourself bleeding to death. Normal people spend Christmas night in the arms of their loved ones, sipping wine and eating crackers and cheese. But not me, I'm here listening to an Alien werewolf dig me out of the snow bank and my crow calling for me.

"Caw."

"Caw, caw, caw!" I can hear his feathers flapping violently. The werewolf roars in painful anger, his blood dripping down onto the snow where I hide.

"Caw." The snow is ripped away from above me, and the werewolf looms inches away, as Caw claws at the back of his head. The good doctor tries to reach up and swipe at him, while wanting to bite into me. His mouth opens, this is it. Right at my chest. Bubba, I'm sorry. "Mook, help me!"

10

Blip!

"The important thing is not to panic, Picasso."

"Where am I?"

"Up here. Almost done."

"I'm back up there?"

"Yep, 'fraid so.

"Why can't you show me? After all I've been through."

"The reality of what we're doing up here has always distorted the human mind into sick violent reactions that are usually detrimental to our existence. We keep those here we bring up and let see. And we're not done with you yet on Earth. When you're up here and you are awake, seeing all this Alien reproduction activity, know they plan to suck the life out you and you'll never leave. You understand?"

"Unfortunately.

"Good. You lost half your arm so we had to find a new one."

"So, I'm not awake again. Yet, I'm talking?"

"Subconsciously speaking, yes. You've had an arm put back on and other things repaired. Simple stuff for us but important to what we need done."

"Did I kill it?"

"What do you think?"

"I hit it. I know I hit it."

"Yeah, down there someone unfortunately jumped and shot the local good doctor on his way home last night. Took all his clothes. It's in all the local papers."

"Someone."

"Don't worry about it now. Your hero alibi was in a station wagon full of happy kids on the Five at the time. You're in the clear."

"That's so comforting."

"We can surgically remove the sarcastic attitude, Picasso. So unless you want more of yourself running around down there, show us some respect."

"Alright, alright. Where did this arm come from?"

"Let's just say you weren't the only one on the menu last night."

"Let's just say you tell me who the hell's arm is attached to me, you bastard."

"Let's just say you ain't as white as you used to be cracker head."

"You son-of-an-alien-bitch! What have you done to me? Help! Someone help me!

Blip!

I open my eyes. I'm yelling while sitting in a living room of what appears to be a very large, upscale log cabin. No lights are on inside. So I can see outside in the still full moon glow that I am not far from where I was when being chased by Dr. James Elwartowski, aka hairy, scary Alien werewolf. Down at the end of the drive someone is there smoking a cigarette. He looks familiar in shape but I can't make out his face. I only see a short fat figure in a gray trench coat. I look down to my right arm, there's a gun in its hand. Good, I might have to shoot myself. I set it down on the table beside me. Even in this light I can see my hands don't match. "Son of an alien bitch!"

"It's only temporary."

I grab up the gun and point it at Mooky's head who is sitting across from me. "You are one lucky hologram."

"Why? Because I have to baby sit your whinny punk human ass. Waa, I'm still alive. The mean old Aliens saved my ass once again from a nasty werewolf. Help me."

I pull the trigger three times, click, click, click! Friggin' empty. "No, because I'd explode your head this time, you yellowed brained Alien freak.

"Look who's talking, Frankenstein?"

"Look what you've done to me. What am I now, part Mexican?"

"Guatemalan, to be exact."

I look around for bullets. "Where's the silver bullet?"

"Relax. The world is a melting pot after all."

"End this now or I'll end this bullshit my way right now. Where's the frigging bullets?"

"Go ahead shoot. They're in your pocket. No one would even know you're gone. Not your friend Erin, J.J., Claire, or Hollywood. Not even your little fur mutt. Real life goes on, Picasso, with or without you.

You humans need to all keep that in mind. There's always a bigger picture. Much like the ever expanding Universe. It doesn't end with us. Makes living a lot less stressful, trust me."

"Bubba is not a mutt." I take the eight non silver bullets out of my pocket and load the gun.

"Whatever, they all taste the same to us."

"You Aliens are eating our dogs, too?"

"Only those of us who eat what you humans cook and don't give a shit where the meat comes from, yes."

"Wait, you said you don't eat, you drink?"

"So you got me there, I've never eaten a dog. But Dr. James Elwartowski has and now you've got to finish this. Even if you have to wait to the next full moon."

"Next? My film will be done in three weeks. I'm supposed to spend New Year's Eve with Claire Davis."

"You are. Sort of."

"Here, shoot me, will ya."

"Maybe later if the need arises. Now let's get down to it. Next to you there are a driver's licenses and a passport. Including a deed to this cabin. Not in your real name. So don't get any ideas of wanting to keep it or use the ID to skip town. This next part is very complicated. Pay attention to everything I say to you. Stop feeling sorry for yourself. Just be happy you are still who you think you are up there inside your white bread head."

"How do you kill Holograms?"

"We'll get to that some other time. Now listen. You, and this person you appear to be, have already befriended the doctor. He wants to buy this place from you for reasons that involve a very beautiful and sexy young thing."

"But I shot this werewolf. What about that?"

"The good doctor is rehabbing nicely, thank you."

"Won't people recognize me as Jozeph Picasso?"

"I doubt it. Take a look in that mirror over there."

"What have you done to me?"

"We didn't do anything. We only repaired what Dr Jekyll did to your arm and face."

"My face?!" I get up and move to the mirror. I'm not sure what to expect. I don't remember anything happening to my face. "Holy shit! Who is this?"

"Check your ID."

"Javier Sanchez? Who the hell is Javier Sanchez?"

"Relax, only until this is over, and then we'll fix things."

"Fix things? How are you gonna fix things?"

"Either way you die, Picasso. Just make sure it's the right you. Not the wrong you who ends up being the living you. If the real you wants to sleep with your little actress or dog again."

"Mooky. I can't do this. I won't do this. Please, I beg of you. Don't make me do this. I'm just starting to get a real life."

"Fine. Then don't be Javier. But keep one thing in mind. Javier is in a deep relocation program with the LA undercover narcotic squad. He is due to testify against his own drug lord family in five weeks. He's been in hiding up here for nearly a year now and he's fallen in love. This is so deep that they couldn't even use guys currently on the force to watch over him. They're all being followed. So you make the call, Javier.

"Stop calling me that. I'm Jozeph Picasso."

Then kill the werewolf and return to your own pathetic self. Or stay as Javier Sanchez. A rat testifying against his own scumbag brothers. He'll end up dead along some lonely gravel road. You know all about gravel roads, don't ya?

"I'm a...." I turn to face the door. Someone is approaching.

"Squealer. You're a no-good dirty rat. Hear those footsteps coming back this way? Those two guys you might remember. Hired privates to keep an eye on Javier. Nobody else wanted the job bad enough to die for it. I'm sure they'd like to know you're really the Picasso who fingered them. The same guy who got them kicked off the force and out of their pension funds.

"I didn't finger... Tucker and MacAroy? The Hansel and Gretel of the LAPD are coming here?"

"Good, you remember them. They're outside right now. Have been here for three weeks. Watching over you like a couple wet nurses."

"Why haven't I read about any of this in the LA Times?"

"This is a very hush-hush situation here, Picasso. This is a big money case for humans and Aliens alike. We can't have one of ours eating their drug case witnesses, drawing attention to the rest of us who are feeding on you dimwits. So, just keep your smart mouth shut this time and stick it out as Sanchez and kill Doctor Elwartowski when we tell you to do it. By the way, you now speak fluent Spanish."

"Si?"

"Si. Now stash the gun. You got visitors coming in. Ironic isn't it? Those two low lives watching over your sorry ass. Making sure you don't accidently die or purposely run for it."

Blip.

I open my mouth to reply and the door opens. Filling it are two of my fattest nightmares. Mike and Mac. How did I get so stinking lucky? I look back at Mooky. He's gone. "Alien Hologram."

"What did you just say?"

"Nothing."

"You hear that?"

"Hell with that," MacAroy says. "Where the hell have you been?"

"I took a walk."

"Don't do it again," Mac tells me. "Looked all over for your ass."

"He said Alien Hologram," Mike says.

"Did you say Alien Hologram?" Mac asks.

"What do you know about Holograms?"

"Nothing. You two stop for Tequila?"

Mac moves over to turn on lights.

I do my best to stay out of the direct light.

"There's a full bar right over here." Mike goes over to it. He turns on the back bar light and looks behind the bar at a row of bottles. "Three kinds of Tequila. You want any, pick one."

"I like fresh bottles. But I changed my mind, I don't need you now." I get up and go to the bar, getting right up into Mike's face, looking him in the eye.

"What the hell. Step back, Poncho."

"You smell like a woman. You have been with my woman?"

"The hell I have. I've been out on the driveway listening to something howling in the night, looking for you. And he just stopped down to the market and back. No one's come in or out but us."

"Then you must be the sweet woman I smell."

"Are you looking for an ass kickin'?"

"The last time I let a woman kick my ass she wore black boots. You got black boots, Mike, you can kick my ass."

"What in hell is going on here?" Mac says. Who do you think you are? Talkin' to us this way. You scumbag?"

"I know you two pinche cabronas. You're both dead beat cops. Out on your fat asses. Having to baby sit some drug lord like me. How low in the scum-pool you two pricks have sunk."

"I'm gonna kick your ass."

"You ain't doing jack shit, Mac. You and Mike are gonna stand there and take my bullshit. Or I'm gonna have my friend the Mook come turn you both into Alien fodder feed."

"What did you just say?"

"You heard me, Mike." Mike looks at me queerly, and then looks at Mac. "You starting to figure it out aren't you, Gretel."

"Picasso?"

"That ain't Picasso. He's a stinkin' Mexican drug punk."

"Technically, part Nicaraguan. The rest, well some of me, is still me. Other parts are Italian. You remember your two boyfriends, the bad actor and his thug brother?" I turn and drop my pants and show them my tattooed ass. The fist sized heart with Debbie does Dallas imprinted in it. "So, how have you two assholes been?"

They both just stare at me with their mouths open.

I pull up my pants. "That's what I thought, dumb as ever."

"Let's kill him."

I pull my gun. "Not so fast, fatsos. Hands on the bar. Let's go. Make it quick. None of me has killed anyone in days and my trigger finger is startin' to twitch from the lack of use."

"Shit, look who's using bad dialogue now."

"If you're really Picasso in there. Then we know you ain't got the balls to shoot us. So cut the crap."

"I don't, but Sanchez does."

"That shit needs us more than we need him."

"Shut up, Milky. I will explain how things are gonna go down around here. Or I plug you now and bury your asses in the basement. Better yet, feed your asses to the werewolf."

"What? Nobody said nothin' about a werewolf."

"Now hand over the guns. Real slow."

"Will you stop with the corny dialogue, for Christ's sakes?"

"It ain't me, it's him, Sanchez."

"Great, now we got two assholes who can't write dick we gotta take shit from."

"I say we strangle them both right now. Tell everyone he offed himself because he couldn't stand his own Hollywood bullshit.

"Just slide the hardware."

11

"This is dumb, Picasso. We're here to protect you. Or him."

I continue to tie up their hands behind them. They sit at a breakfast bar looking into the kitchen. "You should know, Mike. You guys are the kings of dumb."

"Okay, we know you're a little mistrusting of us. On account of what happened between our friends and yours in the past," Mac says.

"You mean like trying to frame me for murder to cover your sorry asses? Or helping bury me in the Magic Man's Magical box?"

"Both, but we ain't those guys we used to be," Mike says.

"You got to admit we met under some unusual circumstances. You know, Jetty and the Mook and all," Mac adds.

"Yeah, we are freelancers. Our own guys now. We don't answer to nobody about anything."

"Really. Only because you two dimwits have screwed up so bad nobody wants you around them, I bet."

"Come on, Picasso. Tying us up like this is a waste of time."

"Yeah, you're gonna need our protection sooner than later."

"I don't need your protection. What I need is for you two guys to stay put while I get me something to eat."

"Hey, now you're talkin'. We got three very juices in that bag out there by the door. There's one in it for you, or Javier, whichever one of yous decides to cook."

I finish with their hands. I add rope to both their feet and tie them together to the foot railing at the base of the breakfast bar. "How much are you two willing to buy into?"

"Shit, Picasso, ain't we seen enough to know that there's something else goin' down around here. Other than you just being some whack-job causing all this shit to happen."

"Yeah, shit, one minute we're dealin' with a drug scum. The next thing we know you're walkin' and talkin' in his skin. Hiding from who knows what this time."

I go back out to the living room and retrieve their bag of goodies. "Beer? You guys plan to protect Javier while drinking beer?" I reenter the kitchen to find them tangled up, face to face, trying to get free. "You two really love each other don't you?"

"Untie us, Picasso. We ain't goin' nowheres."

"You still sound like a dime store thug, you know that, Mike."

"Come on, we need this as much as you probably do."

"More even. Since you screwed us out of our lively hoods. We ain't seen much action. And we only got this because no one else feels like dyin' over protectin' some scumbag like you."

"You're not making me feel better about you two bums looking after me."

"Hey, we ain't talkin' about you. We're talking about Javier. This guy is turnin' on his whole family. To get out of livin' on death row."

"He knows he wouldn't live a day in the joint."

"So, Mook tells me his brothers and I are dealers."

"Kingpins, man. The mother is, too. Coke, pot, heroin. Shit, these guys have so many meth labs set up across the nation they're practically big as Walgreens."

"You hear about them ten bikers found burned in a house out in Palm Dale?"

"Yeah, I read about that." I take down the biggest skillet hanging on a display rack. I fire up the Wolf Range. Then drop in a little olive oil to rub out the skillet. "Nice, I'm gonna fry not grill. Okay?" They don't care. Before me is a rack of seasoning and spices. I pick a blend for red meat and add a little chopped garlic I found in the door of the fridge. "A lab explosion, wasn't it?"

"No, that was them tryin' to cut a new deal. They wanted more of the backend. Prosecutor had the Times down play it because of what they had planned to do with you."

"So we killed them?"

"Burned them. Stacked them on top of each other. Still alive. Doused them with chemicals, man. Set them ablaze. Not a pretty sight. To teach the others watching a lesson."

"This was me, Javier?" I stand back because in my head I can see everything. Smell everything. The flesh burning, chemical fumes. "Shit." I choke up into the sink, running water to wet my face.

47

"Thanks for sharing."

"Shut up. For whatever sick reason these bastards have implanted him inside of me and me inside of him." I choke up again. And run the water before facing them, wiping my face. "This is bad."

"That's Javier, man. He lit the flame according to the Bureau."

"And they're letting him walk?"I get a fresh sense of smell from the roasting garlic and sizzling steak. It hits me like burning flesh, hard and heavy. I lean over the sink and dry heave again. "Holy...."

"What the hell, man?"

"You puss, we're about to eat in here."

"Sense memory. They put his bullshit visions in my head."

"You mean?"

"See, hear, smell... all those things he did and his brothers... it's as though I've done them myself when they flash through my head."

"He testifies and he thinks he's walkin'."

"But he, or you, as things stand, won't get far."

"Wait. After the trial you kill Javier?"

"Well, we ain't been told just yet. Know what I mean?"

"No I don't, Mac. You're hitmen now?"

"Hell no, Picasso. Private security. He hired us himself, through the help of his lawyers and the courts. As part of his deal to testify. He stays out of the local lockups and romances the girl he's got out here. Shit, these relocation programs only work so good, and for so long. Even if you follow all the rules. But this guy seems to think his life is safe up here. So far it has been, by keepin' his people away."

"Until I became him."

"No one said he was lucky," Mike says."Dumbass fell in love with a local honey. We are just to drop Javier off at the trial, and then bring him back here to let him convince his girl to go with him. Good luck with that."

"He's been living a secret life up here. For how long?"

Mac and Mike look at each other, waiting to see who's gonna blab. "He just got back from business travel as far as anyone knows," Mac says. "But he's here on and off for three years now. This past year with her on his arm. Now that she's old enough."

"Had his eye on her the whole time," Mike adds. "No one in his family knows about this place. Not even his crazy momma. We're not sure how that's happening. But no one's shown up lookin' for him."

"Yet."

"Right."

"Don't worry. We ain't the ones to button you, I swear on my mother," Mike promises. "We just do as we're told and step aside and let nature take its course."

"Yeah, it's all we signed on for. Get you to the trial. Make sure your right thumb print matches. Then later bring you back here. From that point he hires whomever he wants. He goes wherever he wants. We couldn't care less."

I look at my new right hand. Thumb prints, huh, "What if I don't testify? I mean, what the hell do I know about any of this stuff?" I look away because in my head I can see a flash of my two brothers standing before me. Money is stacked on the table, stained with blood. Coke is all over the floor and two dead men. An old woman, our mother, Javier's mother, sits off in a rocking chair looking on with a proud smile. As if she stopped seeing what scum we were years ago and only sees us as good loyal boys.

"If we know the Mook.

"And we wish we didn't."

"We're guessing you'll know what you'll need to know when the time comes."

"No, what if I'm not Javier when the time comes."

"You mean, if you go back to being Picasso?"

"Shit, that's a good question. I don't know. What happened to the other Javier to make you become him?"

"We were eaten by a werewolf."

"A what?"

"A hairy, scary werewolf. And it's living right over there, as Doctor James Elwartowski."I point out the window at the cabin up the hill. He's one of them."

"You mean James, the local doc, is one of them?" Mike points up.

"An Alien?" Mac adds.

"Yes, with werewolf tendencies. You heard him howl. There was only enough left for one of us to make it back. I'm not sure if Mook told me the whole truth. The Alien Council wants James the Alien werewolf dead. Because he's eating people instead of saving them."

"Alien Council? What the heck is that?"

"You don't want to know all what I know."

Mike and Mac look at each other, sitting ducks tied to the bar chairs. "What the hell, Picasso. Untie us."

"Relax, I shot him earlier tonight. He's in the local hospital. He ate Javier before he did this to me. Chewed me up pretty good. But I shot him once. Just not good enough."

"You mean?"

"Because he bit you?"

"The next full moon, I might be just like him."

"What did the Mook say? Are you a werewolf or not?"

"He didn't. It just came to me. I've been bitten by a werewolf. My face torn off. My arm bit in two. They need a place to continue hiding Javier away. His death could make a big stink around here. Or they're now using Javier by keeping him alive to help me kill the doctor before he eats anyone else. All I know for sure is they're making me do this if I ever want to be the lovable Picasso again. What happens to Javier after that, I don't know. It's complicated. I'm not calling the shots, they are."

"Shit, Picasso, how do you keep gettin' your ass into these fixes?"

"Yeah, and you might be a werewolf already," Mac says.

"What if we got to shoot you, to stay alive?" Mike asks.

"There's that. So, how do you two want your steaks? Bloody?"

"I ain't so hungry."

"Ain't you supposed to be directing some big Hollywood movie? With the girl Jetty Dazarrio was all busted up about?"Mac asks.

"Somehow I don't see Ern the Burn Burnstein letting you on holiday to go chase Alien werewolves. I think he got enough of your crazy shit last time. Ain't that why he's letting you direct his meal ticket, Claire Davis? With his son, Junior, producing the thing?"

"Oddly, Junior has turned out to be a good producer. Staying out of my way as much as he can, and getting me everything I ask for."

"He's probably scared shitless of you, if he knows about any of this crazy stuff," Mac adds.

"Only enough not to ask for way-out-there details, but not to worry, I'm still directing the film. No matter what happens here." They both look at me, confused. "Well, my clone is, if I don't make it back."

"Shit, Picasso, this deepshit is gettin' smelly complicated."

"Yes, so now you know about the Aliens, werewolves and clones. You still want to help me?"

"Don't forget about your magical horny vampire, Gray McGuiness. He ain't involved is he?" Mike asks.

"Jesus, I hope not," Mac says.

"Him no, Jerry who created him, I'm not so sure yet."

"And now it's a real werewolf?"

"Worse than any back lot horror movie you've ever seen."

"Shit, I wouldn't miss this for anything. I love all those black and white Universal B movies," Mac says.

"So what do we kill him with?"

"You serious, you two still want to help?"

"Picasso, there's a lot of things about us you don't know."

"I know more about you two than I ever wanted to know."

"Untie us."

"Why? All of a sudden you two are my long lost buddies?"

"You're gonna need help with this."

"Aren't you two forgetting something?"

They look at each other. "I don't think so," Mike says.

"The fall guy."

"The what?"

"The fall guy. The patsy. Someone's got to take the fall for killing the doctor. It's not me this time, because technically I'm not here."

"The doc is a friggin' werewolf, so screw 'im."

"And that will be your defense? They won't let this linger a mystery. Someone will either die or see time for killing the doctor."

"Ah... yeah, we get your point. This is really complicated."

"So when they find him he's a dead guy killed by Javier, no big deal," Mac says.

"A well liked dead doctor. Front page news dead guy."

"Why don't they just take him?" Mike asks. "Up there, wherever?"

"Then he's a missing doctor some dumb human keeps looking for. They tend to frown on these kinds of investigations. Besides, the Alien Council can't get involved in this in anyway. Not all of them want him dead or think he should die. It's why they couldn't kill off Jerry's Alien clone. The Magical Man. Aliens can't off Aliens. Clone or otherwise. It could start some awful civil war that none of us humans will survive. That's what I was told. That's why they suck patsies like me in to do their dirty work by holding the end of civilization as we know it over our heads. Even the life of my lucky dog. That's why you're probably here, too."

"We ain't heard any of this, shit."

"Alien Council? Civil Wars? They've got a government?" Mac asks.

"Mac, Mike are you sure you two want to hear all this? Once you're in, you're in and there's no way of getting away, even dead.

Hell they brought me back twice already. This is a mob, from Earth or otherwise. The rules are no different. Only the insurance is out of this world. Once you accept it, they use you. You're valuable. If you fight them being here, freak out in anyway, you're up there feeding babies. They replace you with a nice usable clone, or just make you explainable dead."

They look at each other again. It's comical because they are so close to each other. "Yeah, we're in. If you untie us."

"Never mind, who wants to eat first?"

"Okay, at least untie one hand each so you don't have to spoon feed us."

"Make it fast. I'm startin' to itch here."

"Yeah, Mike gives me the heebeegeebees, too." I go over and untie one of their hands each and retie the others to each other and the back of the stool."

"This isn't necessary."

I cut their meat for them. Beers and meat ain't my best of meals but it's all I've got. "I still might need you for bait."

"The hell you do."

"So tell us. Hey, this ain't half bad, thanks. There's some potato salad there in the fridge."

I open the fridge and pull out the container of potato salad. There are two big ripe tomatoes so I take them too, and green onion. I plop a heaping spoon full on all of our plates. I stand across from them, and start cutting up a tomato. They watch me like two punk kids waiting for Dadda to tell them how his day went.

"Come on, Picasso. Fill us in on everything."

"Are you sure?"

"Hell ya," they answer like I'm about to pop their cherries.

Blip!

"Don't tell them anything else, Picasso." Standing by the fridge is the Mook.

"Thanks for knocking."

"This is a need to know operation boys. Anymore and I'll have to take you both up there."

"You mean. The space ship?"

"Somewhere like that."

"Shit, man, let's go."

"When you get there, Mike, they suck the life out of you through your balls."

"Pass. My wife's got that covered."

"Yeah. Pass the tomatoes. And an onion. Come on."

"Need to know, Picasso."

"I don't get to tell them about all this shit."

"They know enough. Just get the job done. If you two keep him alive we'll make it worth your while."

"We talkin' cash?"

"How much?"

"Enough. No more questions on this. Just continue doing the job we brought you here for. We'll take it from there and make it all go away, when need be."

"Done. Wait, you brought us here?"

The rope drops from their hands and feet. "Fail us by letting harm come to Picasso and you'll end up feeding babies through your nuts."

"Or eaten by a crazed werewolf?"

"Man, this is really getting complicated," Mac says.

"But we're in. Pass the A1 Sauce. Right there in the left fridge door. Second shelf."

"Any chance you can get us fully reinstated?"

"When we finish the job, of course."

"What do you think, Javier?"

"Only if I get my name back."

12

After dinner we sit in front of the fireplace large enough to take a kettle-bath together, but we don't. Instead, we watch the flames devour the logs Mike and Mac brought in from the wood shed. We quaff from a rare bottle of Remy Martin 1965 edition cognac, worth probably around a grand, like it's a four dollar Haller's res blend whisky. We don't bother to take in its bouquet because a twelve-foot Christmas Tree, the only other illumination in the cabin, fills the moment with the overpowering smell of Old St. Nick. What was left of the full moon is the only light coming from outside. It's almost three in the morning.

I haven't had time to take this all in. I'm not even sure if I can sleep or if I can fully trust these two guys. I'm doing my best not to think that I won't personally finish my movie. Trying hard not to foresee my clone spending New Year's Eve with Claire and Bubba, and not the real me ever again. With my luck of late he'll mess up everything. I'll return just in time to take the brunt of everyone's anger, millions of lost dollars and sexual disappointments. Or with my bad luck, he'll knock an extra wanna-share up on the set. I'll get a late night sobbing call on my machine when I get back. Letting me know I'm gonna be a daddy. And that she and her parents are moving into Mystery Towers.

I'm Javier now. His ugly thoughts keep jarring me back to reality. I'm a scumbag drug dealer, a murderer and worse, a rat about to turn the screws on my own family to keep from dying in prison from the hands of one of my own people. Just so that I can stay in the grace of the young woman I love, despite having children and a wife back home in Texas. I'm even lying to the sweet young thing up here in the mountains. I'm now as trustworthy as a fly on dried donkey shit promising not to eat any. "How do I get myself into these things?"

"Why are you asking us?"

"What? Am I thinking out loud again?"

"Yeah, stop it, fly-boy. You're ramblin' in bad Spanish half the time, and givin' us the creeps."

"Your head starts spinnin' around I'm shootin' and askin' Mooky questions later."

"Sorry. This sucks."

"Pays swell."

"If you live to spend it."

"Nothing we ain't lived through before."

"Doesn't any of this Alien shit bother you?"

"What bothers me is you keep complainin' and ruinin' my free expensive buzz from this shit. You think we drink like this at home?"

"Excuse me. I'm a third of the man I used to be."

"Life's a bitch, and then you have kids, right, Mike."

"Shit," Mike answers. "I got three fat assed girls in local high school sittin' around watchin' TV all afternoon because they ain't got one single afterschool talent between them. Plus, an ex-wife who hates the dirt I stand on because she blames me for having to manage a Burger King because I lost my job. If that ain't bad enough, all of them menstruate at the same time, and always when I'm visiting. Being infested with Aliens is almost a relief as an explanation as to why my personal life is so screwed up. So what do I care where the money comes from? As long as it shuts them up."

"You don't care we're not the top of the food chain?"

"He's never been married," Mac replies.

"Sanchez has."

"It's why you're him, up here, chasing around some local rich filly, because Sanchez is married, and not happy about it.

Mike sips his cognac, "Guess he ain't as dumb as us two. Picasso, since some fool invented 'I Do,' man is 'I ain't,' and hasn't seen the top of a food chain. Wife and kids float first, and end up with all your shit, whether you can swim, make it across to the other side or not."

We sit there for a moment before Mac adds, "Food chain. Shit, Picasso. My wife's friggin' cat eats better than me, and has its own toilet. I nearly blow my bladder twice a week just wakin' up knowing I got to wait in line to piss. I added a balcony so I can piss off it. I try not to crap outside."

"Spare me," I say.

"My neighbor would've called the police," Mac continues, "long ago if I wasn't a cop myself. He's tired of me pissing outside on his fence. And my wife's mother even lives with us. Nothin' I do is as good as her husband made it for her and her shithead kids. She's got more money in retirement pay from the government than I made working full time in the LAPD. Takin' from Jetty was the only civilized thing in my life, because I was able to hide that money for myself."

"Okay, I get it."

"No you don't. You don't have kids," Mike says.

"Shit, I got married right out of the academy with my first brat already on the way. My kids don't even see me, unless they need me to pay for somethin' they did wrong. You know what my oldest kid wants to be? A professional skateboarder. He's sixteen years old. Dresses and smells like an Encino bum. Broke half the bones in his body already. And the only thing he's really good at, is smokin' dope. So shut up," Mac says.

"Yeah, I got your food chain right here," Mike says, flipping me the bird.

"I didn't even know you two clods were married or even thought of you dicks as having kids or a life. Thought my life was messed up. Over there, my gun, use it on yourselves before it's too late. Here, give it to me, I'll shoot you both myself."

"Don't tempt me. When I go I'm taken everyone around me with," Mac says.

"See, even my own partner hates me," Mike says.

"Shit, I just know you can't live without me, Mike."

"Not if you don't let me try."

"Told you there were things about us you didn't know. No thanks to you screwin' things up for us."

"You're off the street and out of jail, making more than you had in your whole lives. So you should both be thanking my alien ranting."

"Is that what's eatin' you, Picasso? We're not alone? Lots of people think that. There are all kinds of books and study groups."

"You don't get it, do you, guys? Thinking it is livable, knowing it and not being able to warn anyone that it's really happening is maddening to me. We're not free. We are not living the lives we want to live, that we work for. We're living the lives they want us to live."

"Maybe he is married with kids after all."

"To an Alien Mob."

"Are you sayin' we're slaves or somethin'?"

"Lap dogs. All of us are. Is what I'm saying."

"Speak for yourself."

"I am. They've bred us to be who we are."

"Stupid, no good husbands? Can't wait to tell my wife I have an excuse to who I am in her mother's eyes."

"Exactly. They bred us to be their worker bees, from out of the trees and caves. They even got rid of Neanderthal because they were a mistake. We're creating a paradise that only they can truly enjoy, because our genetic makeup won't let us be totally happy. Even if we get it all, wanting more is part of being human. And getting it all only allows us to destroy ourselves from abundance, destined to die with or without it. It keeps us from seeing the whole picture. Keeps us from knowing that this is it, the only place we'll ever be. This is Heaven on Earth, and all we do is live here as though it's hell."

"Speak for yourself."

"There are happy people out there, Picasso."

"Are there? In peace with themselves, one with the universe?"

"Yeah, I've seen them, arrested them even."

"I hate them, smug little bastards."

"They're Alien. Don't you get it? They're content, because they're one of them. They're not gonna die like us."

"Come on, Picasso, you're talkin' crazy."

"Am I? Next time you see someone perfectly happy, shoot them in the head. He's either an Alien with yellow blood or a clone of some unsuspecting human. Some are just humans taken over by Alien forms. Then run like hell."

"Why ain't this paradise perfect than? Why not make us docile and easy to control?"

"We are to them."

"Why all the war and turmoil? Why can't we just get along?"

"Thank you, Rodney King. It's so they can collect us, take us up there and no one will suspect them of drinking us. In the Milky Way alone, findings suggest, 60 billion planets may be orbiting red dwarf stars in the habitable zone, much like earth. Do you realize how many of those beings are here? A hell of a lot. That's why eight hundred thousand children younger than eighteen are reported missing each year, for an average of over two thousand children reported missing each day. And that's only in America. There's another hundred thousand in the UK alone. That's one kid every five minutes alone. Don't you see? They're taking us, studying us and feeding on us. There's nothing we can do about it. Because we don't know they are here? The three of us know. Thousands more probably do. But we can't tell anyone, because they won't let us tell anyone on a large scale. If we try, we're crazy people, ranting and raving in front of a giant fireplace, drinking hundred dollar cognac, and no matter what we've seen or heard or done, we sound crazy talking about it."

"Don't include us in your dizziness."

"We know. We're good. It doesn't matter, long as it pays the bills."

"Like you said, we're goners anyway."

"Then why fight crime?"

"It's different."

"Is it?"

"Shit, he's got a point. Shut up, you're startin' to make sense."

"Our minds, digestive systems and our sex drives are what separate us from them. Who can prove a thing? No one. Not one shred of evidence that any other form of intelligent life exist in our Universe other than what's already here. Who's kidding whom? Are there those of us who are allowing this to happen? Are there those of us in control not really human, merely human clones? Think about it. Look at me. I have a clone living my life right this very moment, and I'm sitting here now as three living human beings sharing one body."

"Pour me some more of that. Please shut the hell up about this stuff, Picasso. It's Christmas," Mike says.

"Yet, life as we know it may have started from way out there as single organisms crashing to earth on meteorites and asteroids. Still we as humans can't prove that life other than ourselves are here, breeding and feeding on us. Doesn't that drive you mad?"

"You need to stop watching TV, Picasso. And stop over thinkin' all this shit. It will drive you nuts," Mac says.

"Us too, if you keep this up," Mike adds.

"That's my point, Mac. This is not TV. This is real. They're really here, all around us. Worse, not all of the Alien Council wants to stay hidden. There's a faction of them who want to send us back to the Dark Ages before our technology and developing brains let us know they're here and we get out of control. Look at your own life. If you found a way to change it, wouldn't you?"

"In a heartbeat."

"That's my point. They don't want us changing on our own."

"You every meet these Council guys?"

"No. Not yet."

"Was Mary, the one pretending to be from the DA's office, on this Council? That yellow brain thing Mike shot in the head?"

"Bitch sucked us into this mess. Got what she had comin'.""

"I don't know for sure. I've only met Mary, Mooky, Jerry, and now this werewolf. Patty, the tenant who got me out here, she's one."

"That little girl, long brown hair, she's an Alien?"

"Or she's a Human Clone being controlled by an Alien."

"At least you got Alien Health insurance. They took both of ours."

"And our pensions."

"Only they don't give him back his own body parts."

"Parts are parts."Mike and Mac think that's funny.

"Wait until they start working on you, keeping you alive."

"I got a hemorrhoid or two they're welcome to give to someone."

"What are they so worried about?"

"Think about it, you guys. What would happen if the God fearing masses discovered that we are not who we think we are? And that there is real proof we are not alone?" I answer.

"You mean if the Devil isn't real but Aliens are?"

"Revelation will bring revolution," Mac says.

"Yes, fear of evolution is the way it was explained to me by Jerry and Mook. Man is just a few generations away from evolving into a species that can detect the presence of Alien life forms here on Earth. They will be forced to deal with us in a mass destruction that man has never seen before. But dinosaurs have."

"Are we talkin' some kind of extinction?"

"No, those that evolve and accept them as our Supreme Beings will be allowed to live as the Aliens intended us, as working slaves creating a paradise, a heaven in the galaxies away from their harsher home planets. But those that don't… I don't know… some kind of world-size pandemic. Bird flu, swine flu, flea-bitten black plague, or just zap us from up there and take us away. Turn us into frozen dinners, or maybe smoked testicular oysters. I don't know."

"They eat us?"

"Drink us, clone us, eradicate us… take your pick."

"Human smoothes?"

"Ball and ovarian juice cocktails. They keep those they take alive and milk them somehow."

"Christ, Picasso, that's some sick shit."

"He's another story."

"So, none of this is real? You're not just making this up?"

"No, it's all real. It's just more real than you can even imagine. Think about it. What are all these immunizations they're giving our kids? That they gave us when we were kids? Ten, fifteen, twenty shots, what is really happening to the kids? What is really in those shots? And who's really giving them to the kids and why? Don't you see, knowing what we know, there's nothing we can trust anymore. There is no face value. If looking at me now doesn't nail that point home, well, shit, I don't know. Because everything of importance, short of Mother Nature, that happens on this Earth, is caused by them. Is controlled by them, and in the big picture is for them. It's for their happiness here on our planet Earth, and not ours."

"Shit. Please shut up."

"Oh, yeah, they don't shit. And that's why we don't know they're here. No shit and they dissipate, not decay, you saw it firsthand. And they're fascinated by our sexual animal desires because most of them reproduce in a Petri dish at best. They are here for the money and power of living forever in paradise."

"So if your spouse can't reproduce...?"

"It could be one of them."

"Too bad mine wasn't."

"So they're doing us?"

"Some of them are. Jerry, I only know does, when he takes over our bodies or creates people like Gray McGuiness. Beyond that, I don't know what the hell is happening to us. Sometimes when I can't take thinking about it anymore, I pretend this is a great big hoax on all of us and our government is really controlling everything."

"No government on earth did that to you, Picasso. You're right. You're living proof that this shit is all real. That blipping in and out of rooms that Mook does, shit, that still freaks me out. Holograms."

"And you still want to stick around?"

"Where do we have to hide? Mook blips in wherever he wants."

"He blipped in on me while I was peein' once."

"Me too. Wait, you guys are in contact with Mook?"

"Yeah. You know, a little here and there."

"Are you guys in on all this shit?"

"Ah, maybe a little."

"But we don't know jack about what you're trippin' on."

"So shut up about it."

I just look at them. Sons-of-bitches.

"So, what are ya gonna tell her when she comes?"

13

"Who?"

"Your girlfriend. She's due here any minute now. Mooky didn't tell you?"

"Christ, that's right, she's still comin' for Christmas booty. To do you in the snow."

"What? In the snow?"

"It's your booty call. From Javier's list of places to fornicate before I get married. You are so lucky, man. Regardless of how short-lived it ends up being."

"You better hope they gave you Javier's pecker. From what I hear through the walls, he's the man."

"Call her and cancel. She can't see me like this. I only have his face, hair and one of his arms. The rest is half me and a forth Leonie Dazarrio."

"You're not gonna want to cancel this one, Picasso. Believe us, brother. She is so hot the snow melts below her feet on her way up the stoop. Icicles sing her praise as they die from her heavenly heat. And snow angels whistle backbeats into the wind."

"Yeah, and all the more spoiled ripe on the vine. She's got this Javier wrapped around her fingers. She's why he's doing all this. So he can be with her. It's as though he knows it'll kill him. But to him it's worth dying for. Just to be with her for a little while. He wooed her away from Doc, your werewolf next door, who didn't like it."

"Which is my guess why he ate you."

"Latinos, what do they know about stealing werewolves' women? By the way, you've been doin' her stepmom, too."

"What?"

"Relax, she's hot, too. Late thirties. Owns the grocery store and two other businesses in town. Hair and a floral place. The old man doesn't care. He needs your money so bad he'd do you himself if you'd let him."

"And she's just coming up here? What if someone follows her?"

"Relax, she's from Frazer Park, man, reigning Miss Frazer Park. Lives right up that other side of the mountain. You should see the place. This was Javier's little hideaway life away from the wife and kids. Who are still in El Paso, under house arrest. No one knows he's here. Not his wife or kids. No one but us knows she's with him. No one here knows who he really is. That he's a squealing scumbag drug dealer."

"Are you sure?"

"If they did, you'd be dead long ago."

"What time is she due here."

"About...."

Three knocks sound out on the front door.

"Now."

"Shit."

"Hey, she knows none of this. Not sure about the stepmom. As far as she's concern, we are visiting from out-of-town lookin' to invest in this area with you. She knows your sick ass only as a rich well hung businessman who loves her with all your heart. No kids, no wife, no drug family. Oh, and she's plannin' your spring wedding. She knows you as Bolivar Agustin. Don't worry, Javier killed him off the coast of Puerto Rico. Cut him up and used him as bait to fish hammerhead sharks. He assumes his identity in America when hiding from his wife. Feds know it too. It's how they caught up with him. He was shopping at Kmart for sheets and pillows."

"Wait. My what? Wedding?"

"It's going to be a big one, too. Gigantic. Everyone in the town is invited. Just go with it, you won't live that long anyway."

"Thanks. Get the door."

"Get it yourself, lover boy. We did our thing. Kept you here and up, so we're goin' to bed."

"You set me up? You two fatheads sat there and let me rant on, and you knew all along what's happened to me?"

"You heard the Mook about us. We both got to look out for all of yous," Mike says.

"Look, if it makes you feel better, they don't tell us shit. We just know details as we need to know them. Thought implants or something. You heard the Mook. Need to know. Now we know we need to leave," Mac says.

They get up and head to the back of the house. I haven't even looked around. I'm not even sure where I'm sleeping or peeing.

"Bolivar?"

"Wait, you shitheads, what's her name?"

"Olivia Hamilton. Twenty three, a junior at UCLA. Built hot, fast, and sleek like an Indy race car, but twice as dangerous. Her daddy owns most of this town. Of which you are investin' mighty heavily into redevelopin' and savin' his ass from losin' everything. He loves you. Spic dick and all."

"Boli? It's Oli. Open up, I'm naked, remember."

Boli? Oh great. Just what I need, endearing rhyming names.

Blip. "I told you to keep your mouth shut, rainbow boy."

"Mooky, why didn't you tell me about Oli? Or that those two clowns are in on this?"

"You've got enough to worry about, Boli. She's why we had them baby sit you. Not to just sit and listen to you whine. We had to make sure you didn't make a run for it. Now just let her in. Smack her brains out in the snow. She'll run back to her daddy afterwards with a big satisfied smile on her face. It will be okay."

"It will not be okay." Visions of Olivia devouring Javier's manhood fills my brain. "She'll know I'm not Javier."

"You don't have to be Javier. You're Bolivar Agustin, hung like a Conquistador."

"But I'm not. Won't it blow my cover?"

"Trust me, your cover ain't what she's here to blow, dill weed. They're after only your money. Haven't you looked in your pants yet?"

"What? Wait a minute. What have you done? Is she one of you?"

"Not exactly."

"Mooky."

Blip.

"Son-of-an-Alien bitch."

"Bolivar, are you alright?"

"Yes, ah... Oli. I just stubbed my toe in the dark."Oli, Boli, what am I into now?

I open the door. Standing in a full length slate blue chinchilla coat is Olivia Hamilton. Her rich dark hair splashes over her shoulders. Her eyes are so blue and full I could fall into them and swim forever. Unbelievable. Unforgettable. Even more so now that I don't trust any of this, one bit. Now I know what Mooky meant. Holy-Boli-king mackerel-Oli, what have they done to me? I'm as alive as a bobcat in Bermuda shorts. I nearly fall over myself the manly reaction is so painfully thunderous. It's as though I snorted a quart of Viagra.

"What do you think?"

"Nice fur."It's all I can do to stop Boli from pouncing. I literally have to hang onto the door knob to hold us back.

"Not this old thing, this." She peals the fur away to reveal what might be the most perfectly spectacular tanned female body to ever walk modern day Earth.

"Ah… you're so tan." I'm growing so quickly I'm in immense pain, literally and figuratively. Boli's a monster.

"Let me in, silly."She squeezes by rubbing herself on my new found self esteemed. She smells like heaven rained on Earth. "Umm, someone's up. I told you, you sent me to the spa. You don't like?"

"No, no, no, I mean yes, yes, yes. I love it. It's just I didn't expect it to be so deep, beautiful, and so all over."

"I sent you a text, even attached a photo."

"I haven't touched my phone all day." I move out of the way and Olivia comes to me and stands on her tiptoes and gives me a big wet kiss. She grabs Boli's manhood rubbing it threw my pants. Then she looks back up at me once she's back on the flat of her feet, coy young bad girl smile. "Are you taller?"

Am I taller? "What? Me? You don't have shoes on. Come in, come in. Your feet must be freezing. You want something to eat?"

"Eat? Are you joking? I plan to devour you out in the snow."

"Out in the…."

"Honestly, are you not paying attention? You asked me to come over to make love in the snow. I said only at night. Well it's still dark. Take off your clothes and let's do it before I come to my senses."

"In the snow? Are you sure I said that?"

"It's on your list of places you've never had sex. Now come on, the light will be up soon. I've been thinking about this all night, sitting around the fire, drinking with my boring family, with the moon so full. Now do the deed, mister."

"Do her already," Mike's voice comes from down the hall.

"Are they still here?"

"Yes. We can't with them here."

"You two mind your own business. Or I'm coming back there."

"My room's the first on the left. Door's open."

"Shut up, Mike."

"Lucky bastard."

"You too, Mac."

"Really, now off with your pants. Come on, this is your idea. You won't marry me until you've had sex in every place on your bucket list. And I'm not letting you do it with anyone else. Now, drop the pants, mister." She comes to me with hands grouping at my fly.

"Now hold on. I'm not in the mood yet."

"Are you kidding me? Look at this body. You're about to spring across the room."

"I know. Believe me. Would you mind if we…?"

Her eyes light up. "Where is the ring I gave you?" She takes my hand, my real hand, not Javier's. "You promised never to take it off."

"I ah… I was… cleaning…."

"Who are you?"

"What do you mean?"

She covers up. Who are you and what have you done with Boli?"

"Oli, it's me."

She stares at me, searching my eyes until a knowing smile washes across her face. "Come on, Picasso, let me rock you in the snow."

"Jerry?"

"Sssshhh, they don't know I'm here."

"Those guys?"

"No those, guys up there, the council. Only Mook."

"Shit Jerry, what are you doing here?"

"Helping your sorry ass. You need any more shovels?"

"That was you. I knew it."

"Duh, anymore hints I'd have to hit you with one. Now seriously, let me blow you in the snow."

"Will you cut it out? What are you doing here?"

"Keeping your cover, dummy. Come on relax, you're in way over your head on this one. That's why we brought them two dicks in to back you up and me to work on the head part."

I move in close. "Are they aware of what might happen to them?"

"They're aware they don't have a choice this time. Now come here, you're looking really good. They did a great job on your face among other things. I had them tuck your chin a little, and remove a scar." Olivia reaches out to touch Javier's face. "Talk dirty in Spanish, Boli. I just melt all over when you do."

"Will you shut up? Christ, Jerry, cover up."

"Why? I've never looked so pretty. Check this ass. She spins two hours a day. With two hour rub downs three times a week. I just may keep her."

"Give me a break, sit down. This is ridicules."

"You need to kill this doctor for us, Picasso. This is the perfect cover. A win-win for humans and us, all the way around."

"I meant this. You showing up. How will I ever trust a woman again? Knowing at any second she could be your twin butts inside?"

"I haven't fooled you yet, have I? Okay, maybe I have that one time. But hey honestly, do you think she'd buy you being some hot below the border lover. Girls tend to remember these things. You may look like him but you lack the spice. So, I'm making sure she doesn't interfere. It's what I do best. Come on, Mook asked me to help. Said I'd get to do you. So let's go, mister. It's snow time."

"Well, you don't. Now, back off."

"You are so disappointing. Fine, I'll do one of them."

"Have at it."

Olivia looks towards the back of the cabin. "Oh, just forget it." She throws her coat closed and heads for the door. "One of these days, Picasso. I'll get you drunk and I'm gonna rock your world."

"You already have. Remember?"

"Oh yeah, you weren't half bad. Nothing to write across the galaxies about. If my own planet still existed. But surprisingly appreciative." She gives me a great big, mouthwatering grin. So beautiful, with or without Jerry.

"Hey, for the record." Olivia hesitates at the open door. "You're the most beautiful and enticing woman I've ever seen. Even with a two butted pure energy-based Alien inside."

"Even better than your little starlet?"

"Two different planets."

"Ah, you say that to all the Alien possessed women you meet."

"Never. Good night."

"If you hear about the local paperboy claiming molestation on my way home. Don't blame me."

"Beat it."

14

Damn, I wake up on the coach to the smell and sound of sizzling bacon, brewing coffee and boiling water. My gun is on my chest, a finger on the trigger, and my other hand on my deflated crotch. I take note that the gun is pointed at my chin. "Hello?"

"Picasso, you want one or two fried eggs?"

"Just coffee." I let Boli go. I almost miss it.

"Quit playing with yourself and come eat. Look at that sun."

"I'd give a right leg and butt cheek to own this friggin' place."

"Might as well."I get up to go look out the window. It is truly beautiful. The trees are all shinning from the Christmas snow. But that's not what I'm looking at. What catches my eye is the two hundred thousand dollar, all wheel drive, black BMW X5 M Mansory parked out front of the doctor's log mansion. "These werewolves know how to live."

"And stay alive. Wait until you see the inside."

"You've been in?"

"Nope. We snooped around until that beamer pulled up."

"Who is it?"

"It's him."

"The doc?"

"Yeah. And not feelin' too bad. He's all by himself. Walkin' around like nothin' happened."

"I must not have got him very good. Or he's got good friends with healing stones."

"Oh, you got him good alright. Mooky had me go in his room and check while they had him under. You missed his heart by two inches. Punctured a lung," Mac tells me.

"Yeah, but here he is."

"Alien werewolf bastard," Mac says.

"Which means he's got friends around here from faraway places who don't want him dead," Mike says.

"Great, factions of the Alien Council are here, too." I say.

"My guess they're everywhere," Mike says.

"You snore like an in-heat orangutan, by the way. And you even sounded like you stopped breathin' there for a while. I was glad to have to leave," Mac says.

"Yeah, I feel like shit. Why didn't you roll me over, I could've suffocated?"

"Hell, I came out and sat with you. What did you want mouth to mouth? You wanna wake up with my lips on ya, and blow my head off with a laser enhanced silver bullet?"

"Besides you kept grabbin' yourself and moaning Jerry all night."

I put the gun down. "Are you sure?"

"Come on and eat, you crazy bastard." Mike puts a plate out.

I move over to the table and take in the cabin for the first time in the daylight. "Man, this scumbag knows how to live."

"He bought this place as is from your future father-in-law. The old man built it himself. Most of these places on this hill, matter of fact."

"There's got to be close to a mil just in furnishing."

"There's a black 911 in the garage. It's his."

"Mine?"

"And a new Range Rover. We've been usin' that."

"Pass the pepper. Thanks, I could get used to this. My place is haunted." I cut into an over easy fried egg.

"Hurry up. We got to be at your sweetie's place in an hour."

"I'm not going anywhere near her. She's got Jerry inside."

"Yeah, we know. You still should've taken the offer."

"Close your eyes. BJ's a BJ, Alien induced or otherwise."

"You learn that from your cop bodies in the showers?"

"Don't mock the blue."

"I wouldn't pass it up. I don't care what she's possessed with. Long as it ain't catchy."

"She's all yours."

"Don't think so, Boli. Today's your birthday. You're thirty-two."

"Birthday?" I pull out Bolivar Agustin California Driver's license. "Bolivar Agustin. This won't end. How will we keep all this straight?"

"Don't worry. Everyone calls you Bolivar around here. Except for Oli, she prefers Boli. No one but us, Jerry, and Mook knows who you really are. Remember, whatever happens to you next, we didn't know

68

about you joining the party until you was under up there. We were told to see how you handled it, play along, and wait for Mook."

"But they're throwing you a shindig over at her father's place, just over the hill," Mac says.

"Don't worry," Mike says.

"Stop telling me not to worry. There's no way I'll fool these people."

"Just don't act like your asshole self and everything will be fine. People like you here. You got money. You're young and you're happy."

"I still have this gun."

"You just got back in town. You've been away for three, going on four months, living on your yacht, playing with your money. They don't need to know it's been in Federal Prison. Where your family thinks you're still at. As far as all these people know you were out cruisin' the Caribbean. You sold off island investments and raised millions to share with them. It ain't far off the truth. The feds have made sure the transactions have looked legit."

"We think it's the feds. Could be Mook and them."

"One and the same, most likely."

"If Olivia thinks you're him, and we do, they will just go along. Trust us, the old man is so happy you haven't run out on him that he might rock your world himself."

"Watch out for the old lady, though."

"She ain't so old, but plenty inquisitive. Been asking all kinds of questions about us. She's already calculating how we will get in her way if the old man croaks before we leave."

"Can't blame her. You guys reek of dirty cops."

"Yeah, she asked me if I was a cop when I went into her market last night."

"Said she recognizes us from somewhere."

"You think she's on to you from being on the news?"

"Could be. If she figures us out, we'll just say were here on your behalf. For safety reasons. In the meantime we're investors lookin' to see where our money is goin'."

Someone walks past the window. "Oh-oh."

"It's him, at the front of the house."

"The doctor?"

"Yeah. What the hell is he doing?"

I move to the window and watch as the doc seems to calculate how my shot would've traveled last night. Why didn't we think of that?

Mook or Jerry leaving it there? Are they setting me up? He digs something out of a post on the front veranda, with his finger nails.

"He find something?"

"Stop sneaking up on me."

"Mooky told us to leave it be."

"Why?"

Out the window, I watch him put the silver bullet in his pocket and make his way around the veranda to the back of the cabin.

"Here he comes."

"I asked, why."

"We don't know."

A knock comes on the kitchen door. "Bolivar, you up?"

"Just a minute. What should I do?"

"What normal people do after they shoot someone on Christmas, answer the door and pretend you got no idea what he's talkin' about."

I get up and move to the backdoor. The doc looms there, waiting. He's handsome and smart looking, about mid thirties, light brown shaggy dog hair. "Damn Doc, why are you out of the hospital?"

"What, and miss your birthday party?"

"You okay? You look great for getting shot in the chest."

"Just a flesh wound."

I hold the door open and he comes in. He's just a few inches taller than me, maybe six-three. He's dressed in a red ski vest, black hiking boots and plaid shorts, showing off his overly hairy muscular legs. In Alien reality, depending on how he traveled, he's a thousand.

"Hey, Mike, Mac... it's a beautiful day, huh?"

"Sorry to hear you were in the hospital for Christmas."

"I heard you stopped by to check on me, though, Mike, thanks."

"Yeah, you know, just checkin' out the local nurses. Nurse I met said you where pretty bad."

"Ah, what do they know? Here, this is for you, Boli. A bribe, cigars. I figure you wouldn't want to share them with those hicks at the party. Just mull over my offer while you smoke them. When that box is empty, I withdraw my offer on this cabin."

I open the package. "Havana. Doc, you shouldn't have."

"Oh, yeah he should've. I see one with my name on it."

"Listen, another reason I stopped by. Did you guys hear or see anything strange last night?"

"What do you mean?"

"Well, shooting, screaming, anyone running around these cabins on Christmas night?"

"Ah..." I look at Mike and Mac. "You guys hear anything?"

"Not a thing."

"You think it was someone local who shot you?"

"I don't know actually. I don't remember a thing. I heard there were a lot of out-of-towners stuck up here in the snow. Could've been someone looking for gas money home," the doc says.

Mike hands me the local paper. "You see the paper, Bolivar? Says here some director guy, a Jozeph Picasso, helped them get out of the snow. Take a look. Someone snapped a shot of him driving a carload of kids down the mountain."

I take the paper. Sure enough, there I am, being a big hero. Only I don't recall anyone taking my picture. "He must be one hell of a guy."

"I met him. He's a typical overpaid Hollywood bullshit artist. A flash in the fish pan."

I look at Mac. "Why so, because he's successful?"

"No, because he's full of himself. Has a nasty attitude towards authority. And he treats his dog like it's a human."

"Leave his dog out of this." I look back at the local paper, "Said you were naked, Doc."

"Yeah, imagine that. I'll probably end up on YouTube. Well look, enjoy the smokes. Think it over. I'll catch you later today."

"Okay then, thanks for the gift. Hey Doc, you should take it easy, you don't have to come to the party."

"What, and miss another opportunity to pinch my Oli back from you. Not a chance."

"Hell, you're gonna have to fight through us first."

"You're a lucky man, Bolivar. I'm not sure how you got Oli away from me. But when I figure it out, I'm taking her back, married to you or otherwise."

"I'd say you're the one with all the luck. Taking a bullet in the chest and living to tell us about it."

"Want to hear something really strange about all this?"

"Stranger than you walking and talking about it?"

"Yeah, the bullet was silver."

"Silver?" I look at Mike and Mac. "Silver. You believe that?"

"He's pulling your leg."

The doc reaches into his pocket and pulls out the silver bullet. "Take a look. That's pure silver."

"That's the bullet they took out of you?"

"This is the bullet that passed right through me and lodged into the post outside your front door. But take a closer look."

We lean in to take a closer look.

"See there, not a single mark. Not a sign that it was fired from a gun. Nor that it hit anything. No way of tracing it."

"Maybe it ain't the one."

"It's the one."

"Won't they need it for forensic?"

"Maybe. I'll stop by the sheriff's office and give it to him."

"Hell, if a silver bullet can't kill you. What can?"

"I guess the next time someone points a gun at me, I'll have to rip his arm off. What do you think, Bolivar?"

"That's a good plan, Doc. You need help home?"

"Got it. Going for a run. See you guys later."

"We'll be there."

The doc makes his way down the back steps, easing his way into the snow and takes off on a run up the hill. I close the door, watching him speed up like running up hill for him was running down hill for me. No human could do that. He looks back at me. He catches me watching, waving as he makes the bend behind the pines.

"Shit, does he know it was me who shot him?"

"He knows he ate Boli, and yet you're here now. Unless he knows you ain't just Boli now. Did he get a good look at you last night?"

"He ate my face. So I'd say so. This ain't good."

"He won't be a werewolf for another month now."

"You better get some of Oli while you can, Picasso."

"Yeah. Before Doc gets another taste of you."

15

I'm standing here with the feeling I've been here before. I'm not talking about déjà vu. I'm talking about really-really having been here before. As I sip a Corona, I run Boli's fingers along the forty foot peacock green Chinese marble bar. I know exactly what his hand is touching and how much it costs. I sure didn't before touching it. But now I do. The Picasso in me is still in awe of Oli's father's gigantic log cabin. It overlooks a vast snow covered pine forest, so incredibly scenic it could be a ski lodge in some faraway mountain resort.

As amazed as I am, I still can't escape the feeling of knowing this place. Right down to how much it cost to build. It's to the point of planning to own it someday. Everywhere I turn I've seen this place. I've been here. I've sat here. I've eaten here. I've laughed here. I thought of killing here. I even got head here. Not really, but really. It's because Javier knows this place. That's obviously it. The details are floating in our head. He's been here so I've been here, and all the things he's done here I've done here. His memories are becoming my memories? Or is he becoming me the more I become him. Crap, what am I saying? I have no idea.

All these people look familiar because I know them. Yet, I have no clue as to who they are until the moment I hear their voice or their name. At that moment our past relations pop into my memory bank. Do I have part of his brain? Or am I being fed these things? It makes my frontal lobe tingle. I need to scratch it from the inside. It's maddening at best. To a point of wanting to stick a tooth brush up my nose to scrub away the sordid thoughts of the life he's lived.

I've had dinner with them. I've... oh-oh, have had sex with Oli's stepmother, right here on the couch, many times. Holy crap, I see her across the room looking back at me over her cocktail. The image of me, Javier, Bolivar, feasting on her body, multiple noisy orgasmic fills my head. I want her right now, so bad my groan aches. Javier is an animal. Crap. "What have I gotten myself into?"

"You better stop saying that, Bolivar. People are gonna get the wrong idea."

"Yeah, you look like you're about to run for it, lover boy."

I turn to face Mike and Mac sitting on the stools next to me. "I've slept with Oli's stepmother."

"That ain't all they did."

"Bolivar got into her pants. Both up at the cabin and right here in this room."

"Yeah, like we don't know. She drops by twice a week to have you run your mustache up and down her butt, while Olivia is spinning her ass into perfection for you. She gets you over here as much as she can to meet with the old man. He ends up knapping while you two screw the dust mites out of the cushions."

"This is crazy."

"What's crazy is the old man knows you're doing his young wife and still wants you to marry his dazzling daughter. I'd cut your nuts off if I could find a way to use them myself."

"I'd cut my own nuts off. How long has this been going on?"

"Since Bolivar paid cash for the house up above the canyon and committed to financially redeveloping this valley for Olivia. You're about to drop ten million in development money with another twenty after the wedding. Hard cash. What you might call a reverse dowry for being allowed to marry Olivia. Miss Olivia Hamilton. God, I love saying that name. Olivia Hamilton and her eyes are intoxicating."

"How about you lettin' us watch one of these nights?"

"Forget it. Remember, for me, a pinch of Oli is a smile of Jerry. So we won't be taking that voyage any time soon."

"Don't be surprised if the old man is recording you two up here, to use against his hot wife when he croaks. To make sure Oli gets what she's supposed to get. Or against you to make sure you pay up or he shows it to Oli."

"Great, I'm now a porn star?"

"Relax, we ain't found the tapes, and it wasn't you yet."

"Here comes Candy, as you know, Oli's stepmom. She's as smart as she is sticky. Watch out for her."

"She's pushing forty but her body is tight as a teenager. You could bounce a golf ball off her chest. And that blond hair is real to the roots, all the way around. We found photos in the old man's desk."

The thought of her naked body spread across my bearskin rug splashes across my mind. Candy steps up to me and runs her hand up and down my backside.

"Bolivar, why are you being so shy?"

"Shy?"

"By now you'd have the room taken over or me out back on my knees. What's the matter? Can't handle getting older?"

"Believe me, being thirty-two is a pleasure. It's just I haven't been feeling my best."

"Come to think of it, you do look a little off. Did you get some work done while you were away? You did, didn't you?"

"Sssshhh, don't tell anyone. How did you notice?"

"The scar just under you left eye, it's gone. You got a peel and a tuck. Christ, Bolivar you're still a kid. How vain can you get?"

"Hey, keeping up with dangerous animals like you will coerce a man to do crazy things. But truth, I had skin cancer from living on my boat. They had to graft some skin around my nose and eyes."

"Oh, I'm sorry to hear that. You look wonderful. Smell divine. But you two, rummies. I figured out where I've seen you both."

"Watch her, Mike, she's on to us."

"We didn't do it."

"You were the two cops who got let go by the LAPD for trying to kill Jozeph Picasso. He's the one in the papers this morning who helped all those people out of the mountain last night."

"Isn't he directing a film? I hear he's a hell of a guy," I add.

"I'd do him. If he had enough money," Candy adds.

"Trust us he ain't worth screwin'."

"Are you saying he got away with killing his tenants?"

"We ain't sayin', we know he did."

"So, you are those two low-life cops. Those two who helped bury him in a magical chest of some sort?"

"Guilty as charged. Keep in mind we were at gunpoint when doing the dastardly deed."

"So, what's it like being low-life cops, guys?"I ask.

"We ain't cops no more, Boli.., we're investors, remember."

"But you're still low-lives, I can tell. Bolivar, would you like me to have Arthur remove them from your birthday party?"

"It's okay, Candy, these guys are with me now. They're both reformed low-lives. Kind 've born again good-guys for hire. Half-empty- lives now. They're on the mend character types with their heads just out of the septic tank of respectability."

"You are too funny."

"We're making sure our funny man here doesn't get molested out of all his money."

"I got my eye on both of you, stinkers."

"Feel free to watch us all you want."

"Sure, stop by my room next time you drop by to give out some free candy. I'll give you a peep-matinee."

"Watch it fellows. I pack a gun, in and out of bed."

Mike shows her his. "See, we got something in common already."

"Thugs. I knew it. Here's Oli, our very own beauty-bride to be." Candy smiles at me, grabbing my ass harder this time. She shoots a snooty look at Mike and Mac as she goes.

"She wants my stump, I can tell," Mike says.

"Yeah, stumpy fat guys who dress poorly are just what she dreams about the most."

"At least I ain't livin' a Hollywood lie. I y'am what I y'am."

"Thanks Popeye. You mind giving us a minute?"

Mike and Mac head towards the kitchen door, pulling out a couple of my stogies the doc gave me. Just then, Oli storms up to the bar and gives me the biggest, wettest, Frenchiest, and nastiest kiss I've ever had the displeasure of getting splashed by."

"Oli... your breath smells like a dead Alien."

"Oh, Humus. I've missed you, so much, lover boy."

"Cut it out, Jerry?"

"Come on let's dance. I love this song."

"But we...."

Oli takes my hand and drags me across the enormous living room to an almost as big empty room. In this room a dance floor has been laid with a disk jockey at the far end that overlooks a ten foot high bulletproof bay window. Outside, it drops sheer off into a crevasse three hundred feet below. Breathe taking I know, because Bolivar had Candy butt naked, holding onto its wood frame, screaming bloody murder not to stop, and more than once.

"Are you sure you don't mind getting married here?"

"No, it's great. This is a great idea."

"What's the matter?"

"Jerry?"

"Don't freak out."

"I'm not dancing with you."

"I didn't bring you here to dance, dummy. They're making a move on you when you leave here."

"Who?"

"Them, your new south of the border family. They're out there right now waiting for you."

"Javier's two brothers?"

"No, they're in Mexico for now hiding out at your ranch in Ciudad Juárez. They were doing horrible things to your people trying to make you come home to face them and your mother. They know what has happened here. There are four of your brothers' cartel-hopefuls outside right now with machine guns. And plan to burn this house down if they have to."

"So what do we do?"

"Well, if it were up to me, I'd drop this girl in your arms and I'd go out there to make sure they're not waiting for you when you leave."

"What are the other options?"

"They storm the place. Take out as many of this family as needed to get to you. Or you slip out the back, and hike down the face of the mountainside, just beyond that bay window, to get to them first."

"Are you insane? I've seen how far that drops?"

"My father has an escape harness in a metal box. Just outside the window. All you have to do is climb out, slip it on, let go and it automatically lowers you to the ground."

"Fat chance of that happening."

"Or you can wait for me to finish things on our end."

"You mean, up there?"

"I told you no one but the Mook knows I'm involved. I sure can't be sending people up anywhere until they give us the okay on what we are doing here. What I can do is make those guys miss things they wouldn't normally miss. To give you time to make your move."

"Well, fix it so I can walk out the door I came in. I'm sure as hell not leaping out that window or killing people."

"Where's your sense of adventure?"

"Where it should be. Set in reality. How'd they find Javier?"

"My guess is him. Seeing you come back, he knows something's up. We let him find the bullet so he knows the Council voted against him. He knows it's you or him at this point. He's brought Javier's people in so he doesn't have to do it himself because now you're part Alien werewolf. See how complicated this is getting?"

I look across both rooms and standing there at the marble bar is the Doc with a drink in one hand and Oli's stepmother in the other. He's watching us, with a big grin on his face.

"Are you saying the doctor can't kill me himself now?"

"Yes, he knows the Picasso in you was sent here to kill him. Javier just stole his girl? Both of you coming back alive as the same Alien enhance person is keeping him from taking you both out again."

"So me being part Alien now is a good thing?"

"Yes, you and Javier were both human when he attacked you? We can't have him going around eating anyone else now that he's had a taste of human flesh. So the Council wants him out. Gone for good. Not all voted against him. Those who didn't brought him a stone. Personally, Alien werewolf or not, I think he's an animal and I just love cheating behind your back whenever I can get alone with him."

"You're doing him, Jerry. As Oli? Shame on you."

"Making love is what I do best. This war stuff is for you humans. Why do you think old Candy there can't get enough of Bolivar?"

"Jerry, you're despicable."

"I know. I just love humans though. But I miss my Gray." Tears of sorrow well up in Oli's eyes. The fading sunlight dances off them. It's amazing to watch. For this moment, it's almost worth being here.

"Come on, don't cry over dead clones. How many Aliens are in this room right now?"

"Four. Me, Doc and those two over there."

I look over and find two very average looking men standing up against the wall talking with Oli's father, Arthur Hamilton. "How do they fit in?"

"That one's a very powerful local banker. Has Arthur under his thumb and is twisting it good. He's making him sell his daughter off to a scumbag like you to stay solvent so he can leave all this to me. That one in the tacky green Christmas sweater is a realtor who stands to make millions on this deal just for being a middle man. Arthur does all the work, you spend all the money, and they take most of the profit."

"You guys get us coming and going."

"More than you know."

"So which one has stones?"

"That's just it. We don't know where they came from. So there's more to this than even we know about. But you don't just walk out of a hospital after being shot in the chest by a laser driven pure solar-silver bullet without causing a stir. Now he's eaten people, Bolivar in particular. It won't end. So he's gone as soon as you can stomach it."

"Wait, solar-silver? What's that?"

"Many of the precious metals we use in our weapons are not from Earth. They are from planets with much more gravity and thus much denser and purer than anything possibly found here on Earth."

"You mean like Kryptonite?"

Oli laughs. I'm funny. Family, friends and neighbors turn and smile as they see the lovebirds touching and laughing. "You are so cute when you want to be."

"At this rate I won't last to another full moon."

"We're aware. It's a matter of how much of this you can stomach."

"Okay, stomach what? What's up?"

"Mooky didn't tell you?"

"No, Mooky didn't tell me."

"Then you didn't hear it from me."

"Shit, Jerry, what do I do next?"

"You as Picasso or Bolivar don't do anything. Javier infused with Alien werewolf blood does. He's a sick, evil, murderous scumbag all by himself. He catches his young bride to be in a car with her former boyfriend, Doctor Elwartowski."

"Wait, isn't that what you did with Gray? Dismembered him?"

"Unless you want to wait until the next full moon, or sever his head as Picasso hiding in Javier, portraying Bolivar, then just let it happen as we planned. It's why I'm here getting them all sexed up. Javier gets blamed, Alien werewolf is gone, case closed."

"But I can't do this. I won't do this."

"Within hours, if all goes as planned, you won't remember anything other than being Javier. Surely, you see his visions of us already. Like us against those windows. Or Boli and me, as Candy, of course. I just love you hot Latin lovers."

"Shut up. Yes, I see his thoughts. I smell and taste his sordid life."

"Picasso as you know him is going away."

"Wait. I don't want to go away. I like being what's left of me."

"I'm sorry, Picasso. This body will never be all you again."

"Then who will I be?"

"Javier. It takes a few hours but it moves faster and faster, until piff, you as you know you are gone. These kinds of surgeries almost always work. It's really up to the human involved. But there's sometimes things that look human in nature, but are really Alien defects."

"Are you shitting me!?"

"Keep your voice down. We have a clean slate of you in backup."

"My clone?"

"Yes. Almost. You'll be you. Only you won't remember any of this. Right now your memory bank is home with your dog working on your film. Last I heard, playing with yourself way more than usual."

"I won't be me. I'll be him."

"No, he'll be you. Entirely, almost cell for cell. If this goes as planned, all of you will be gone from your consciousness. Everything that happens to Javier will happen to him, not you."

"But I'm inside. I'll feel it. I'll know what I've done."

"Javier, will feel it. He'll know what he's done. The Picasso, as we know you, will dissipate and return to your clone."

"When does he do this?"

"You won't be aware that it's happening. You'll be him, taken over by his evil instincts. It's setup to happen that way. You've got extra subconscious backup in that noggin in case we need to draw upon it."

"Subconscious backup. Jerry. There's more to this? To me?"

"You'll be okay, Picasso. We've got you covered. I'll be right there with you. Oli won't remember a thing. When it's over, you'll be as good as new. Not even the tattoo. Think about it. We'll be gone from your knowledge of what life is to you. You will be free from us. From me." Oli's eyes well up with tears again. "I'll miss you."

"But...."

"Go with the flow, and tonight I'll give you the best BJ you'll ever dream of getting. Just out of this world."

"You're killing me, Jerry."

"Not until you take out Doc for us. Don't worry, all the loose ends will be tied real tight. It will end up being a lovers' spat gone very-very bloody. Your true identity will be revealed and they'll take you out. Or at least that's what it will look like. If all goes as planned."

"You keep saying if. When will this take place?"

"In time to spend New Year's Eve with your sweetie."

"There's too many ifs here, Jerry."

"If I'm in complete control. Now hold Oli, so I can go out and set up what's waiting out there. What happens next is a test. We need to see how Javier will handle this step before we move forward. If he passes we know we've got our man. What we've done to you works for our needs. Once he takes over, Picasso should not resurface. He'll be too deep inside. Oh, and don't smoke those cigars. They're laced to temporally paralyze you so that they can overtake you with ease."

"Wait. Mike and Mac... they went out."Oli falls into my arms.

"Oh my god, Boli, you dance so smoothly. I barely remember a thing. Did I fall asleep?"

"Yeah, I'm Mr. Smooth. Do you mind, I need fresh air?"

"Not at all, thanks for the dance." She plants another kiss on me, this time less Alien tongue-ish and real lady like. "I love you."

"Thanks."

"Thanks?"

"I meant for the dance. I love you, too. With all my heart."

"That's better. Now, we make love in the snow tonight or never."

"Okay."

"Yes or no?"

"We'll see."

"You are acting very strange, mister."

"Jet lagged."

"I know men who would fly around the world for some of this."

"Baby, I have. I'm here. In the snow, tonight. Boots on."

I give her a kiss on her lips and walk away. Mike and Mac could be passé by now.

I cut through the bar area heading for the kitchen, passing by a gigantic birthday cake in the shape of a log cabin. There's one large candle in place of every fireplace. My new face is in the icing roof tiles. Happy birthday, Boli is written in the smoke.

By the time I get to the door I can feel something's wrong.

16

Crap, I'm still here.

The snow has arrived again. Nothing heavy, just enough to add to the fray of what is taking place. But what's surreal, is that all my actions are quickly dissolving into involuntary motions without giving me options. I'm sure it has something to do with the Alien bullshit thrust inside of me. At the same time I don't care or want to stop my actions, even if I could, as I move toward being we.

As far as we know it's Javier making these decisions. Maybe it's not. It could be just them, meaning Mooky or Jerry. If it is, why go through this charade of me being just a piece of what I once was? We can see everything that takes place. Why and how we can do any of these disgusting actions our mind is planning to bestow upon other human beings is beyond Picasso. Even though, these other humans are nothing more than paid killers here to assassinate the being that possesses us. My sole input is in thinking how I'll explain all this mayhem while trapped inside the locked local police station without admitting that I'm completely nuts.

Under dance music, we sneak past chefs, and stop to find the two bodies of Mike and MacAroy. We feel their pulses. They are not dead but in no shape to dance. The cigars they were smoking are nowhere to be found. Not even ashes. They've been cleaned and left to die by one of them on the other side of the council.

We open Mac's eye and if he sees us we can't tell. We take out Mike's phone using Javier's hanky and dial 911 with Mike's finger. Using Jozeph's voice, "Yes, come quickly to the back veranda of the Hamilton Estates. There are two private security guards in need of immediate attention. Poisoning, I think. Yes." We hang up and give the phone back to Mike and take his leather gloves. We pull Mac out of his navy blue pea jacket. Making the call shows we haven't at least lost all our human compassion for our fellow man, even though we're thieving this poor man's jacket, and leaving him to freeze in the snow. Or is this just part of Javier's evolving plan?

What little that is left of Picasso wants to scream and cry, but any human emotion left belonging to me is suppressed deep down inside a dark forbidden passage. It's somehow hidden away, as though to protect my creative soul so it can find its way back home again. I'm lost in Plato's Cave, and portions of my life are left like bread crumbs on the path to reality. Back to me, to whom I really am, Jozeph Picasso, working writer, fledgling director of my first Hollywood film; about to spend New Year's Eve with the woman of my dreams and my beloved dog, Bubba.

I can't let them take that from me. It must hide. It must remain safe. Or the sum of who I ever was will be gone. My creative passion left to be owned by him, my clone, that bastard who has stolen who I was. He is now writing the future of who I will become. I have to get back, at all cost, back to who I was. They've made me Javier Sanchez, aka Boli, possessed by Alain werewolf blood; a drug selling, rat fink murderer. As him I am a predator of man, the worse kind, a life taker with no remorse to the loss of countless souls.

Putting on the gloves I say, "Hang in there, guys."

We look through the slats of the timber railing. We immediately see three men off to the left and another off to the right, standing way down the slope. There's only one reason they are here. They don't expect us to know they're here. Surely they don't expect us to come out this soon under the cover of the new snow. It appears they have themselves in position to ambush us getting into our Range Rover or as we exit out the front door. We can only guess which one Jerry is possessing first. The furthest one away from us is our final guess.

Regardless, they aren't expecting us to make it back to our cabin. Which is directly up the canyon about three hundred yards. We take both Mike and Mac's handguns and place them in the belt of Javier's black Brioni winter suit and place one Kitzbuhel Nappa boot into the snow to kneel down for cover. Like a snake we slither along the snow covered veranda. This Javier is catlike nimble. He appears to have had some first world military training.

The thoughts going through our mind are no longer the petrifying fears of Jozeph Picasso. They are the exhilarating survival tactics of a python on the hunt. An animal so attuned to his surroundings that a startled field mouse can't out run our grasps as we reach, snatch it, and bite off its head. The rodent's blood spurts into our hand and we take the blood and wipe it all over our face. Javier seems to have a plan set to keep us alive, an element of disgusting surprise.

At the end of the Veranda, the gorge drops three hundred feet. We ease between the railings to hang and plop nearly fifty feet into a drift of snow. We use Mac's jacket as a makeshift parachute to slow our decent. But we still sink nearly to our neck with our arms out stretched. Somehow this doesn't seem to bother the new us a bit.

The old us, the Picasso would've screamed all the way down. But the Javier in us reaches up with both our arms and starts making a snow angel. He's using our arm motion to lift our body up out of the snow and push it along the top of the drift until we are literally flat on the top of the snow. Now he's using our arms to drag ourselves back to hard ground. From there he lifts our feet up over our head and with one quick tumble backwards we are again standing on our feet. We move quickly down the north-slope amongst the trees and backtrack towards where the lowest marksmen awaits with his high-powered scoped rifle. Somehow this is exhilarating yet completely terrifying as it unfolds, even though every move is planned and calculated just before it happens. It's still new to the old me in us.

We are about eighty yards from where we parked and are moving up from behind this guy. The closer we get the further Jozeph pulls back and the more Javier takes over. Until Javier, clearly on his own, floats up on his boots and stands so close behind his soon-to-be-victim that we can still smell spices he had for breakfast. Javier taps this young man on the back of his hooded head with Mike's revolver.

He turns to see the blood stained face of Javier glaring up at him. His mouth opens up to scream Jerryless to his friends. But nothing can get out before Javier shoves nearly half the revolver in his mouth, shattering his front decaying teeth. Javier throws the jacket over the guy's head, and pushes him down into the knee deep snow. He uses the jacket to silence the slight pop that blows the back of his head off. This turns the whole disgusting event into some crazy kind of human bloodstained flavored snow cone.

Javier picks up the body, running it to the edge, and throws it off the ravine. It drops nearly the full three hundred feet and sinks into the drifted snow. Leaving just a slight hole before the snow is pulled down from above. It fills it up and even covers the slick of blood.

What we're doing now doesn't cross our mind as savage or insane. Only that we have ten to fifteen seconds to make it up the slope to reposition ourselves behind the other three waiting for us, before they realize their buddy below is further below than he ever imagined.

Just as we get there, one of them turns to us. Javier knows him, because he waves us over with a big smile. Jerry's got this one is all we can think of, though this bit of info doesn't seem to faze Javier in the slightest. Somehow he's still filtering what's left of me inside him to fit the situation as the facts roll in.

I'm a duel personality running concurrently in the same body and mind. Though be it pieced together in thirds, we're somehow still able to micromanage the impulses of each of us. We are somehow filtering the useable incoming data back into the right person. Knowing this is happening and being aware enough to acknowledge it, is mind-blowing. Hopefully, Jetty's big thug brother and his ass tattoo won't wade in anytime soon. We don't need him pushing his mobbish personality to the surface and making things worse by asking dumb questions about what the hell is going on.

Javier doesn't get closer. He takes Mac's jacket, wraps it around Mac's gun and fires ten bullets into the heads and backs of the three assassins. They drop into the snow. Javier wastes no time in covering them with snow this time. Instead he jogs us back up the road to the back veranda where we wipe the guns and place them back where we found them, along with the jacket and gloves. We then take us to the sink just inside the door in a mudroom and wash our face and hands.

We take off our shirt to make sure it doesn't have any stains. Finding a little blood, we rinse the stain out with bottled hand soap. We can see that we've got full pecks that we never had before, and abs of steal. Looking at our new self, we're not complaining. We look good, we look athletic, and we look manly, if not somewhat two-toned like a Fifties Buick. The only thing is, we did not look like this when we got undressed to redress for the party. Our body is evolving.

Back dressed, I feel my real self coming back and taking over until it's just me again. I'm like an Alien induced monstrous Cybil. But I'm pumped and feel like I could chew bamboo floors. I finish buttoning up and reenter the party. I slide in behind the bar, pour me a double Tequila neat and down it without hesitation. By my estimates we were out of this room less than five minutes. It's a new found personal bad behavior low for me. But just the high to a day's activity for my new found personality, Javier Sanchez. Who knows what supernatural Alien blood was influencing us.

If nothing else, I know I'm much more than what I used to be.

17

"Don't panic, Picasso."

"What the...?"I turn and standing beside me is the Mook. "Jesus, Mooky, what are you doing here out in the open like this?"

"Keep your voice down. No one but you can see me. So you'll look like you're talking to yourself, which you do quite often by the way. Here, put this behind your ear." He hands me an ear phone that clips behind my ear like an oversized hearing aid. "Relax, it's a specialized Bluetooth phone, to replace that handheld I gave you. You're gonna need your hands free. We got these out worldwide. Soon everyone who we want to have one will want one. Until they find out twenty years from now what these did to your brains on our behalf."

"Fried them?"

"Yes partly, but most significantly, they give us total access to everything you think, do or say. They are also programmable to effectively slow down developmental behavior and desires to want more than you need."

"The phone companies are spying on us and using these to keep us stupid and satisfied? I thought that's what pot was for."

"Hardly, those of us involved use those gadgets in other ways then what they let phone companies build them for. The phone companies, those who think they are running them, have no idea what the Alien Council is doing with them.

All supposedly modern human manufactured technologies being developed across the globe today, including all government special projects, from the very beginning of the industrial revolution, are secretly used by the Alien Council to control you. Think of where all the war money is really going. In Alien pockets lined with power and greed. That's why the money trail always dies. War, Wall Street, even banking bailouts. All Alien moves to lead humans in the direction we need them to go. The Aliens involved make most of the money from the sales to you humans. If they didn't you'd still be stabbing each other with sticks and pounding your loincloths with rocks."

"Some of us still do, especially in Hollywood."

"Proof to what I say."

"Stop the Alien Council is doing it to us bullshit, Mooky. You're as Alien as the rest of these shitheads. You're profiting as much as any of them on what they're doing to us. So don't think you're any different than them in my eyes."

"Fine, dill weed, we're breeding you. We only share with you what we can control for our own use, like advancements in TV. To you it's great big entertainment. To us it's research in surveillance of human behavior and simple migration control. You ever wonder why the volume goes up in commercials and kids suddenly jump around the room like monkeys? It's a test to see who is mental suggestible."

"Why are you telling me this?"

"If you accomplish what they have set for you, you won't remember anything we're talking about. And if you don't succeed, you are dead and gone anyway."

"So why bother?"

"You might need to know some of this before the deed is done. If nothing more than to know why you must get it done."

"It's important that I know you're herding us?"

"It's important that you know what is happening to you inside personally because it might have some value to those of us who are positioning themselves to be involved with what you're becoming."

"How so?"

"Would you live in Afghanistan or Iraq if you had a choice?"

"Probably not if I wasn't born there."

"Humans do because we need them there to service us. They adapt to the world's climates very easily over time. It has evolved in their blood, their souls, and their beliefs that the ground they sleep on is sacred, so they fight to remain there. We encourage it, and allow it only because the heat, the arid climate suits only some of us. So we breed humans to be able to tolerate it as well. In the meantime we extract from the ground what you humans think you need to power the world. In reality, we make billions and you heat up the Earth for some of us. This keeps the economy rich countries dependent, socially poor and in inner turmoil."

"Like America. Wait. Evolving blood? My blood, what you've done to me, this mixing of my blood, does this have Alien value?"

"Don't let on to Jerry that you know this. Just stay away from digital TVs until this is all over. And no matter what, when this is all over, do the right thing."

"What is the right thing?"

"You'll know when the time comes. I don't want you thinking about it now. Just stay away from TVs."

"Let me guess, cartoon programming rotting our kids' brains isn't the big news?"

"No, TV is not only giving us access to you in your homes. We also watch your every cell function from our side of the screen. We speak to your Junk DNA.

"Should I ask."

"Don't. LED to us stands for Life Energy Design. Think about what's happening as digital TV spreads across the US as mandatory programming. Other smaller countries are already ahead of you. From the advent of digital technology on, we have you wired tight, coast to coast. You use ten percent, we use the other ninety percent to talk to you and control you. Humans are just getting to know this about yourselves. We don't know if you're getting it from us or not. But your Junk DNA is not only responsible for the construction of your bodies but also serves as data storage and in communication. We've been using it from the beginning. But you knowing it's there could cause us a problem very quickly. So it's important that we move faster than humans can learn about themselves. Or life is over as we all know it. You know the routine. I'm not telling you anything I haven't told you before.

Someone helped Russian linguists find out that the genetic code, in what they thought was a useless 90% of human DNA, follows the same rules as all our human languages. They started comparing these rules of syntax, the way words are put together to form phrases and sentences.

"You mean semantics, the study of meaning in language forms?"

"Yes, and the basic rules of grammar. These Russians found that the alkalines of your DNA follow a regular grammar and have set rules just like your languages."

"So human languages didn't appear coincidentally but were a reflection of our inherent DNA?"

"You see where this is going? We can simply use words and sentences of the human language to train you. Humans have proved this now. Someone from our world had to help them.

"Jerry?"

"We don't think so. But someone is gearing up to make a move on the rest of us. You can imagine where the council sits with all this."

"Humans are screwed."

"Always. Living DNA substance, in living tissue, not in vitro, will always react to language-modulated laser rays and even to radio waves, if the proper frequencies are being used. If we are left alone to continue, even the poor dirt farmers will be monitored right down to their very carbon fibers for advancement in cell activity. So that we can take those we want out of the gene pool before those humans mutate into something beyond who we want them to be. Just keep sitting in front of your computers, posting on Facebook, Tweeting, watching TV, playing Xbox or Wii, at least three hours nightly, and soon you will be carrying these things wherever you go. Think I'm bullshiting? More humans have cell phones than toilets."

"Shut up, Mook, before I moe you again."

"You'll thank me later. Just think IPods, Kindles, Nooks and Smartphone. It's all for us. So that we can watch your every move, monitor your every thought, see everything you see, know everything you know and everything you don't know about yourselves. The more advanced the culture is, the more of you who use these technologies, the more we can monitor your evolvements. Even your own governments are listening in.

You don't believe me, go to any Asian country where their youth are more technically advanced, and see for yourself. While you text, we monitor your fingers' blood pulses and record your finger prints. Even your secretions are added into genetic data files so we can track your movements worldwide.

We've had to wait for your technology to catch up with ours. At least enough so we can do what we need to do to keep you under our thumbs at this level without sending up red flags by advancing you too quickly. But it's all working out just as we've planned. With every new development in your technology, even in cars, monitoring you gets easier for us because we are able to use more of our hidden observation technology behind it. Eventually it will be automatically done from birth to death for any person using your modern technology. All the others will have our implanted tissue-based technology without their knowledge."

"I suppose Aliens are behind Amazon taking over the book world."

"Yes, and note that movie theaters are going digital as well. While you all sit on your fat asses sipping lattés, guzzling soda, and eating popcorn, the real world is collecting data on you."

"We must really have you scared. Big brother, right out of science fiction books, not very original, Mook. Only it's not our government that is watching us, it's yours. That's a nice twist on all this Alien sorted shit. So quit messing with me before I make a scene and make them put me somewhere I can't be of any use to you creeps."

"I'm not messin' with you, melting pot head. Like I told you before, go ahead and write your own book based on what you've learned so far. Just call it sci-fi, don't try to make people think it's real. Put it out there as fiction and nobody will ever believe it's all really happening. Who do you think gave you the ability to create fictional stories and write them down in books?

"Let me guess, you did Mook."

"Don't be a smart ass. They did. They bred it into you. Taking what Jerry started to levels he never intended, for their own entertainment, and to help keep this all just one big crazy fictional story. Why do you suppose they developed so many different languages?

"To divide us."

"Yes, to categorize you. It's to keep humans from grouping all of your collective thoughts into one cohesive movement against us. But times are changing. English is quickly becoming the universal language and computers and Internet are pushing this forward as the universal language of music has for centuries."

"So dancing to Beethoven, Rock & Roll, and disco is our path to salvation and out from under your dragnet feet? I can dig that."

"Don't try to be cool, Picasso, you ain't got the wit to be part of the beat generation. Music has helped humans advance more than you're supposed to know. The more we discover about you dumb shits now, the better we can protect ourselves from those of you who are...."

"Yeah, yeah, I know, those of us who are evolving into knowing you are here. Breeding and eating us. Seeing beyond all the fictional adaptations of the horrible truth of what you're doing to us. You horse tick. Stop telling me all this shit before I take this cork screw and uncap my jugular with it."

90

"Go ahead. Eventually, the one we're looking for will logon to our system. So we're sharing with you today what we need in place tomorrow to keep you where we need you, under our thumbs. You ever hear of a project called the Matrix?"

"Yeah, a friend of mine starred in all three. A woman sued the producers over stealing her idea and won. I suppose it's real."

"Something like that. But simpler. Hollywood never gets it right because we don't let them."

"Let me guess. You can only advance us so fast, or the technical breakthroughs will seem out of proportion to how our minds function and attract way too much attention to the new technology than you want. Or someone smart will control way too much of how our world operates, like Microsoft."

"You're catching on."

"Can't have too many Steve Jobs in the world capable of figuring out what's really going on behind the panels of his ideas."

"No we can't. Electronic trade shows are as fast as we can humanly move on the surface. There's way more going on out there than any of you know from how we see things. But the little things we let you see are very affective in spreading what we need marketed across the globe in a nice orderly, human like manner. While you're listening to music, we're listening to you from the inside out. Rock on, Picasso."

"What appears as free trade is only Alien domination of our every move and thought. I get it. Is Bill Gates one of you? Was Steve Jobs? What about the rest of these billionaires?"

"They don't all have to be, do they, Picasso? We allow the right thoughts to appear in the right minds to make sure what we want done gets done the way we want it done."

"So people with high IQs could be cloned already or just Jerry playing hide the Pogo Stick as far as anyone knows."

"Some people know. You should know by now. You are a prime example of a crazy human who knows way too much already. That also makes you expendable when this is done. So watch your back to the very end of this. Regardless of what Jerry tells you. Got me?"

"I feel so privileged. Honestly."

"Don't be a smartass. I'm telling you this so you'll understand why you must follow through with what we're asking you to do. Every human of power and financial prominence is merely a clone of himself. Genetically altered to be what we need them to be. They

91

mess up. We take them out. To keep life as it is. Ours and yours, or they are given the information to be themselves, because they know we are here and accept us. It's a privilege we are extending to you. Even though you are a nobody, just a hack filmmaker, living with his dog, now directing your very first movie because of us.

Some humans even allow us access to them, knowing the tradeoff is that they'll live longer, better lives. Don't blow it. We can't tip the status quo, or the Council will be forced to reevaluate how we live here. Remember, it's Aliens like Dr. James Elwartowski and his two friends over there that want to come out in the open and send you humans that don't accept us being in charge back into the Dark Ages. So think about what you're doing for the rest of mankind by sacrificing who you are today. And you will be your better self tomorrow."

"I'm really an intergalactic hero like you. Not a mass murdering slime bag human like Javier? Gee, that makes it okay. Let's do it."

"If I could reach into that thick skull of yours and squeeze to death the smartass Picasso hiding in there, I would. Just try to see it from our point of view for once before you do anything stupid. By the way, that was nice work outside."

"I had nothing to do with it."

"Yeah, we know, but calling 911 was still a nice human touch. It showed heart on your part. One of the reasons I can put up with your bullshit. It could still cause us some problems, though."

"I couldn't just let them die without trying to help."

"I'm not talking about why you helped, it's that you helped."

"You're losing me."

"Exactly."

"If I can see you, can I moe you?"

"Your transformation isn't fully taking. We shouldn't even have this irritating conversation as Picasso and Mook. This conversation, all that I told you was a test. Something has gone wrong."

"Because I'm still me?"

"Because you still remember who me is. By the time you hit that backdoor, Picasso as you knew him should've been gone from your mind and body. And none of what I just told you should've made the slightest sense to you."

"But I thought...."

"You must take the doctor out tonight at the very latest."

"But how? I'm still me."

"You know."

"You mean, off with his head? When did I become Medieval Picasso and your go to whack guy?"

"When you found that first stone and touched it. By doing so you began all this Alien activity that is happening to you. And no, you don't have to separate the head and body from each other. He's an Alien not a clone. Just stick a blade you'll receive as a birthday gift into his head. Stay with him long enough to make sure he dissipates like Mary and those in your foyer did the first time. Or his buddies over there watching you will fix him again. We have to end this now because they know we have successfully removed his entire clone-able DNA from the data bank. This is the end of the line for him. There will be no further cloning of him to bring him back from the dead. If you get the job done right this time."

"Do they know you're here?"

"This isn't a parlor game. They know as little as possible. They know who you are and thought you're only here for the girl. But now know there's something up because you've come back after being torn to shreds by you-know-who. So don't drop the ball again. They've let Javier's family know where you are to get you out of the way without drawing any further attention to themselves. By tomorrow morning fortune hunters will be all over this town, if not sooner. Those guys out there were just the first wave because they were the closest. Some of them will not be fully human, but clones working for them."

"What about killing Javier's mother and brothers. Wouldn't that put a stop to the hunt for me by the Mexican drug cartel?"

"Good, Picasso. If it comes to that, but even in that there's more to know if and when the time comes. It won't end the hunt by others who want an end to you for other reasons. Remember there's more to you than Javier, and things are constantly changing within you. This is drawing attention to you for reasons that are just now coming to light for even us. We don't know if Jerry actually intended this or not. But it's very interesting."

"Not to me. Does the doc know you're involved?"

"Nobody really knows me. Not even you. Understand that."

"But...."

"I'm top secret, my man. I answer to only one Supreme Being, myself. Now stop with all the stupid questions. I've given you everything you need to know up to this point."

"Yeah okay. Do they have stones?"

"They got one somehow. We're still tracking where it came from. Our only hope is Doc won't have it on him when you make your move tonight. Or you'll have to take it from him, and we don't want you to have it either. It could prove to be a disaster for all of us, top to bottom in this adventure."

"Don't worry, this adventure is over. I'm not making a move on anyone tonight. As soon as you leave I'm getting the hell out of here."

"Yes you will and no you won't. We still have your dog's safety in questions. And your girlfriend is with two of ours right now."

"You've taken Bubba again?"

"Not yet, but fail us again and we will, your clone, and all your friends, too. Your movie will go unfinished and you'll disappear into nothingness as one of the biggest losers ever to exit Follywood."

"You're a creep, Mook."

"Only when I need to be, Picasso. So don't push those buttons. Now Jerry is taking your squeeze to meet Dr. Elwartowski in the parking lot of the hospital after this farce of a birthday party is over and he's done with Mike and Mac. We have to do this while your two cop pals are still in the hospital pretending to be big heroes for taking out those guys you killed with their guns. Everyone is paying attention to them. The sight of Oli and the doctor screwing in his BMW should set off an implanted primeval response that will put Javier into an out of control jealous rage."

"With all your interglacial otherworldly intelligence I find it insulting you'd use stupid human jealously again."

"See, it works all the time. Man's biggest weakness. Jealousy is our greatest weapon for motive to get you humans to do our dirty work, next to revenge and fear. She sleeps with him out of revenge for you hurting her heart by screwing Candy. You kill the doc out of jealousy for screwing Oli, because you fear losing her to him. It's all a very human like tragedy rewritten over and over since the beginning of time. Haven't you ever read Homer?"

"I don't recall any Alien Werewolves dissipating while mutilated and naked in the back seat of his BMW in The Iliad."

"You get what I mean though, Picasso. If Jerry does his job, Doc will be at least partially naked. The stone will still be in his discarded clothes away from his body. Don't touch it for any reason. I'll pick up the stone and leave a replacement dead human body for the cops to find. When our Alien werewolf doctor is gone from the car allow Mike or Mac to shoot you in the heart with the gun I gave you. Do it right there in the parking lot and it will be over."

"But Oli, what about her? Surely this will mess with her head."

"When she drives away to meet you, you'll do your thing."

"Is there any way I can survive all this?"

"You as you are now in this makeshift body can't, Picasso. I thought Jerry explained all that to you."

"Why are you doing this to me, Mooky? Really, despite some early misunderstanding of what you were, I've done everything you've asked. What you're doing to me. Chopping me up and putting me back together distorted. Mentally disturbed like this. With these despicable murderous people inside of me, is above and beyond being just cruel Alien bastards."

"We know how it looks to you from the inside because you can't see the whole picture from the outside. That's why Jerry made us clone you. Before we kill you, so that you see that you live on with a long happy life. If you let things happen the way we have it planned. Trust me, if it was up to the Alien Council you'd all be pulverized into Alien fodder when we're done with you. That'd be the end of it. But Jerry insists that you be taken care of in a respectful method. He's constantly doing this, getting involved and making sure we clone you humans and give you a chance to live on if you succeed. For an Alien Being with absolutely no physical presence, he's got the biggest heart and can be a bigger pain in the ass than anything else on this planet. You can tell him I said so."

"Cloning me, distorting who I really am, is respectful?"

"Yes, in the highest form, from our perspective."

"But he's not me."

"Yes he is. Minus all this Alien espionage bullshit."

"He, I, Jerry said my clone won't remember any of this stuff."

"From the moment your clone got back into that station wagon and drove away, your life continued on as though you never met me. And the moment this Frankenstein you've become ceases to mentally function, the very last of you will be automatically transferred to him. You will be complete again. Minus the memories of us. It should've already automatically taken place while you were out there in the snow. But it hasn't for unforeseen reasons. So we've got to end it tonight before things get more complicated than they already have."

"Turning me into some psycho killer isn't complicated enough?"

"Hardly, the hardest thing to kill in you humans is your conscious intellect's will to live. Your Alien enhanced will to live has complicated things by hiding somewhere deep inside your prefrontal cortex, where we can't find it. It won't get released until you're actually dead and you let it go by yourself. In more human terms, envision this in kin to being protected and hidden by your enhanced human spirit. Something that is as random as the one walnut in a bushel that is unwilling to be opened and be eaten. It fights to the very end only ultimately to be found rotten, uneatable, and usually not worth my time cracking."

"Great, my whole existence here on Earth is finally reduced to the value of a tough, sour nut to crack."

"Pretty much. Though, you wouldn't be so damn sour if you didn't bitch so much."

"So, if I let what's left of this me go, I'll be free to go away from you, back to my life, and hide inside my clone?"

"Yes, it's that simple. No Aliens, no vampires, no werewolves. No feeding our babies through your testacies."

"No Mook, no Jerry?"

"We'll still keep an eye on you, but you won't know it ever again."

"And Jerry will be free to molest me whenever he wants."

"He's fond of you. What can we say?"

"What happens to this me?

"I told you, they kill you right there in the parking lot. Look, it's not you, it's him. Javier. Keep that in mind."

"They, after I, you know...."

"Yes, Mac and Mike gun Javier down. They don't know yet. It's their payoff for being involved. It'll make them big shot heroes who save Frazer Park from a band of scumbags. They kill Javier, who stabbed to death the beloved local doctor in a fit of green-eyed rage. It might even lead them back to being reinstated onto the force with full pension, if it all works out right. They're deep undercover. So deep no one knows who put them there, not even them. See how it works. It'll just all fall in place."

"You haven't told them this yet?"

"This is a need to know operation, Picasso. Just like you and me talking now. They just think they're here to protect scumbag Javier who turned out to be werewolf enhanced you. Knowing they have to kill you will come to them when it comes from me. We don't want them going rogue on you before we need it done, just in case."

"Okay, I get it, but what about Oli?"

"She's Jerry's problem, not mine. That's why I brought him in. But there's still a big problem with all this."

"I'd say so, I don't want to die."

"Exactly, dummy. You're still in there. You're still talkin' to me as the pain in the ass Jozeph Picasso. Anyone who knows you will be able to see that you're still in there. And so will those cops. We can't have Mike or Mac, whichever one ends up takin' you out, hesitate. Or they will be dead, first. The Council will not be happy with more bodies to deal with. Therefore yours truly will be in deep shit, trying to make all this killing bullshit look like a human calamity. I'll have to pin it on someone logically involved, and the only three left are Candy, Oli, and the Old man. I might have to take one of them out."

"I need to be all of Javier to make this work right?"

"Maybe. You shouldn't have come back into this house with any of Picasso left in you. The fact that you can see me is proof that you're still in there hiding. I'm a programmed hologram so that only Jozeph Picasso's DNA can see or hear me."

"How is this happening? Is there a chance that I can get myself back out of this body?"

"Picasso, you don't want to get this self back. You'll be good as new. Better, your movie will be a smash, and you'll get the girl. You've got to let us go. Or you'll end up looking like this until someone from Javier's past hunts you down and buries you in a pile of sand, or worse."

"There's worse?"

"Trust me on this one."

"Why is someone always burying me in sand?"

"Let them kill you with the gun I gave you or this will get very complicated by the next full moon."

"You mean... so it's confirmed?"

"We weren't sure. We tried to clear it before it got in the way. But yeah, it was too late. You probably are."

"A werewolf?"

"An Alien Werewolf, Picasso. You understand the irony."

"This is no joke, Mooky."

"We're not laughing. You'll be a thousand times stronger, smarter, and more deadly than anything you can imagine walking this earth. It's why you're already able to hide from us. You're now part Alien. So we can't risk you getting loose or getting your hands on that stone.

97

We have no idea what you'll be capable of as the blood inside you morphs into who knows what, or how fast. You might not even need the draw of the moon to pull your werewolf out."

"This is really happening inside of me?"

"Yes. There are those of us who want to study you. And there are those of us who want to make sure they don't get the chance. You see how complicated this is getting by the minute?"

"I think. So I could have the power to get away? Or some kind of evolving value if kept alive as I am now."

"You won't. I'll take you down myself in person if I have to. Even if it puts an end to me as we know it."

"But, what if I do get away from you and become a hideous killing monster?"

"You already are. You saw what you did out there."

"And I'll be worse during the full moon?"

"Much, with teeth and claws. You saw what bit you. You'll view the world like you were never meant to see it. At first it will drive you mad, eating at your flesh with such pain and anger that you'll just need to howl at the moon. Then after you've fully transformed into what we aren't sure of yet, instinctively you'll be out to kill and take back the one thing you know is yours."

"My dog?"

"Your life. You'll hunt yourself down and eat your clone, probably your little dog too. You might not even remember why. Only that you have to. So you will. Unless they stop you first. But if they don't, you, the Picasso we all love to mess with, will be nevermore."

"Wouldn't you just be able to make a new one? A new me, you have several clones. Why not me?"

"They degenerate at times. Especially in humans, not always turning out good, even mine, but especially traumatized humans. Ask Jerry about that. So there's no guarantee they would be exact, retain memories or talents completely or even last long. You could be shortening your life considerably. We've had this conversation before. But listen, Picasso, no bullshit, this one living your life right now is as perfect a clone as clones get. Jerry saw to it himself, became the doctors who did this to you. You could live well into your hundreds with him. He's a no wrinkle ready to wear as is clone. You don't want to end that life, Picasso. You'll regret it to the end of this life.

Remember, you wanted a life when I met you. You've finally got one fully worth living. Just finish this one last thing for us and you're

98

free to walk away. What's best, you won't remember a damn thing about us. We removed any potential mutating genes and your extra vertebra. We only left your genius bump, your apophyseal, because we couldn't remove it without affecting your brain significantly. Don't mess this chance up."

"So, you won't try again."

"No. Sorry. This is your one last shot to get your life back as you. Living dumb as a human, unaware that we are here. Jerry couldn't stand the imperfection that could happen in you if we tried again."

"I don't understand why I am so special to him."

"Ask him sometime."

"I will. So, Mike and Mac live on as is and will remember?"

"They'll be fine. We'll take care of them as soon as the paramedics you called for them get here. We'll take over and they'll be out later tonight if nobody gets in the way."

"What's taking them so long? We've been talking for nearly ten minutes. They could be dead by now."

"In real time you'll stand here alone for 10 seconds."

"I just wish I had time to poke you in the eyes once more."

"Shooting me in the chest wasn't good enough, white boy?"

"Not nearly as satisfying. And I ain't so white no more."

"That's right. Don't think about all this too much. Let go. Go with the flow. Do it tonight in that parking lot. If you want your life back. Or anything can and will happen next beyond all of our wildest fears. We don't want that."

"I got your we right here."

Blip.

"Damn." I look at the clock behind the bar. Ten seconds have past.

18

I can hear sirens pulling up out back. They're here. I have never dreaded the future like I dread these next twenty-four hours. That thing, that it, that clone has my life. And I have to let go of what part of me I still possess, so that the other me can have it all. Have it all. All of my life. Everything that is me. I grip my head and involuntarily try to squeeze the thoughts out of me. Great, they've turned me into a mass murdering Golem.

"We'll see about that."

"See about what?"

"Oli. Where have you been?"

"Where have I been? I think I should be asking that question."

"What do you mean?"

"I know damn well you've been with her."

"I have not."

"She even had the nerve to tell me all about the two of you."

I look over at Candy and she's smiling at us. What the hell? Jerry is setting me up. "I was in the kitchen all this time."

"Don't lie, you've been schtooping her behind my back, all this time, and look at you, what is that on your collar, her slut lipstick?"

"A blood stain. A rodent, I grabbed up a mouse in the kitchen and must have squeezed it too hard when it bit me. It exploded in my hand. I was in there cleaning my shirt. Ask the help."

"That's disgusting, you liar."

"Why can't you believe me?"

"Because she flaunts being with you every chance she gets. She's such a whore. I don't know what my father sees in her."

"It's obvious don't you think. Older guy, younger girl."

"Are you mocking me?"

"I meant your father. How can he keep up with her?"

"She doesn't have to go after my men. First James, and now you. She hated my mother. Now she hates me because I'm younger and more beautiful. She's no longer the fair maiden of Frazer Park."

"You are the most beautiful maiden in all the land."

She smiles slightly. "It's just not fair, you big dwarf."

"Oli, I wasn't with her. I haven't been with her." As the words come out of my mouth I know they are a lie and a big mistake.

Slap, Oli clobbers me across the face. "You pig! I saw you both in this room myself, remember. Up against that window, butt naked so anyone could see it."

"Ouch, I meant tonight. Oil, I love you."

"So you weren't with her again?"

"She's lying if she says I was."

"That heartless bitch. I'll make sure she doesn't see a penny of Daddy's money, ever. We won't give them a penny to develop this town, unless it's in writing that she is out of his will and I get everything. She'll have to go back to blowing men for nickels and dimes when I'm done with her."

"Now you're talking. I'll make sure it's in the contract. Now, do you believe me? I never left the kitchen."

"When I found her with James, I thought my life had ended until I found you. Don't play with my heart, Boli. I don't think I can take it. I'm so confused. James was the man of my dreams… until you came along and convinced my father to let me marry you."

"Oli, there's no one but you. I loved you from the day we met."

"Then why do you test me? This stupid list of yours of places to have sex before you get married, I hate it."

"It's gone, torn up. Okay. Come on, it's my birthday. I've grown."

"I still want to do the nasty in the snow, Picasso."

This takes me by complete surprise. Why, I don't know after all I've seen. "I'm gonna kick your asses, Jerry."

"Promises, promises. Just setting the tone, Jozeph. It's nothing personal." And it's Oli again. "What's going on out there?"

"I don't know, look at all the lights."

Olivia heads back towards the kitchen. I look across the room at Doctor Elwartowski to see his reaction. James immediately makes his way toward us. He's following Oli into the kitchen, stopping just slightly to look me in the eye. "Happy birthday, Boli."

"Isn't it?"

He goes in, leaving me there, as Candy comes up behind me. "Looks like the cat's out of the bag again."

"What did you tell her, Jerry?"

"Will you stop calling me that? I'm Candy. Don't you want to suck on me?"

"It's been awhile since I spanked a woman, so don't push me."

"I liked you better when you weren't part werewolf."

"Me, too." So I leave her, and follow Oli into the kitchen.

Just outside the backdoor, two young paramedics check Mike and Mac for vital signs. They are not happy with what they're finding.

Doc moves to the backdoor where he looks down on the paramedics who shake their heads.

"Some kind of toxic shock comma or something. Could be poisoning," Terry, the slightly older of the two, says.

Oli turns to Doc, "Do something, James."

I see him hesitate, he knows these guys. He glances up at the two I know to be Aliens, then back at me, "Get me a syringe, Terry."

"Wait a minute, Doc? Let's take them down...."

"No time. Make it two syringes. Now!"

Terry looks up to see the faces of the Frazer Park elite looking down at him, his credibility at the balance. He turns to the younger paramedic for advice.

Oli's father, Mr. Hamilton, sticks his head in the door from outside. "Give him what he wants, Terry, the man's a genius."

Doc moves to the refrigerator and takes out five or six different items, mostly spicy liquid and begins mixing something in a glass. He works very quickly, but measuring precisely, finally cutting a lemon and squeezes two drops in. I do my best not to laugh out loud and mutter bullshit.

The syringes are placed before him on a cloth towel. Into which he pours the concoction. He kneels down just inside the door and sticks a needle in and shoots the first one into Mikes' calf and then the other into Mac's.

But only I and his two special Alien friends can see what he's really doing. He has reached into his side pocket of his jacket and has what appears to be a small shinny purple glass stone in his hand. He presses it first against Mike's bare chest, then Mac's bare chest, flush up against the skin, pretending to feel for vital signs. Three seconds tops for each guy. He then checks their pulse. He opens one eye on each with the stone in that hand.

"Okay, they'll make it. Just give them a moment."

"What?" Terry asks very skeptically. "What'd you shoot them up with, Doc?"

"Hot sauce."

"Hot sauce?"

"And a few other natural spices to get the blood moving."Dr. Elwartowski stands up. His job is done here. He hands the syringes back to the younger paramedic, who looks at them like he's seeing his career flash before his eyes for letting Doc shoot the two guys up with spices. "Take them to the hospital, and put them on saline IV. I'll be right there."

"Saline? Look, Doc, these guys need...."

Mike sits up, then MacAroy, "Heartburn! Give me water."

"Sorry?"Dr. Elwartowski asks.

Everyone breaks out in applause. The paramedics, I think might have stopped breathing. These two were way into a comma. And good old Doc brings them back with kitchen spices and a need for drink.

A Spanish member of the kitchen staff cutting salad stops and hands them both bottled water from the refrigerator.

But Oli involuntarily plants a great big kiss on the Doc's mouth. "Oh, my god, James, you're brilliant. You saved them both."

"It's nothing. They'll be fine as soon as we get fluids in them, and run some blood tests to see what caused this."

The two paramedics look at each other again, wanting so much to leave. It's over is all they seem to care about. They recheck Mike and Mac's vital signs."They're normal."The one says to the other.

"Thanks, Doc."

"What the hell happened? We were out here smokin' and next thing I know, you were callin' 911." Mike points at me.

"I ah, okay, I called 911. I went to throw a mouse I caught out the back door and they were lying there."

"You left them out here? They could've frozen to death," Oli says.

"What, I was with them, I ah... called 911. I didn't want to move them. I'm not a doctor."

"No you're not," Oli says, gripping the doctor harder.

"Keeping them cold might have saved their lives, Miss Hamilton. Slowing the blood down may have prevented any toxic shock," Terry says. "What do you think, Doc?"

"Sounds like he did the right thing, Oli," Mr. Hamilton says.

Everyone looks at me. I shrug.

"Maybe so. Good going, Bolivar. Now everyone, back to the party," Doc says. "Birthday boy hasn't had his spankings yet."

Laughter breaks out at my expense. Doc gives me that knowing smile, mocking me, stealing my girl back from me as we stand there.

Oli hangs on to him, hugging Dr. James Elwartowski as hard as she can, rubbing her young luscious body up against him; a cat in heat, just short of purring. So hot in fact, that the only thing I can envision clearly at this moment, as the others in me percolate to the surface, is us splitting his head open with a blade! Oli looks at us, smiling into our insanely jealous eyes, darting out her tongue, tormenting the fully us now. You are a bastard, Jerry.

"Oli come," her father calls to her. "It's time to cut the cake and open presents. Move it, Bolivar, let these guys take care of this mess. Let's go get drunk."

I clamp down on my emotions and the Picasso in us resurfaces just enough to answer civilly, "Right behind you, Dick." I take Oli, nearly having to peal her off Doc. "Shall we?" She looks up at me. At that very moment I can tell she no longer loves Boli, no longer wants to marry Boli, and she will be back in the doctor's arms as soon as she can get away.

I don't want it to make me sad, angry, humiliated or homicidal, but Javier does because this act is for him, not me. Javier probably will seek revenge, despite all of my efforts to stop him. So what's left of my mind starts calculating how I'm to get away afterwards, before Mac and Mike gun me down for what we are destined to do.

At the door Oli leans into us. "I'm gonna rock his world so crazy tonight, Boli. While you can only wait for me to come home to spank me for being such a bad, bad girl."

"Shut up, Jerry."

"You okay, Bolivar."

I look up and Dick is watching us. "Right there, Dick."

19

After cake and ice cream, I open all my presents. Good old Boli must have some reputation. Besides expensive winter clothing and unusual cabin kitchen knickknacks, he got six bottles of tequila and a shinny ten-inch elk-bone handle hunting knife. It is from Boli's uphill neighbor, Buckley Jones, who keeps hiding behind a black Stetson cowboy hat. The blade is supposedly in case Bolivar hits a deer again while driving drunk on tequila.

But I am pretty sure Buckley, and maybe a few Aliens, really know what it's for. Boli got a very nice Rolex from Dick with a card from Candy saying it's to make sure Boli gets to the church on time. Add the poisoned cigars from the good doctor, and hell, I'm a trapped dead man in another man's life.

From there, still in control, I leave Oli behind in the dark to freshen up before she joins me for perhaps a romp in the snow, or a goodbye speech. I don't know which to expect at this point. She and I both know she has other plans before Boli sees her again. I know because I was told. Boli knows because his heart is hurting.

I drive back to Boli's cabin, trying not to think too much about her, knowing it will cause internal steaming and flushing with anger. A black F250 with a plow attached, still running, and still pushing against a fifty foot Frazer Pine catches my full attention once I get there. So I pull Boli's Range Rover into the garage. Taking my new knife, I climb out the back hatch window and slither into the snow. I don't know if anyone is still waiting for me, but the Javier or the werewolf in us seems to think there is. So we go around the house checking every window.

Everything seems to be in order until I make my way to the back den overlooking the town. Sitting in there is someone watching ESPN and doesn't seem to care if anyone knows it. I'm thinking it's probably the Mook. But from what I can see by the cobra skinned cowboy boots, and black Stetson hat, it's the owner of the F-250, my knife gifting uphill neighbor, Buckley Jones. I didn't see him leave Oli's, so who knows how long he's been here, how he got here so fast, or why.

Fighting Javier from taking over, I'm still doing things I know I wouldn't do as myself. I move cat like to the kitchen door and find it open. Buckley must have a key because I know I locked it. As I make my way through the house I begin to see and smell an increasing amount of blood. Bodies spread about the place in many forms of deadliness pop into view, followed by wild potshot bullet holes that puncture everything else.

It's weird how the selective eyesight just happens. It's almost as though I'm racking a motion camera lens to focus a shot. I know it's not all me it's happening to. I forget about it by the time I get up behind Buckley. Remembering the new knife, I slide it up under his stubbly chin. Buckley's already not going anywhere. His front jacket is covered in blood that pools in his lap where he has all four of his right hand fingers stuck in a matching set of holes. The other hand holds a neat half filled glass of Scotch. From the looks of the red blood he's not Alien, or at least not a yellow blooded one.

"Are you dead?" I ask.

"Close as I plan to get," he says.

"You took them on all by yourself?"

"They were layin' in wait when I got here. Six of 'em."

"I only count five bodies."

"The sixth one got away. He drove off in my truck bleedin' as bad as me, after ruining my good Stetson. Put a hole clear through."

"I see that. What are you doing here?"

"Hold on." He clicks off the TV. "They listen. What they sent me here to do. Clean the house. Make sure you still have what you need when you leave here."

"The knife."

"From them."

"You know?"

"I know who you're supposed to be. Javier Sanchez, a scumbag drug cartel's brother in hiding. You were supposed to be just Javier, but they told me something went wrong last night and you might try to run because you're part someone else now. I stopped tryin' to figure it out years ago, so whatever, whenever. Long as they don't eat me. Or suck on my balls."

"You're human, then."

"What's left of me."

"Will they be back to help you?"

"End of the road for me, partner. I'm expendable, now that I've paid them back."

"When you say them, are you talking about the Mook?"

"Never heard of anyone, or thing by that name."

"How bad you hit?

"If I remove my fingers from these four holes, I'll bleed out."

"They sent you here to save me?"

"I came to save my family from what they'd do to them if I failed."

"Bastards." I look at the TV and stand away from it. Just in case.

"They're everywhere, running everything. I tried hiding, but they know my every move. I think they've got somethin' hid in me."

"Listen, I'm supposed to kill Doc, he's got a stone that could fix all this. I saw him use it today on Mac and Mike. If I make it out of that parking lot with it, I'll double back here and give it to you."

"You'd do that for me? Why?"

"Because you're human, it's not what they expect me to do. I can't just leave you here. Despite what they've done to me, I'm still part human inside. You saved me from these guys. So, I'll need help out of the parking lot. If you give that help to me, I'll make it back. If I can."

"Healing stones. I've seen them work on Ma. It's how they sucked me into their world. They let me see just enough to drive me mad as a hatter if I think about it too much. Saved her from sure hell on earth though, she was a heavy smoker. I couldn't get her to quite them for nothin'. She's healthier than both of us now and a pain in the ass tryin' to keep up with. But she's Ma. You know?"

"Not really, didn't know mine very long."

"Sorry."

"Guess I was probably too young to barter for her life with them, even if I had the chance."

"Yeah, some flowers flourish, some don't. It's the good ones that get picked young to decorate the world."

"Their world, from what I've heard."

"Yeah, got to love Ma though. She's nearly a hundred years old and could still drive if DMV let her. I secretly take her huntin', her eyes sharp as rabbits."

"Do you have any idea what's going on?"

"You're here to kill Doc 'cause the Alien Council wants him gone."

"So you know he's a werewolf? A very powerful Alien one?'"

"Don't I. I've been hearin' the howlin' ever so often. Started findin' my cattle mutilated by somethin'. I was told not to mention it to anyone. Just to dig holes and plant the bones and they would give me back two more. I sell one. He eats one. A good livin'. I think they're clonin' mine anyway 'cause they all look alike. So it ain't no sweat off their butts, either way."

"You've been feeding him, keeping him at bay until they figured out a way to get some fool like me up here to do their dirty deed."

"You ain't Boli or Javier right now are ya."

I show him my other arm. "Only part of him. I've got the leg and butt of someone else. The rest of me, is Jozeph Picasso. They keep dragging me back and stitching me together with other people's body parts and blood. My mind is so twisted up I'm not sure who I am at times. Especially while I do horrible things to other people."

"Bastards are turnin' ya into some kind of Frankenstein's Monster for their own benefit. When they could've just cloned new body parts from you all along."

"They did this to me on purpose? Why?"

"Probably so when the time came you won't argue about leavin' this wreck behind when you're done with what they made it possible for you to accomplish."

"Sons-of-a-bitches."

"Treatin' us like dogs. Breedin' us, bein' us, eatin' us. I swear if I could track them all down and cut off their heads one at a time, I'd never stop until they were all gone. Or I was too dead to care."

"Yeah, you might have heard of me showing up as a leg in the Tujunga Wash last year. That Jozeph Picasso?"

"Naw, but I read that a Jozeph Picasso, the Hollywood guy, in the local papers this mornin'. He helped all those people get out of these mountains on Christmas day. Is that you?"

"It's how they got me up here. I got invited by one of my neighbors who is one of them. They sent my clone back in my place to live the life I created. A complete set up."

"Clones. My mom is a clone. It's why she's so young for her age, 'cause she ain't as old as anyone thinks."

"You know these hills?" I ask.

"Like the back of my hand. Hunt this place dry if I could. Killin' critters keeps me from killin' myself, knowin' what I know."

"Knowin' what we know. It's been hell. We can't trust anyone."

"Yeah, some of them leap from person to person. I never know who I'm talkin' to half the time. Wait, you ain't messin' with me?"

"Look at me."

"Yeah, sorry, I can't even tell Ma who she really is. She'd put me away somewhere, throw away the key. She thinks Jesus saved her from all her misery. Been givin' her church all her earthly belongings ever since. Her Reverend's been eatin' it up and keeps referrin' to her every time he hands out his basket. I had to take him aside and threaten' him, if he didn't keep his hands out of my family's pockets, I'd introduce him to what really saved my mother."

"He get it?"

"He will."

"Yeah, trust me, my friends and dog think I'm a little weird."

"A little, have you looked in the mirror lately?"

"Look who's talking. What are you, Dutch?"

Buckley looks down at his fingers stuck in the blood dike. Laughing only makes him spit blood. "Yeah, a little. Mostly inbred hillbilly."

"How do I get out of that hospital parking lot and back up here without taking any of the roads?"

"You'll bring me that stone?"

"If Doc still has it. He used it on those two in the kitchen."

"Yeah, I figured there was more to that. You know the canyon you tossed that body into?"

"You saw that?"

"I watched the whole thing in Technicolor from the bay window. You're quick. You're a real killin' machine."

"So I'm finding out."

"You didn't move like any human I ever seen hunt."

"Yeah, I got that too. I got bit."

"By the werewolf?"

"Yes, but when they kill me what's left of Picasso will go to my clone and it will be done. So they tell me. I just need to get back here first to help you before they catch up with me while I have the stone."

"No funny stuff?"

"I don't want to live with them hunting me."

"At the base of the canyon, over two meters north of where the house overlooks it, is a passage to a water drainage viaduct. You'll have to break in. It's sealed with a special metal door. It runs deep and dark. Take a flashlight. Be careful to keep turning left. You'll

109

round your way up the ridge just a hundred yards short of my cabin where it once emptied a massive water drainage basin.

Turn right once and you're dead, no matter what you are. Very Greek lookin' or Roman in its design and I've got a hunch it wasn't designed by modern humans. If it was, it could've been here since before Indians ran these mountains. It's a nasty climb though, nearly straight up, but I've done it many times, it's secure. No outsiders have lived to tell about it. The door will have snow and ice holding it closed. There's a lock on both ends so you'll have to figure out a way to open it. The guy in my truck has my keys if you plan on using it."

I pull out the knife. "Can I cut through the door with this?"

"Good idea, that ain't no ordinary knife as you probably already figured. That thing will cut through steal like it's butter. Watch you don't cut your leg off."

"I'll keep it sheaved until I need to use it."

"Good luck."

"Stay alive."

"Takes more than six hombres to kill a redneck like me. But hey, if you don't make it back, I'm to set this place on fire before I die. So if it's a blaze by the time you get here, don't come inside."

"If I'm not back by midnight, there's a Zippo right above the fireplace. If you come across Cuban cigars, don't smoke them."

"He removes the brass-based Zippo and two cigars from his jacket.

"They're lased with something deadly."

"Might just be what the doctor ordered, case I need 'em."

"Could be. Buckley...."

"It's okay."

"I don't control most of what I do. Only when I seem to be talking to humans do I have much say. So I'm sorry for anything that might happen in the next hour or two. I wouldn't do any of the things on my own. Make sure people understand that. If they find out it's me doing this, and know I'm still in here, the human in here is still me."

"I won't kill you unless I have to... if they make me, I mean."

"Fair."

"Hey, Jozeph, you ever hear of a Blue Moon?"

"It's rare, but yeah two full moons in one month."

"Bastards didn't tell you, did they? This is that month."

"It must have slipped their yellow brained, ball-sucking minds."

20

Two full moons, I'll be a werewolf's victim. No wonder they're making their move on Doc tonight. I'm getting the queasy feeling that my concerns don't count. That I'm merely an infected host organism for their virus-like behavior.

After changing into something more fitting for murdering in the snow, I leave the way I came in, with full intentions on finding a cure to what ails me. I grab up a ski jacket on the way out, planning on taking Javier's Land Rover. But when I look across the snowy road into the dark I can just make out the pickup truck running with its break lights on. I don't know why I need it yet, but Javier does. It's Buckley's, and likely crashed by the sixth assassin here to kill me. I guess he wasn't Dutch enough to plug the dike that leaked from him.

The snow is coming down harder. Big white flakes meaning it's not as cold as last night, not that it matters to us. I am now dressed in the world's best winter sports outerwear. Javier may be who he is, as might I, but at least he buys only the best of clothes.

Just ten feet away from the Ford F250 we involuntarily make a simple bound that I know doesn't come from Picasso or Javier and we're in the bed of the truck, looking into the back window. The dead hombre is slumped to the side of the seat, making a mess of the leather. Damn. But I now know that driving this truck will give me just the amount of cover I need to sneak up on the doctor. So I'll have to deal with the mess.

As disgusting as I find planning to hideously stab an Alien in the brain, I somehow can only feel the rising rage that is filling our every fiber. The thought of Olivia and Doc huddled together in his BMW fills our mind. Just as Jerry knew it would.

What's really weird is that I know Oli is probably already there with the doctor. They are pleasuring each other in ways only Jerry could imagine. I know it's supposed to trigger a primeval rage within Javier, and does. Still, I can't help knowing that the real sense of rage that keeps bubbling to the surface of the part of our mind I control is that I want to get home and take my life back from that son-of–clone who is living it. He's set to direct my movie, from my script, romance my girl and sleep in my bed. Visions of mutilating him is so frighteningly 3D because I actually see myself being torn to bits by what's left of this me. Not by Javier, not by the Alien werewolf, but by me, the real Jozeph Picasso. So vivid is the vision, that it jolts me back to the moment at hand.

I must focus. Step by step, I fight to keep remembering that I do these things to get free of those who occupy me and use me for their dirty work. Kill the doctor, take the stone, and come back here for Buckley who will help me run for it out of these hills. I must be free to get my life back. I must, I must, I must do these things to be free, free from what they have done to me. This demon self-mutilating mantra marches through my head. But it's fair to say it's actually the sanest amongst many sick thoughts that keeps us movin forward.

Opening the truck door, I realize I saw this same truck plowing last night as I lay in the snow bleeding to death. I pull the dead body out. With one clean swipe of my boot I cover him with fresh snow. None of this matters to me now, as I see that there is still a snow plow, despite the tree, firmly attached to the front of the truck. My cover for being in the lot unfolds.

I'll simply start to plow it, getting closer and closer until I pounce to do my dastardly thing. A perfect cover for me the killing thing. I look at the seat. There's lots of fresh blood where I need to sit. It doesn't faze me a bit. I merely take the floor mat and cover the blood. That doesn't work. So I dig my nails into the seat pad, ripping away the leather and jump in. The truck's already running. I throw it into reverse and the big Ford V8 rumbles to life. At least what's left of Jozeph Picasso has proven by now, even in print, if not yet cut in ice that I can definitely drive in the snow.

I look at the cabin as I put the truck in drive, knowing I promised to make it back. I also know I might not be in this much control of myself when I try to make it back. All I know for sure is that I need that stone. And if I kill the doctor and take it, I'll have a chance to make it back to my life. Taking my life from the Alien-created-bastard who is living in my place seems to be the growing motivation that is propelling me down the hill. Having envisioned my true inner desires to kill my outer-self, I know I'm in terrible trouble.

From what happened to me before, I know that from this moment forward something bigger and stronger will take over my movements. Something more powerful than any of Javier sicknesses could muster. I or Leonie Dazarrio will never be able to fully control this body again unless they let us. The blood of the Alien werewolf is taking over, just like Mooky feared. Will this interfere with us being able to kill another Alien? Is this why there's such a rush? The mystery lies within who will survive. Me or me, or will Mooky have to sacrifice himself to take me out when the deed is done? A result to which both of me and him loose what time we have left on this Heaven of the Universe, Mother Earth; the vacation destination to all the rich and powerful cannibalistic Space Travelers from all other galaxies.

A thought pops into my mind. If this little bit of werewolf blood can do this to the three of us partly inhabiting this body, than what kind of abnormal powers does the doctor posses while not a full-fledged werewolf? How will I ever creep up on him? How will I ever over take him? Unless Jerry is doing his job. Jerry, Oli, screwing the doctor, "I'm gonna kill that bastard!"Through the snow we go as we drop the snowplow into action and proceed on down the hill. Who would suspect it's not redneck Buckley doing his nightly job?

There are so many powers pulling at our brain from all directions. If we explode from the inner brain outward, splattering all our evil thoughts on the windshield before us, we wouldn't be surprised. I must concentrate on being Picasso. "Live, I must live to get my life back. My life back. I want my life back!"

In the end of all this mayhem, the single most important event must take place, the clone of Jozeph Picasso, must die!

21

We pull into the parking lot of the hospital. It's more of a doctor's complex than what we city slickers would consider a hospital. The parking lot is overly large with enough snow to need plowing. So following the lines of what had been plowed before, we go about Buckley's work.

At the middle of the parking lot far away from any lights are two segregated cars. A black GLK350 Mercedes Benz not running and a blue BMW 535i sedan that is. As much as Javier would just love us to drive the truck over there and literally plow right into the cars, we refrain and continue on our way. We plow the parking lot, inching closer and closer until we see Oli pop out of the BMW, pulling her fur coat around her lusciously tanned body.

The Picasso in us knows she's as naked as she was when she showed up to do Javier in the snow. I can feel the switch click on in our head. The fire in our belly turns on the instant steam. Our eyes watch through murderous slits as Olivia scampers barefoot to her Mercedes and fires it up.

Her window rolls down as she glances back at the plow truck. It's Jerry inside her, licking the sex off her face and fingers, the bitch. She can't see us glaring at her, but Jerry knows we're here watching her every teasing move. She turns to blow the doctor a farewell kiss, and whispers with those sumptuous lips, "I love you."She glances mercilessly back at us with those sky blue eyes, as she rolls up her window and drives away. Knowing exactly the fire she has lit in us.

That's all Javier needs to set us into action. The Aliens knew this. It doesn't matter if I think of myself as me, I, us or them, we're all the same. The next 30 seconds are completely out of my control. Javier sets the plow into a slow full length course across the parking lot. After dismantling the dome light by ripping it from the ceiling, we climb out the passenger side door. As the truck approaches the BMW, about twenty yards away, we hang onto its side like a salamander hiding from a hawk. We drop, tucking-and-rolling, until we are up behind the doctor's trunk, secure that the steamed windows are blocking our movements, and the snow is smothering any sound.

Unsheathing the Alien hunting blade, with one swift move, we bound up on the trunk, even quicker and faster than we did the bed of the truck. One quick motion and the knife slashes, cutting quickly and effortlessly through the sheet metal of the Beamer's top, carving away a two foot hole with hardly a noise.

Doc looks up at us, as we toss the cut metal away. He's still in the back seat, half undressed, fighting to pull on his pants while sitting down. Perfect timing, as we plant the eight inch blade an inch above his forehead. We drive it in down to the ivory handle, slashing the blade upward before pulling it out, slicing his skull and right brain from his left. His dead eyes stare at us reflecting nothing, expecting nothing, never having a chance. The life drains from him evenly as his Alien yellow substance flows over his bare shoulders.

We don't stop to admire our work. Instead we do what we really came here for. What they feared Picasso would come here for. And we reach down to grab up his coat. We poke inside to a shallow pocket where we saw him draw his stone earlier and pull out the wrapped object in a strange, almost alive, tingling fabric. Something protectively Alien we're sure. We know the instructions are to wait for the body to dissipate and leave the stone behind. But we've done enough of what they wanted. To hell with Mooky. It's time to do what we really came here for. The stone is ours now and we are getting our lives back with it. We sheathe the blade and put the stone into our own jacket pocket, cloth and all. And leap from the car, to sprint after the plowing pickup truck, still doing a descent job.

We are moving so fast we are barely leaving foot prints as we make the Ford F250 just before it runs out of parking lot. Jumping back in we step on the break, slamming it in reverse and head back towards the exit.

Blip! "Hand over the stone and the knife, Picasso."

"I'm part Alien now, you can't touch me." I drop it into drive and speed off.

"That's where you got it wrong, Picasso. Officially, you don't exist anymore than I do." Mook points his laser gun at me.

I stomp on the gas, down to the metal and cut the wheel sharply to the right. The Ford smashes immediately into a very large square cement lamp pole base, taking out the whole right side of the pickup truck. This sends all those that compile my body through the windshield, over the plow and face down into the snow. We've lost most of an eyebrow, leaving large open wounds down the side of our head as blood rains down from multiple lacerations.

But we don't look back as three laser shots beam over head. The fourth takes off the left earlobe, leaving an open wound in our cheek. We leap up and with inhuman bounds are up a tree swinging from branch to branch as if possessed by some great, almost white ape.

If the I in us wasn't doing my part by helping to navigate, I'd be dumb founded. But knowing it's not me, Leonie or Javier powering these super primate movements, the Picasso in us just points us deep into the woods as far as we need to go to get to the hidden door.

Now out of lazar sight, we force our other nearly useless arm into our pocket and grip the stone, fumbling to get it out of its Alien cloth. We hold it in our palm. The tingling continues until our whole body vibrates with near orgasmic pleasing energy. We can feel our broken collarbone mend nearly immediately while we climb the snowbound mountainside. The warm blood that gushes from our face stops and flakes away. Our wounded flesh flushes, and heals with the supernatural feeling of thousands of hairy spiders crawling, stitching us together with their spindly webs.

We adjust our path toward Oli's mountain resort-size cabin. Making the good half mile length of the three hundred foot deep canyon, cut all the way back to the base of her father's majestic cabin pillar supports, in a matter of minutes. It would've taken a normal none Alien-werewolf-infested man nearly an hour, if accomplishable at all in this snow.

Looking up at Oli's cabin the Javier in us is fighting the rest of us to scale the cliff and do to her what we had done to her Alien doctor lover. We pull the blade as we near where the tunnel door should be hidden when "Blip." Crap. But we don't look back, we react. With one sudden swoop of our left hand we cut Mooky's arm in two. The laser gun he tries to point at us drops into the snow. We pick it up, plying it from his death grip, and point it at the Mook.

No need for words. We pull the trigger. This puts a sizzling six inch hole right through his chest. This burns a hole into the metal door behind him. Leaving his black duster smoldering. All taking place before he finishes reacting to missing his arm just below the elbow. Why he'd show up in the flesh and not a hologram to go up against what we've turned into is questionable. We look him in the eyes, knowing we could mend him with the stone in our pocket, but we don't. Instead we leave Mook to sit down on his ass and plop back on his yellow blood soaked duster. Screw him. Let Alien Insurance mend him. Maybe they'll put someone else's arm on him for a change.

I know for sure I'm not controlling these actions or emotions. Even though I'd love to have done that on my own, I know that the Picasso still left in us wouldn't have pulled the trigger or severed his arm. Well maybe, considering I have shot him once in the past.

My guess is that Mooky knows. He's here to kill us all himself. In person, no hologram or kindred spirit to do the Alien Council's dirty work this time, because we took off with the stone. Proving only how important it is to end what is left of me before we get completely out of control.

How taking us out could be so important to their survival on our planet is also questionable. We're sure we've only seen but a sliver of what is really going on within the Alien dominance. So, we're even more tempted to put the next laser shot between Mooky's eyes. But the I in us fights Javier the best I can to keep us moving just in case we end up needing the Mook down the road.

As it turns out, Mook knows where the channel door is. He is indeed sprawled in front of it. So we kick him out of the way. And use the blade to cut a hole as easy as butter. Big enough for us to climb into. A thought occurs from somewhere, making us adjust the power on the laser gun. With inhuman accuracy we reattach the metal hole cut in the door. This will slow down anyone taking the dead Mook's place in coming after us. Making sure we don't sever our fingers in the process.

Once the laser stops it turns to pitch black beyond the reflected snow coming through a seam we left in the cut. It's scary in itself. But with powers that behoove a werewolf, our eyes quickly adjust and we can make out enough to keep us moving. We still have no idea how any of this will turn out. Only the I in us knows that we are hell bent on getting my life back. Stopping the imposter from enjoying the life I created.

As far as we know, Leonie's leg and butt really have no say in this adventure and are just along for a leg up. Javier's face, arm and killer instincts control most of our emotions, while the Alien werewolf blood running in our veins is juicing us with superpowers. We're feeling so groovy with having the stone, we're almost looking forward to living a life of violent mutilating, cannibalistic crime.

Knowing this, the I, the fall guy of the millennium, the Cybil of the Alien Council, Joe filmmaker-schmuck, manages to direct our movements deeper into this frozen channel. I strongly borrow what I can from the inherent Alain navigator skills. I point us home, taking each left in the climb back to the life I left behind. We're still wearing Javier's babies, and they make the going at least comfortable and somewhat civilized. In thinking this, as though my comfort is of any importance on this trip up the channel, even I want to punch us all in the mouth.

22

As Buckley Jones said, by keeping a constant left in the channel we briskly climb up the inside of the mountainside. Until we come to a dead-end at what appears to be a very large caldron hollowed out about five hundred feet down to draw a water flow from an ancient dead lake. The stone work here is immaculate, even in today's terms. How did primitive people do this? It's much easier to envision the possibilities knowing what we know now, figuring the mathematics and laser like cutting tools that must have been used to accomplish such an enormous engineering feat. Given that we're now holding such an Alien tool and using it to cut our why out of here.

Without damaging anything other than the man made door that somehow Buckley attained keys to, we step out into a now half-filled valley that once must have been a great basin filled with water. A dead stream that once filled the bowl is now just a path leading up to Buckley's cabin. Seeing the beauty of this, a giant calm washes over me. As though the we drains out of us and I, Jozeph Picasso, have retained possession of our mind.

At Buckley's cabin, I take a moment to think. Do I make my way to where Buckley is waiting, chancing that he is already dead and something else is waiting for me? Or do I take the Corvette parked in his garage and head to LA to avenge myself on my own?

In the end, being still part human wins over. I ignore the old lady watching out the window, and let Javier hotwire the Corvette. I drive it through the snow, down to Javier's cabin just in case what Buckley knows can help save me. Buckley will not be happy about me driving his Corvette in the snow. Would it matter to him if I were to just take off and let him bleed out? Probably not. I park up under the pines where I found his F-250 and make my way back to the blood splattered, and body-filled cabin. I'm not sure why, but I'm feeling very much myself. So I'm on guard as to why.

I can't see anything else lurking about. No Mooky, or any of his Alien kind. That doesn't necessarily mean they're not here to take the stone back. Laser in hand, I make my way back through the kitchen. All the bodies are still here. Is it a good sign? I'm not sure. The place hasn't been touched. Only a flame in the fireplace lights the room I left Buckley in.

Buckley is still there, fingers in his gut, watching me.

"You made it."

"So far," he says.

"You're in better condition than I expected."

"Thick fingers. How did it go?"

"Gruesome as expected with a few unexpected horror attractions."

"Had a yellow brain and what not?"

"Yes, a mess. The things these Aliens make me do."

"You didn't stick around to make the body exchange?"

"No. I took the stone instead."

"You wouldn't have gotten out of that parking lot without it."

"They knew I would take the stone. I don't think they planned to wait for Mike and Mac."

"Mook is pretty pissed off."

"You heard?"

"He was here."

"So they fixed him."

"Of course."

"What now?"

"Give me the stone, and let me fix myself."

I look at Buckley closely. Damn, so it's Jerry inside keeping him alive. "I can't give you the stone, Jerry."

"Yes you can, Jozeph."

"After what I went through with the clone and sexual abuse, I don't think that's a good idea."

"You'll let Buckley die?"

"Of course not."

"Let them kill you, Jozeph."

"I can't."

"Your will to live will lead to a no good end for you."

"It's still my life."

"Your life is waiting for you. Back home. Let this thing you've become go. The longer you live with that werewolf blood in you the harder it will be to take you out. The stone will only complicate things. They'll have to behead you to take you out unless they wait for you to turn into a werewolf, or whatever mutated version it becomes. There's really no telling what you'll morph into."

"I'm starting to like it, Jerry. So it doesn't really matter."

"You see our point."

"I'm part Alien now. Where does the Council sit with me?"

"They don't at the moment. But that will change shortly. That's why Mook came for you himself. This was very hush-hush, unless the bodies lying about this town start showing up. Mooky is out there in the cold taking care of that right now. And none too happy about it."

"Can I fix him while you're in him?"

"Not without me taking possession of that stone. If you try to leave I'll fry you, and maybe him."

"Then pick one of these bodies. Hurry up, we're leaving."

Jerry jumps into the nearest body and he sits up, blood still dripping from his head and chest. He's a real bad zombie horror film in the making. "I love it when you're so forceful. You brute."

Buckley, opens his eyes, back to himself now. He looks at me, smiling slightly. "Better hurry."

I move quickly and place the stone over his heart.

"Better pull your fingers or they'll seal up in there," Jerry the Mexican zombie tells him."

Buckley grabs his gun, "Jesus!"

I take it from him. "Sit still. He's an Alien friend inside."

"Alien zombie, what next?" Buckley stands. "What do we do now?"

"We're taking off?"

"The three of us," the zombie says.

"Sorry, Jerry, I can't leave with you looking like that. I've only got two seats. They'll be looking for all the other vehicles."

The dead Mexican drops back to the floor and Buckley's demeanor changes slightly. "Let's, go Jozeph."

My hand stings sharply and the knife dissipates into nothingness. "Ouch. Warn me next time."

"Give me the stone."

"No."

"Give it to me."

"Bite me."

"Be careful what you ask for."

"You'll get in trouble with the Council if you stay with me."

"I started this by insisting on your clone. If you're hell bent on ending what I created for you, then I should at least be there to see that you don't turn this into an international fiasco. Besides, it's cold up here. Let's get back to some of that fine ass floatin' around good old smoggy L.A."

"I don't know about this, Jerry."

"Or I can just toast you now. And forget this ever happened."

"I'm driving."

"The hell you are, technically, that's my Corvette. With a wave of Buckley's hand, the room bursts into flames. Smoke and the smells of burning flesh, wood and plastic fill the air.

We beat hell out of there. Jerry, still inside Buckley Jones, materializes right beside the car as I reach it.

"You cheated."

"Running is for humans."

As the fire alarms burst through the early morning darkness we jump into the Corvette and head out of the mountains on freshly plowed roads.

None too soon as far as I'm concerned.

23

We make LA in less than an hour, and the sun is just coming up. The whole time I have Mooky's laser gun pointed at Jerry's side. I'm trying not to laugh. Jerry the two butted electric Alien is wearing Buckley's big black cowboy hat with a bullet hole through it. Not easy to pull off in a black Corvette.

He knows this laser wouldn't do any good on him. But Jerry hates killing anything human. So I hold Buckley's body he's using as a hostage. I don't know if Jerry has influence on anyone around us, but cars seem to partway as we zoom by. Cops merely watch us pass. It's good to be an Alien sometimes, even so slightly.

Maybe being covered in blood has something to do with it. And all the other drivers think we are famous stuntmen or possibly real zombies. It's hard to say where respect comes from in Hollyweirdness Land when out-of-the-ordinary is the ordinary and anything less than bizarre is stuck in blasé land. I'm betting on his Jerryness and his inert desire to make everyone around him feel groovy.

"Where to, Jozeph?"

"Mystery Towers."

"Not a good idea."

"I want to check on my place. Post how you look on Facebook."

"It's not your place anymore, smartass."

"We'll see about that."

"Why bother? You know everything has gone on as though you went home Christmas night. Minus all this mess we're in. Just leave it be for now."

"I want my life back, Jerry. All of it."

"You can't just take it back anymore. If you do, everything that you know to be Jozeph Picasso's life ends. I have to see to that."

"You'll have them take me out if I make a fuss?"

"No, I will. You can't expose us being here. You've seen the extent we're willing to go to. Even bringing humans like you in to take some of us out doesn't touch the surface of what we've gone through to keep our silent status of being in control of everything on Earth. You've got to learn to accept this, Jozeph, if you really want your life back."

"It's the gap between him being me and me still not being him that's got me crazed in my head over this. It's borderline insanity fearing the unknown. It's that final leap from one of me to the other me. Though perhaps a simple mental petaflop in real time, it still gapes like the Grand Canyon before me, when I think of not being in control of any of what is happening to me. The mere thought of it makes me fear I'm tilting off the edge of reality about to crash to my death on the rocks of distrust, a thousand unseen feet below."

He smiles knowing I'm being overly dramatic. "Yes, Jozeph, it is the born writer in you that keeps these silly fears so vivid in your mind. You should try putting some of these thoughts down on paper before they too dissipate. Quit trying to understand everything that is happening to you, because yes, you have no control. You are completely and utterly being used by us. And not just me anymore. There's now others, many others involved in all this, thanks to you touching that stone. And I know, I have no room to talk after what I've done and tried to do in the past. I understand the sickness.

I will have to take you out first by using Buckley here. Then your clone and all those you expose to what is really happening on Earth next. Some of them who qualify in fulfilling our needs will actually go up there, you know, to feed babies. Buckley will have no idea why he did what he did and they would put him away with all the other unexplainable criminally insane. His mother would be left all alone. Do you want all that to happen to all these others? Just because you can't get a grip on what's happening to you?"

"I'll be much more discreet then you were. A lot less blood sucking and buggery will occur."

"Hah! Jozeph, you are too funny. They won't know you as who you are. You'll be Javier, drug cartel leader, a marked bad man. You could get your friends and your dog hurt in so many unforeseen and nasty ways. In the big picture, we Aliens do not make very good humans. To them you are all expendable. And for the most part, I am the only reason they don't just get rid of most of you."

"Fine, I get it. But don't use my dog against me. I mean it."

"He won't even know who you are, Jozeph. Not even by smell. Your blood and sent has changed in ways I couldn't even begin to explain to you. To Bubba Dog you slept together last night. Contacting him like this will only confuse him at best."

"Okay, what do you think I should do?"

"Sit back, join in, and observe how your life will be. I'm sure you'll understand that dying as this you will only make the new you live a more fulfilling life as a better you. Consider it a rebirthing process, a second chance to get it right. To do so, you'll have to pay the price."

"What does that mean?"

"We'll get into that later. I don't have any firm answers yet of what they expect from you now."

"Mooky told me those that know me will see I'm still in here. Bubba will know, too."

"Perhaps yesterday, not many today, and even less tomorrow will sense who you really are, but not know why. Really, do you want to drag, Bubba, Claire, Erin, J.J., your movie crew, and all those above the line clowns into all this? After all we've gone through to make them see you in a respectable light? If those above don't keep them, they'll be forced to take them and clone everyone and put them back. Abducting them and clearing their memories in the past has only caused crazy roomers of being probed and studied due to the advancements in human retention and verbal skills. Do you really want that for them? Living with those shadows of doubt of what really happened to them?"

"No. But I still want my life back."

"Then let's wait it out."

"Wait what out?"

"Wait for what comes next."

"What, Jerry?"

"I'm not calling all the shots. I only promised to clean up the mess if one occurs. One has. I'm so sorry, Jozeph. Not dying like you were supposed to changes the game I bartered for you. I don't know all the new rules yet. I can only control the here and now. Not the past or the future of you any longer."His eyes well up.

"Don't cry, you big sissy. People will think we're breaking up, with you wearing that ten gallon hat in this part of town."

"Oh, shut up."He wipes his cowboy eyes on his bloody sleeve, smiling at me now with a rugged, teary, bloodstained face. Like we just survived a popular gay bar brawl at Oil Can Harry's, and now we qualify as hardcore buckskin-lovers.

"Reel it in, or I'll smack the forlorn prairie-smirk off your face."

"Whatever. You understand, right? We need to quickly move on to what happens next if you want your life back. What's going on inside you is changing rapidly. Not even we know the value of it yet. The end results could have profound, far-reaching effects on the future of both human and alien science."

"He's spending New Years with Claire. I can't bare knowing he's touching her in my name. I'll rip him apart."

"You're so mean."

"I'm a mass murdering Alien werewolf–slash–sometimes writer/ director now with hell bent self-destructive tendencies. What do you want from me, a hug?"

Jerry stops crying and puts Buckley's hand in my lap. "And you are making me so hot."

"I'll break that off and beat all your clones with it."

He withdraws it. "Tease."

We get off the 101 Freeway at Woodman and head south.

"Those two who were with the doctor, the Aliens at Olivia's, who are they in all this, where are they from?"

"Investors mainly, there are those who are insanely cutthroat in running the financial world here on Earth. They are very angry that Boli isn't putting up the money they expected. Doc screwed them big time by eating Boli. And now you're on the run. Olivia's father will awaken to find his financial future crumbling by a horrible crime caused by two men squabbling over his daughter. Yes, he will be devastated and ridiculed by what he's done in selling his daughter to the highest bidder. These two, these Alien investor types, will swoop in like vultures and heartlessly ruin him with the help of the Feds."

"You knew this going in. That Oli would suffer from all this."

"Yes. It would've happened anyway once it was revealed who Boli really was publically when Javier was killed. The Feds would've seized everything to cover their end of what they were doing. By ending it before the money was transferred Olivia's father has a fighting chance. I've got someone in mind that could help now that I've gotten to know them. But you see how it works? Doc's two Alien financial friends win no matter which way it goes."

"These financial Aliens, are we talking Scottish Freemason, New World Order, and stuff like that?"

"Very good, Jozeph, in part that is true, but not fully. What those who are still humans, not even clones, think they are secretly doing as Freemasons is fools play in comparison to what they don't know."

"What's this I hear about the Denver Airport and why it took so long and why it's so big? Something about what the Freemasons built underneath. Is that true?"

"You surprise me sometimes, Jozeph."

"Don't be impressed, it was on TV."

"But still, let me just say, no you haven't been there yet, and no they didn't do this to you there. Okay?"

"Okay. Do they let you there?"

"Good question. No. If I can't penetrate it, then you can imagine that humans will never find it."

"So it's dimensional?"

"Let's just say you are not wrong. Now listen, these Aliens really running the financial holdings here on Earth own and operate complete planets out there. They're greedy bastards, all of them, and as clever and cunning as they are dangerous. They're utterly heartless to their Alien marrow, mostly posing as bankers, Wall Street bloodsuckers, lawyers, and even leaders of whole countries. You know the type, hording all the money, allowing their people to starve and suffer while they live lavishly in palaces. They really can't help it. It's who they are. Sometimes we've had to make human wars to dispose of them before they became anymore dangerous to us."

"Are we talking about the Middle East Wars? The uprising of the general public to oust them from power?"

"Well, we are and we aren't. You'll stop asking these kinds of questions if you just keep in mind that nothing you see from a human standpoint is really what's happening. There's always something deeper, driven by one of us making it happen for our whole or personal benefit. You've heard the concept of the Fourth Dimension."

"Yes, since the theory of relativity it has been orthodox to treat time alongside the other three spatial dimensions, as the fourth dimension of a unified space-time."

"So you did read Geometry, Relativity, and the Fourth Dimension by Rudolf V. B. Rucker?"

"Oddly, yes. I found it on a park bench back in college."

"I know. I left it there for you."

"So you've been feeding me information?"

"Sometimes. Preparing you. You don't even have to read now. We just put it in your head so you have it when needed."

"I knew it. Why?"

"Ask again, later at dinner. Just keep in mind that as early as the late 19th century, physicists such as Helmholtz popularized work of Riemann that suggested that there might be a fourth spatial dimension, into which things might disappear, only to reappear elsewhere."

"What about the incongruent counterparts theory that if there were a fourth dimension of space, we could in principle disappear from the three familiar dimensions, flip round, and return with our hearts on the right hand side of our bodies?"

"Let me just say, my favored number of dimensions is ten."

"How many dimensions are there?"

"Everything is relative to where you are from. You are from here; therefore you can only see the three dimensions your limited brains will allow you to see. I am the most advanced being on Earth, for now, and ten is my comfort zone. I'm basically a form of light, very much like a rainbow, or ray of sunlight. Beyond that, I fragment and things start to die around me from radiation."

"For now."

"Yes, Jozeph. As long as they control which ones of you humans live and prosper, I am the most powerful being here."

"Yeah, yeah the Alien man is keeping us down."

"The Aliens are, but not me."

"Why not?"

"There is nothing anyone or thing can do to harm me any longer short of a black hole appearing here on Earth. As you know I am the only one left of my kind. There's no players left on the playing board who can harm me. So I do not fear what so many of us do."

"Anarchy, revelation, annihilation?

"Yes, it would be so sad, but humans in the future, way-way in the future, in an almost whole different evolutionary form, can and will surpass all of those Alien bastards, accept me. Because you will always be fundamentally able to survive wherever you go better. It's your basic evolutionary process of adapting your DNA to the ever changing environment. It's your destiny.

Humans in the big picture of things are very much like roaches, minus wings and a few legs of course. It's part of what makes you so special in this Universe. As a species, you have an uncanny ability to overcome environments and survive a punch in the mouth by Mother Nature. Oh, by the way, if allowed, wings would've been possible. But not anymore, it's too late. Your bones won't allow it. And the thought of you all migrating around was too annoying and uncontrollable."

"We surpass them because we are still evolving."

"Bingo, and the others, those from out there, are trying to restart their evolving process over again by studying you, your blood, your DNA. So they can survive here like you do. It's why they both fear and loath you. They envy you lowly humans and are unwilling to admit it because of their sad superiority complexes and insecurities of not belonging here."

"Are we talking hundreds of millions of years?"

"No, silly, we'll all be out of here by then, and need to repopulate another Earth if one still exists out there with those we can save. It will be a natural disaster thing, nothing man-made. Plate shifting, causing massive volcanoes and earthquakes in the likes Earth hasn't seen in a billion years. Earth is a living growing thing with enormous energy trapped under its thin skin. She's very sensitive to what is happening to the weather up here. The drying and dampening of the bedrock. You've studied history, so you've seen the changes that have occurred over Earth's 4 billion years."

"When will that be?"

"Don't worry, you won't be here. You would mutate much quicker than you are now if left alone. Your brains are under used, so under developed because they inhibit your use of it. You would really be surprised. Frightened mostly at how powerful your brains are. But the notion that you only use ten percent of your brains is such a misnomer. They know this. But make you think it's true. With your natural killing instincts life for most of us staying behind would end. So we control you, keeping you who you are for as long as we can. Survival of the fittest, if you think about it as such. Your kind is not much unlike that of the dinosaurs, eat or be eaten, copulate or be copulated, shitting and breeding, there's not much more to life on Earth beyond the power of your imaginations."

"But not you."

"But not me. Humans fascinate me. As you know, I brought you this far, and I'll take you with me to another dimension to help you survive everything if I can, but not them, and they know it. Before any of them came here. Before they knew that I was here playing with you. Mixing and molding your minds. You have no idea how hard it was to find the right ones to breed."

"You've known me my whole life, haven't you."

"I gave birth to you. That is, I was in the doctor who delivered you. Due to things you don't need to know at this time, there were complications that I had to make sure would be taken care of."

"I was a sickly baby."

"Yes. Not in ways you think. But I took care of that."

"You saved me from my natural self?"

"Now isn't the time, Jozeph. Just keep in mind that everything down to what you eat on a daily bases has some kind of influence put upon it by us. Not just you, everyone. Even your supercomputers really work for us. Though still appear to enhance human needs."

I reach up and suddenly realize I still have the ear piece Mooky gave me. I take it off and show it to Jerry. "Mooky gave this to me."

"Yes, I know. Unless you consciously think about it, you forget it's even there."

I roll down my window and pitch it out.

"Your entire food chain is designed for us. It's controlled by us more and more as the little guy, the independent farmer, is pushed out of the loop of feeding America. By using patents, like in soy seed and financial strain like in raising chickens against them. To the point humans have to do it the way those Aliens want it done. In part for Alien financial gain and in part so they can control what kinds of foods humans in many countries eat. There's more of this going on in America than anywhere else because of the advancements in the centralization of the industrialization of the major four or five food processers.

They are all controlled by a handful of Aliens using the cheapest labor possible. That's why there's so much food available here for so little. If Aliens could control the seed the poorer nations grew to eat to benefit us, they would suddenly find themselves with more food to eat, altered by us to benefit us. But it's not as easy as it is here. So we concentrate on controlling the seeds here first. And let the other countries fend for themselves unless they buy foods or seeds grown or processed here. Otherwise they'd let them starve if it weren't for bleeding heart humans influenced by me stepping in the way of them disappearing. Nature's primitives are far more advanced then you'd think. They are far more superior than you so called civilized people.

The key is in the processing of foods and the basic genetic altering of the seed. That is where they hide what they are doing to all of you. It's in what you eat. If you don't like it, then eat organic as much as you can. There are still those out there resisting us, even though most don't fully know why they are. Most farmers are in fear so they don't talk about what's happening to them."

"So, America is an increasingly fat nation because Aliens are controlling our food chain to benefit themselves by what is put in it."

"Yes. They've made it cheaper for the poor to buy fast foods made primarily out of genetically altered corn products, than it is for them to buy fresh vegetables and fruit. What this is doing to human bodies is better for Aliens when they grab them up and feed off them.

Our study shows the fatty tissues of humans harbor genetically altered nutrients that we have added to the foods. We are finding that there are beneficial possibilities of re-harvesting these nutrients to alter Alien DNA during the cloning process to enhance our ability to live here naturally like humans do. I say we, but I mean them. Those that feed upon you. And when I say us, I mean those who are running the day to day activity of all that is human. Both good and bad. They don't really allow me to fully participate because I'm not one of them, holding your complete destruction over my head. I let them think it's working.

It's part of what makes you humans so easy to manipulate. You're still cavemen at heart, hunters and gatherers of food and water. Just like dogs are instinctively still wolves and will hunt in packs if left to go back to the wild. Even dogs are smart enough to use humans to live better lives. Offer a human just enough food and water to survive and they will do just about anything to get it on a daily bases. Even when knowing they are shortening their lives in the process."

"Like mining coal and digging for diamonds."

"Much worse. Believe me. Consider the history of human wars. Modern human technology has finally evolved enough for us to make our move. Soon we will allow you to break the petaflop barrier. When you do, humans will think they see more into real-time nuclear magnetic resonance, computer-based drug designs and astrophysical simulation. When in fact we will be able to use this computer speed to make sure you see even less of us and what we are doing to you."

"But how?"

"There will be no human on earth not in our DNA data bank. We will be in complete control forever of your evolutionary changes."

"How close are we to this? Why didn't you tell me this before?"

"Very close, you weren't ready. When we last really talked about these kinds of things, I had stitches up my ass."

"I recall you did that to yourself."

"Listen closely, funny-guy, China coming on board with their supercomputers will finally set the stage for us to allow complete control of humans to happen worldwide. Without my energy being involved, it would not be possible."

"You're helping them?"

"I have to. Otherwise they will keep trying to destroy everything I love, including you. It also keeps me not only in the loop, but able to manipulate it for my own benefit. When the time comes to move to another dimension with those I wish to take with me."

"You're making a list and checking it twice, Santa."

"You betcha. Keep that in mind next time you eat Mickey D's. Fast foods are leading the way. The US Government is subsidizing this for us. Because we tell them to, believing if they feed the poor, the poor will not rise up and overthrow those running this country. Keep them fat, quiet, and on the couch in front of TVs, and hope they don't live long enough to collect social security. Do you understand?"

"Regardless of how free we think we are because we can shop at Walmart and eat at McDonalds, we are, and always will be, just lapdogs slaves to make this the vacation away from vacations for the Alien space travelers. Yeah, Mook told me all about it."

"I'm sure he has. Don't believe every view you hear from Mooky. He's a mercenary of the worse kind and lies like a scuttle fish."

"About what?"

"About why we're here."

"Okay, why are you here, besides to mess up our lives?"

"We have nowhere else to go at this time. We're trapped here, as much as you are, waiting for the next big event. Only we know it and you dear fools think there's somewhere else better than here if you die. We instilled that one in you to keep you under our control by manipulating religions and superstitions. It's to help you bear the turmoil that all humans face here on Earth, rich or poor, handsome or ugly. Life is a bitch and then you die worldwide from the beginning of time to the end of time. Tucking that one away for a rainy day, Jozeph, might keep you from pulling the trigger someday."

"It's all a mind game."

"Very much so."

"But not all of us believe in heaven and hell. Why?"

"Atheism. Yes, pagans, demon children. Many of them believe in Mother Earth or the Sun. Whatever floats their boats to the other side of happiness. The truth is all the same."

"That you and they are here."

"Yes. We are here. For the good and bad of it all."

"So why are you stuck here if you're so advanced?"

"Most of our places of origin no longer exist. Destroyed or in the process of being, or are so far away, or brutal it's not worth trying to get back. Even if they own the whole planet. We are the chosen ones to keep our civilizations alive. Why do you think man desires to live outside the gravity pull of Earth?"

"To keep mankind alive?"

"Ultimately, yes. Your governments don't tell you that so bluntly. But yes, to keep at least the ability to repopulate either here or somewhere else alive. Away from a worldwide calamity."

"Like nuclear war and Earthy disasters'?"

"Yes."

"Then why let us have these abilities?"

"In case we need them. Trust me, it won't be you humans who use them in the end, if it comes to that."

"What about Milicalazarra, that planet I was invited to."

"Ah, good point there. You see, Milicalazarra is merely a figment of human's imagination while we keep them captive."

"Losing me. Where did my friend J.J. go?"

"Enjoyed himself with that redhead, in whatever form his mind allowed him to see Milicalazarra. Surfing, fornicating and creating his own future in the form of what he felt his life should be. He did what I needed him to do. Sacrificed himself for the good of all without really knowing it. You saw the tan, and in return we gave him what his wildest dreams were. His own TV series, created by you."

"My lame surfer detective series, Consider It Done, Matt Dunn?"

"Yes, he's back, happy and only thinks he had the time of his life by meeting the right people while there."

"Why spare him?"

"We haven't. Everything we do is by design. He fulfilled a basic need of ours on his vacation. Very shortly he'll have no idea beyond what is humanly possible. He'll appear perfectly normal as J.J. gets."

"Losing me again."

"You'll see, just be patient. Everything is in the works."

24

The sun is coming up over the condos across the street as we pull up in front of Mystery Towers. Standing outside the spooky place is me, the clone of me, waiting for Bubba to do his doody dance. I look good, peaceful, content even, almost younger, and better fit somehow. What have they done to me?

Jerry slows down and Jozeph turns to us and waves. It's a nice wave, being neighborly, so I wave back. I hate him even more. Shit, I'm a nice friendly guy living the Hollywood dream. Damn me, how can I eat a guy like that? Bubba hasn't a clue about this me. He doesn't even turn to watch us go by as we move on up the street toward Ventura Boulevard.

"It's okay, Jozeph. You're happy, you're finally getting all that you dreamed of when you first road into Hollywood on your motorcycle that fall, thinking that UCLA was the door into this town. Your two friends who did not survive the Hollywood journey and succumbed to human diseases would, and are, proud of you for sticking it out."

"Michael and Roger? You knew of them."

"They were your good friends and want you to have all that you guys dreamed of. They are happy for you."

"But, wait, what are you telling me? Did you do something to them to get them away from me?"

"Jozeph, how can you say such a thing?"

"Because nothing in my life is what it seems, Jerry. You've said so many times. How can I trust you haven't purposely isolated me from my friends by killing them? Even my mother at an early age?"

"Because you're an asshole for even implying I would."

"You're twice the asshole for making me think you could."

"I can see where this is going, so let it be. We've got so much more to cover. You'll see. It's okay. They are okay."

"But...."

"Not now, Jozeph!"A flash of energy abruptly pushes me against the window as though he reached over with a great big powerful hand and mashed my face against the glass. I am powerless to move as he reaches in and takes the stone, still in the cloth, from my pocket. With a flash the stone is gone from the car. "Thank you."

He lets me go. I feel an instant emotional letdown of not having the stone on me. I felt this before. So I understand the power shift.

I've hit a nerve if he's got one. Roger and Michael. They didn't make it this far. I miss them so much. They left us way too early in life. We were the three Amigos. Now there's just me, and being the lone Amigo isn't nearly as much fun. What did Jerry mean by they are proud of me? Are, not would've. What is he up to now?

"It's okay, Jozeph, you'll see."

"Stay out of my head, Jerry."

"You were so naïve when you first came to town. You all were, so hopeful and clueless. Look at you now. Think of all the things you know. What life experiences, both wins and losses, that you can draw upon to write your stories. People would kill to know what you know, feel what you've felt, be in your position. Hollywood respects you and everyone is waiting to see how your film comes out. You're just weird enough to be somebody special. You'll live a long happy life if something stupid doesn't happen."

"Like what's left of this me getting in the way of that me."

"Look, I know how it hurts to let something go that is part of you."

"Too bad what I know will be gone if I let myself become him."

"Still you've lived beyond what most writers will ever know. Even without all this Alien crap to suck the sanity out of your brain. Your ability to tap into those deeper emotions will still be there."

We make a right onto Ventura Boulevard. "Let's eat. There's a deli in the supermarket."We stop at the light in front of Ralphs.

"I know a place."Jerry makes a left up into the Sherman Oaks hills. I have a place up here I use while taking over an agent and have some fun with him."

'Funny my agent, Jerold Zeiger lives up this way, too."

"Isn't it?"

We turn onto my agent's street.

"Shit, you are my agent? I knew it."

"I use him once in a while. He's fun and the life of a party. Nobody says no to Jerold Zeiger, and I like the name, don't you."

"Fits you."

"Don't mock what he's done for you and J.J. already. This is just the beginning. If you let it all run its natural course."

"I knew you were involved. Why didn't you just tell me?"

"I didn't want to. Why spoil it? You won't remember any of this by the time we're through, one way or the other. So it doesn't matter what you know now. There's people here I want you to meet."

"Great, we're not breaking in are we?"

"Of course not. This is my place."

We drive all the way up Deep Canyon. Just before Mulholland we pull into a gaited drive, security cameras and lights are everywhere. I've been up here but never beyond the front door. It's amazing how an hour drive can change the temp. It's seventy-five degrees and we are in bloody winter wonderland clothing.

Jerry lowers his window and reaches over and waves his hand. The heavy stained wood gates open up into a lavish hacienda style compound that could've been in Spain or built hundreds of years ago. Two feet thick cement walls surround what appears to be at least ten acres of manicured property flowing straight up the hillside. So lush and perfectly designed that trying to take it in at once is stupefying. So I turn and twist as we move up the drive, to take it in bit by bit.

"Some Aliens know how to live."

"You like?"

"What's not to? Even McGuiness' Castle had nothing on this."

"Please don't mention his name again. But thanks, it's my little LA getaway."

"Does Gerald know you borrow him?"

"Let's just say he's enjoying his long healthy life. At eighty-eight he can still get it up without Viagra and has multiple orgasms. You could too, Jozeph."

"Stay out of me. I mean it."

"Don't worry, being you isn't what intrigues me."

"Why be me when you can do me?"

"You are such a tease."

"Stay out of my women, Jerry."

"Now, that I can't promise you. Claire is a lot of fun."

"You've got her confused."

"Not as much as you think."

"You turn her into a lesbian I'll never speak to you again."

We pull up to two heavy wood doors, at least twenty feet tall and eight feet wide each, with heavy bronze bolts, ornaments and hinges. They could've been stolen from one of the 16th Century abandoned and dismantled Spanish castles, from all I know.

"They were."

"Stay out of my head, Jerry."

Standing before them is a young Mediterranean houseman. He looks in his early twenties. He had greeted me at night once before and has a voice of a snotty grown miniature man. He never let me get out of my car. He just handed me a contract package. He's now dressed in a natural grain houseboy getup. He scampers to the Corvette driver's door and opens it. He bows as Jerry gets out, standing under the Stetson. He somehow knows it's his Jerryness. In a very over the top fake south of the boarder accent he says, "Your Excellency, welcome home."

"It's okay, Manuel, we are amongst friends."

He drops the servitude, and springs into a bossy, flamboyant nag, "Where the hell have you been?"

"On adventures, as usual. You remember, Jozeph."

He drops back into this fake Spanish accent. It's already boring. "No, this is Jozeph? The Jozeph Picasso you've spoken so highly about? The young filmmaker I met just the once? What have you done to him?"

"He's still in there somewhere."

"Ay, caramba! I know this face, a horrible face. He is very bad man. What have you brought into this house? This filth, with those mortal eyes. Ay-ay-ay, you make me so loco, Jerry."

"Yes, the face is from a horrible man. But we are with Jozeph now who is using it. He's our honored guest. As much as I'm using this person, Buckley Jones. So prepare a befitting brunch, and save the drama for your acting coach."

"And who is this hick Buckley Jones? Why do you bring such a bloody cracker into this home? When you could easily stay here as Gerald and live a civilized life with me, and find me acting work."

"I know, I know. I'll introduce you both later. Let us get inside and out of these bloody clothes."

"Fine. I'll have baths in ten minutes and feast of food in an hour."

"Sounds delightful."

"I'll take mine alone. The bath. Thanks."

"Cheeky."

"A pain in the ass, but we love him still. Now run along, Manuel."

We go into the hacienda. Magnificent in every way, matching down to the door knobs in both class and design, everything we saw outside. Only in here there's probably twenty million spent on just this single room alone. I stand at the door looking at everything at once, breath taking, and a burglar's paradise.

"You like?"

"Looks like a movie set."

"Better, everything here is priceless and most of it is original one of a kind art."

"Wait a minute. I was in here before. I entered from that door over there. I had dinner with McGuiness, sitting naked at an enormous wood table with my feet on the priceless rug. I had a drink with Stacey Carson over there."

I look around, and yes this is the same room, multiple pool tables and bar, the painting on the ceiling.

"I don't get it."

"It's all relative, Jozeph, to space and time. Those dimensional things we spoke about. We, you, I, and everyone here are and are not anywhere in any given moment, while anywhere in my home."

"Did you do this? Decorate all this?"

"Of course, I've bought, inherited, pillaged, collected or commissioned all of these things throughout the ages. Look, this is the very first wheel honed in stone by man himself."

I'm in complete awe. There in a glass square is a hand carved stone wheel, nearly perfectly round. "Is that...?" I point to two stuffed hairy cavemen in animal clothing.

"Yes, taxidermies. My first two best friends. Dumb as you can imagine. But great hunting fun. Had no clue I was there inside them. Making them do what they never imagined they could. Discovering fire was our greatest achievement. Look at their burned fingers."

"These are the guys who discovered fire? Really?"

"Yes, well, how to use it, with my help, to cook and stay warm. There was a woman but she burned to death while celebrating."

"I didn't take time to really look at it before. It was dark, thinking I was in some magical place. Plus I was naked and waiting for that dog nabbing Stacey Carson to try to kill me again. But this woodwork is unbelievable."

"It's all from Fifteen Century Spanish ships. Not a single nail. Check out the bar."

"This I did see."

"Roman. Literally, I've had it in storage since the fall."

"This is a Roman Ship Galley?"

"Yes, that is real roman blood stains. Sealed with the heat enhanced petrified sap, fruit tree resin. Now known as amber, and reused to make what we modern-day Aliens consider appropriate."

"These are real Roman battle garments? Their beautiful."

"Thank you. I wore them myself. Well, as you know, the man I inhabited while at war, dressed in them. But I had them designed. So that you know, I never killed anyone while wearing them. I couldn't bear it. I looked so dazzling and virile. The Romans were so beautiful, the men so strong and manly. The women were just awe inspiringly feminine. Only it was hot, unlike the Aliens, the humans all stank to high hell. I could barely get out of the baths."

"Don't get yourself all worked up, Jerry. I'm sleeping alone."

"Yes, I know you prefer sleeping with dogs."

"Dog, and leave Bubba out of this. Anyone coming in here would know that this isn't something you'd find in the real world today."

"Very few are allowed, I assure you. Now look at this. Cleopatra actually sat naked in this chair as a child. Her little bottom touched this very spot as she grew. Feel the camel leather. It's as though it's new. Smell, you can almost sense her charisma. It's addicting."

He smiles at me. I'm not sure if he's kidding.

"Pass. But I'm honored to be in the presence of all this. Holy crap, I forgot about that."

I point to a life size gold statue of a naked male statue standing across the room of what must be a very well endowed, yet dusty Greek Saint.

"You should be honored. Yes, Ancient Greek, it's from the period when I was still working on my perfect clone. Not gold from Earth either. I had it taken from passing asteroids, very rare indeed."

"Solid? Damn, if that much gold got out into the open market all at once it could cause shockwaves to the value of gold."

"Possibly, yes, I had it done because that was me, or you know, whom I lived as, part of the time. Murdered by a Diocletian."

"Roman Emperor Diocletian?"

"Very good again, Jozeph. See, you know more about me than you even knew. Diocletian was a despicable cowardly man, who murdered us while I was away, and I could not save myself. Such sorrow that it drove me to create, you know who."

"The Magical Man."

"Cruel bastard Alien clone, Diocletian was."

His eyes water up.

"It's okay, Jerry. It happened years ago."

"It's like yesterday to me. Jerry leans in like this next bit is a big secret. "He's inside, perfectly preserved as we lived. You are one of the very few who have seen it since the fall of Rome."

Manual comes out of a hallway. "Your baths are drawn and new clothes are on the beds. I want a full explanation."

"Relax, I only have his arm and face."

"And his penis plus the better parts of his torso. I couldn't let those go to waste," Jerry smiles.

"Disgusting."Manual glides away, eyeing me with distain. He disappears by seemingly dissipating before my very eyes.

"He should see things from my end."

"He'll get over it. I'll have drinks sent out to the veranda. How about Mimosa? I grow the oranges. Literally out of this world."

"Beer."

"Live a little."

"I would if you'd leave me alone."

"Fine, beer it is. From a hop you have never experienced before, such delicacy your tongue will feel withdraws with every swallow."

"Whatever is cold, Jerry."

"You have much to learn, Jozeph."

"Why is Manual pretending to be Spanish? He's obviously not?"

"I know. His acting sucks. Don't say anything to him though. His ancestors were from Spain, and brought to Greece as slaves. He's still bitter about it. Now he's trying to find his roots and fit into being in LA. He hopes Gerald will get him on TV if he finds a niche."

"Just another Hollywood dream dashed on the rocks of Malibu."

"You want me to have Manual come in and scrub your back."

"Fat chance, Jerry."

"I hope your clone isn't so boring."

"Don't even think about it."

"I haven't even met him."

"I'll introduce you when I take my life back."

"It's his life now."

"We'll see about that."

25

Shit, showered, shaved, and dressed, literally, in flowing sage green robes, I reenter the bar area to find Buckley Jones dressed in flowing apricot robes, minus his cowboy hat with the hole in it. We look like two Hare Krishna wannabes, in need of a head shave, seeking the meaning of life from the afternoon light.

He sits just outside the open double glass French doors on the cut stone veranda overlooking the entire San Fernando Valley. His feet are strapped in matching Roman sandals as are mine. His long black hair is braided down his back and held in place with a strand of deep brown leather. I have no idea how old he is. He talks with a thick country accent befitting a Nashville hopeful, so it's hard to tell.

He looks calmly at my feet as I stand before him. "Not sure why I know this," he says. "But you ever notice you've got an Egyptian foot, the great toe longer than the second toe, on that leg? And a Greek foot, where the great toe is shorter than the second toe, on that one? While I have two normal square hick feet where the great toe is the same length as the second?"

"Yes, thank you. They are gifts from our friends piecing me back together. Note I also have two colors of hands and sizes. If you want I'll flash the tat on my ass I got with the foot."

"Maybe later. Nice nails on that one."

"The reference to Egyptian is due to the fact that in Egyptian paintings feet usually were shown from a profile point of view. The great toe appeared longer than the second toe. The reference to Greece is due to the fact that Greek statues showed feet having the second toe longer than the great toe. Nearly all the Roman statues, often copies of Greek originals, have Greek feet. Look at that one."

He studies the gold statue and both our feet.

"I'll be damned."

"Nice, view."

"It ain't Kentucky bluegrass but it'll do."

"How'd a country boy like you end up in Frazer Park?'

"It's where they put us after they saved Ma."

"How'd you know to ask for help?"

"Didn't. A young filly brought it up one drunken late night I was moonin' over her near passing."

"She told you she knew a doctor who could fix her?"

"Yes. I was drunk and stupid, and just thought I was gettin' her in bed. Next thing I know, I'm feedin' that werewolf, hidin' Ma from the rest of our kin. They all think she's dead. I send her on trips when they come visit me. Answer her mail myself."

"Nice big funeral?"

"Just local folk."

"Where's Jerry?

"Shithead left me in the Roman-size Jacuzzi tub and nearly drowned my ass until that little Chihuahua of his pulled me out by my hair and gave me mouth to mouth."

"That would most likely have been Jerry."

"Yeah, well he's feelin' it now. I popped him good. Had his hands all over me, if you grasp what I'm gettin' at."

"Jerry's a little friendly."

"He ain't no friend of mine."

"You actually hit him?"

"Real good. He's got a showcase shiner, is my guess."

"You're lucky he didn't fry you on the spot."

"Let him try."

"You know he kept you alive until I brought you the stone."

"It's why I didn't hit him with the left, too."

"Where is he?"

"I heard the doorbell chime when I was gettin' dressed. More voices, one a female from what I could tell. They seemed real pleased to see each other."

"So, whoever it was is still here?"

"Be my guess. Try the kitchen. It's that way over about three rooms. Massive place, Ma would love to see. That's your beer."

"Thanks." I pick up my Genuine Draft Light out of an ice bucket and go back inside, moving across the living room. I'm still in awe of the art work everywhere I look. It's beyond fitting of any major city's museum of art. I look up at the ceiling and almost pass out seeing the painting in this light. There in all its glory is the fresco painting only a master like Michelangelo could've created. It's a love scene in the middle of an endless sea of battle. The likes of which only someone with unmatched talents could've projected, with its light, the color the human's and steeds so lifelike. I nearly hit the door because I can't take my eyes off the painting.

"Isn't it outrageous?

"Stacey Carson?"

"Do I know you?"

"Stacey, it's me, Jozeph."

Stacey walks over to me and plants a great big kiss on my lips, no tongue but she's glad to see me." Then pulls back, looking me in the eyes and slaps me. "You son of a bitch."

"What did you do that for?"

"I'm just messing with you. How are you? Jerry tells me you're hung like a bull now. Let me look."

"Step back. What happened to your hair?"

"It was too hot to keep it long. You like?"

"Absolutely, it's a great cut. Fits your face perfectly. But it makes your asses look bigger, Jerry." She swings at me again, but this time I'm waiting for it.

"You bastard."

"Cut it out."

"I can never fool you."

"Try not kissing me so much."

"I can't help myself."

"Who painted this? It looks like a real Michelangelo."

"All those art books paid off."

"The milk crate of art history at a garage sale was from you?"

"Of course. Do you still have them?"

"No, they were stolen from my storage, about twelve years ago."

"Were they?" Stacey points to a shelf incased in mother of pearl, gaudy and expensive just the same.

"You stole them back?"

"They were mine. I only loaned them to you."

"I paid a hundred dollars. Those are all first additions. I could've paid for my entire UCLA education and then some."

"Yes I know, but you would've been arrested for possessing them. Call it an intervention. I saved you ten years of imprisonment."

"I kept finding one open on my bed at night."

143

"Yes. Not your father. Me."

"He thought I was nuts accusing him of coming into my room when I had the door locked."

"That was pretty funny. You never saw this in any of those books, I'm sure. This was from my living room in Rome in the fifteen hundreds. Yes, painted just after he finished the Sistine Chapel for Pope Julius II. He resented the commission, believing his work was only to serve the Pope's grandeur. As so did I, and though many still believe that work was his crowning achievements in paintings, I believe it is this, completely private. It's me and my beloved wife, Ophelia, well you know, who I inhabited at the time, look closely."

"Gray?"

"Yes. We were immaculate together. There is no record of it outside of this room. This was hidden many times under lesser paintings, by lesser artists, to keep it safe and secretly mine. I had it shipped, well Blipped here."

"You don't just ship these kinds of things, it's painted plaster. How could you remove this and... never mind. Why do I ask?"

"Are you hungry?"

"Of course, but my stomach's a little jittery."

"Hold my hand." I take Stacey's hand and immediately my stomach calms down and I let out a boisterous burp."

"Christ, Picasso, you share that with all your girlfriends," Buckley asks from the veranda door.

"Sorry, have you met?"

"Stacey." Stacey walks right over with her hand outstretched and Buckley attempts to take it.

"Watch out." Slap! Stacey clobbers Buckley.

"What the hell?"

"Jerry."

"Oh, you friggin' weirdo."

"You ever hit anyone I'm in again I'll set your balls on fire, in or out of water."

"Then keep your hands and tongue to yourself."

"I wouldn't touch you with Picasso's dick."

"Will you two cut it out? Come on, Jerry, let's eat."

"Call me Stacey. And follow me."

Suddenly Stacey Carson is standing there without Jerry inside her. "God, that's distracting. Who are you?"

"Two strangers, whom you're about to show to food."

"Good, I'm starved. Do you know how far away Milicalazarra is?"

"Light years?"

"So, you've been?"

"Not us."

"But a friend of ours went."

"Really? Who?"

"One of my tenants, J.J., has."

Stacey wheels on me. Staring me in the face. "Jozeph?"

"Somewhere inside here, yes."

She throws her arms around me. "Oh, my god… it's…. Dogman? What have they done to you?"

"You don't want to know."

She pulls back examining all my parts. "You're right. These Alien things are freaky. Did you hear what they did to J.J.?"

"I saw, he looks like a baked ham. He wouldn't say a thing about it. I don't think he even knows. He likes it even. I only saw him the one time. He showed up on Christmas Eve out of the blue with a TV series. What happened to him?"

"You better ask Jerry. It was disgustingly, heroic, but just mean spirited if you think about it. Come on, Jerry's probably with that Manual character, cooking. I liked him much better as Gray."

"Me, too."

26

When we enter the dining room, I'm taken back by the sheer fact that I've also been in here before. The room is the very same medieval castle where I shared the last dinner with Gray McGinnis. We sat at this very same ancient wood table spanning about twenty yards.

I look down. "Unbelievable." The rug from a series of seven priceless tapestries dating from the 1500's from a culture in the Southern Netherlands is still there under the head of the table.

"Cool, huh?"

"I thought this was in the hills of Scotland."

"It is."

"Blyme, take a look out this window. This is a shithouse, isn't it? Look at that, you crap in the hole cut in the stone. Makes you want to wear plaid and dance a jig," Buckley says.

I move over to Buckley and look behind the curtain. "It's called a garderobe. Don't use it. His Jerryness watches."

"It looks cold and drafty. Look, drops right out. Feel that? Talk about blowin' air up your buttocks."

"What's with the accent?"

"What accent?"

We stop and look out a three foot thick glassless window and sure enough the view overlooks the Atlantic Ocean from the mountain side of a Scottish Castle, and smells like it. "We're in McGinnis Castle?"

"It's a state of mind, Jozeph. Haven't you learned anything?"

"Yes, Jerry has altered the dimension, so therefore we are?"

"We are wherever he says we are," Stacey answers.

"Who's controlling this? Our minds or Jerry's weirdness?"

"Oh, it's real, Jozeph. Everything is actually here. Look at this gold. Christ, there's millions of dollars in this stuff. Look at this."

Buckley holds up a solid gold hand mirror. "This thing must weigh ten pounds. Holy crap, are these diamonds?"

"They are if his Jerryness says they are," Stacey says.

"Where's Jerry? Jerry? Hey, Jerry, where in hell are we?"

Just then Manuel enters, sporting a shiner under his left eye. He's followed by a five course meal on silver platters and china bowls this time, the fancy stuff. They float on thin air. Right out of Harry Potter. There's enough food to feed twelve plus people. Its delectable mixed aromas fill the room. Our eyes get bigger with anticipation of tasting all of it."

"I hope everyone is still hungry."

"Very funny, Dumbledore. Where the hell are we, Jerry?"

"Sorry, Jerry isn't with us," Manual says minus the fake accent. "He'll be down in a minute, mister hotshot director, who doesn't like fake accents, behind that mean face. He's got someone he wants you to meet before I kick you and your slaphappy friend's ass out of here."

Sounds like Manual heard me talking about him. "Like whom?"

"You'll see. Everyone, look for your name tags. Chop-chop, I can't float this food all day, or it will get cold," Manuel says as he moves to what looks to be a fifth-century side table carved by hand from hardwood. While he moves the delicious smelling foods place themselves perfectly upon hand carved oak serving plates.

I know the value of some of this furnishing and the rug because of the books Jerry had me buy and read as a kid. Some of those vary pictures are photos of pieces in this room. I hadn't really looked at it last time I blipped in to eat with McGuiness. There was just too much freaky stuff going on. But looking at it now, really looking at it this time, the craftsmanship of everything is matchless, flawless and priceless. Jerry may not embody a human as himself but his human tastes are beyond compare.

From a stack of china on the side table, plates, bowls, flatware, napkins, and glasses that are being filled by levitating water pourers, all float up and over head. They ascend to a designated perfect place on the table before each chair.

"Are you doing this?"

"What?"

"Levitation?"

"No, Jerry has everything wired so that if I look at it and want it to move, it does. He's the man, you know."

"Wired? Possessed?"

"Really, he's not a witch. He just fills them with love, his energy. Don't ask me how it works. Everything in this room, including us, holds a part of what is Jerry. Pure energy, it's not unlike the sun itself. He just channels it to make them do what he wants them to do. All I know is it makes my life easier. They even clean themselves. Hence, I have stopped trying to kill myself centuries ago."

"Are you human, or one of them?"

"Does it really matter?"

"Only if we go on an Alien killing frenzy," Buckley answers.

"In that case, neither. I'm a clone of someone who lived many, many years ago. A young servant that washed the feet of the man inside that gold statue. I'm actually the third clone out of six, three were let go after he whipped them to death. He couldn't grasp why I kept coming back to life to haunt him. Eventually he stopped killing me. We nearly drove him mad. You might've noticed he's dusty. I spit at his feet whenever I can. And have been known to publically urinate on him in given drunken stupors."

"Too much information."

"Sorry, I've been in therapy."

"Whipped? Wait, I thought Jerry was in him?"

"Sometimes, not always, and not nearly enough to save me. I was let go, fired, terminated, and beaten to death, who really knows way back then. It wasn't just a job it was usually a cruel sexual abduction, known today as statutory rape. Not always unpleasant when no scars are left behind. Jerry always made things right, when he was there. Kept bringing me back, and back. I'd be just dead without him."

"Touché."

Just then, a man dressed in fifth century robes, much like Buckley and I, but with much more flare and elegance, enters the room from the open hall. I once heard the vampire girls' giggling echoes from there. His dark hair streams down around his shoulders much like Jim Morrison of the Doors back in the sixties. I look at him because I've looked at him many times in my art books. It's Michelangelo in the flesh, The Michelangelo, not just some Hollywood look alike. "Jerry, is that you?"

"Sorry, not I. Jerry said that he'd be joining us after dinner. He doesn't eat you know, unless in someone. But he's all around us, so he's listening. You were saying?"

"Are you...."

"Many years ago, yes. I haven't painted since losing my painting talents during my second cloning."

"You're Michelangelo's clone?"

"Yes. One of them. Jerry said you wanted to meet me. That you once studied my past work. Thank you, I'm flattered."

"Ah, well, yeah, I guess so. You're a clone of Michelangelo but obviously aren't living as him."

"My name is Mick Lang. If I were to go around telling people I was a clone of Michelangelo, how long do you think I'd stay out of the booby trap? Besides, as I am now, the mutation in mutable cloning, I can no longer paint, and have no passion to do so. Therefore I don't."

"You are him and know you are him, but you live over and over as someone else?"

"Yes, it's not that hard, Jozeph. Jerry wanted you to see what it is like to live beyond your expected life span, if you chose to play along. I'm a fourth clone now."

"So you are a happy clone."

Not a perfect clone, but living large, shooting nudie art here in Hollywood. I'm having a blast at it, too. I get to test tomorrow's photo technology. I make big bucks. Lots and lots of young women float in and out of this world. Some at will enjoying the one light that travels all the way around the planet."

"Let's eat," Stacey says.

Stacey, this is…."

"We've met. He's the one who came and took J.J. with him."

"It was a job, a photo shoot." Mick says.

"So, what the hell happened to J.J.?"

"Jerry revealed himself during the photo shoot."

"Flashed him and gave J.J. a permanent tan?"

"He's going to die, Picasso," Stacey says.

"We're all gonna die, unless they keep cloning us. He'll be fine," Mick Lang clarifies.

Buckley scratches his head. "So you get paid to test tomorrow's photo tech on nudes?"

"Yeah, it's called fine art in some circles. Porn in others."

"They haven't offered me something like that with guns?"

"They can't control you, Buckley. You're not a clone. Yet."

"Those five guys you took out were your doing, using your human guns. This is an Alien Gun."

We turn and standing there are McGinnis's two Vampires, Amanda and Brenda in stunning see-through black flowing silk dresses, revealing almost everything a man needs to know. They are both spectacularly backlit from the setting light outside the window. A sense of peacefulness washes over me.

I can't take my eyes off the evolving reflective gold and blue that is hovering over the ocean. It shimmers just below painted pink and purple bilious clouds that are too beautiful to be real. Because they are just flamboyant enough to let you know, it's all Jerry's making.

"Okay, enough shop talk. Stacey's right, let's eat," Brenda says in her heavy Russian accent. "We're starving."

"Vampires eat?" I ask.

"These vampires do. I can't keep them out of the walk-in fridge," Manuel says.

"So, it's a nice dark, cool place to sleep."

As confused as I am, I can't help but laugh with the others at what should be just a ridicules comment. But for them and now us, it's probably the truth.

27

We eat for nearly twenty minutes before I break the silence. "So tell me, what's really going on with J.J.?"

"Radiation," Stacey says.

"Why would Jerry do that to him?"

"It was a job he agreed to do," Brenda says.

"A job. So it wasn't Jerry himself that did that to him?"

"Not exactly, but sort of," Stacey says.

"He'll be fine. They've harvested the necessary stem cells before he went in," Brenda says.

"In where? Just tell me what happened to him."

"J.J. did an extraction job for Jerry," Mick says.

"Extraction? Extraction of what?"

"Apparently it was necessary for the Council to get Jerry involved in a matter that was of international importance. Jerry got J.J. to see it through. And it fried him," Stacey says.

"When he's ready, he'll be taken care of," Brenda says.

"He knows this?"

"No, he's unaware of what's happened to him. Only that his life has changed for the better after meeting someone."

Just then, Jerry enters the room by taking over Amanda, "Relax, Jozeph. J.J. did us a little favor and in return I've done him one."

"What kind of little favor?"

"Gave him what he wanted, a TV series. Now, is everyone ready to move on to dessert?"

"I don't think I can eat another bite," Stacey says.

"Me neither."

"Fine, then after dinner drinks."

Half filled crystal cognac snifters float into the room and place themselves before us.

"Now, Jozeph, we need to get down to it. What do you want to do with the last few moments in this body?"

"Excuse me?"

"Before you are live samples of what being cloned can do for you. I can make you live forever if you want. Or just the one normal life span if that's what you prefer. In any case, you may not stay who you are at this moment."

"You brought me here to kill me?"

"Of course not. To show you what life could be if you just let your old-self go. The body is just a vessel to transport the self. And it's the self we are offering you to keep."

"I don't want to let my old body go. I want it back. I want to be me. The whole me, and nothing but me. Put me back the way I was."

"We are, Jozeph. We are offering you just that. You need to understand that what is left in this body is just a shadow, an echo of who you were in this body. We are seeing it now because we recognize it and want to see you as Picasso. Others, who do not know you as well as we do, will see you for who they want to see in you. You know there are people in you even you don't want to hang out with."

"Why have you done this to me?"

"Because a job had to be done. You were chosen to do it. Not because you're being punished or deserve it or any of the paranoid conclusions your mind has conjured. You were the right human for the job under the circumstances."

"This sounds a lot like bullshit to me."

"It is, they screwed you, Picasso," Buckley says.

"You let them screw me, Jerry."

"No I didn't. They brought you in because they know you are close to me, and that I would never harm you."

"But look at me. I'm a monster."

"Yes, rather handsome, and hung like a bull. Shame on me."

"Wait. I just need to see my life. See how it's going. Say goodbye to me, my life if you want, whatever. I just need to see for myself what my life will be. Just once, please."

"Jozeph, that's not a good idea. You know what's going on inside you. And what could happen if you don't allow us to stop it properly."

"He's part Alien Werewolf."

"How horrid. I met up with a full blooded Alien Werewolf once back in Gévaudan, in the Margeride Mountains of south-central France. I think it was during my second clone, around 1764 or so.

Nasty thing, The Beast of Gévaudan they called him. It attacked at least 162 women and children peasants and killed 113 of them. He kept at it until a local blacksmith rammed it with a silver stake. Not sure where he got the idea from but the damn animal appeared to morph back into a passing nobleman I knew socially. Right before our eyes. Sadly, it is the moon you know.

It has something to do with gravitational forces pulling it out of them. These types of Aliens had no idea when they arrived here on Earth that it was happening to them. But get this. The poor fool who killed the wolf was later burnt at the stake for claiming Alien voices from up there sent him to do their bidding. That we were not alone here on Earth. Imagine that?"

We all watch Mick Lang to see if he'd smirk. But he doesn't. He's perfectly serious. Then their eyes shift to me.

"I'm not eating anyone."

"You say that now. Probably will deny it afterwards and actually believe it. But the truth is, Jozeph, you will have no control over what you do if we let you live like this much longer."

"But the full moon is days away."

"Yes, but the will to live as you is here right now, and we recognize Jozeph Picasso. But it will be harder and harder to keep you from running amuck in any of the forms that you possess. There's no telling when and how long you may stay Javier Sanchez, possessed by Alien werewolf blood, or Bolivar, Jozeph Picasso and who knows at this point Leonie Dazarrio could show up in the mix of all this."

"I only have his leg."

"To those who see you as Leonie, it won't matter to them. They'll see who they think they see. Leonie alive and you'll have to explain it to them. I understand those east-coast Jersey associates have little if no sense of humor when it comes to killing their people, dicing them up, parting them out, and feeding Alien babies through their testicles. At least I've been told this."

"If you were there when Leonie tried to kill me, why not help?"

"Caw and I did help. Do you know how horribly shocking it is to be inside someone and take a bullet point blank in the face? It wasn't at all pleasant."

"They won't let you run free, Jozeph. You might as well come to grips with that," Stacey tells me.

"If I let you leave this room, Javier's family will look for you. We'll look for you. If humans find you, you'll end up surrounded by crack pots just like you who rant and rave of being victims controlled by Aliens. Souls who are trapped in someone else's body, and for some of them, it will be true."

"In fact, I think I saw that movie. What was that?" Buckley asks.

"The Fly."

"That's disgusting," Manual says.

"And not a good example. The fly was a man-made machine accident, not Alien induced."

"You're more Frankenstein meets the Werewolf possessed by an Alien Mob kind of thing. You know, you may be unique, your own horror genre. A high concept pitch that will never get made because it's too far out there," Stacey says.

"And a Jack the Ripper," Brenda adds.

"Yes, let's not forget that, Jerry," I say. "I'm a monster."

"Regardless, you're not you any longer. You're an It. And not an It you should keep any longer than you have to."

"Please, I get it. Just let me see myself in action one more time. See what I'll do with my life. What the other me will do. I just need some time. Some closure on this."

Blip!

"Sorry. We can't have that, you dumbshit." The Mook stands before me. He's got a laser gun. "On your feet, White Boy, let's go."

"Screw you, Mook. If you're gonna take me out, do it now."

"Take him down to the dungeon. The rest of us are having dessert drinks. I don't want to damage anything in this room," Brenda says.

"Come on, Jerry, you can't just let him take me out like this."

"I'm sorry, Jozeph. You have a choice to make. Die peacefully like I'd end it. Or die extremely violent Mooky's way. Apparently, he's still upset at how you left him up in the snow. Sliced up and with a hole in his chest, from what I heard. Very messy and uncivilized."

"Jozeph, let go of this self. I promise, it's painless," Stacey says.

"How would you know, are you a clone?"

"Yes," Stacey says. "It's really no big deal. Look, they even gave me a facelift and perkier tits. Here feel."

I don't move. So, Buckley reaches over and gives them both a solid squeeze. "Nice. And real, too."

"Thank you."

"You're welcome," Brenda says.

Mooky reaches out and grabs me by the neck. "Get up."

And I do, straight up, with one great big leap. I cling to the wall by my protruding raiser sharp nails. I make a run for it by scampering across the ceiling. I have no idea how I changed so quickly. I burst back into the living room, leaping over Michelangelo's painting and past the Roman bar. I make the door in seconds. At least I'm still civilized enough to recognize great art.

Once out the front door, I'm suddenly standing on an empty Sherman Oaks bone-dry hill, dumbfounded and overlooking a sheer drop back into the valley. No hacienda, no magnificent grounds. Nothing to give me any idea of where I just came from.

If what I just experienced was within a different dimension, it didn't keep Mooky from following me out.

Blip!

Mooky pops in right beside me. Laser gun in hand. I'm dead to right. So I leap toward what I'm about to hit two hundred feet below.

"Ahhhhhhhhhhhhhhhhhhhhhhhhhhhhhhhhhhhhhh!"

I'm freeeeee faaaaaalliiiiiing. It's as though I'm standing still and the scrub brush and rocks are racing up to squash me. Faster and faster until my mind starts to black out. Twenty, ten, five, one. What the hell was I thinking?

28

Plop, right back into my Gray McGuiness castle dining room chair. "Ummph!" I look at everyone watching me, expecting me. There's even more, and they burst out in laughter at the look on my face. Mooky is there too, pointing a finger at me.

"What a drama queen," Manual says.

"What the hell is this?"

"It's an intervention, dumbass."

"Do you really think we're gonna let you run wild-ass, Picasso?"

"If this is a joke, I'm not getting it."

"Jozeph, we can do anything. If you want to see your life, fine, we'll go. Just stop being so dramatic about all this shit."

"I'm not being dramatic."

"Yes you are. What is done is done. You have two choices, die like this, or live as your clone. You have absolutely no say in the matter."

"Are you telling me I can't get away?"

"What I'm telling you is that you don't have to. We won't harm you."

"But Mooky, you said...."

"Playin' with you, White Boy. You did one hell of a job with Doc. And we appreciate it all the way around."

"But I shot you. Cut your arm off. Kept the stones."

"Yeah, so?"

"And you were there to kill me."

"Not me, the other Mook. Clones. He's fine, pissed. But he's still salvageable. Think about it. Do you imagine that I'd show up for real and give you a second shot at the real me? Shit, I'm not even here."

"Coming back to save me with the stone was a nice human touch," Buckley says.

"And the Alien Council's safety net of getting their stone back," Brenda says.

"This was all a setup? Some kind of stupid Alien test?"

"Not a test, an option. If you would've agreed to let us take you out, we'd have done it. But not here, and not like this against your will. We'd take you up there, dissect you cell by cell, and figure out where you were hiding on us. See what's happening to your blood, and test your bone marrow to determine if we can use it."

"My brain?"

"You'd be gone. This would be over."

"So I'm sticking around?"

"Jerry says it's your call. You're his boy," Mooky says.

"Not sure I like that."

Jerry turns Amanda's vampire smile on me. "Jozeph, you saw how hard it was for me to lose Gray. I've known you your whole life. Watched you grow up into who you are. Remember that time you fell in the ocean while feeding sharks?"

"Five years old, while throwing fish heads off Pop's boat?"

"You walked on water."

"That was you holding me up?"

"Of course. Do you really think you can walk on water?"

"They called me Jesus all summer. Pop stopped sleeping in the cabin with me the rest of the trip. Said he wasn't sure what he'd seen, but it was unnatural."

"How about when you fell thirty feet out of a tree?"

"I fell in an angle and landed on my stomach on a branch that stopped my fall from plopping on the hard stone ground. They called me Rocky the Flying Squirrel."

"Yes, that was me. I pushed you over to it."

"So, you're my Bullwinkle?"

"There's lots more, Picasso. Remember the horse, Sandy, that reared over on top of you when you were twelve? She would've split you in half, if I weren't there. Instead you got only that little dead spot on your calf. How about Buck, who held a gun to your head when you were hitching across the USA back when you were nineteen? You got away in a set of oncoming headlights. You ever wonder why he didn't come back? Or why he didn't pull the trigger when he had the chance to kill you? Remember all those times you came close to dying on your motorcycle?"

"Yes."

"Part of me was there for you each time, hanging in the light. I am doing it again now, keeping you alive. You are my boy, like a son to me. Everything has led up to this moment, right now. I can tell you this. I love you like a father. So if you want to see your life again, get closure, fine, we'll go see it."

I'm not sure what to say. So I say nothing.

"Yummy, drink up, we've got time," Stacey says.

"But my clone will be leaving for Connecticut first thing in the morning."

"We'll be waiting for your clone to arrive. In fact, we'll meet your clone on the train. What do you say?"

"Train? My clone isn't flying?"

"Bubba doesn't like to fly."

"He's taking a train because of… that's right Bubba won't fly. I've never taken a trip with him. He prefers a crew camper."

"Train works better for us."

"Us?"

"Us, I'll be going with," Buckley says."

"Thanks, but no. I'm serious, really you don't have to help me, I'd much rather do this on my own."

"He's tagging along to kill you the moment you appear as the werewolf," Jerry says as Amanda.

"The next moon."

"Bang bang." Buckley looks at me. "Jerry, would you mind bringing that body into play at the pool table?"

"Right in there." Stacey points back towards the bar.

"Come on," Buckley says, "let me kickass, one at a time."

"I just need sleep." I stand up. This is so much to take. Everyone seems so at peace with what they've been given. But I feel as though my skin is crawling. "I'm gonna need something to help me relax."

"I'm available."

"Thanks, Stacey. I'm thinking sleeping pills."

"That's right, you prefer sleeping with dogs."

"I wish he were here."

"You want me to bring him here?"

"No, let's leave Bubba out of this crazy stuff. How about some pills, though?"

"I'll bring them to your room."

"Thank you, Manual. Jerry, I'll eat anyone you show up in."

"Sweet dreams, Jozeph."

158

29

I've got his sweet dreams, right here.

I open a bedroom closet. Inside is enough clothing to clothe ten men in high style. Rows and rows of suits and jeans, dress slacks, dress shoes, boats shoes, ties, belts, sport jackets, leathers. All my size. Out of my price range by hundreds. I pull out a built-in drawer. Stacked inside are new, in the package, socks and underwear. Again they are my size. None of which I wouldn't wear. The shoes and boots are meant for me as well. "Damn, someone's got taste, and apparently shopped for me."

"What did you expect?"

"Get out, Jerry."

"Rude. Jerry's not here. Just you and me."

"Come on, Amanda. How can I trust any of this?"

"What? I came in to give you a rubdown. See, oil and hot towels. All you have to do is go in there and take a nice relaxing shower. I'll be back after I smoke a joint."

"Really, it's not necessary."

"Yes it is."

"No it's not."

"Jozeph. Haven't you learned anything? I've been told to come in here and rub you down. That is what will happen. I don't care if you're conscious or not."

"You're going to knock me out?"

"If I have to, yes."

"No Jerry business."

"No Jerry business. Happy endings are up to you, yours or mine."

"Fine. I'll take a shower."

"I'll be back. Afterwards, I'm supposed to help you pack."

"Okay."

"Good."

"You can go now."

"Don't be shy. You're not my blood type. Garlic boy."

"I'm not shy, cautious and untrusting is more like it. The last time I was with you I literally ended up with a head."

"Yes, losing Gray was a very sad thing. You did good by all of us. Thank you for that."

"Just keep in mind that Alien molestation isn't my bag, conscious or otherwise."

"How do you feel about vampire seductions?"

"How do you feel about werewolf mutilations?"

"I'll be back to find out."

"Fine."

"Yes."

Amanda leaves, closing the door softly behind her. Vampires. Why is there always a weird twist to my dirty pleasures? I have news for her. She's not sucking on any part of me.

I go into the bathroom. Suddenly I'm standing outside in a wooded area. A braided leather pull string hangs over head, leading to a large overly-shinny wood rain barrel. A thick, soft lavender cotton towel and washcloth hang from a peg on a varnished wood stick. A fresh bar of soap sits in a large mother of pearl soap dish. Perhaps elves shower here. "Very funny."

I look back at the door, and sure enough the night lit bedroom is still inside it. But there is no sign of the house beyond the door. Just the frame and what can be seen inside it. I look around and I am standing in the foothills of the Daniel Boone National Forest overlooking the Cumberland Falls, sometimes called the Little Niagara.

I know all this backwoods geographical detail because before me is a plaque personally welcoming Jozeph Picasso to this very historical spot. Apparently, the real Daniel Boone once crapped here and wiped his ass on leaves from these very trees. Why this bit of information is worth telling me is probably lost somewhere in Jerryness. But to just make sure the joke isn't on me, I check my toes to make sure I'm not touching anything from inside D. Boone. Poop free, I look around and there's no one else, just me and the wilderness.

I step back inside the door frame and peak my head outside. On the outside the sun shines warmly through the trees, a perfect ambiance to shoot in, yet me with only my bellybutton to push. The sweet smell of honeysuckle mingles with the light and I get the feeling as if I'm walking inside a soap commercial. The single rawhide braided chain hanging from the water barrel above is still just above my head. This is ridicules. But what the hell, I could use a shower with all the tension in my back after nearly leaping to my death trying to run from all this nonsense.

I shed my flowing green robes, making sure my balls aren't about to be exposed to some wild Alien raccoon's malicious lunch attack and stand below the barrel upon a warm slab of light brown sandstone. Sure that Daniel Boon himself isn't about to join me, I grab the pull string, expecting frigid river water. What I get is a sun baked stream of heaven. So perfect in temperature that I stand there with tingling toes and cry. My life is so messed up, yet so amazing at this very moment. My emotions run out of me and stream down my face. Being lost in the falling shower drops, as my entire body lets go of all its troubles. I pee with what appears to be an eternity of indigestion, regret, and Alien induced bullshit.

"They always do that."

I nearly jump out of my skin. "Who's there?"

"Don't freak. It's just me. I live here, thanks to them."

I turn to find a Unicorn standing under a tree just to the left of the barrel. "Give me a break."

"I know, people always take me for some kind of hallucination."

"I'm not hallucinating?"

"No, you are. Let go of the string."

I do and now before me is a hairless white man completely naked. His saggy skin droops from his bones, possibly a thousand years old.

"Which do you prefer?"

I pull the rawhide again and the talking Unicorn is back. "Okay, I get it. What do you want?"

"I've come to warn you."

"Are you about to inform me that my future is in danger? If so, you're way too late, Marley."

"No, I'm here to tell you that you must never tell anyone about any of this. That you must make sure your clone knows nothing of anything that goes on here. The future will not bode well for him if he tries to insist that there are others on this planet controlling what is happing to humans."

"You are from the future?"

"No, I'm from right here and now in a different dimension. I live here, have for many centuries."

"Where is here? Kentucky? Are we actually at the Denial Boone National Forest, according to that sign?"

"Come with me."

"Not on your life. If I let go of this string I'm following the naked ass of some crazy old man."

"Yes. Precisely, but you must, you must, you must. Keep in mind we are both buck naked. If it makes you feel better."

He has a point. I let go of the draw string and the soothing water stops pouring down. I'm standing there naked with an old man in the middle of a long hallway. The walls, doors, and window frames are all white. We are not alone. Walking up and down the hallway are men and women in white uniforms completely unaware of our presence. This must be some kind of hospital. The little old man points to a viewing window. So I step up and look inside. I'm blown back onto my naked heels. "What the hell?"

The old man touches the window and we can hear Jozeph Picasso looking at us and then saying, "I'm not alone."

"You recognize him?" he asks. The old man removes his hand from the window, we can no longer hear inside. "You recognize him?"

"Of course, it's me." I step away so Jozeph can't see us.

"You, but not you. He's your unaware of who we are clone."

"What happens to me if this all goes wrong and this me takes over the clone, and I can remember all of this? Won't that bring me back into all this?"

"Possibly. I've never seen it happen. Most likely they will suck you back in, or just kill you. Once you possess proof of them, they don't let you go very often without controls in place. This is Jerry's gift to you. Your innocent life back. This wouldn't be possible without his help. You could blow it if you allow this self to know the truth. This is January first, the day after one of you dies. What you want to do. What you need to see before you let go of this self, with what's left of this life, could cause this for the rest of that life. Sounds ridicules, I know, and it's a tongue twister every time I have to say it. I'm here to show you this in hope that you decide not to go through with what you want to do. Let us end it now."

"But they promised me that I could view my life."

"There's a very likely chance you will interfere. With what's going on inside you, this blood in your veins, you might not be able to help yourself. They will do test to try to install stop actions. You are still evolving with all these different types of bloods in you. You are on course to collide irreversibly with the life Jerry has set up for you. Do you understand?"

"Yes, but I must see myself again. I must know who I am."

"You must not go on this adventure. You must let Mooky take you out, or let Jerry put you to sleep before it's too late. You must let them, up there, dissect your brain and learn why you are still in there. Let them have your blood. You must not leave Jerry's house looking to find out what your life will be if you let go."

"I get it. I still don't want to let this me go. Not like this."

"Nothing you do will come out better than what is going on with your life right now. You are not in control of your clone's life until you fully let go of this life and join him. There are powers that be that are involved in all this. Dark things, dark beings, that you don't know about. That you shouldn't know about. That will only cause you and him great personal harm. You could end up in there, completely out of your gourd, screaming and believing that you are not alone, that there's Aliens, vampires, clones, werewolves, and more.

Your friends will be of no help. Jerry will be of no help. Mooky will be of no help. Once you cross that line of trying to reveal that we are here, you will be thrown away. Like so many of the others in places like these, controlled by them. You'll be of no use to anyone up there because you will be a clone so you will not be allowed to feed their babies. You will never be trusted again to keep the secret of what is really here on Earth. Why they are here on Earth. Life as you know it will be over."

"This could be me. Not is me yet, though. Right?"

"Correct. This is how your present existence, as is, calculates to a natural end. It's a very complex mathematical equation of your life with present set variables. You could be diagnosed as schizophrenic by your own kind. Dangerous to yourself and those around you. Made to wear that jacket and take all kinds of experimental drugs. You will once again be labeled a murderer for killing a man whom you thought was there to eat you. Even though he himself is but a bad man as despicable as Javier Sanchez. Self defense will not get you freed.

No matter what, no one will believe you. They will make sure of it. Justice will not prevail. It never does in these cases. Your best friends will be forced to turn their backs and won't even have a choice to save you from yourself. You'll die a lonely soul who knows the truth. A truth that will eat away at your sanity until your own father will be forced to let you go, knowing he's leaving you in this place all alone. No one, not even Jerry, will be able to bring you back from here."

"I'll kill both selves?"

"Eventually you will, if you continue on this path."

"But how do I stop this and still get closure?"

"We don't think it's possible. We will do our best to help you. Who you are now, what you will be then is an unknown fraction of the equation that even we can't calculate accurately at this time. Your only guarantee is that you let yourself go now while we have the correct answer." He turns to go.

"Wait. Who are you?"

"You still don't recognize me?"

I look closer. I take his left hand and look at his thumb. The length of it from wrist to second knuckle has a scar I put there with a razorblade when I was ten making smoke bombs out of walnut shells and gun powder from firecrackers. It can't be. "You're me?"

"In another dimension. In yours, I'm not real or possible."

Something moves behind me. I turn to find the bedroom door frame is there again. I look back and I'm nakedly alone. The old man, and the Unicorn are gone. The white hall of padded cells are nowhere in sight. I reach to grab the draw string and there's nothing there but a very mean looking snake. Okay, I get it, shower's over. I reenter the bedroom door.

"Crap, my neck is still as stiff as a giraffe's hard on."

"Good, you're ready."

"How long have I been gone?"

"Gone? You haven't gone anywhere. You were in the shower."

"Have you been in there?"

"Of course. Now lay down. I'll cover you with a sheet if you like."

"Thanks. This is so crazy."

"Sssshhh. Don't think about anything."

"I wish."

"Close your eyes."

I close my eyes as her oil slick fingers touch me. A warm calming rainbow of sensations rush over my body, not unlike that of the water from the rain barrow.

I'm sound asleep before she can suck one drop of my blood.

164

30

I stretch out my toes and hit cool varnished wood with my stocking feet. In the dark I think it's just the end of the bed, but then I realize I'm being softly jostled as though I'm being carried inside.... no!

"Let me out!"

I reach up and my hands hit the top of whatever I'm in. A coffin! I'm being carried to my grave!

"Help, let me out. I'm not dead. Help me!"

The panic that rushes over me is so overwhelming, having been this way before. I can't control myself. How? The rubdown was so relaxing I slipped into death. No!

"Help me. I'm still alive in here!"

Suddenly, a hand is put over my mouth, a man's hand. Christ, I'm not alone in here... again!

"Shut up, Boli, you'll have the whole friggin' train awake."

"Train?"

Buckley Jones lights the brass-based case Zippo. "Yes, dummy, the train. Remember?"

"But?"

"You talk in your sleep. For two days now. Yap-yap-yap. Haven't caught a wink myself, stickin' around you to watch your back. Nearly offed myself and you, I'm so friggin' tired."

"I was getting a rubdown."

"We know. She had her way with you. Not silent about it during or afterwards. Apparently, you're quite the man, Boli."

"Not me, Bolivar Agustin or Javier. They changed me."

"Yeah, I asked for a little help and got nothing. So consider your newfound manliness as lucky."

"I'm thrilled."

"You've got a nasty hickey right there on your lower neck?"

"What? Bruise? Bite marks?!"

"Yeah, looky there. Those are fang marks."

"She bit me, sucked my blood?"

"Weird chick she was."

"Weird, she's a vampire."

"Come on, vampire, werewolves, make up your mind."

"But she bit me. She could've infected me."

"I'd check your pecker for love bites to make sure it's still there before I'd go frettin' about a hickey on your neck. When she came out of that room she wasn't what I saw goin' in."

"Why did you let this happen to me?"

"I was in no position to change anything. Her friend had me pinned to a chair and wasn't about to let me up. I think Jerry had his way with me after all."

"This is… you know what, screw it, where are we?"

"North of Colorado, heading east."

"We've been on the train the whole time?"

"Na, they put us here about thirty hours ago. You've been out cold since we left. Your bags are under your bed. I've searched the train and the guy you're looking for is two cars up with a little white poodle. Is that what you looked like, before?"

"I guess."

"Not a bad lookin' guy. As guys with little white dogs go."

"Thanks."

"You hungry?"

"Starving."

"Good, Picasso is about to have dinner in the dining car if all plays out the same as last night. You want to meet him?"

"Why not?"

"Don't pull anything monstrous on me, werewolf, vampire or otherwise weird. Or I'll have to use this." He pulls out a laser handgun.

"Is that thing loaded?"

"No, but this is."He pulls out an even bigger handgun."

"What are you doing with all that? We're on a train."

"Yeah, but we ain't alone. There's two guys sitting down on the last car who I think might be some of your guys?"

"You mean Javier's?"

"Yeah. They got on a couple stops back."

"How would they know that I'm… or Javier is here?"

"As Jerry said, there are things goin' on here we don't know about. People, Aliens, and whatnot involved that we don't want to know about. Your ticket says you're Bolivar Agustin. When we meet up with this other you, just play the game. Jerry says film distribution will work well."

"What are we supposed to do about the other guys?"

"Play it safe. Stay in crowded areas. Don't give them a chance to make a move on us. This Picasso guy is a minor celebrity. They might not make a move on us while we're with him."

"Won't people recognize me? I'm a wanted man, aren't I?"

"You mean cops? There's that. Keep in mind you don't exactly look the way most people would expect you to look."

"But anyone expecting me, looking for me, will see me for whom they are looking for. Javier, Jozeph even Leonie Dazarrio, from what Jerry says."

"Don't forget Bolivar Agustin. He's a man about old-town, very wealthy. We don't know who or what he's been in contact with."

"I'd laugh if I remotely found any of this shit funny."

"Keep in mind which one of us is expendable and think how funny it seems to me."

"Yeah, sorry."

"You hungry, Cybil?"

"Kiss Jerry's asses."

He spits. "Might have."

31

Entering the dining car, Jozeph Picasso isn't hard to spot. He's the only one with a dog. Bubba Dog is eating up the attention from a young girl sitting behind them who keeps reaching over and patting him. Bubba's no fool, have fur will travel. A pat's a pat in his book. Dogman isn't paying much attention beyond his newspaper and coffee. Envy runs through me to my very soul. Regardless of what I am or have inside me the news ink pangs and coffee addiction kicks in full force. I am overwhelmed to off myself right now so that I can jump back into my comfort zone, the clueless Jozeph Picasso, man about Follywood, without an Alien worry in his bones.

"Excuse me," Buckley says. "Buckley Jones. Isn't that Bubba Dog from the Claire Davis show?"

Jozeph looks up from his ink, annoyed. Doing his best not to show how much when he gets a load of Buckley and his new black hat.

"He sure is," the little girl answers.

Buckley fixes her with a mean stare. She turns around and starts eating. Glancing back only quickly at me before forgetting us.

Bubba snaps to, tail wagging and tongue hanging out, waiting perhaps for a photo opp. The ham. "Sorry?" Jozeph puts his paper down, looking from Buckley to me and back.

Buckley sticks out his hand. "Howdy. Mind if we join ya?"

"Ah...."

"You're Jozeph, Jozeph Picasso, the filmmaker, ain't ya? That there is Bubba Dog. It's a pleasure to meet ya."

Jozeph finally takes Buckley's hand. "Do I know you guys?"

"Sorry, I and my friend here, Bolivar Agustin, couldn't help but notice you both."

"Well, it was...."

"Mind?" Buckley sits down pushing a chair out for me to sit across from Jozeph. "Sit down, Boli, don't be rude."

I sit down. "Hi, how are ya, Bolivar Agustin?"

Jozeph looks at me then at Buckley, trying to think of why he's getting bothered this far from home. "Have we met?"

"Once, but you wouldn't remember. American Film Market. Back I think two, three years ago," I answer.

"Really?" he says. "You have a good memory. I don't seem to place the conversation."

"Wasn't much, just in passing at the lobby bar. I just remember the name, sticks out. You were there with other people, two guys named Tim and J.J., I think."

"Sure, okay."

"So what brings you on the train, Jozeph?"

"Bubba doesn't fly. We're visiting friends for the holidays."

"Congrats on your picture deal. How's that going?"

"Good."He looks at me again. "What was your name?"

"My friends call me Boli."

"Really, well two of your possible friends, who just walked in, seem to be overly interested in this table. I've never seen them before. My guess is that they are looking for you guys."

I don't turn around. "What do they look like?"

"Trouble."

"Nobody I know. I'm not looking for trouble."

"Sometimes it finds you anyway," Jozeph answers.

I look at the darkened window, noting that I do not see my own reflection. Jozeph doesn't see this, yet. Good. Buckley does.

What we do see, not far behind us, are two young Latin American men sticking out like sore thumbs. They sit down, wearing matching brown leather jackets and overly white Nikes. Probably the first things they bought after making the American border. They glance our way again. None of me knows them. But we know them well enough to know they know us, or think they do.

"Mr. Jones here is my bodyguard. Whoever those guys are won't be any trouble. I'm well-known from where I come from. Money does that to a face."

"Speaking of your face, are you sure we haven't met more than in passing. I'm flashing on something that I can't put my finger on."

"I'm a film buyer and foreign distribution south of the border. You've probably seen me around town. Perhaps Sundance? I'm in LA all the time, at the film marts and local haunts. I stay and hang out at the Sportsmen Lodge a lot. Outside bar. Maybe around the pool? Picture this face in a Speedo. I've seen you there eating soup before. So maybe that's it."

Jozeph's face registers displeasure at the thought of my ass and package slinking around the pool. "Why do I get the feeling this isn't a meeting in passing?"

"You are a smart man, Jozeph. May I call you Jozeph?"

"Believe you just did."

"I'm here to get you to convince your partners, the Burnsteins, to allow me to distribute your first film in South America."

"That's pretty aggressive. What's the catch?"

"I want to see the footage first."

"I'm not ready to show anyone."

"I know. I want to see it anyway."

"Have you spoken to Ernie? Did he put you up to this? This is bullshit. He saw the rough cut already. Everyone's happy with it." Bubba barks in agreement.

"Hold on, relax, nothing like that. I'm a gambler. I like your personal story. I know I can sell the shit out of it without even showing anyone the film."

"This is about my life? My life is pretty boring."

Crap, it just occurs to me he knows nothing about any of the real shit that has happened to him over the past two years. I'm forced to back pedal fast. "Your story, young kid comes to Hollywood, pays his dues while nobody wants him. Finally gets his first chance to direct his own script without having to kiss ass. Not easy in this town."

Jozeph looks at Buckley as if for an explanation, because surely I've blown it. "Can I call you Boli?"

"Why not?"

"Thanks. Boli, I don't know who you and your bodyguard are, but take your bullshit and get out of my face. And take those two thugs with you." Bubba starts barking, backing Jozeph up with a wary eye on a door to escape. "Ease up. Dogman, they're armed."

"Hold on now."

"It ain't like that," Buckley says.

"I thought you were just the bodyguard."

"He is. What he means, I'd like to have the first crack at your film. Distribution wise and I'm willing to pay top dollar if you let me see what you've shot so far."

"Why should I even be talking to you?"

"Listen, where we sell films is a very difficult cutthroat market. There are people down there that have gotten in my way for many years. I like your star. I like that it's your first film. I remember meeting you when you were a never-was, now you're famous. I like that. I can sell that."

"Never was?"

Oh-oh. Crap I pulled something out of my own head. He's on to me. I can see it.

"Where'd you hear that expression about me?"

"Come on, I don't know. I think I read it in the paper, an article on you, I'm not sure."

"Is this about the boot in the river, and bodies in my apartment?"

"Si, I can market the shit out of all that."

"I was cleared of all that. I have no idea why it happened, or what it was all about. Are you New Jersey friends of Jetty?"

"What? That punk? Hell no. All I ask is that you give me a glimpse of the film before I cut a check."

"I just started piecing it together. I've got two weeks of interiors left to shoot. It wouldn't make any sense to you."

"Crazy Kind Of Love. Are you kidding me? I could sell that title in my sleep. Loco Amor. Claire Davis in a bathing suit, playing a sexy murderous bitch. With spooky Jozeph Picasso writing and directing the dark comedy. Come on, give me first crack at that."

Jozeph looks at us for a moment. "Piss off. And get away from us, now. Waiter. These guys are bothering us."

"Yes sir, Mr. Picasso. Gentlemen, please follow me out of the car?"

We stand up and Buckley leans into the waiter and opens his coat and whispers something threatening. The waiter's face turns ashen and he backs away without a word. Money moves the world forward but guns will make you walk backwards.

"Forgive us. I'll catch up with you in LA."

"Don't."

"Perhaps in Connecticut?"

This stops Jozeph cold. "Stop! Do you have a card?"

"Ah...."

"I didn't think so. Look, I don't know what makes you think I'd go for this. I'm not taking any strong armed bullshit. My partners are as connected as you two punks ever will want to be. I suggest you beat it out of here before I start calling them."

I want to punch myself in the mouth. Calling the Burn for help. What a dick I am. Instead I lean into his face, looking him square in the eyes. "No bullshit. I want to see your film. If I like it I'll buy the distribution rights for all of South America. If I don't, I walk away."

Jozeph doesn't flinch. "Okay, tell you what. You contact Junior Burnstein. Not his dad. Set up a meeting with us when I get back in town. If you two thugs turn out to be half legit, I'll meet with you only in LA. But if I catch either of you anywhere near where I'm going in Connecticut the deal is off. I don't care how much money you throw at this picture, who you know or who you're in bed with. I will have you barred from this film until it hits Telemundo. You understand me?"

I keep a steady soft gaze into his eyes. It's fascinating to look at myself without a mirror reversing what I see. Technically I want to rip my own throat out. "The real question is who will you sleep with?"

"None of your business."

I stand back up and look at the reflection at the booth the two men were in. It's empty. I look around the diner car and people are all staring at us. "Come on. See you in LA."

"I'm serious."

"So am I. Enjoy New Years with your girl and her two friends."

This stops him cold, again. He pulls Bubba near as Bubba starts to bark again. "You tell him, Bubba. Hey, Claire is his girl, not mine."

I look back at him. "Be smart, keep it that way."

"What did you say?"

"I was talking to the dog."

He looks at Bubba, glancing up at Buckley's reflection. I can see in his reflection that he does not see mine. He doesn't overly react. He just turns to face us, holding Bubba close. Conversation is over.

So we go out the way we came in. From the other end, security shows up with the waiter and they go right to Jozeph's table. He points our way, but waves them off. What he's saying I can't hear, but watching him through the glass in the door I can tell this is not old me. This is more than I ever was. This me was never a never- was. They've made some changes in how I see myself, and I'm not un-liking them. He had balls telling us to piss off. Not seeing my reflection. I've got to say, he did both with as much flare as needed. No over excitement, just told us where to go. It worked this time. Even though he has no idea of how close he came to being ripped to shreds by an Alien werewolf trapped in his old mutilated body.

32

"Me? You were in there face first."

"Yeah well, sit back, we've got company."

"Who…?"

"Shhh, those two. Jump up in your bed."But when he turns to look at me, I know he's surprised that I'm not there. I can hear him. "What the hell?"

I don't even know how I'm doing this again. I'm up on the ceiling of the train's passage way, crawling, like I had at Jerry's. I know I'm not doing it, nor Boli or Javier. This Alien werewolf shit is freaky.

When I drop down behind the two scared young men and hand the second one the first one's head, he spits out his false teeth and runs down the passageway, only to find me waiting for him as I reach into his chest and pull out his heart. I'm so grossed-out by this and yet enthralled by the site of it being a human heart in my hand that I nearly faint and fly at the same time. What is happening to me?

The young man drops into my arms and I step back out the train's door where fresh air hits me between cars. Without hesitation I fling his body over the railing and he disappears into the frigid night air. I fling his heart after him and can't believe that I lick my hands clean. That is when Buckley enters with the other body and head. "What the hell, man? Are you completely mad?"

"I don't think I need to answer that. Do I?"

"You ripped his head clear off and left him lying about the passage way. There's blood all over the place in there. Look at you. You've got it all over yourself. How can we go back in there?"

"What should we do?"

"We get off this train."

"Great, have Jerry pop us out."

"I don't exactly have his cell phone, now do I."

"If you're gonna get bent out of shape every time I protect myself, maybe you should stay out of this."

Just leave the killin' to me from now on so we don't have such a friggin' mess to clean up."

"People are coming." Screams from inside the car come from just where I offed the two men. "We've got to jump."

"We're not dressed for this. Look at the snow," he says.

"Screw it. Come on." When he hesitates, I grab the body from him and heave it over the rail, followed by his head.

"I don't even know you, do I?"

"I'm not sure I know myself."I grab him. With one quick, nearly effortless, leap we are off the train sliding down a snow bank until we tumble into a salty plowed service road.

"Touch me, and make me jump again, I'll blow your brains out!"

I look up and grab him, tackling him into the snow bank as a snow plow rumbles around the bend nearly cutting us in two. We pull our faces out of the salty snow, looking at each other, both half covered in brackish silt, slush and mud. We burst out laughing.

"What are we laughing about?"

"Hell if I know, but thanks. That truck had us. Shit, it's cold."

"Come on, there's lights up there." I point straight up a cliff.

"Are you kidding? That's nearly three hundred feet straight up."

I look at him. "So?"

"Shit."

I grab him and throw him over my shoulder. Without breaking a sweat, I have us all the way up the sheer cliff standing before a dreary gray log cabin. There's a faint glow from a window. Smoke rises out of its chimney.

"What do you think?"

"Someone's home."

"You want to risk it?"

"I'll freeze out here if we don't.

33

I reach to knock on the door and it opens all by itself with an over-the-top chilling squeak. Fitting for the walking-talking horror film I've become. Buckley and I look at each other, still not wanting to go beyond the door frame, knowing that I'm probably as scary as a killing machine gets.

"Come on you pussies, it's a squeaky door. Get in here, it's cold."

"Mac?"

"You're letting all the heat out."

"What the hell, Mike?"

"What the hell is right, Picasso. I'm gettin' tired of being popped in and out of places on account of your stupidity."

"What are you talking about?"

"What, you don't think they know what the hell is going on."

"They've got people on the train cleaning up your bloody mess."

"Come in, shut the damn door," Mac says.

We step into the dimly lit room and it's empty. "Mike, Mac? Where the hell are you?"

"We're standing right here in front of the fire."

Neither of us can see them. Yet the light from the fireplace is slightly shadowed. "What's the matter?"

"No you're not," Buckley says.

"I can see him and me. Look, there's my hand. I got a drink in it. Scotch on the rocks."

"As far as we can see, you aren't here. Neither is your drink. Please tell us you're not naked," Buckley says.

"Look." I hold up a silver spoon for them to look in.

"He's right. What is goin' on?" Mike asks.

"You tell us," Buckley answers.

"I'm just glad we have our clothes on," Mac says. "When they plopped me home from the hospital, I was still in my gown."

"Thanks for callin' for help by the way."

"You're welcome. Were you given any instructions?"

"Yeah, kill Picasso, but only if we have to," Mike says.

"Otherwise we hang here to make sure you two stay put until someone comes and gets us."

"How'd you get here?"

"Hell if I know. After we were released from the hospital, I was sittin' down eatin' with my family. When they finally filed out of the room, givin' me some time to think, I was here," Mac says. "I'm gonna catch hell when I get back for leavin' without askin' the old lady."

"If we get back, after the mess you've got us into."

"Yeah, there's a huge manhunt out for you."

"Me? Why?"

"Think about it," Mike says. "You killed that doctor back in Frazer Park after he saved our lives. He was a big hero. You're a scumbag in the eyes of everyone. Now you rip those two down on the train. They got your clone with your dog right now, grillin' his ass because he was seen talkin' with the both of you."

"He don't know shit," Mac adds. "So don't worry. The waiter confirmed that you told yourself to piss off."

"Are you believin' we're saying these things again," Mike says.

"How do you know all this," I ask?

"We got him bugged," Mac says.

"Actually the dog. His neck thing, it's got a camera and mic on it. Here, listen in," Mike says. A small monitor turns on next to a chair on a small wood side table made from a stump of wood.

The voices are clear as day.

"So, Mr. Picasso, what you're saying is that you've seen this person before. But you're not sure where."

"You want me to say it again," Jozeph says?

"No. I've got it. The two last seen going into the hall, you saw for the first time in this car?"

"They seemed to know the guy who sat with me. This Bolivar whatever. I only saw them the one time."

"Did he give you anything? This Bolivar guy."

"You mean besides the creeps?"

"Ha ha, he's got your ass pegged," Mike says.

"Shuddup," I tell him.

"Yes," the investigator answers.

"No, he wanted to buy my film. He didn't offer money. He wanted to be the first to see the raw footage. I think he meant this weekend."

"I'm not a filmmaker. But isn't that highly unusual?"

"I don't know. It's my first film. Through most of my film career people have avoided me and my work like the plague. Having someone actually want to know me and buy my work is still a novelty."

"I see."

"I doubt it."

"Don't get smart, Mr. Picasso. We're here to help protect you."

"Fine, didn't mean to. Can we go? You've got what I know?"

"Don't get off the train."

"I'll be departing in Connecticut. Don't wake me to talk to me. Or you'll have to answer to Bubba."

"Would Bubba recognize these men if he were to see them again?"

"I don't know, ask him."

"Goodnight, Mr. Picasso."

"Fat chance."

I reach up and turn off the monitor. It's nothing I've ever seen before. "Where'd this come from?"

"Was here when we walked in. Fire just like this. We haven't added a single log in two hours."

"Gas?"

"No, we checked."

"Is there anything to eat?"

"That's the good news. Place is completely stocked."

"What about clothing?"

"Yeah, I'm covered...."Buckley looks down at our clothes and they are perfectly clean. "What the hell...?"

"We're clean, were they Aliens?" I ask.

"Maybe," Mac says.

"No way were they Aliens. Red blood all over," Buckley says.

"Clones then?"

"This cabin is givin' me the creeps as it is," Mike says.

"Those two back at Olivia's, the banker and real-estate guy. Jerry told me there were two of them. They must be feeding Javier's family my whereabouts."

"So, what do we do now?"

"We eat and sleep until someone comes to get us."

34

Damn, I wake up around four am on the bearskin rug with one of those dry throats and dull heads I get when on my back snoring most of the night. I'm even more whipped from sleeping than being awake half the night. Dull head, dull head, dull-Picasso head, as dull as the bear looking up at me as if waiting for me to finally get off him. I haven't had this much mind-numbing in a while. Distorted like a Picasso portrait describes how I feel inside.

The atmosphere in here isn't just some mildewed cabin-dump overlooking a train track on a snow packed cliff. In fact, I don't recall hearing a single train passing by the whole night, unless I drowned it out with my near-suffocating snoring. So where we really are, the Colorado Mountains, or Jerry's backyard, is up for grabs.

The fire is burning steadily, apparently still on the one fire log. It's filled the cabin with that nostalgic smoky scent of my childhood mornings of waking up with Pop to fish before first light. I almost expect to find him there waiting for me to open my eyes. He's not.

It's very cozy, all things considered. I sit up on the floor to get some blood to my neck to find Mooky instead. He's dressed in his habitual black duster sitting in a rickety wood armchair, watching me. I know Mac tried to go to sleep in it, because I could hear him fussing to get comfortable. I look around and Mac is nowhere in my sight. Of course, he and Mike were invisible last I heard from them before nodding off. So it's a jump ball as to if they are both still here or not. Buckley Jones is unquestionably not in the room. It's just me and the Mook so far. Not a settling thought considering our combustible relationship.

"Good morning, Picasso, you snore like a dying yak."

"I feel like one, too. Four a.m., what?"

"You ready?"

"Maybe. How much of any of this is real?"

"Enough to keep you warm and fed. You're officially approved to view your film and see your doggy and girl. Deal got cut this morning in front of the whole Council. Congrats."

"I don't need anybody's goddamn approval, Mooky."

"You don't need to blow attitude at me either, Picasso."

"What is mine is mine. I'm not giving up what's left to anyone without a fight. You can tell all those Alien pricks that."

For some reason I must be popping funny because the Mook is laughing at me. "Relax, tough guy, Jerry's got your back. A little bit of Alien werewolf suits you though. I'm gonna miss it a little, even if I have to crush the life out of your chest to stand being near your big mouth. Now listen up, it's all very complicated. A lot more goin' down with the Council over all this bullshit than you can begin to imagine.

So this is how it's going down from here. Nobody is happy with what you did on that train. You hear me? Stinking mess is what it ended up being. To make up for it, you are doing a little job for them, the Council, on your way to Connecticut. You get in return what you make happen with Claire, your dog, and Jozeph when you get there."

I open my big mouth to say something smart I'm sure, but Mook holds up his hand and pulls out one of those laser guns I've seen and used before. So I shut up.

"You want to see the girl? See your baby's rough cut? Pet your poodle? Or maybe just spy on her while she sacks your other self?"

"I can't just walk…."

"Make it happen when you get there, Picasso. We'll help if we can. First you're making a drop at a lab on the way. So get your head out of your pants so you don't screw this up."

"Eat me, Alien bastard."

"By the way, whatever this you're morphing into has given you some real tiresome form of human Tourette Syndrome. So think, bite your tongue before you talk, Picasso. Or I'll dig out what's left of you in that distorted mind of yours with this thing."He shows the laser.

"Did you implant something in me? What is it? Don't be messing with me, Mook."

"I'm not messing with you. Neither are they. Why would we mess with you this far into the game? Why would they spend the time? Think about it. Think about who you are now."

Point taken, so I do. I think about me. Awe shit, they're using me. Why not? Like this, what's happened to me, I'm still of value. I'm unique, unusual, a one of a kind, and a pain in the ass to most human and Aliens alike. I'm a mutable-personality, nasty killing machine. Genetically, I may or may not have incubated into something of far more useful. I not only think this, I know just enough about this. So someone has given me this information. Or the Alien werewolf doctor in me knows this. It's my blood they want. They don't want me.

"I get it. Good or bad in human terms, I am being used by Aliens who are looking for a way to live here on Earth as we humans do."

"That's not a given, Picasso. Parts of the Council, the scientific ones, the take-the-human-apart and see-how-he-works portion of the Council, wants you to work for what the human part of you wants. They are hedging their bets. To make sure they get something they want out of what you've become. Before someone else's devious wants wastes your blood out in the snow."

"So they're offering me a blood transfusion, a swap of some kind. They use my blood, study it or whatever. I get to see my film, pet my dog, and possibly watch my potential girlfriend bed another me."

"You're a walking-talking germ beaker. Think of the dirty mixed bag of blood running through you."

"I have. It's got me doing some crazy shit."

"Good. They want it. Want to examine it. Play with it. See what they can make of it. They want to see if it can mutate into something that can harm them or save them. Either way be careful. They start digging into your marrow, they'll lame you, turn you into a cripple."

"I thought Jerry was helping me get what I want."

"Yes, but they want your blood making abilities, not just the blood. They want this as much as Jerry wants you to live the life you desire once this is over. Do you not recall how hard it was for It to let go of Gray? I'm sure Jerry's told you this is not an easy process.

"Do we have to call him It? Seems disrespectful, all considering."

Fine. He has issues of letting go of humans he is fond of. It's his Achilles Heel. How they control him. They even had Jerry bite you while inside one of his things, his very hot vampire. Just to speed up the mix. A payback for you not dying as planned in the parking lot."

"Then what gives Jerry his power, his control over all of you?"

"Jerry has the ability to be any one of us at anytime. Jerry makes us do whatever he wants, whenever he wants. He plays Mr. Kind Guy to you humans yet he makes us do horrible, degrading things to each other. Including voting his way on the Alien Council. Whatever he needs or has a whim for at the moment. Even killing ourselves if we don't give him what he wants. He leaves us and humans at the moment of destruction that he creates. Remember that little guy at the bar? The one who nearly took off your head? Jerry put him there."

"Jerry told me what he was about to do."

"Claire sleeping with women is another example."

"I get it."

"Hologramming is the only way to keep him from controlling me right now if he wanted to. It allows us to control the light, bend it in ways he can't control, because I'm not really here. It's why we developed it along with the portal holes. To keep him from manipulating us physically and mentally like he does you humans."

"He can't talk through you as long as you're a hologram. I'm an Alien Frankenstiened werewolf-vampire so he can take me."

"Yes. As a filmmaker, you get the erotic high concept hook."

"Hollywood Director/Writer infected with Alien werewolf and vampire blood goes on a rampage to kill everyone in this cabin."

"Don't forget the three human beings inside of you."

"My blood type changes so often I have my own ethnic background. Is that it?"

"I knew you'd see the irony in it eventually. Let's go."

"Screw you, Mook. Are you up there? Or down in some secret chamber underground? Say under the new Denver Airport?"

Mooky looks at me for a moment. "Which do you prefer?"

"The truth."

"I'm not in Colorado. They don't accept me there."

"So it's true. There is a place?"

"You'll have to find out for yourself."

"What does that mean?"

"I'm not controlling any of this, Picasso. I'm just the middle-Alien on this one. Now let's go."

"Wait, where are the others?"

"They're setting things up for you. Don't worry. Nothing will go wrong on our end."

"Oh yeah, this has all gone just as you planned thus far."

"How do you know it hasn't?"

"Come on, Mook. Admit it. You guys screwed up real bad and now I'm me. Just admit it. Something has gone wrong. Just like what happened to J.J., when Jerry gave him that permanent tan."

"Think of it this way. There is more than one side pulling you humans in directions you have no idea you're going in. It's often more political than even in this case. This is nothing in the big picture of what's really going on. As I told you before, you're nothing but a finger puppet to a small little part of it. You all are. That's the way it is. Always has been. And will be forever, as long as we are here."

"You know I don't believe that. We have a chance."

"No you don't. We just let those of you who know we are in control think there is some grand evolution-revolution or world fairness someday. Not going to happen. There will be no ninth inning human rally to beat us. Stuff has to get done. Someone's got to do it for them. Someone they can count on not to say anything if others find out. Someone like you, Picasso. A reliable human bagman to the Alien Mob, who knows we'll kill his dog and friends if he talks or fails.

In the big picture, you are willing to put up with what you've become, to stay out of the loony bin, by unconsciously suppressing the psychotic disorders we've given you. But you and I both know, you'll end up there, in that straightjacket, before this is all good and done, a clone or otherwise. You saw it. So yeah, I guess there is a chance you escape us Picasso, but not to a better place, trust me."

"If you ask me to trust you again, I'm gonna rip your head off."

"Hologram. Give it a shot."

"Okay, wait... I give my blood and bone marrow and then we go see my film and Claire. How much of my blood and marrow?"

"Enough, and not in that order. Claire first, film later that night."

"What about Jozeph?"

"Yes, what about Jozeph?"

"He suspects nothing?"

"He knows you are a murderer. Reintroduce that. I think he'll be more than glad to listen. So will Claire if you talk with her first."

"Does Jerry have her?"

"When the time is right."

"I force them?"

"Convince Jozeph to cooperate. His little dog, too. Be you, as Boli the land investor. You're a Central American film distributor, who is pretending not to be scumbag Javier, the murdering, on the run drug-lord rat fink, wanted dead by his own brothers. Keep it simple."

"Wait, so leaving out the Alien crap makes that tangled up bullshit simple? Come on, what planet did you say you fell off?"

"Simpler, complicated bullshit, yes."

"And the invisible Mike and Mac and gun happy Buckley Jones, my side kicks, are setting this up?"

"Making sure your other friends don't interrupt. To give you time to watch your film and pet your dog. That is the best we can do."

"What about Claire?"

"Jerry said he'd gladly make that hookup happen all weekend."

"I'll take my chances. I want to see my film. I want to see Claire with Jozeph, with me... to see for myself. I want to know what she feels about what you've done to me. Without Jerry using her."

"She may love you, Picasso. Or him, now. Who can say? You sappy humans and these mushy drive-in emotions are hard to figure."

"She may love me for how long? Until the end of production?"

"That's the question, isn't it? Hollywood romance isn't real love. That suspicion is always there. You're weak, Picasso, you're still a man, a human, well okay mostly. This Javier, that part of you, your manhood, your sexual drive, is dangerously obsessive, and the reason why we chose him for you. Use that, but be careful you don't damage things that don't need fixing. You know what I mean. Her body and mind, Claire's, is fragile and Jozeph's mind is innocent to all this other worldly drama. Both are clear of this Alien Horror film tooth and dagger stuff. So, don't mess that up, or you will be sorry for a long time. I know I'm not the first to tell you."

"I'll carve it in your back."

"Just scare the piss out of him as a murdering thug. Oh, and one more thing. These lab people are willing to do some things to help you mask what is happening to you. It will only be temporary and most importantly experimental at best. So if you don't watch your film before midnight, things could get very ugly, hairy even, in that rental home. You understand me, Cinderella? We very much doubt that you will have time or the patience to sit and watch it all the way to the end. So we will take you out, one way or the other, before you start wanting to eat everyone in there."

"Watch film. Don't eat anyone. Then die. Got it."

"Good. We be out of here, Frankenwolf."

35

My eyes open. Oh-oh. This isn't good. They want my blood machine, my bone marrow, the spongy tissue found inside my bones. That's gonna hurt taking it out. It's likely the bone marrow in the breast bone, skull, hips, ribs or spine that they'll want because it contains stem cells that produce my body's blood cells.

These blood cells include white blood cells that fight infection; red blood cells that carry oxygen to and remove waste products from my organs and tissues; and platelets that enable my blood to clot. Mine mutates at an alarming speed. So fast that not even they know what I'm turning into yet. But are probably willing to kill or disfigure me to find out. I'm not even surprised, considering I'm strapped to a surgical bed with tubes in both arms.

My vision is impaired. From what I see, I'm in a very normal looking surgical room. An IV is in my right arm slowly draining my blood. While in my left arm, a clear yellowish liquid is slowly seeping back into me. Are they really doing this to me? Replacing my Alien enhanced red human blood with their yellow yuck? Is there no end to the sick distortion they'll bestow upon this body for their own desires?

The air smells clean. It's neither cold nor warm. The only sound is my pulse from within me. Who knows how long I've been in here. Or how many pints they've taken out and put back in already. The two young doctors, in blurring white, seemingly roll about the room monitoring what is happening to me. They slide in and out of my mushy vision of flashing white and flickering colors as they pass in front of what could be colorfully lit blinking panels. They could be from Earth, or any far away planet from what I can tell. Is this where they've taken me before to do their dirty work on me, to piece me back together? Is this the place? Is Jerry letting me see this?

Then one of the blurs stops in front of me and reaches down to examine my eyes.

"Good morning," she says. Her lips are freshly painted a familiar burnt red. "How do you feel?"

Holy crap! Ms. Mary Devonshire? The DA imposter or the Alien using her clone? "Is that you Hot Lips?"

"Are we doing this again?"

"Damn straight."

"Still the foulmouthed filmmaker. Some things never mutate."

"Yes, inside here is still the lucky guy who watched your head splash something nasty all over my walls. The human who got to watch as your yellow Alien goulash dissipated from my painting. I fantasize about it all the time. How nice you're back and I get to have you violently killed again. It's sad what some humans have to go through to get rid of a nasty-stalking chick like you?"

"What are clones for? Regardless, as you can see, I am very much with you now."

I squint and my eyes begin to focus despite my loss of fluids. "Are you still as hot as you were in that interrogation room?"

"You can fake a lady out of losing her mind but you can't make her stop wearing heels once she re-clones herself."

"Hot doctor, now, Mary Devonshire? I doubt that's your name. I'm sure you're still just some parasitic Alien using Mary's clones. You got a thing for Alien werewolves?"

"My name isn't what's important here."

"It is to me, since you seem to be draining the life out of me."

"I won't kill you, Picasso, not yet. As much as it would please me to no end to see you withering into a smoldering pile of human flesh out in the desert sand."

"So it was you who killed the Essinolas and set me up to be the fall guy of the galaxy. That's why you kept letting me go."

"Of course. I blipped in, got your gun while you were walking that insipid little furry poo-machine and drove those lowlifes out there myself. They thought they were finally getting their big payoff. But they didn't have the stones. They left them in their cocker spaniel. So they got the payoff they had coming. Now it's your turn."

"Still got the hots for me, huh, you black widow."

"Go ahead and talk smart, Picasso. Now that I have you in my control again, I'm gonna scrape your marrow out with a scalpel while you are fully awake. I'll take some from your chest, and the rest from your thick skull."

"So, you getting shot in the head by my two buddies, Mike Tucker and Leonard MacAroy didn't fit into your grand scheme of things."

"Let's just say with those stones I'd have no need to stand here jibber-jabbing with the likes of what's left of you."

"You could've been somebody, instead of remaining some Alien intestinal maggot-like-creature at heart. Is that it?"

"Something much like that, yes."

"Since you brought it up, where are you from?"

"I was cloned many times right here on Earth."

"Okay, I asked for that. Where was the first of you hatched?"

"Twenty of what is really me ago came from a planet about twice the size of Earth, five galaxies from here. Called Airotalogatu, in a very loose translation. A somewhat gassy planet. Something I'm sure you'd appreciate from your flatulent human nature. In our case, from high levels of evaporations. There was no solid land and the air we breathed would set you on fire."

I already know these details. They've been implanted. "Hydrogen based life form. No wonder you're such a frigged bitch. Ouch! Did you really grab my IV?"

"I'm sorry, did I do this?"

"Ouch, you bitch."

"You know what fowl language does to me."

"Listen, if you're here to shoot me again, get it over with. I'm tired of all you whackos prodding and probing me and telling me what to do and not to do. I'm at the point where I might off myself just to end the speculation of what I might or might not do next."

"You're calling me a whacko? You're the monster who rips their heads off and pulls their hearts out on public trains."

"That's not me. Jozeph Picasso would never do those things. You know that. That's what they've done to me."

"What about you leaping three hundred foot cliffs at a single bound? Or killing beautiful doctors? That's not you either?"

"I get winded running up my stairs to answer the phone. I certainly wouldn't go around murdering your boyfriends if I wasn't infected by what that creature did to me."

"Ex-boyfriend many clones ago. That's not the point either. The point of you being here now is that despite your annoying personality you're potentially mutating into something very useful to me."

"In what way?"

"That's not a concern of yours."

"It wasn't, until I heard your voice again. Now I'm thinking that letting you have any of my blood isn't in the best of my interest."

"You're most certainly right. I am and always will be your worst Alien nightmare, Picasso. From the day you first crossed me until I dance upon your and all your clone's ashes. You and your meddling dog have caused me my irreplaceable station in life. I'm vaulted from the Alien Advisory Board, shunned from the Alien Council, and thrown into eternal exile like some beaten egg-laying insect.

I and others stuck our necks out to acquire those stones for reason you have no idea of the meaning. Yet an imbecilic lowly Hollywood dog-loving filmmaker, an unemployable hack writer/director-slash-apartment manager, stood in our way of my greatest conquest."

By the time she's done letting me know how much she admires me, we're nearly touching noses as she examines my eyes.

"You harm me beyond the agreement, and you know Jerry will be very unhappy."

Mary drops a liquid into my eyes and her face comes into clear focus for the first time. Full painted red lips. A yellowish glow in her razor-sharp eyes. Long blond hair pulled back tight and held with a solid pearl hair pin. Yes as hot as she ever was, if not even a few years younger. "You had plastic surgery. Why you little minx."

"Look who's talking, Frankie. At least I'm still all me."

"At least I don't suck the juice from strangers' balls so that I can breathe here on earth and walk around dressed in their clones."

"Shut up, you filthy pig!"

"Jerry won't like you messing with me. When he gets inside you I'm gonna take you out in some stinking grease stained Pacoima ally and make you sing like a hungry cat. Ouch. You bitch!"

"That's three. You are very lucky your friend the Mook warned me about your dirty-mouth side effect, Picasso. Or I'd dig out your heart with a spoon and squeeze your blood into an eyedropper."

"That backstabbing Mook gave me up to you?"

"Yes, of course. You have no real friends in this game. But don't worry about little cloned me and your friend Jerry. He will never know I have you, not down here, where we are now. This place is Jerryless. I'm as untouchable by him here, as a black hole. As long as I have control of you, I'm gonna milk your marrow until you morph into something I no longer need. Or your bones turn to mush. I will watch with Alien glee, as you suffer a very protracted death."

"Alien glee? Give me a break, you corny bitch."

"Shut up. You foul mouthed freak! I'm gonna test your blood drop by drop as it morphs inside the guinea pig humans I've got stored down here. Until I come up with just the right blood cell mixture and DNA I need to keep me from dissipating on earth every time I die. I'll be super- strong, terrorizingly-stealth and nearly unstoppable by any human or Alien hand. Even by friends of your guardian, Jerry, who keep trying to kill me and my clones off. As you can see, thanks to my alliance with the Mook, they have failed once again."

"Did you just make up a new word? Terrorizingly? OUCH! You are truly certified crazy."

"Perhaps, but once I've achieved my bloodletting goal, they will have no choice other than to accept me back in the Alien Council's fold as a new and improved Alien life form. I'll have, thanks to you, all reinstated inoculations against unlawful Alien termination."

"So it's you feeding Russian scientist this DNA information."

"Yes. I will become the richest being in the Universe."

"Including his Jerryness?"

"Untouchably rich. Now for the record, since we're expressing our true inner feelings. Jerry's real name is Jerithizugludimi, from not a living planet but an exploding galaxy, nearly pure gamma-rays. And so that you know, there's a reason there is only one of him. It's because Jerry is all of them. Black holed the rest of his kind before they could overtake him. He sucked in their Gamma-Rays until he was the only one, as strong and powerful as your Sun's inner core.

"I'm glad you don't call him an It."

"He, her, It, or Geraldine is made of the matter as old as the universe. An equation of a being so deadly he's forced to store his energy far-far beyond the moon or the entire planet would burst into flames. Harvesting a dominate portion of his on-Earth energy would be the only way of controlling him."

"You mean imprison him in a battery cell?"

"It didn't work. But like many of us not from here, his only way of walking amongst you is to become one of you, or many of you. The Council has put a ban on him becoming one of us, though he still tries. And succeeds way too often.

So don't think your pal, your benefactor, is such a nice harmless little thing who weeps because he has two lonely butts. He's a user, a power-hungry source. Pure evil in the eyes of most of us. He's the deadliest thing on this earth, including sunlight, and anything living in these galaxies anywhere. He's pure, one hundred percent, made from the gamma-ray energy that created this whole big bang thing. A sun, a star, and a son-of-bitch goner as soon as I and my friends can figure out how to suck him back into a black hole, and take control of his powers.

"So Mooky is in on this double-cross?"

"Of course."

"Figures."

"Yes, and when we finally have control of Jerry you humans will experience the true terror of what life across the Universe is really all about. It's a constant expanding terror of destruction. So great and so emanate that nothing beyond infinity of time will escape its creation of the next space. A dimension few of us will survive to see. And that, you tricked out-joke of a human, is what it's all really about. Which of us will somehow get to that safe dimension and see the next Universe form when this one implodes to a tinny anatomical spec and reboots itself again. Something only your Jerryness has the ability to do right now. Something he is hording for himself and those he plans to take with him."

"Us?"

"Yes, you soul forsaken humans. He's leaving the rest of us Space Travelers to dissipate into blistering dust particles. Become part of the new expanding Universe in forms that would put an end to all that we were and ever will be. We will cease to exist, taking billions of light years to repopulate the new Universe in whatever form occurs. He wants a simpler Universe controlled by Humans so that It can continue to have Its way with you lowlife, fornicating, defecating, decaying, lumps of protoplasmic waste of everlasting time."

"So, you want to hit Star Bucks after this, or what?"

"Be silent!"

It clicks to mind, perhaps through my Junk DNA, that I know why I'm here. Why Jerry allowed me to come. Why Mooky was given permission to feed me to this horrible deed doer. Why they put me in the hands of this pestilent of a clone. They are controlling me still. It's to do their dirty work. Do the Alien Council's dirty work. I am after all, in all my incarnations still their bagman. So, without much effort, I break my restraining straps and clamp my Alien werewolf fingers around her throat and start to squeeze. Just enough to make her eyes protrude and wipe that dastardly smile off her heavenly face. "Screw you and all your clones, bitch! Jerry sends his farewells and I'm takin' my blood with me." I kiss her hard, rubbing a rash on her mouth with my heavy wolf stubble.

"You pig. Let me go. You have no idea what you're doing. I'm the only hope to put an end to him."

I turn. Standing at the door are two more Marys. So I snap this one's neck pulling her spine out of her body with her smashed head, like boning a boiled fish. I yank the IVs from my arms in one motion.

"Shoot him, shoot him," the closest Mary yells!

In a single leap I am on top of them both. Grabbing them by the foreheads, gripping their eye sockets like an ambidextrous bowler. I twist quickly, popping their heads off, pulling both their spines out with them. Horrific!

Jerry you sick bastard for sending me here to do this. If my own hand, along with Sanchez's were not doing this horrible thing I'd be puking in them.

Mary's human cloned flesh crumbles into mushy piles of spineless blobs. Yellow ugliness flows from their cavities, their spines having pulled out like deboned boiled salmon. I'm enthralled and appalled at the same time.

Two of the male white uniforms still in the room crouch behind counters with what appear to be lasers pointed at me. So I grab up the nearest table and throw it against a bank of highly-powered computers. Sparks fly everywhere causing both of the armed technicians to expose themselves to my brutality. But something stops me from outright killing them once I have them in my grasps.

"Take me to the humans she was telling me about. The ones you're doing tests on. I'll let you live."

"That door," the first tech says.

I realize at this time that neither one of them is anymore than a mechanical technician.

"Is there any of my blood outside of this room?"

"No, every drop is in those beakers."

I turn and under a small flame five rows of beakers of my blood are slowly stirring and evaporating into long glass tubes. "Has any of this been tested on anyone yet?"

"Not yet. It's not ready. We are waiting for it to mutate further."

"Pick up the beakers. How do we destroy these?"

"There. Acid. To kill off the blood residue and you once we are done with draining what we can. You and it must be burned in a vacuum chamber when the time comes. We are to pour it on you until you dissolve completely away. It would take less than thirty seconds for your body and flesh to dissipate inside that vacuumed chamber. The blood instantly."

"I wasn't making it out? Not seeing my movie? My dog, my girl?"

The two droids look at each other. "Nothing ever leaves here. Not even her."

"Dispose of all of my blood, now."Without letting go of either, I allow them to reach over and pick up all the beakers, one at a time. They place a container of acid with all of what dripped from me inside a small vacuum chamber. "Activate it."

The nearest droid pushes a button. With a sizzling puff of searing smoke my blood and the beakers they are in dissipate to nothing.

"What were they pumping back into me?"

"Nutrients to keep you making more blood and your heart pumping to the end. So we could drain you dry without killing you first."

"Will it harm me?"

"No one's ever walked away from this process. So we don't know what the Alien defects to your human cells will be in the long term. You're mutating so fast."

"Great. How many Marys are there left?"

"None in here, but there are those who are capable of cloning her again outside of here. And will unless they are stopped."

"They? Are any of these Aliens here?"

"No."

"Where are we?"

"Down here. We don't know exact location. For security reasons."

"How do I get these other people out?"I realize now why Picasso was still in charge throughout this murderous ordeal. For the other humans. Jerry wanted me to bring the other humans out with me. Okay, I get it.

"Portal bumps, the lump on your head. If they didn't have one, they wouldn't be here."

"You brought them here by using their own portal lumps?"

"Yes, bumps. May I?" The droid in my right grasp reaches up and touches my genius bump. "Yes, it's how you came here."

"How do I get those others to use theirs?"

"If you do not destroy us, we will take care of it. Get you all out. But we warn you, you will not like where you will emerge. They are programmed to return from whence they came, if they weren't used."

"I'll worry about that when I get there. Take me to them."

In a Blip we are standing in front of twenty glass-enclosed female humans mostly in their teens and early twenties. All are modestly dressed Mexican or possibly Central American, who for the most part appear to be completely asleep and oddly familiar."

"Do they know they are here?"

"No. They are unaware of what is happening to them."

"What will happen when they wake up?"

"Nothing has happened yet. They will remember nothing."

"How do I explain where we are when they wake up?"

"We can't help you there."

"Okay. Let's do this. Wait, I know these people."

The same droid reaches up and touches my portal lump.

Blip.

And the droid is more than right. I do not like where I am. "Holy Salsa, Dogman."

36

I'm in some exceptionally stinky Third World barnyard-basement-stall-like prison cell. It's full of shadowy human forms clinging to the damp slimy river rock walls. They smartly stay as far away from scary old me as they can. Who could blame them? The other twenty young women who popped in here with me lay prone at my feet. Their eyes randomly open to see me standing over them.

I know them, because each of them works in my whore houses or are daughters of my ranch hands. That is, Javier's family drug cartel ranch and drug emporiums. We are in Ciudad Juarez, right on the border between the United States and Mexico. Javier's ancestors have owned this land since it was founded in the 17th century. Accumulating it by deals, marriages, and murders. It's mostly hard-accessible land without burros and airplanes. But perfect for pulling the guts out of its soil by growing marijuana and coco plants with the hands of peasants living meagerly off the operation.

These days Ciudad Juarez is mostly full of irate guerrilla fighters. It's clogged by desperate Catholic congregations siphoning pesos through the dirty fingers of the fearful poor. It's overrun by merciless revolutionary armies itching to kill someone. These brutal armies are financed mostly by scumbag drug traffickers like me and my two brothers. Of course, there's still room for the modern day honest and dishonest federal armed forces. I know this because I was given this information. It's all in my head maybe because Javier is part of me. Maybe it's because they, meaning Jerry, has sent me here to do what I'm about to do. Kill Javier's two brothers and their hag mother, too.

Although the number of drug cartel members is not known with precision, I can tell that by the time I leave here there will be a handful less living ones. I know that both of my brothers have five armed men around them at all times. Those guys they sent my way were strangers to me. They were most likely mercenaries from this crowd, looking to make a buck off the price on my head. Bounty hunters, trained killers, or wannabe cartel members, even their Alien clones, it doesn't really matter. They will harshly die and won't be part of Jerry's plan to help humans escape this exploding dimension.

I'm sure the horrible news of the last two dying on the rails made it back here. I've got a good idea there will be more waiting for me and looking for me if I don't end it right here, right now. If Jerry sent me here, I'm sure that's why. I, Jozeph Picasso, of course want nothing to do with any of this. However, those residing inside me, Javier and the good doctor the Alien werewolf, know that Jozeph will not be able to sit with Claire Davis and watch our film together while these people are sending their troops out to kill us. The only way to survive this ordeal, and not put Claire Davis in danger, is to become the greater more aggressive killer.

The plan that is going through my melting pot of a brain is simple. Once the heart of the money to kill Javier stops, it will end the hunt. And that is what I'm here for. To still the heart of those who mean all of me harm.

Is it just Jerry, Mooky, and the Council making this all come true. Or is the US and Mexico Governments aware of what I'm doing down here? Am I creating this adventure on my own to save myself? I don't know. It's no secret the Sinaloa Cartel is at the center of the problem in Ciudad Juarez. Are they run by a faction of the Alien Mob, a part of the Alien Council who is designed to create havoc amongst the Third World humans, to make it easier to take them and suck on them? Is this a three-for-one deal? Everyone getting a piece of me before I'm given my life back? Sure feels like I'm cheap disposable labor looking for a way to cross the border to my better life.

That's a fair and wise question in light of what I've seen. Aliens control everything on Earth, good or bad. What is bad for humans doesn't have to be bad for Aliens. Crafting and supporting vicious cartels and regimes creates mayhem and chaotic consequences. Hundreds of people go missing for no apparent reason, other than they are here today and gone tomorrow. If all their loved ones and village members are gone too, who would stand up for them and notice they are gone?

How many of us are cloned already? Designed replicas of us, as our birthed-selves are feeding the needy Aliens? That's the real question. Bloodlines do end. More often than we know. Civilizations

194

cease to exist, leaving no explanation to how they managed to accomplish what they did with supposedly so little mechanical knowledge or tools. There are ancient books and drawings of seemingly Alien flying machines, resembling modern-day jets and planes but crafted into gold jewelry thousands of years ago. With no earthly explanation as to what they were modeled after.

Some have even proven scientifically able to fly without altering their basic design. Down here is ripe with these kinds of mysteries. Why and how did their civilizations end? Did they find out what was happening to them? Did they revolt against the man-eaters? Did they evolve into something too close to what the Aliens fear? Did someone walk in on mommy and daddy and realize that Santa wasn't who he said he was and all Alien made gifts were taken away?

Who can stop this from happening? Not I, not Javier, he might be in on it. Or he may not be able to go through with it and they'll expect me to do it, and I know I can't. The thought of what they'll do to me if I fail is paralyzing. In thinking, if Javier isn't in on all this, he's of no value to the Alien Council. He's either a clone already or a made man by some faction doing Alien biz for the Alien Mob. Have they sent him back with me and the werewolf attached, to clean up his mess once and for all? Is this so they can put rumors of unusual local disappearances to rest and possibly hide what they are really doing down here from everyone else? "Shut up, Picasso!"

Cartels are making and selling drugs, yes. But Aliens cultivating and stealing people for food and science projects are far more real than any other scenario in the light of what I've seen thus far. How much of all this involves Mary Davenport's faction of the dismembered Alien Council? Just how desperate is Jerry and his faction in using me to rid themselves of her kind and all this killing of innocent humans? The hypocrisy of it all is mind-numbing and not too unlike our own government. It's all about how to get those who support you what they want without losing your place in life, the Council, Congress, or the Senate. Aliens and humans are not so far apart as one would think and probably have very similar retirement plans based upon milking the middleclass cloaked as government subsidies.

Indeed, Javier, his brothers and other smaller cartels have been warring over this strategic city for many months. They have caused thousands of unsolved deaths, the resignation of police commanders and officers, as well as numerous kidnappings and blatant murders.

The city is also infamous for the disappearance of thousands of women over the last few years. Now the problem is likely to spillover to the United States. So the question still is, is this part of the grand Alien plan to cover up the taking of humans for their crazy tests and feeding? Or is the US Government also involved? Are they using me to end this Cartel stronghold from within because it's gotten out of hand? Is the Alien Council unable to control it on their own because they would have to openly appose each other? Is all this fundamentally against their Alien bylaws of not harming each other? Therefore causing Jerry to allow them to drag the likes of me, Jozeph Picasso, Javier Sanchez, and the rest of who embodies me into the crapper to do their shitty work.

How much does our government, or portions of it, know about them, those who feed upon us? What are they feeding their Junk DNA? Somehow I don't see even our President knowing any of this. How could he function knowing they are hiding this? Unless, they too are either cloned or actually Aliens themselves already. In that case, we are cork screwed from the top down and bottled into this mess beyond any simple person's control.

My guess is that Jerry and the Alien Council are getting what they need from what I've become, their Alien Mobster, before they have me end it and gain my innocent, non Alien Mobbish life back. Cleaning up a few loose ends as last minute favors and the fact that I'm solving more than one Alien problem is just pork belly on the deal of allowing me to get my life back.

If they do give it back. Jerry likes me, created me by supposedly breeding my parents. But how far will this carry me back to what I was? And how much of me do I want back? Has this been my destiny all along? Do the numbers all add up to this moment? Or are these acts of Alien espionage as haphazard as human life seems to be? And my involvement in them only progresses as Alien crisis arise? Creating a need for a button man like me to take action?

My heart is racing. I need to sit down. The thought of this murderous price to pay, just to escape what they have done to me, is mind-bending. All I have to do is eventually murder myself or at the very least allow it to happen by the hands of others.

I am no toga-clad Caesar. I care not to die by hands of my said co-conspiratoring-peers. I care not to feel the Ides of March in the dead of winter. I want to live on deep inside of me beyond the next full moon. I want my life back as it was, tedious, unknowing and simple.

While thinking of all this bullshit, the peasants before me look on with amazed eyes as though I am the second coming of Aztec Sun God, a real life saint. And one by one they get on their knees in the wet mildewed straw and start to pray before me.

"What the hell? Get on your feet." I'm speaking in Spanish of course, though the putrid urine smell is grabbing at my gag reflexes, and making my eyes water as though I'm crying for their pain.

"Si, Senior Sanchez," says an astonished little man with brackish matted hair spilling down to his bony filthy shoulders. He speaks through spittle-caked whiskers that hang and mingle with his thick grimy gray chest hairs. "You have come, appearing before our very eyes, back to free us. It is truly a miracle. They keep us here trapped like wild pigs. Some of us for months, with barely enough food and water to feed the rats that fight us for it. We are forgotten people in a cruel world of wasted lives. Yet, you have finally come back as you promised to set us free? You even bring us back our missing loved ones. Just as you promised you would."

"Where are we?"

"Home, Senior Sanchez, you are home. We are home. This is our home that you provide for us. We are locked in what once was a pigsty, but now a jail cell for human swine like us. But up there, out that door is home to us all."

"So I am in Mexico on my ranch?"

"Si, Senior. They are looking for you and have taken us out of the fields after they burnt them and our homes. They have taken all our young women and are killing us hombres two by two until you show your face. Now you are here to save us. Appearing before our very eyes. A vision of saintly hope. Fulfilling our so many prayers, and a few castration threats I might add."

"I get it."

"Understand, we are hurt and angry. This is your entire fault. Regardless, mostly we pray for you to come back and help us. We were disheartened when you abandoned us here to rot. We heard you were in prison in America. Now this, you return to us like magic. They will surely kill you for showing your face here again. You are a great and brave man to come back now to see that we are free to go home again by sacrificing yourself for us."

"What's your name?"

"Roberto, I am your cook, surely you remember me. I raised you from a little snot-nosed boy. You were like a son to me. Only you were spoiled and ruthless and my children are kind and caring. So, I even beat you when no one was looking. Mostly I punish you to keep you out of the sugar jar and from rotting your teeth. Surely you remember. See, you have all your fine teeth. And I must say a lot more hair. I don't recall you being so hairy."

I look at my arms and sure enough they are twice as hairy.

"They've got you all here because they thought I'd come back?"

"Si, your two brothers and your mother, they still work together on killing you. It is her idea. I hear them say so myself. She's still very silent but continues to raise your brothers like pit bulls. Even more so after you left. She had them take your land and they have put us here because they thought you would not be able to stay away once you found out they were killing us and your dogs because of you. And here you are. To save us just as you had promised."

"I promised, how did I make this promise?"

"Your voice came out of this mute boy's mouth. He broke a fever after three days of sickness, near death, when your voice possessed him. It was very late last night. If I myself hadn't heard the voice and witness the boy come back to life, I too would have your very look on my face. But your voice told us all to wait patiently for your return and to help you in any way you need. You said you would be here to end all this, to give us back what we have lost."

"Your freedom?"

"Si, our lives and our loved ones' lives. You are a miracle worker that only we shall know about. For we were warned that we would all perish in hell if we were to ever mention outside this cell that we knew you were coming to save us. You promised that our girls would be returned to us if we kept this vow of silence for evermore."

"Did this voice tell you his name?"

"Si. Your name, Javier Sanchez."

"Figures. So we are on the grounds of my family's estate?"

"Si, you remember this cell? It's where you put my brother's son for stealing your best hunting dog. You dragged him here yourself and showed him where you'd put him if he ever did it again."

"My dog?"

"The finest hunting dogs in all the land. They kill them all, and they hang now in the courtyard because they cannot find you."

"Great. How many of us are in here?"

"Many, thirty, thirty five. Not including these girls we thought gone forever. But you have brought them back to us."

"I'm not so sure I did them any favors."

"Tell us what you need," the old cook says.

"How many are there watching this room?"

"There are twenty armed men at all times on the grounds."

"Five on each end of the compound." The longer I stand here the more I remember of Javier's former life he left behind for Boli.

"There is one more thing you should know. If you haven't known this yet. There's a very beautiful woman, so hot she catches the straw on fire. With a very foul mouth. Just three doors down, at the end of the hall. Your youngest brother, Pauleto, he has attempted to have her twice. Both times he came out of the room holding his balls.

"Olivia?"

"Si, she very fine. Tidbit of an Americana bitch, but honey drips from her breast. Stars shine from her teeth. Her eyes are the path to the sky. She no like it here and has stated so rather colorfully."

"Someone will let you out."

"No get killed."

"No get killed. Words to live by. Thank you."

I walk to the bars and reach out and pull them apart. The men and women behind me gawk at me like I'm a giant. I bend the bars back. "I won't be back."

"We wait in our stink and filth."

"When I'm done, there will be a mess to clean up. I want you to take care of this mess for me. And for that, I give you this house and land. You, Roberto, will be the new owner of this home, the master of all this land. It will be yours. My brothers' land as well. Grow food for others not drugs, and the title deed is yours. If you grow drugs I'll be back and do to you what I'm about to do to them."

"But your mother, your brothers, they kill me if you fail."

"No one will bother you ever again by the time I get done."

"Hell be thy name."

"Worse, much-much worse. But I must hurry. I need to get to Connecticut by nightfall."

They all cross themselves as if they understood what awaits me there. As I turn my back, I hear the young, once mute, boy who Saint Javier spoke through. "He's as crazy as they say."

"Worse. But we are his people. And he will see we are freed. As he fixed you, he offers us a life we could only dream of."

"What if they kill him first?"

"Then of course, we are, how do they say in San Diego... screwed."

37

I'm not running down the puddle-filled hall, hands held out wide, like some crazy love-lost fool, barefoot on a sandy beach. Not I, because I, meaning we, know who's waiting for us behind door number three when we get to Oli. His Jerryness. We know this not because they have told any of us. But plainly because that's the logical thing for Jerry to do. Take possession of someone I know.

Sure enough, as I near the last wood gate at the far end of the underground tunnel-like hall, leading to the other stalls, it opens Alien-magically. "Boli!" She starts slapping at me. I have to fend her off with all my mutable-might. Not to mention she's really extraordinarily hot, sweaty, musty smilingly-beautiful to the point my groin pangs like a cast-iron Mexican church bell. I'm sure Jerry's got her all worked up and pissed off at the world.

"Stop it, Jerry!" Wishing it wasn't him to the point of almost not caring. Old Boli is fully fighting the rest of us mightily to get his grubby hands on her. He's an animal, I'm a hairy animal. But I know it's not all her. I think.

"Jerry? Who the hell is Jerry? Oh my god, what has happened to you? You're a talking chimpanzee in tacky shoes with all this hair. And you smell something much worse, almost gorillaish. Oh Boli, what have you done to us? I was just trying to make you jealous. I didn't expect you to murder Doc. My god, now someone grabbed me up and tried to rape me in a pigsty?"Oli goes for the slap again. I have to fend her off with a right hairy forearm chop this time because she surprises me with her ferociousness, bouncing her ass back against the wet stone wall.

"Yeah, yeah, settle down."

"How dare you hit me?"

Oh-oh, she's really offended, or Jerry's a great actor, and knowing his Greek days he's classically trained. "Cut it out, where do we go from here?"

"Home, you dumb son-of-a-bitch. What is the matter with you? What the hell have you gotten me into, you hairball prick? Your family is crazy. They kill people, sell drugs, own whore houses. You are all scumbags and you're the biggest scumbag for fooling me. You son-of-a-maniac. You're not even trusted by your own mother. Who, by the way, is completely out of her evil little mind! There's definitely something wrong with her. I mean, why didn't someone kill that woman before she multiplied? I've never met a woman so hateful, so spiteful, and so set on killing the man I thought I loved. She kept watching me, waiting for something to happen. I couldn't even take a pee in private, like you might miraculously drop out of my ass or something"

"Okay, okay, okay, relax will ya, Oli. Things aren't close to what they seem to be."

"No shit. Really? There's actually an explanation to all this?"

"Just give me a moment to think this out."

"Bullshit, think what out? You're a backstabbing son-of-a-witch who better get my ass out of this pigsty immediately or I will kick you in the balls so hard you'll hear the North Pole bells chime. Like I did to your stupid brother. You've ruined my father. The banks will take everything thanks to you, you murderous pig. If you don't come up with the money you promised us, I will hunt you down no matter where they bury you and I will feed your carcass to werewolves."

"Come on, seriously, there's way more to all this, things you don't understand that's going on. You remember reading about that writer on Christmas, the one who helped those people out of Frazer Park? Wait a minute. Werewolves?"

"If you're gonna stand there and tell me you're also him... some lowlife mass murdering filmmaker, well... forget it, I already know, Hollywood big shot director. You ready for this one, Picasso?"

"I knew it, you bodysnatching butt sniffer."

"Bullshit, you thought I was her. Little spoiled Oli, bitching you out. And it turned you on. Tell me I'm not hot in these pajamas."

"Shut up. You're not hot, Jerry, Oli is."

She frowns. "Here, put these on. Your eyes look like crap." Jerry hands me a very nice, very dark, very cool pair of sunglasses. I admit she's hot in torn winter pink and green paisley cotton pajamas. They must have grabbed her up and blipped her out of the states. From the looks of things she put up one snowball of a fight.

"Okay, you fooled me a little bit, Jerry, and you're hot... as Oli. Even my old cook at the end of the hall wants you."

"Jozeph, you are evolving rapidly into a valuable creature, a commodity on the open Alien blood and bone marrow market. It's very big news."

"Yeah, I can't wait to read my LA Times over a cup of joe."

"Now put those on, we're gonna need them."

I put the shades on without thinking about the why or about the we part involved in all this yet. I'm sure he has some Alien vortex mind-sucking reason that I don't really want to know the details of until after it happens to me. I'm too busy being insulted anyway.

"Creature? So that's it now, I'm a hairy creature to you? I'm no longer a human? I'm now just some monstrous creature from the deep Alien faux pas lagoon."

"Jozeph, you are evolving so fast that you're even starting to scare us. It's your fault for touching and mending yourself with the stone. You have blood and organs that are completely out of human nature. Remember, you carried stones once before. It increased the effect of the stone on you this time. Your liver is twice the size it was and filtering so much blood that we can't fathom where it will end. Your muscle tissue is already nearly ten times denser than normal human tissue. To the point that your weight is now eight times heavier than you were the last time I saw you. Look at your footprints."

I look down and yes I have left deep impressions in the wet dirt floor of the hall. "Great, my life has become such a running gag, I'm doing stupid impressions of myself everywhere I go."

"Your heart is already six times stronger, yet half the size, with a capacity to pump enough blood to sustain a pregnant Yulacannenite."

I just look at him. I'm sure that meant something, somewhere.

"Something the size of an elephant. Only with smaller ears, two added arms, and tastes delightful if cooked with the equivalent of garlic and potatoes. Feel the bump on your chest."

I feel. "Yes, feels like a great big syst."

"Puss filled. Your system is eliminating functional waste through puss holes. You've probably already stopped defecating."

"You're killing us, Jerry."

"Anyway creepo, there's a slim chance that with your blood, an Alien arriving here would be able to live as close to being a super human as any of us have come. Do you realize the value in that?"

"To me or the world?"

"Is there any difference?"

"Yes."

"The value would be in the quality of life we Aliens live while here on Earth, in comparison to how easy you Humans live here.

"Is this gonna be a long Alien whine?"

"This is your next decision, Picasso, so you need to know this."

"Why is it my decision? Aren't you controlling all this and I'm just a puppet on an Alien string of Violent Behavior."

"Very nice, Jozeph, you worked your script title into that bullshit comment. By the way, it's still in turnaround over at Paramount. However, if Crazy Kind Of Love opens well, meaning if you live to finish it, it could resurface with a new title. Possibly with you directing. That's what Gerald has in the works."

"Yeah, thanks."

"Thank him."

"I did."

"Now shut up. Does this outfit make me look fat?"

"Whatever. I need air, Jerry. Let's get out of here. I don't care about the whys anymore. Let's just move on. I'm starting to itch in this stinking humidity in places I didn't know we had follicles. This hair, I'm a friggin' south of the border Chia Pet."

"Don't be a bore, you grumbler. The point being, some of the others on the Alien Council, most of the ones who oppose me and my friends, would love to control, exploit, and explore your blood tests for their own benefit. They want out of the Alien closet."

"Oh, and that's another thing. What's with sending me in there to kill more Marys who are not so merry after all? That was sick. Pulling her spine out like that."

"That was poetry. We just taught you that before sending you in. Purely for self-preservation. Not mine, yours."

"Mary gave me an earful on you."

"She's just hurt because many clones ago I wooed her into thinking I was human. It broke her heart when she found out the Magical Man was just me playing her. But watch her. If you think I'm rough in bed, she's a real monster. Few humans escape her clutches and live to tell their friends about Mary-one-nighters. Even McGuiness was left with a few emotional scars."

"Gosh, Uncle Jerry, that's romantic. But I don't give a rat's ass right now if she is a black widow. Let's get to someplace cooler."

Oli slaps me. Hard. "This, this that you have become, Jozeph, will not be wasted. We have an opportunity here to better the world. But that bitch must never get a single drop of your blood. If I can't have it all and do what's best for human and Aliens alike, then nobody gets it and I'll fry it up myself."

"Wait a minute, this is my blood, and I'm keeping it as long as I want. So keep your electros off it."

Oli's eyes quiver, I'm sure of it. "We'll see."

"I mean it, Jerry. I decide to go, when and where I go."

"Don't let them keep your blood. Stay as you are. But if you let them have any of your blood, I'll never talk to you again. You'll be on the run until they find you, and they will find you, Jozeph. With your evolving skills you could hide for a while. Maybe longer if you learn how to use that genius bump on your own. But it won't last forever. Not from me. Ask Mary about finding her."

"Give me a break, Jerry."

"I made you. Oh never mind. You're so ungrateful, Jozeph. I gave you a life. You're living it, on your way to Connecticut with your dog, of which you will be arriving in two point seven hours. End this life. This mutated mass murdering life is just a tool, a byproduct that bought you the life you've always wanted. A successful Hollywood career, writing and directing your visions into masterpieces. I bought you that with this you are now. I bought you out of knowing we are here so that you could live free of all this again.

I made you, and now I'm finally setting you free. This is goodbye. I'm letting you go, Jozeph. Don't you understand that? I truly love you for what you really are. Just remember that. None of your mental freedom from all this will come without payment by both of us. So I used you to make some of those payments to others. Such as what we are about to do. What you did to those Marys. It's all paybacks to the Alien Council and a few other involved Governments on the way to you being free of us. What's it to you if you end up with the happy life you've only dreamed of?"

I knew it. I'm standing here hairy as a chimp and I'm actually feeling bad that I'm not appreciating what he's done for me. "Look, Jerry, Mary came very close to getting my blood. I had to destroy several beakers of it in acid. We almost blew it. Why risk sending me there? What happened to me just walking away?"

Pouting, "That is still our goal. We don't know how that will go down, yet. They could still just kill your clone and it'd be done with."

"How much more of your Alien dirty work do I have to do to get what I want out of all this?"

"Just one more for them. The last thing you'll do, you'll do for us both. But it's undecided at this time because of you. And I mean both of you will have to decide which one of you lives. All I want is for you to walk away, to be happy. So I won't make that decision. I can't, even though they expect me to."

"Happy? All you want for me is to be happy? Are you kidding me? I'm as far from happy as you are from human."

"Okay, now that was just uncaring."

"Don't tell me you care for me after doing all this to me. Mary filled me in on what you did with love ones from where you're from."

"Did she tell you why I did what I did?"

"That you're a hypocrite? Not willing to kill humans or Aliens but willing to devour your whole species?

"If you survive any of this, I'll tell you the truth about me."

"If I survive any of this, Jerry, I don't want to know that any of this is going on around me. I want to be left to live my life as naively as humanly possible.

"I am doing the best I can, Jozeph."

"Just leave me alone when I get there and I'll be just fine."

"Will you? Are you aware that by the time you arrive in Connecticut you will not need to be wearing clothing. You'll have pretty much your own fur coat."

"But there's no full moon, not for weeks."

"Yes, well about that. You are becoming what appears to be a fulltime, full-blooded, Human-slash-Alien werewolf."

I just stand there, stupefied. This is just too frigging perfect. A fulltime Human- slash-Alien Werewolf? How will I explain this to my barber? "Yo Bill, you mind, just taking a little off my back?"

"Listen you can't show this hairiness to anyone. You can't expose yourself, and I mean to your other self, to any of this or you will have to deal with the circumstances no matter which life you keep."

"Oh, and another thing, thanks for the bite on the neck."

"You're welcome."

"No seriously, I'm not happy with you injecting me with your Vampire Alien Clone bullshit. What's the matter with you?"

"It was my part of the Council's deal. I bite you, or my girl does, to add to the mix. I've hidden them from the others. Remember she was created by Gray. They wanted to see what would happen. Study the effect to see if his influence would make it all move faster.

Don't you see? They, and we're talking Mary's allies, thought they were getting your blood? And they needed you to fully mutate before the night was over. So I bit you, letting them thinking it would.

That's why I sent you in. To take as many Marys and whoever was with her out. And bring those girls back with you. By the way, you should've taken out the droids. That's another matter I'm sure we'll have to deal with down the road. I made this deal in exchange for them not killing you before letting you see your dog, girl or movie one last time. Yes, I used you again. It was our only access to her. You did well, but it's not over. Not by a long shot. We'll have to see if it buys you enough time to watch your film and say your goodbyes before Mary catches up with you again."

"Are you kidding me? All this shit is happening to me because I want to see my life again? They are and you are taking advantage of a simple human trait still lurking somewhere deep inside my head?"

"Not your head, your heart."

"What if I had failed?"

"We were in complete control."

"You were in me?"

"Of course not. We just implanted the info you needed."

"You made me to kill her?"

"Nothing is ever what it seems. I thought we covered that."

"Yes dimensions. Planes of actions. We humans have no free will. It's all right out of sci-fi novels and sounds stupid coming from you."

"Trust me. Most humans are a waste of time, so we let them be. It's the ones we want, the leaders we use to control the others. It's those like you that we cultivate on lifelong bases."

"I'm just lucky. I'm special. I'm so happy for me. Yay, Picasso, you go used leader-boy."

"You'll thank me in few minutes."

"Why wait? Thank you, Jerry. Thank you for breeding me into this pile of hairy shit so that you could attempt to sexually abuse me every chance you get while you turn me into a real, smelly, modern-day Sasquatch. Thank you so much, I love what you've done to my life, and all this hair is to die for. Who wouldn't want a full body perm like this?"

"Smart ass, you need to be who you are right now to be able to withstand what we are about to do to you next. The genetically altered hair is more than what you think it is, and will help you through this next event."

"Kiss my asses if you think I'm letting you alter one more hair."

"Oli just looks at me. "Oh please, Boli, get a grip. You don't have a single choice."

Jerry suddenly jumps into me. My body is completely out of my control. I get a warm, yet slightly slimy, though comfortably reassuring feeling up and down my spine to the base of my skull. Soothing even, kind of like peeing myself in a cold ocean. My mind is attentive but I'm only watching Olivia's body fall, then Blip, she's gone, before she hits the dirty straw covered floor.

From there I leave the room and reach the cellar stairs when a young Mexican cowboy tries to stop me. Oddly enough, I don't kill him. Instead I allow this teenage kid to manhandle me up the stairs until I'm thrust into a room with at least thirty to forty angry men arguing about what they are to do next.

In the middle of this chaotic barnlike room is a little old hag lady, Javier's mother. She sits on a wooden chair made from old grapevines that once grew on these hills before the plight of drugs ravage the lands. My father, Javier's father, twisted them into that chair many years before while wooing her.

The visual is touching, maybe to the Javier in me, but not helpful knowledge under our circumstances. The crowd parts as they turn to the door we are standing in. Javier's two younger brothers holding the mob off their mother step aside so that the old hag could lock her wicked eyes on me. A penetrating wickedness I've never seen before. Not even in Javier, not even in Mary or Mooky. This is not the vision of his kindly mother Javier had been sharing with me.

There is no love here. No sibling tearfulness of long lost lives. She wants Javier dead. She knows I'm no longer just her human son. I know this, Jerry knows this, and she and the two boys know that I am now a mutated Alien Werewolf with Vampire quickness here to kill them. They have been waiting for this very moment.

The others, the humans in the room, are plainly stupefied that a bushy Javier is standing before them. After all the senseless killing, to have Javier simply appear before them is borderline supernatural.

Karl J. Niemiec

It's far more complicated than they'll ever know. In that reasoning is the mistake Javier's family makes. They think no Alien, possessed human or otherwise, would so blatantly take them out in front of so many humans.

To the others in the room, I am just human, yet very hairy Javier who had turned on his mother, the family, and the rest of these local thugs. Javier being the eldest of the three boys, no less the killer by any means, but what is considered here the weakest for ratting them out to the gringos.

Apparently, Jerry's got news for them.

Speaking in Spanish, Javier's mother carefully chooses her words, "You lowly dog, you have the spine to show your face around here? Letting a woman take you from us. You chose this whore over me? Over your wife and kids? You throw away everything your father gave and I gave you, your brothers helped build for you. You turn on us? You testify against the family for her? To be with her?"

"It won't come to that." Come on Jerry, we sound weak.

"Si, you won't live that long."

"Si, but you will die first, hag."

The entire room reacts to the old hag pointing her foreboding finger at us by pointing their foreboding guns. Then it happens. A light emitting from my body, a modified gamma-ray burst, yet so bright that everything turns instantly opaque. I see this even though I'm wearing deep thickly dark sunglasses.

I'm thinking they have some very special powers, because just as quickly, the light disappears back into me and every person in the room has vanished; except for the two brothers and our mother. Without this full body armor hair-suit, I'm sure I'd be parboiled. Which means Javier's family is at least Aliens using human clones, if not full yellow blooded Aliens.

My skin tingles something awful from the blast of radiation. I think I'm gonna vomit, which I do, as do the other three before us. A nasty sight on my part since I am still part human and digest foods. Though I haven't eaten in quite some time. Yet a sickening chunky like dry heave on their part. I know, because I'm told, that this indicates they are Aliens using human clones. Ah, the fine effects of radiation poisoning. What a pleasure. I'm thinking this is what must have happened to J.J., being used by his Jerryness, like he's using me now, to eradicate pest needing to be eliminated from Earth.

208

Recovering fast, they now know that Jerry's involved. They make a move to attack us but Jerry stops them cold in their tracks with a quick wave of our left hand. Even the old hag is motionless, her mouth stuck stonily in a snarly, near toothless frown. We walk to them and stop within two feet. Jerry leaps to the old hag, leaving me barely able to stand.

"Kill us."

It freaks me, coming back to take control of myself. "Come on, Jerry. She's his mother,"

"You must kill us, Jozeph. It's part of the deal with the Council."

"You got rid of the others. Get rid of these."

"I can't. The others I sent up there. I did not kill any of them."

"I am not your Alien Mobster, your button man. Make Javier or the werewolf doctor do it."

"You must do it, the human in you."

"I'm not a killer, Jerry. Ask Mook."

"Javier will not be able to kill his own mother, or his brothers while facing them. They're his Achilles Heel. He's a momma's boy. Even though he knows this bitch is an Alien form as nasty and blood thirsty as they come, as well as his two brothers inside these human clones. He won't do it. Not like this. They left him as a human to do their dirty work against other Aliens who are their natural enemies. Until he fell in love with another human and walked out on them. He won't kill them, won't kill his family, even though they have tried to kill him. And they know it."

"I can't, Jerry."

"The good doctor, the Alien in you, cannot because of our unbreakable bylaws implanted in all of us, making us genetically unable to harm one another without the threat of being shunned by the Alien Council and expelled from Earth forever. So you must. You must Jozeph, now. Draw upon Leonie Dazarrio if you have to."

"But I...." And like that, Leonie surfaces from deep within us. We yank their heads and spines right out of their bodies. Severing Alien brains from their human clone necks. We crush their skulls in our hands like we had done to Mary's. One head effortlessly after the other. It's just awful to watch as their lifeless human bodies slump to the floor, while the yellowness from their brains oozes through our fingers like squeezing a bunch of Chiquita Bananas. We let their skeletons drop to the floor with the crushed skulls. "Oh my Buddha, I thought it was the werewolf doing that."

Jerry jumps back into me. So it's as though I'm talking to myself.

"Why do you think we gave him to you?"

"I only was given Leonie's leg and ass."

"And Leonie's blood. Plus a smidgeon of his killer psyche. Remember your blood type changed? We had to do that so you couldn't reject what we really wanted you to have of his. A backup for just this moment in case it arose."

"This was planned long ago?"

"Something that was on the table but I nixed until now."

"Jetty and I were more like brothers than we thought?"

"There are master plans. Some things play out, some don't. We had to make sure you could do what we needed done. We took from Leonie what you needed. We gave you his ability to kill and his leg and butt because you needed those to walk. When we had you under a second time, after the mauling, we added a little more will to live of Leonie just in case he had problems surfacing when called upon. I threw in his tattoo the first time because I couldn't resist the irony of us both having two butts."

"That's right, we both have two butts. Aliens have sense of humors. My life is but a space traveler's butt joke after all. What now?"

"We go."

"Connecticut?"

"Happy New Year, Jozeph. You've earned it." We watch the three bodies dissipate beyond repairing before anyone else enters the room.

"So, the old man and his family will get everything?"

"If that's what you want. So be it."

Jerry has sent the other men, the bad humans, up there to feed Alien babies. He left me to kill the Alien possessed clones of Javier's family. I, Jozeph Picasso, Allen Mobster, the button man, and all my counterparts, have fulfilled our side of the deal.

"That's what I want."

Blip. And we're there. Happy New Year to us.

38

Snow fills the air with imposing flakes. All bravely independent from the other until they pat the ground and instantly meld into one with the Earth. They become a blanket of glistening white beauty and peacefulness. A life unknown to us humans and Alien alike. Not a creature stirs, none but Jozeph Picasso and company of merry Alien infused, pillaged human body parts. We hairy hobgoblin, bred killing machine, suddenly home for the holiday in this rolling mountain countryside of Danbury, Connecticut.

I am not sure what they did to me on my way here. I sense that once again Jozeph Picasso is no longer alone in controlling our moves. We are much more than that, yet different than before. Perhaps it's the evolving of the blood that keeps changing me. Or I am what they need me to be. It's hard to say.

Our overly weighted footprints are as subtle as jackhammers in wet cement as we push through the hip-deep-snow. Our clothing nearly laying waste around us, save a camel hair overcoat with hood I stole from a parked Jeep at the top of the hill. Parked in a place I'm sure its owner never suspected it would be vandalized by a fulltime werewolf like us.

Unfortunately, Jerry was dead on in his assessment of our evolving into something in need of its own flea collar. We are the true meaning of America's melting pot dream. We are a full-blown werewolf, Alien or otherwise, without even the hope of a new moon in sight to blame all our troubles away. Our multiple human parts make us a modern day Frankenstein, covered by Alien werewolf wool on the outside and its blood on the inside, while our vampire clone bite is somehow causing our every evolving process to speed up as the mixed juices percolate inside us. We are no longer me, myself, nor I. It is fully we, ourselves, and us. The lack of moon is causing us no distress due to our ability to see as if we had night vision, which of course we have, now that we are a frigging fulltime nocturnal button man-beast from the Universe's Horror Back Lot.

When not being able to see our hideous reflection in the Jeep's side mirror, because of being bit by a vampire, we tore it off to break the window. As we stand here, we are so extraordinarily monstrously hairy, I'm sweating.

After doing an endless battery of tests on us, while keeping us penned like a wild dog in a different Alienated-dimension, they fed our evolving blood nothing but nearly raw deer meat. They did this purely to see if we could still hold down solid foods and not upchuck on it. Sticking it in our face on a pole through an electrically charged exotic metal bars for what could've been hours or minutes, for all we know, they had us so sedated.

Finally Portal Lumping our hairball-ass down into what appears to be the wilderness of a sparsely populated winter vacation nook overlooking the East Lake Reservoir. We know the lay of the land because they briefed us in the same way they always do. We just know what we need to know when we need to use the information, 'Speak Thinking,' Jerry called it. Talking to our Junk DNA.

If Jerry is still controlling all this free flowing info into my Junk DNA and chilling snowdrift action we don't know. We hope he can hear what we are Speak Thinking about his butts right now. Other than our appearance and seemingly limited mobility, nothing has changed on this mission. We are assuming, everything and everyone is still in the game, and we are still the Alien Mobster on a marionette string.

Smoke is in only two of the chimneys of the six rental homes we can see. There's light in every window of the three facing the lake. They portal lumped us a half mile trek down a wooded hillside in what is ending up at times to be waste deep snow that is quickly getting deeper, making us stumble over fallen trees and stumps.

We clump like this from tree to tree making sure we're not spotted by owls or dogs. When Doc and Javier were controlling our wild escapism movements all of this outer space exertion seemed effortless. Now that we've evolved into a fulltime earthbound werewolf, somehow our ability to simply leap into the trees and fling our body about with the ease of a Vegas trapezes artist has left us on planetary footing. Very big beefcake footing at that, with toenails that unfortunately match our finger nails. Long, yellowish gray and sharp enough to instantly neuter us if we're not careful where to scratch.

We say this because we're standing behind the strong hardwood of a white oak, the same wood used to build the outer hull of the Revolutionary War frigate, the U.S.S. Constitution. When British cannonballs were deflected by the ship's resilient hull in the War of 1812, she was nicknamed "Old Ironsides. Though, we just use this one to hide behind, while writing our new name in the snow. "Monster!" Finally the human in us is having the need to empty our bladder. At least I still have control of our bowl movements, though the bump on our chest is oozing whitish yuck that freezes and flakes away in our hair. We were starting to wonder if we had lost all need.

The temperature being in the low teens has kept all the New Year's Eve revelers inside their rental homes. Even the sad-suck balcony smokers must be snug around the fireplace. No doubt sipping eggnog and butter rum, smoking dope or snorting away their children's inheritance. Actually being discovered by humans isn't really our concern until two men step out from behind another white oak, nearly making us involuntarily pluck their heads off.

"Friggin' a, Picasso. You are one hairy bastard."

"Sasquatch lives. What big teeth you got, grandma."

"Happy screw-off to you, both, thanks. And don't bother, Mac, you don't want to hurt yourself trying to wax clever. We know what we look like. Alien bastards."

"I can't wait to see you reintroduce yourself to that mutt of yours. Jesus, the little guy's liable to have an aneurism trying to hump your furry knees."

"Did you really come all this way to bust our balls?"

"Wouldn't touch them with a hot fire poker. You mind coverin' them."

"How come you don't look like a werewolf? Just a circus freak?"

"It's the blood mixture running through me."We pull the jacket closed. "Sorry, we were taking a long overdue pee when you showed up. Mind if we finish?" We turn and continue to pee. Bigfoot good, Sasquatch fun.

"What's all this 'we' shit?" Mike asks.

"I need to explain this shit to you guys?"

"More than one of yous in there. We get it," Mac says.

"Whatever."We finish pissing, and turn back around.

213

"You know what, after meetin' the other one, I ain't gonna miss this Picasso one minute."

"Yeah, Picasso, this clone of yours ain't such a bad raw egg. You should try bein' as likeable some of the time. You might even get somewhere in life."

"Likeable? You don't want to hug me, Mike?"

"Puttin' some pants on would help me not want to shoot your ass and hang your one-of-a-kind head on my wife's living room wall."

"How much you think we can get for him all taxidermied?"

"Cute. Our torn clothes dropped off down at the bottom of the hill. We're still growing. We got this coat out of a Maroon Jeep."

Mike looks at MacAroy. "You asshole, Picasso, that's my coat."

"Yeah, and my truck, they just gave it to me."

"Really, well thanks. I'll give it back when I'm done with it."

"Keep it. Cost me a fortune to get the hair and stink out."

"Thanks. Good thing you're still fat, Mike."

"Look, got a message from the Mook. He says your film is on its way here and bein' hand-delivered by that fruit-brat kid you're making the film with.

"Junior? He's delivering it personally?"

"Yeah, he and you know who?"

"You ask who, we're supposed to shoot you in the big foot."

"His Jerryness."

"You got it. We're to meet the kid at the door as security. But truth bein', once he's inside we go way undercover like you didn't see us before. We're to shoot anything that tries coming in after you."

"You know, bang-bang, in the head, drag them out into the snow and watch them dissipate-dead."

"We talking Mary's gang?"

"Yeah. Apparently you stuck your pecker in a hornet's nest and didn't get them all. Jerry ain't so sure Mary won't show up trying to take what's left of you with them. Seein' we done it before, we get to do it again."

"There's another Mook character you don't want to meet again," Mac says. "The one that got away from your apartment that night. Not the one you chopped up in Fraser Park."

"He's one of his bad clones."

"Yeah, he's bringin' in a chopper, or what looks like one."

"It ain't our Mook, so off his ass."

"Why are they being so visible?"

"Why not just Blip in and Blip away?"

"You asking us these questions, Mr. Think Speak?" Mike looks at Mac. "Maybe not all of them can Blip, not all of them are able to function as holograms. As we were warned, it's a Jerryless grid you got to get let on."

"We don't know all the details, Picasso. Something about being exiled from it thanks to you and your pooch."

The answer comes to me. "You're right. You guys seem to be cozy with all this Alien stuff. What gives? Are you guys clones already?"

This thought startles them. "Hell no," Mac says. "Are we?"

"You hear something like that?"Mike asks.

"It's just that you guys are so eager to put your lives on the line."

"You get your life back, we get ours back. Only we don't get to walk like you do. We just get reinstated back onto the force with all retirement and promotions back in place if all goes as planned."

"As planned? Are there plans I don't know about?"

"You know these freaks. They give you just what they want you to know at the moment you need to know it. We're thinkin' you know the score. One of yous doesn't leave in the condition you arrived.

"Great. What's next?"

"You wait for the film. You watch the film. You die laughin'. We laugh last."

"This Jozeph guy, so you have met him?"

"Yeah, he ain't so bad. Not as big of a wise guy as you. He doesn't seem to have the big chip on the shoulder that I'd like to knock off yours at least twice a week just lookin' at you."

"So he remembers you guys?"

"Sure, he knows we're involved with that last thing," Mike says. "Only he seems to have a twisted recollection of it. He seems to think Jetty had a nervous breakdown and offed himself over losing Claire to your dog and failing to kill you."

"Only us know it was Jerry, the Magical Man, givin' him the high hard one. He probably jumped for the tree and killed himself trying to get away," Mac says.

"Jozeph thinks we're there to protect him from a certain dangerous guy askin' to see the film tonight because the Burn sent us. The guy he met on the train. The one that offed them other two guys and threw them out in the mountain snow like some mass murdering maniac, we both always knew you were."

"Very funny. So, he's expecting Boli?"

"Yeah, he only knows this person is dangerous and that he should carry a gun we got him permitted locally for."

"And made sure he knew how to use it. Which he does nicely on his own accord since you practiced, remember."

"So Jozeph is packing?"

"He ain't got the balls to use it if you ask me. But yeah, that's the scenario so far."

"So far? This is sounding weak."

"Shit happens. Jerry just said to make sure you go down for the count unless you decide to walk away right now. But to make sure nobody but him gets the body when it's done."

"I'm not walking away without seeing Bubba, Claire, and the cut film footage."

"Then you got to decide which one of yous will walk back out of that house when it's finished."

"One way or the other, Picasso. You understand? Nothing is personal this time. We bring Javier in, dead or alive, we're back on the official radar. You get away from us, even hairy like this, we're in it for everything on paper. But all this other worldly shit goin' down continues and you know Mary and her kind will catch up with you eventually. And you know what we mean."

"She's got the Russians working with her, talking to our DNA."

"She wants your blood. Dead or alive."

"So, you ready for this?

"I think so," I tell them.

"He thinks so."

"There's one more thing. Jerry said that your inability to do the things that you used to do, you know climb trees and fly like a winged squirrel, is only temporary and will be back to normal."

"See ya across the road," Mac says.

"Hey, if either of you don't make it home in one piece, I'm sorry, okay, I never meant for you guys to be involved in any of this."

"Shit, Jozeph, we brought this on ourselves. We made a choice years ago when Jetty came knockin' to fill our pockets and keep our mouths shut. Shootin' down that little guy at the bar that night, that nut case, shit, how could we know it would lead us all to this?"

"We all lied. It bound us together," we say, knowing that there is more truth to it than we all care to know.

"This is a good opportunity for us to put things back where they should be. All three of us."

"You get out of line on the other side of this night and we'll bust your butt straight up. No specials, down the straight and narrow, with us."

"I'll look forward to it."

"Good."

"Then let the New Year's bell toll for those who don't walk out."

They turn away, faces sadden, knowing this is the end of the road for at least one of me, if not all of us. I watch them go down the last part of the hill until they get to the house and stand at the door facing the street. Apparently, they already introduced themselves and are just getting back at their post.

In the windows we can see movement in front of the lights but we can't make what merriment is going on inside.

39

Once a property manager always a property manager. So we take in the furnished four-bedroom, two and a half bath. It's a funtastic waterfront tri-level home with a great long distance view over the sound to the adjacent mountains. There's also a furnished lakeside three-season cabana overlooking a new deep water dock for swimming, fishing, and boating.

But now, the house is a frozen no-vacancy this New Year. It's filled to the brim with the beautiful, the adorable, the voice and body of Claire Davis. With her is Bubba Dog, the snugglest non-shedding actor in showbiz, plus two young butchy-cute, but snooty lesbian production types, and my one and only clone, the ever so naive, Jozeph Picasso. He's now formally listed in the Trades as the hot, not so young Hollywood writer/director, slash suspected murderer that supposedly got away with killing four of his piglet tenants.

Wish we had bought something like this instead of our Alien Vortex of an apartment building, The Mystery Towers Magical Tour. If renters stayed away in droves before, wait until they get a load of us now. Only the sick need apply, and usually that's all that do.

"Here they come, Picasso."

"Mook?"

"It's me. Don't turn around."

"What's happening?"

"Take this."

"What is it?"

"It'll lighten your load. Eat it quick."

Floating in front of us is a piece of what looks like chocolate. We pop it into our mouth and it dissolves' immediately. My feet are no longer rooted to the ground. Note, I said my. Not ours, apparently whatever they gave me, put me back on top of the sensory chain.

"You're not here?"

"Not since you poked my eyes, Picasso. But there's that other me. I want you to take him out. Hear me. Do not let him get out of this mountain resort. I want him out of our way, once and for all."

"I'm not doing your dirty work."

"Picasso, if you don't get him here, he's to go to LA next to take out your friends. Make you come get him."

"Shit."

"Yes, and you're in it very deep. Now, Mary's got three other guys with her. All Alien. All inhabiting clones of someone you know. This will end nothing, but will get you in and out of the house."

"You can't help me?"

"You know I can't."

"But she tried to take you out. Shot you long distance. Isn't that against the Alien Council rules?"

"Mary is no longer playing by the rules. She's desperate and has no plans of letting us take her out completely or ban her from the planet, without a complete drag down cat fight. She'll expose us all if she has to. That's why she wants to test your blood. She needs all the help she can get. She thinks your blood will make her legally, if not logically, loveable to the Council again."

"Yeah-yeah, I heard all the good news."

"Turn around now."

I turn around and coming my way is a laser shot that nips me in the thigh as I bound fifteen feet up into the tree above me.

Man, that stings, and smells of smoldering hair that follows me all the way up here. The person pointing his lazar at me is not the Mook's clone, only one of Mary's Alien clone friends. But Mooky is right as usual, I've seen and feared him before. It's Victor Castro, crazy dog shit man, who last left his dissipating forehead parts all over my Corvair's dashboard. Could this be? Why do I ask these insipid things knowing what I know now? Of course this is why he could take so much punishment and keep on running. He was a human clone being used by an Alien. This is just another Victor Castro looking to give me more shit, and most likely being used by the same Alien. For all I know, there could be tens of him running around or waiting to be occupied. A depressing thought at best.

I can't hang around to find out. So with a single leap I land behind him. Before he can turn to laser off my arm, I pull his head and neck out of his body. Red blood, this one is still human. What a mess. But I don't have time to think about it because before the body hits the ground a laser cuts him in half and takes off three of my fingers on my right hand. "Son-of-a-bitch!"

I turn and a second Victor is standing in the road pointing his weapon at me, lasering away an eight foot pine that I'm trying to hide behind. I'm dead to right. Before I can do a thing about it, some kind of net is thrown over me and I'm dragged back up the hill. What the hell is this? I fight with all my might but even with all my Alien Werewolf powers I'm unable to break free. I reach up and touch my portal lump and I'm out. Holy shit, did that just work? Did I just learn how to use my portal lump? I touch it again, and I'm twenty yards back up the hill. Shit this is working. Could the Alien in me be using my lump to survive?

"Are you controlling this Mook?"

"Keep moving, Picasso."

"Shit, it's not me. I follow the line to where the net was dragging me. There is no cable, wire or rope. But the net still drags up the hill to what looks like a normal soundless helicopter. I touch my lump, and feel myself settle into one of its seats behind the unsuspecting Mook. I sense that this machine is far from being anything manmade. It has a succinct sensation of being motorized by a powerful soundless turbine engine, spinning main rotor blades with absolutely no change in torque. Definitely not manmade.

The Mook Clone continues to reel in the net having no idea I'm not in it. He pulls it inside wanting to stick me with something narcotic and stops when realizing he's not alone. He lunges at me and I grab his hand with the needle, pulling his arm out of his socket and hit him with it. The needle plops to the flooring as the second Castro makes the door. I scoop the needle up and stab his forehead with it. He drops, his face skimming the door jam, his laser gun landing in the Mook Clone's lap.

The Mook Clone picks it up with his working hand, yellow yuck dripping from this armless shoulder and I grab him, turning the laser gun back at him and split his head in two. Whatever the electrical panel was behind us also takes a direct hit. A hissing starts out of the damage. So I dive out, when Blip the whole contraption is transported somewhere else.

"Can't have Alien War Ships lying junked in wooded areas now, can we, Jozeph? You stupid, troublesome prick."

Crap, she's got the drop on me from behind. "Mary, we need to talk this out."

"We're way beyond talking."

"If you want my blood, I'll give it to you."

"Yes, you will. Hold your hand out."

I do and a laser skims the missing finger joints and the bleeding nearly stops, but the pain is like picking up a hot bacon fry plate. "Thanks, a lot."

"Can't have you wasting all that blood."

"I'm willing to help you if you help me."

"I'd rather split you in half. Pull out your heart and teach it to run my refrigerator. Or should I simply pull out your vertebra like you did to my best two clones? You filthy canine beast."

"Let's work this out. I'm serious."

"So am I. You've destroyed centuries of my work. I plan to get even one bone at a time. Don't turn around. Just know I've got you dead to right. You understand how hard it is to create a perfect clone? A clone that retains everything about you, past, present and future?"

"I just want to watch my film."

"Fine, I'll get you a copy and make you watch it a thousand times as you bleed out."

"Please, Mary."

"Yes, beg, Picasso. I want to hear you beg."

"I want to see my dog one more time. I want to say goodbye to Claire Davis and watch my film before you take me. Just don't take me alive."

"Do you think I'm gonna let you join that other pain in the ass in there. Let you become whole again, after what you've done to my last two good clones?"

"Please?"

"Take one step back. Don't turn. One step."

"Jerry won't let you take me alive. You've got to know he's watching all this."

"Of course I do."

"I don't get it."

"You never will, Jozeph. Take that step and we are out of here."

I take that step and two silenced shots fire to either side of me and a yellow yuck washes over me from behind. "Oh, shit."

"You okay, Picasso?"

"Yeah, but I'm bleeding pretty good."

"This shit is already dissipating. Give it a few seconds. Okay, she's beyond coming back."

"Where you hit?"

"The thigh. My fingers."

"Shit."

"What's the matter?"

"You've lost a lot of blood from the looks of things."

"I'm feeling a little light headed."

"What do we do?"

"Here, take my belt, tie it around there."

MacAroy pulls his belt off and hands it to me. I sit down and have a look. Oh damn, my muscle is showing, but the lazar seemed to have cauterized a lot of the damage. "Wasn't there another one?"

"We took him out."

"You've got five minutes before your film arrives. How do you suppose you get your girl and dog alone?"

"My guess is Junior has already seen it. And the two production girls won't be allowed."

"Are you telling us Jerry's setting that kid up with them?"

"I don't know. He's the producer, but they are lesbians."

"Shit, we gotta start producing films. This security shit ain't paying off with any of the special dividends."

"Try unemployable filmmaker and see how much loving you get."

"Your little buddy ain't doing so bad."

"He's had her?"

"Calm down, Romeo. We don't think so."

"He's only been here since this morning."

"Did she kiss him when he showed up?"

"Kiss? No I didn't see anything like that. A hug and she took the dog. But I'm pretty sure she kissed the dog."

"Bubba, she kissed Bubba and not me?"

"Look at him, he's jelly-belly of his own dog."

"You guys don't understand. I don't know where this relationship is heading."

"My guess, she'll tell you tonight. She put your shit in her room."

"She did?"

"His bag and computer."

"If you want, we'll tape it for you. We still got the bug on the dog."

"Thanks. No."

"How about for ourselves?"

"Shut up."

"Come on, we're playing."

"Well stop. This is serious."

"It's just sex, Picasso, happens all the time in Hollywood."

"Exactly. This is Hollywood. A successful Hollywood relationship lasts about as long as a good paying production and publicity tour."

"You think she's playing you?"

"I don't know. I haven't been there. He has."

"Well, the new Picasso doesn't seem to be sweatin' it out. He's having a good time."

"I need to know if she loves me."

"What you need to do is get her in bed and make her love you."

"Or, you know, the clone, but by then you'll be there, all of you. If you play your cards right."

"That's right. I'll be there by then. If I go through with it."

"Then you'll know."

"I need to know first."

"Shit, Picasso, why complicate things? Just go in there, watch the film and we end things neatly. Don't mess this up."

"Shut up. It's not that easy. I'm confused. I need to know if she loves me, or if this is just a Hollywood fling because we're in a film together."

"Why?"

"I love her. Jozeph loves her. I don't want her crushing me if I'm all of me or not. Not after what I've gone through to get me all here."

"You're messed up, Picasso. You need to just take it easy or you'll put pressure on this and she'll know you're weak. It's a big turn off."

"Thank you, Dear Flabby."

"Suit yourself."

"I can't go in there looking like this."

"They're expecting Boli, right?"

"Shave."

"That's your answer? Shave? I'll grow this back sitting here."

"Look, unless you've got a better idea, there's a balcony access to the second floor landing. We left it open. You've got to be quick because they'll feel the chill. But if you're quiet you can hang up there and watch the film."

"What about your dog?"

"If I know Bubba he's curled up asleep, somewhere warm."

"Good luck."

"I'd have my head in her lap if I was him."

"If I was Jozeph, too."

"Wait. If Boli isn't there, they won't show the film."

Just then, a shiny black Land Rover pulls up out front and Junior Burnstein jumps out, lugging a backpack.

"He's got it on DVDs."

"What did you expect?"

"I don't know. Certainly not being a Bipedal Humanoid."

"Jesus Christ...."

"What?"

"You're shedding."

"What?" I look down and sure enough the hair on my body is dropping off in clumps into the snow. I open the coat and I'm nearly naked flesh. Pubic hair and all.

"Have some respect, Picasso."

"Cover up, for Christ's sakes."

"What the hell is going on?"

"My guess is Jerry is inviting you in for a drink."

The tailgate door opens on the Land Rover and in it is a suit case. "You don't suppose?"

"I'm sure he'd rather you walk in like that, but I'm bettin' Jozeph and the others would prefer if you put some clothes on."

"But I'm...." I look at my hand and it's stopped bleeding. I look at my leg and it's stopped too. ".... a fast healer."

"Ain't you cold? You're standing in the friggin' snow."

"Cold? Oh, shit! Cold, cold, cold!" I touch my portal lump, and as fast as I can say portal lump I'm standing behind the Land Rover doing my best to find something to stand on before I freeze to death or my toes fall off.

Blip. I look up and the Mook is standing there beside me.

"Don't say thanks."

"I won't, I'm freezing to death, you alienator."

"Use your time wisely, Picasso. You only have a couple hours max and what's going on with you will reverse itself."

"This is temporary? Why are you messing with me, Mooky?"

"I'm not, it's from those test they did on you. What I gave you will only mask the appearance of not being who you are inside. It's a derivative of something the original four Alien Werewolves have worked on since they've been here. Only it hasn't worked so well on them. Instead it killed them. But the key here is that they will not see the Jozeph Picasso inside you. Only Bolivar Agustin, AKA, Javier Sanchez, dirt bag drug Mexican Cartel Don. So you're good for as long as this stuff lasts."

"Killing them? You gave me something that could've killed me?"

"Relax, it works on you. I knew that before I gave it to you. You have no idea how excited some Aliens are about this development."

"Yeah, I'm getting warm and fuzzy all over about this, you Alien cold sore."

"Apparently, there's no effect on your big mouth syndrome."

"Hand me that."

Mook hands me a scarf and I cover my privates. "Look, you still have all the abilities inside of you and they will come back as will the hair and nails. Instantly, if you call upon them."

"What do you mean?"

"You know what I mean. Don't call upon them in there."

I look at my hands. My two kinds of fingernails are back to being at least human again. Both my feet are too.

"Okay. Thanks." I step to the open tailgate and smack my forehead. I step back. "Ah, shit. What the hell?"

"You didn't notice that you're almost six foot five?"

"Crap, these growing pains hurt." I start to shiver and shake into slow convulsions. So I climb in back of the truck.

"Help before I freeze to death." I put on socks. I pull on a black sweater next, then dark green slacks, bypassing underwear. Finally furry lined boots and a ski coat. I'm starting to feel human again. My shivering slows down as I hug myself. There's a benefit to being an Alien werewolf-slash-apelike creature in the winter, but I'll trade them all in for being a frozen human lollypop anytime.

"Jozeph, it was nice knowing you."

"What? Wait, Mook, this is it? This is goodbye?"

"Yeah. Don't act all teary eyed. You go in, you stay in and your clone walks out after bagging your girl. Boli is captured and killed before he turns back into your hairiness and dies. You don't need me anymore. If I reintroduce myself to you, you won't know me, so I won't. Watch yourself, okay. Don't let Hollyweird bullshit get to you. Many of them aren't human anyway. Sell that building as soon as you can. Mystery Towers is a vortex, in case you haven't noticed, into something deeper and darker than anything you ever can imagine."

"I knew there was something weird about it. Who really built it?"

"Who do you think?"

"Jerry?"

"He had it built by someone he possessed for a woman he never acquired. It's a very small portion in this dimension that links itself to a much larger, brighter dimension then any of us have ever seen."

"You mean...?

"Where Jerry lives, and stores himself away?"

"Up there?"

"Maybe. No one else knows. Jerry is kind of like the Universe itself. It's there, we can see it, travel in it, but we don't know why or how it ends. It's even a mystery to us. As is Jerry. We only know we are part of something bigger than all of us. I will be sending two friends of yours by to suggest you sell it and buy a house. You will. Relax, you're meant to sell it as part of the deal. Move out, you won't even rent there, your tenants will no longer be your concern."

"Wait, I've got people there who depend on me."

"It's business, Jozeph, they will get over it. They always do or move on."

"But, there's...."

"There's Erin, we know."

"Yes.

"Take her with you, if this actress thing doesn't work out."

"Come on."

"Then don't. It's only a suggestion. She's a good person for you, Jozeph. Put the thought in your head now and act on it when it comes back to haunt you."

"Haunt me?"

"It will be as close to a contact from me as you're gonna get.

It's a gift from both Jerry and I, to say thanks. Without love the Universe has no meaning. Jerry told me that once. It's something to think about. Even for someone beautiful like me."

"Wait. What about all that stuff about me killing you eventually? How does it end this way?"

"Who do you think you stabbed in the forehead with that syringe, beating him with his own arm? That was very sick by the way. Even for a vampire infested werewolf."

"Oh yeah, that was your clone. So this is it. You finally saw me naked, now you're out the door?"

"Bite me, werewolf boy. This is it because they'll assign me to some other human stiff to make sure he stays on track. But let me tell you this, and know this, Picasso, you're one lucky human. No other human I know has ever walked away this cleanly from as deep as you are in all this. Cloned or otherwise. I've buried them all or they live on as clones in places they were never meant to live. Not all of them good and not all of them here. You're unique to me so I congratulate you on surviving all this. You got Jerry vouching for you. That you'll somehow keep your mouth shut, and that you'll never know any of this happened to you."

"What about those around me? Some of them know all of this."

"Mike and MacAroy? They made their own deal with the Council. They mess up, step out of line, or let anything happen to you, we take them out. If you don't speak of it to Erin, she will soon let it go."

"What about J.J., he had that sun burn from working with Jerry? What about him."

"Cloned. His human form died two days ago. No one, not even Erin knows about it. He never knew what happened to him in the first place, outside of getting a perfect tan and a Hollywood deal."

"Stacey Carson does?"

"Stacey is now a clone and one of us. She has been since she messed with you and that dog of yours."

"What happened there, to J.J.?"

"Jerry used him to transport people, like he did you. There's an after burn. You got one too, apparently, the Alien hair protected you. It looks good on you without the hair. Makes you look rich. Relax, J.J. didn't know what he was getting into, didn't know Jerry used him. His perfect clone is getting his own series on NBC for it, right. He's a surfing detective, in an action dramedy. He gets superpowers from some kind of chemical waste that was dumped in barrels back in the forties. They are leaking into the ocean off the cost of Santa Monica. "Consider It Done, Matt Dunn."

"Are you kidding? Who the hell changed it into a sci-fi concept?"

"Don't laugh. Your agent sold it on a one-line pitch and you got two networks bidding over it. You'll get both created by and executive producer credits. That is, if your clone walks out of here."

"Wait. I have no say in the matter of someone rewriting my idea?"

"Wasn't your deal. It was his, J.J.'s. He changed it."

"Why sci-fi?"

"That's the concept he wanted to do. He waved your okay, so you had no say in the matter. It's already in development as you Hollywood clods say."

"But I'm directing films."

"Yeah, white boy, you got a hell of a life ahead of you. Destiny is only the direction we set for you. Everything else is just pure hard work or luck on your part. Congrats."

"So none of this, all the bullshit and my success in Hollywood, meeting Claire Davis, Bubba getting his acting job on her show, it wouldn't 've come about if that Cocker Spaniel hadn't crapped healing stones inside my apartment building?"

"Things would've been different. That's all. You still had Uncle Jerry watching and using you. You still will. You just won't know it."

"The first time we talked, and you mentioned, It. You knew all this connection between Jerry and me, and how he taught me through my Junk DNA, didn't you."

"Some, not everything, I learned shit, too. And yeah, I lied to you. Had to. Telling you too much would've freaked you out. Jerry and I go way back. We're not always on the same side. But now you know how complicated this all is. This little bit of your life, this moment, is just a pin prick to what is really happening around you."

"I'll never know if and when he's doing me, will I?"

"Not the slightest idea. But there might be moments in your life when the physical pleasure is just too great to bear and your bliss will be too intense to be really true, and that moment most likely will be Jerry jumping your bones."

"He's not just doing this for me, is he? That sick bastard."

"Hologramming is the only way to travel, my human. Like I said, it's why we developed the network to this level to keep him at bay and out of our pants."

"Why would Mary's clones show up here without one?"

"We are keeping her out of the system. She hasn't completed a data base on her own yet. We need to find her before she develops one and logs on. Which you will continue to do, hunt her, if you walk out of the house like this."

"What about the Russian Scientist knowing about our DNA?"

"They've gone public with what Mary's group told them, so we're dealing with it internally."

"You've taken them, cloned them?"

"Something like that."

"How am I safe, either way, with Mary out there?"

"That's a good question. Just know we are monitoring her movements. And we'll grab you up without you knowing it if she tries anything. You'll find her for us if you stay as you are."

"Comforting."

"Once you leave this behind, you are worthless to her and her people. It wouldn't be worth the revenge and chance loosing what Jerry will do to her supporters every chance he gets. I'm sure you know by now that Jerry can be very loving. But he's the most dangerous thing on this planet, on any planet."

"I need to get out of this cold."

"Listen, really listen. Focus on what I'm saying to you."

So I do. It's very quite up here.

"What do you hear?"

"Ringing, chirping in my ears like I'm standing in a bug filled woods. It's been there since Stacey Carson tried to take my head off with a revolver. She punched a hole into my kitchen. It's maddening. I had it looked at. The doctors call it tinnitus. There's no cure."

"You sure?"

"Do I want to know?"

"That's us. Your subconscious is aware of us and that's what you've been told it is to keep it from driving you nuts."

"You mean like lopping off an ear or nose?"

"We'll be in there, monitoring you if you stay like you are now."

"Great, I'm feeling all warm and fuzzy again."

"Feel your right ear."

I do, knowing there's a lump in there, some kind of cyst I've had since I was just a kid out on the Michigan farm. "Let me guess."

"What looks and appears to be just tissue is really a tracking and monitoring devise comprised of human DNA in your tissue. Your clone has all of this. He, like millions of human clones or otherwise, have no idea why these things appear. It's us."

"But I've heard...."

"You've heard rumors at Alien conventions, Contact in the Desert, at Joshua Tree, weekends of exploration into ancient aliens, human origins, UFO sightings, and the need to know if this tissue in your ear is something we Aliens put there."

"Yes. I've also read about it, even heard a DR. Steven Greer speak once at a writers group at UCLA. I've seen the websites and Facebook pages. But I never attended a UFO conference or thought about it."

"And that is what we want, you not to think about it. Trust me, they don't know squat about anything that is really going on. They don't know what you know. What you're about to forget."

"You feed them false information to dilute the truth?"

"At its best. There are thousands of books about us, but no proof."

"There's a market for false information, you mean."

"Yes, they're called novels. Never think or say it's real."

"I won't remember anyway, right?"

"That is the plan."

"Wait. It might not work?"

"At worse you both will die. You were right in the cabin. But right now, if you don't mess it up, your clone will live a long prosperous life, kids and all that upper middleclass life style."

"But if you add crazy me to the mix, then what?"

"Yes, then what is right."

"I'm freezing. Is there a point to this that I need to worry about?"

"Don't be so sensitive to what people think about you. Walk the world being who you want to be as if every day is a new invention of yourself. No matter what your failures have been in the past. Wake up every morning with a clean slate. And sleep like there's no tomorrow. The world is a paradise if you let it. It's hell if you make it. You dig, white boy?"

"I dig, Mooky. So long."

"One last thing. If you discover that any of these dark memories of this life haunts your clone, don't let on. Don't acknowledge it or express it in anyway. Don't even think about telling anyone. Or you will be back. I'll be back and all this will be back like a hurricane of trouble, an earthquake of pain, and a tsunami of consequences. It will end up with them sucking you back into all this or they will put you away like all the others. Then Mary will come looking for you, to see if any DNA of this form was transferred by charged memory electrolytes to your clone when your final being shifted over to him."

"The others, you mean locked in a white cell in fetal positions."

"Go pet your dog, Jozeph. Just keep in mind that Jerry picked this house out personally for this vacation. Did you hear me?"

"Wait, that was this me huddled down whimpering, and not him?"

"Hey, the hot bet amongst the Council is that you blow this."

"So, say I die in there, what happens to this body, this mutated blood? Wait, did they take samples already?"

Mooky gives me his knowing smile. "I'm betting on you, Jozeph. You were the first to make Mystery Towers work. The revolution of evolution is coming. Don't make us losers. Don't let them try again."

Blip! And the Mook is gone.

Don't let them try again? My blood didn't work for them yet!

40

My whole life people have bet on me to fail. But I stand here at the door that leads to the end of my torment and the beginning of a new life for me. Jozeph Picasso, fledging Hollywood filmmaker is about to take flight into the rest of his unaware-of-the-truth-life.

I'm about to leave a past life not designed by me. One built by the circumstance thrust upon me by buying Mystery Towers and taking the Magical Mystery Towers Tour into the Alien Underworld. I, Alien Mobster, on my very final mission for the Alien Council, am to kill myself and give them my morphing blood to study. Science Fiction at its very worst because for me, for this composite me, it has turned out to be the worst kind of nonfiction... the happening to me right now variety.

Knowing I can't enter the house until I'm invited in due to the vampire in me, I look closely for my distorted reflection in the beveled window beside the door. How fitting to not be able to see my face and body contorted in the frosted glass. I have no reflection, therefore I do not shine. A pity, considering this may be my last chance to see myself, after having dressed in a hurry, while freezing in the dark.

I probably wouldn't look half bad in a funhouse kind of reflection. Say what you want about Jerry, he's got great taste in clothing. Being six foot five weighing at least two fifty is a little strange at best. I'm wondering if the Jozeph Picasso who met me on the train just that once will notice that I am now five inches taller. He was sitting while telling me to f-off, so maybe he won't. But knowing myself, I will. Or he will. Maybe Bubba will. It's complicated.

Do I knock or ring the bell? I can't sneak around back where Mike and MacAroy left the second landing door open. I want to see my film. Maybe I should've asked how this was arranged. I hear voices from inside, raised voices so I put my ear to the door. Very cold, but it's not hard to figure who is saying what.

"He's coming here, why?"Jozeph is not happy.

"I told you, my dad and his people met and he set it up." Junior is defending himself. "I had nothing to do with any of this shit, I swear."

"You should've talked him out of it."

"I tried. Do you actually think I wanted to fly in from LA on a private jet to watch your stinkin' PG-13 movie again on New Year's Eve? I had plans. Great plans, involving elicit triple-x sex and illegal drugs with many beautiful people I don't know or will ever see again. I'm talking bodacious worldwide women that only we young rich and blameless can afford."

"Didn't you hear me, peter brain? Are we clear on what I saw and heard on the train here? I told the Burn this. This guy, this Bolivar, if that's even his real name, is nuts, dangerous, an animal, capable of killing all of us with his bare hands."

"You're freakin' out, Picasso."

"You're damn right I am. I'm tired of people trying to kill me for no apparent reason."

"Then we're on the same page. This guy says he wants to distribute the film and is offering a large sum of money to just have the first look. Why piss him off?"

"So it's about the money. It figures, dealing with the Burn and his boys, it's always about the money."

"How much money," Claire asks?

"It's a nonrefundable deposit towards the distribution south of the border. Only the Spanish version."

"Even the Burn wouldn't be greedy enough to pull a fast one on this guy," Jozeph says.

"Are you kidding, he set it up. Some guy with a black hat showed up, a Buckley Jones. The money is all real. It's on hold in our production account. I'll show you if you want to see it. Cashable at the bank in the morning."

"How much, Junior?" Jozeph has had enough of this game. This is art to him. He knows what kind of killer game Boli is playing.

"The shooting budget of the film, not post."

The room goes silent. For a long time, so I pull my ear away and look into the window. Golden light flickers just inside to the right of the door. I can smell that it's a fireplace.

232

Jozeph is pacing the room looking out the back patio door overlooking the lake. I can see his reflection but not quite enough to see what he's thinking. Knowing myself, he's kicking himself for okaying what's about to happen. He turns from the window. He looks at Claire, saying something I can't hear but my guess is he wants to know if she is in on it. She shakes her head and comes to him and stands before him, looking him in the eyes to make her point. I can see Jozeph falling for the baby blues. Shit, he's gonna invite me in to see the film. The real Crazy Kind Of Love.

So, I go to ring the bell but my index finger is missing so I ring the door bell with my thumb. Seconds go by as I wait. I'm sure they are scrambling to figure out who will open it. Until finally someone loses, and it opens to reveal the unfriendly production assistant who scorned me many times. She stands there blocking the door.

"Can I help you?"

"I would appreciate it, Debbie. You mind?"

"Excuse me. What do you want?"

"I want for you to back out of the door and invite me in." What I'd really like is to show her that I have her name tattooed on my ass. But I don't go there.

"How do you know my name?"

"If you want I'll leave it out of the Spanish credits. Now back off."

"How rude."

"It's okay, Debbie, let him in," Junior says.

"He hasn't even introduced himself yet."

"Bolivar Agustin." I lean in closer to Debbie so only she and I can hear. "Now step aside before I twist off your arm and stick it up your uptight bottom."

"Excuse me!"

"Debbie, let him in, you're letting out the heat," Jozeph yells as he comes to the foyer to save me. "Come in, come in," he invites me, catching bad eyes from Debbie. Good, she doesn't even like my clone.

Debbie fights the urge to slam the door in my face and steps aside. Her short cropped dikish hair beading at the hairline with angry sweat. I can tell she still likes me. Some things never change regardless of whose skin I'm wearing.

Jozeph moves over to me as I step inside. A roaring see-through fire place is right there warming me to the bone. I step as close to it as I can as Jozeph leans in close, then leans back as if he suddenly realizes that I'm much taller than he remembers, looking up at me.

"Listen, I don't care what you're offering for my film. You are not getting in bed with this picture."

"Is that so?"

"I know what you did on that train and there's no way I'm letting a murdering scumbag like you profit from my hard work."

"Perhaps I should just kill you right now then and finish the film myself."

"Did you just threaten me?" Jozeph is actually surprised. Great, they made me naive and stupid.

"I'm gonna make you the same offer my boys gave Burnstein. Show me the film or I will make sure you don't finish it."

"Listen... Burn said yes because you threaten to kill me not him?"

I push him out of the way and walk into the room where I find Junior and Claire waiting for me. Ah Claire Davis, a sight for werewolf eyes. The dawn-shimmer off an ocean blue. "Hello, sorry to barge in on you all like this. As you've heard I'm only in America for a short time and I'm looking to take this film's distribution rights with me."

"Hi, ah, Junior. Ernie Burnstein is my father."

"I won't hold your father being a prick against you."

"Thanks."

"Hello, I'm Claire Davis."

"Yes you are. I'm a big-big wolfish fan of yours."

"Mine? Why thank you."

"I love your standup. I've seen you live a dozen times. Your show with Bubba, I even cross the border to watch it."

"You do not."

"Sure I do. Sometimes I even have to shoot at people to make it to a decent TV set on time." I can see in the corner of my eye that Jozeph has had enough of this crap already. But Claire for some reason is eating it up. My guess is Jerry has her and if I were to squat and take a dump on the entry rug right in front of everyone she would find it charming, animalistic, and nostalgic of bygone gene pools.

"Come on, let's get this over with."

"Wait, I want to meet Bubba. Is he here?"

"Bubba." Claire calls softly and from behind an overstuffed chair a sleepy grunt emerges. "The poor thing didn't sleep a wink on the train. He's not feeling well."

"He's fine, just tired, aren't you, Bubba?"Picasso assures us.

Bubba grunts in agreement and blows snot.

234

"The wood fireplace is bothering him."

"What?"

"I, ah...." Crap, I said too much. "It's probably the fireplace. I can smell it. The wood smoke. You've got the flame up too high. Smoke is escaping the flue. It's getting into his nose."

"You've got dogs?"

"I did. Many. My brothers killed them. But the same thing would happen to one of mine."

"You pour man."

"I fixed all of them, trust me."

"Good."Claire is moving closer to me with every comment. Until she's nearly up against me. She's whispering in her softest of tones, as if we were all alone. "Did you really kill those men on the train?"

I move away from her and go over to kneel down next to Bubba. "Hey, boy." I reach out to him and he surprisingly rolls over and lets me give him scrubs. He suddenly sits up and looks at me strangely. Those scrubs are feeling way too familiar. I pet his head with my real hand. "It's okay, Bubba, daddy loves you."He looks at me. "Dogman?" I wink and stand back up. Bubba looks at me again, sneaking yet another peak around the chair as I move back closer to Claire.

"Which men are we talking about killing?"

"You mean there were others."She's actually getting turned on from the thought of Boli's violent nature. Oddly, I remember thinking the possibility of me as Picasso killing my tenants seemed to perk her interest when we first met. Her being involved with the likes of Jetty and his people. I'm starting to sense an underlining gun moll trend.

Looking at Jozeph, he's thinking the same thing. The first flaw we've seen in Claire's armor since she quoted the Burn over my script when this whole movie deal started. Just before I ended up a floater in the Tujunga Wash on my way to Hollywood oblivion. I look back at Claire and she's smiling up at me like she did that first time we met in her dressing room, with clear pools, a smile peeking on her lips.

I'll be damned. Jerry set this all up from the very beginning. I'll be an Alien's sister. Holy Follywood, Dogman, even that first time meeting with her in her dressing room for lunch. Maybe even all those wet days on the set when she seemed to want to help me get over my feelings of being put-upon by Hollywood's silver spoon spongers. She was there for me as I was shunned by anyone else worth doing show business with. It was her who held my hand during my deep dark Alien secret days. She could've even made me do my part in ridding Claire of Jetty Dazarrio.

Maybe Jerry arranged the deal with Burnstein by being Claire, and playing them, too, to get at Jetty all along. If so, then probably all those caps to go. The quick peeks of her ass in hot shorts while ordering at Aroma Coffee and Tea in Studio City. Was it all a very long intricate setup by Jerry to lock me into Claire? To implant the fantasy of me being with her? Even her dog walking, her falling for Bubba, was it all an Alien subterfuge? Shit, it's almost funny it's so clear to who I am now. But not to Jozeph. I can see he's taking all this real hard because he doesn't know the whole truth, the whole Alien back story, the Jerryness of it all. But I do. So I smile.

Could that be possible? Why not, my whole life has been one long Alien mockery of Jerry interventions. From the first time my mother and father laid eyes on each other out on the lake. To my first spark of life in my mother's womb. My haunting lonely childhood. All the way up to even this New Year's weekend dream of the impossible dream, of being loved by Claire Davis.

The Claire Davis interested in me is Jerry. Those lesbian interludes she was having during my last adventure with his Jerryness were all part of the long-term game. Is this truly why she so readily entered my life, hired my dog, and helped me get off the Hollywood never was list?

Looking at Jozeph, the poor sap hasn't a clue. He's a goner, setup for this moment, this purpose, to kill the man getting in his way of having Claire to himself. I pity him, because I pity myself. If I fall for this, I'm no better a man than Jetty. Is it possible they, these Aliens, Jerry, could be this devious, this farsighted into how to use me? Or is this just a random result of ongoing developing catastrophic events that has led us all to this Connecticut rental home tonight?

Are we all here as planned to witness me murdering myself? Is all of this misadventure to keep my rapidly evolving alienated blood from falling into the wrong hands? Does this blood pouring through my veins right now truly lead to Aliens of unscrupulous desires living openly here on Earth? Like we humans do, breathing, fornicating, and defecating our way into Heaven and/or Hell? Am I really the one? Am I the one human that gives them the key to unlock humankind as we know it? Do they fear a super race with humans knowing about our Junk DNA? Will they use my blood to stop this from happening?

Is this a test to see if Picasso has the capability of killing someone, even himself? If he's animal enough? Is it? Have they added that gene in him? The killer gene? Look at me, my clone. He's smitten, having ridden across the country with his dog on a rattling, drafty train in the middle of the winter so she could be with Bubba and not him. The Dogman Cometh after all.

The two lesbians stare me down, wishing I would just melt away. Why are they really here? Is it random? Are they part of the big picture? Being used, lied to like the rest of us? Are they even human? I stare back at them. They hate me, and fear the attention Claire gives me as much as Jozeph does. Damn, they're here for her, not just for each other.

"Jerry, you bastard."

Claire, is watching me have this revelation, this Alien epiphany, and leans in close. She's standing on her dainty tiptoes now to look into my eyes. These eyes are seeing the real deal now of why we are here. My eyes have the situation into an evenly stacked pile of Hollywood bullshit scripts. They are seeing the magic ink appear on pages where only I can see that the real gag is on me and my shadow, my clone, Jozeph Picasso. We Alien Mobsters."You figured it out quick, Boli. I'm proud."

"Kiss your ugly asses, Jerry."

"Put the DVD in, Junior," Jozeph says, watching us.

"Okay, but I'm not sticking around for this shit. I've seen it three times already. The guy gets the girl, and the other two get stuck with each other and a baby. And Debbie, Carmon, if you don't mind, the Burn said no one else sees the footage until he signs off on it."

"But...." Debbie says.

"Come on, I've got pot," Junior says pulling out a baggie.

"You've been in town two hours and you already scored?" Jozeph scorns him.

"I'm a rich spoiled Jewish kid. I can buy and sell anything I want wherever I am. But no, I brought with. Private plane, remember?"

"Try buying some brain cells. And take that shit outside."

"I'm in," Carmon says. Looking at Claire for approval.

"It's New Years. We'll have champagne in a bit."

"Come on, girls, I want to show you something."

I watch them climb the stairs. It's a big house and knowing Junior he'll have them both naked and laughing, showing them his private parts, before they come back down. Say what you want about the droopy-pants dip, he's got a self-possessed way into women's panties that neither I nor my clone have found.

"Can I get you something?" Claire asks me.

"I'll have a beer."

"Come on over here, the bar is stocked with at least ten kinds of bottled beer."

I follow her behind the bar, keeping an eye on Jozeph. He does not like this one bit. There's nothing he can do about it, so he turns his back to find a seat. I see him stop to watch the reflections in the glass doors. In particular, the lack of my reflection. His neck stiffens in silent alarm. Had he forgotten about the train? Or is he just concerned that I now know that he knows, and he knows that's not good for anyone in the house.

He doesn't turn to look at me. I see him doing his best to see why I'm not there, putting two and two together. What does he remember about Gray McGuiness being a real vampire? Had he doubted himself on the train? What did they leave him with to explain all that? My guess is enough, because he sees and knows that I am a vampire, and doesn't freak out about it, yet.

What would he do if he found out what I really am? Knowing me, I would be skeptical but cautious just the same. He reaches into his pocket and pulls out what I thought would be a weapon. It turns out to be a pen and note pad. He sits on a bar stool, facing the TV, waiting to take notes.

Claire turns to me, "Let me take your coat." She reaches out and cups my manhood. I'm not sure what to do so I don't move. Her hand travels up and takes my coat. Now I know why he gave me Boli's manhood. Not for me, not for Oli, for himself, the ultimate Alien pervert. She points to a bar refrigerator, "MGD?" I reach in for one as she takes my coat over to an entry closet. Leaving me snug in a naval blue turtleneck sweater, just a step away from the roaring fireplace that divides the entry bar area and the kitchen.

Looking through the flames I can see the kitchen is set up with snacks on the counters and desserts served up on trays. It's a little New Year's celebration in the waiting. Broken up by the arrival of mean old me. I sit as close to the fire as I can. The chill in my bones seeks out its oversized see-through hearth. From the looks of it, a man-size kettle would fit nicely. Perhaps that is what has happened in the past and why it's positioned up against the kitchen. Close to an entry door where I saw a high wood pile in the carport.

"I'll take a beer if anyone is offering," Jozeph says.

I can see it in Jozeph's eyes, hear it in his voice. The game is on already and Jerry is setting the rules. We're playing the basest game of all human traits, jealousy, and envy, the sinful coveting between two men over one woman. The Helen of Troy, the naval Battle of Actium over the love of Cleopatra, tinged even with a little of a Romeo and Juliet motif of men killing men, and even ourselves over an alluring woman pulling our manhood strings. She's turning us into murderous loutish medieval marionettes. Making us play that age old game of sexual conflict sprayed upon us in undetectable blood, like an animal sexual scent, us unsuspecting snappish male humans.

All done by a dastardly manipulating Alien bisexual cad, purely to pleasure Its own otherworldly control freak needs. A game It has honed from the beginning of time. From the time we first swung from trees as apes and lived in caves as sub-humans. It bred us like dogs to service Alien Kind as slaves and sex toys. Alien the Alfa and the most dangerous amongst us. Jerry is Claire now and I know Jerry shall not parish with us no matter how heartbroken It is in the end over both my pending demises. Jozeph doesn't see it as clear in his own eyes, but I do, through both our eyes. The game is on. The end of one of me is upon us. We are about to change our worlds forevermore.

The real question, the five hundred pound gorilla in this room is, can Jozeph pull the trigger? For sure, it's an Alien game of death and destruction. If I had my way there'd be nothing left of this me to leave the Alien pursuit to become human like Jozeph. All of this craziness is because in the end, they are not one of us. One of us whom they loath, collect, train, use, abuse, and deflower in so many ways it's nearly unimaginable to fathom the depths of their depravities.

I hate to think of all the travesties they've inflicted on humans over the centuries since Jerry found this planet. This Heaven of the Universe, this place they control but cannot yet truly inhabit. All because in the end of all ends, they are simply not one of us. They are not of human, Earth indigenes evolving DNA. This makes me smile, and even a small laugh bubbles out from my lips, knowing that perhaps they, without the blood in this sick evolving me, are still light years away from calling this paradise home. If only....

"Genuine Draft?"

"Yes, thanks."

"I'm drinking champagne. That's my glass." She points, so I fill it for her from the bottle stuck in the ice bucket.

41

The giant Alien pisser, if these bastards could relieve themselves again, is that I'm actually enjoying myself for the first time since this crazy holiday adventure started. Truly, sitting here, eating popcorn, drinking a beer with the woman I'd fancy falling crazy in love with while ravishing her body from head to toe endlessly until both our hearts sputtered to a stop. I would, if only I weren't a freak of Alien Nature, afraid to expose myself to myself.

Believe me, good old Boli and his prowess is spry and active inside of me, fighting like a mad man, trying to surface and take over. I'm in heat here. I can sense his animal instincts oozing from my every pore, that musk, that breeding tension that only the subconscious can detect or secret. I'm injected with Boli's brute nature, Alien Werewolf juiced, wanting, having to mate. I'm fighting it with all my Jozeph Picasso human rational not to grab hands full of her beautiful naturally blond curly hair and drag her away to my man cave. Caveman liveth inside of me and wants woman to make him cometh.

What's even weirder, is with the werewolf in me suppressed, I have this uncontrollable feminine urge to morph into something bat-like and flutter about the room. I suspect my visit into vampirism. I'm almost lit with glee. Worse, his Jerryness knows this. He is using this to tease me silly with knowing smiles gripped by just the two of us. No including Jozeph Picasso, the unfortunate sap. Just Claire Davis, fascinatingly sensual film goddess, the beauty, and who I am, the beast within, waiting to disintegrate into death by my own hands.

Whether or not Claire is really still human or a clone or just Jerithizugludimi using a human's body to get to me and my clone is in question. That matters not to me right now. I want her no matter what the stakes are. I want her in so many ways that I'm actually blushing under all this George Hamilton tan.

Claire sits way too close on the couch for just having met me. I'm a dangerous stranger, sharing her popcorn, knuckles brushing, fighting for a single kernel, giggling at all the right places in the script. Us watching her blossom on screen, tearing hell out of my script with her own style of brilliant adlibs. I almost forgot how delightfully talented she really is. Getting a chance to finally step out of her goodie-goodie sitcom role and actually play someone with vibrancy and nasty sex appeal.

Even though, in this script, Crazy Kind Of Love, she gets her comeuppance by getting caught cheating on her husband while trying to set him up to be murdered by the man she's having an affair with. All the while she is unwilling to admit that she has secretly loved the other man for many years. She comes in and out of his life, only when she's safely hidden in a committed relationship of marriage. At times I even find myself forgetting that I wrote and directed this footage. I can tell we've really got a shot at something good here, more so because of her wit than my script or directing. She is a natural, a truly gifted actress, a super star in the making... and perhaps Jerry's manipulative opportunity to shine on film.

Jozeph doesn't see it this way. He sits behind us on a barstool muttering and taking notes. In thinking, he's directed none of this on his own since being cloned from my lost leg, he sits there stewing about what he's seeing develop on the couch before him.

Claire is seducing this stranger, this madman who forced his presence into their lives. Who is ruining any chance of him spending the night with her in the same bed without his dog, and is looking to take over distribution rights to his baby. It's Jerry pulling the spider strings inside Claire. I'm just falling into the tangled web he's constructing. Jozeph is sadly falling full face into wanting to get me out of his life. Before I end up in that very bed with the woman of what he thinks his dreams are made from.

In truth, one of us must die, predestined, regardless, fools all of us, drifting on deadly currents of sexual foreplay. It's a pathetic tragedy of historic proportions in the making. Worse, all of this is happening to both of me simultaneously. I am the recipient of both results of pain and pleasure, hate and lust. Knowing this makes my flesh crawl with frustration. Oh, Jerry, you are a shitty Super Being.

Mooky knew this game was about to be played. I'm sure it's why he told me to invite Erin out of Mystery Towers with me when he sends someone around to buy me out. He knew what Jerry would do with Claire. He knew the whole game. It's why he knew about her from the get go, that day he left the gun under Erin's truck seat. He knew Claire wasn't the true girl for me. He knew. Mook is the matchmaker of the galaxy. He knew that it was Erin all along.

I see that now. It was Erin who Jozeph should pay his attention to. Trust his heart to, not Claire. Jozeph knows none of this. He knows not what's good for him. He knows only that before him tumbles any chance of him being with Claire Davis ever again. That it's me, creature of the night, sitting eating popcorn, watching his movie, in his way of what he thinks is his happy ever after.

Poor, and pathetic, human fool am I, Jozeph Picasso.

Bubba peaks back around the chair. He's not doing well. Perhaps the stress of winter train travel has him weary. Perhaps it's the cold, or all the people in his sleep zone. I don't really know how old he is. He's no pup that I'm sure of, maybe ten to twelve years old. My ex never really cleared that up trying to hide her own age probably. Her wild showbiz stories of Bubba and her on the road all seemed to blend into a blur of inconsistent resume hype after awhile, so I let it go.

Regardless, Bubba looks from Jozeph to me sensing that something is awry with this mounting situation. Even though Jozeph is sitting plainly in his eyesight, all his poodle animal instincts bred from the wild wolf deep inside him is telling him that the Dogman who he's come to love is sitting on the coach, as a wolf in lamb's wool. Bubba barks, testing the waters, and both Jozeph and I say exactly the same, "It's okay, Bubba." This fully confuses the poor old boy and he backs away to lie down. He keeps an eye on us, probably trying to figure which one of us he'd have to bite if it came down to deciding.

But Jozeph doesn't miss this. He looks at me closer. I can feel his eyes burning into the back of my head. I can see his reflection in the glass before me, and not my own. "Who the hell are you?"

"You know who I am."

"No I don't," he says, standing up and reaching into his coat.

So I get up. "Take it easy, Jozeph."

Jozeph pulls out a gun, that I knew was given to him by Mike and MacAroy, for his own protection and to kill me.

"Jozeph, what the hell are you doing?" Claire exclaims. "Put that gun away."

"Shut up, Claire."

"What did you say?"

"Move away from her. You heard me, whoever and whatever you are. Move away from her now," Jozeph demands.

"Jozeph, don't."

"Claire, I don't know what's going on. You know damn well that this man is a no good killer. He knows way too much about me, about both of us, to make this a simple film distribution buy. He's some kind of crazy stalker or worse a psychopath here to kill us both."

"He's probably had his people investigate everything about us. It's called due diligence. He's trying to make money off our film."

"She's right, Jozeph," I tell him. I glance back at my film as it plays. This is happening too quickly. I haven't seen half the footage.

"Shut up."

"Look, I want to see these shots."

"I said shut up, and move over there," Jozeph raises his voice.

So I shut up and move over to the open kitchen where the fireplace dividing the kitchen from the front door continues to burn on. I can feel the heat increase as I back towards it, step by step, degree by degree, until I'm up against the footing of the river rock fireplace.

"Turn around. Face the fireplace. Now!"

Shit, Jozeph is really pissed. I got to hold it to myself, I'm meaning business. Jozeph comes up behind me and starts to pat me down.

"Where's your wallet?"

"Out in my car." Crap something is happening to me. I look at my hands and my nails are starting to grow back. Whatever they did to me, that thing Mook had me eat, is wearing off and I'm returning to hairiness. Or am I calling upon this because of my natural survival instincts are kicking in. Taking over because I'm being threatened. They'll see me change. I've got to stop this from happening. It's got to stop right now. "Claire, stop him."

I've got me dead to right, pointing the gun at my own back. Jozeph's hand is shaking, trying to pull the trigger.

Claire is right up behind Jozeph. She grabs for the gun and fights with Jozeph not to shoot me. I can see from the look in her eyes that she's not really trying to stop him. She's trying to make him shoot me. Jerry is making sure Jozeph finishes the job. Jozeph is not trying to kill me. He's trying to see me. His eyes lock onto me changing back into what I am inside, a fulltime Alien Werewolf. Jerry is trying to prevent it from happening. But Jozeph is fighting her hard.

Claire pulls Jozeph over the coach trying to keep him from seeing what's happening to me. "He's going to kill us!"

Jozeph pulls the gun away and comes back over the top of the couch and his eyes are as wide open as can be because we are full on Chia Petting before his very eyes. Our nails are popping out, fangs growing, and we are gonna live through this now.

We are gonna take him out. We've got to kill Jozeph before he kills us. We all know this now. It's us that must live. We must stop all that is happening to us. Live to take our life back from him. There's more inside of us, pulling us to survive than even we have the power to stop now. This isn't sexual this is survival of the fittest. We are gonna rip Jozeph's head right off and pull his spine out.

We make a motion to leap towards him. But two thuds hit our chest with such a force we spin around. We've been hit twice in the heart, and twice more that passes through us from the back as we spin.

There's no way Jozeph pulled the trigger that fast with accuracy. As we spin around we see from the top landing, both Mike and MacAroy pointing their guns at us. Both hit us twice pointblank in the heart. I'm falling backwards. Everything is moving in slow-motion, as two more bullets rip through us. Our eyes lock upon Jozeph's face, he's stunned. He looks up at Mac and Mike while Claire pops her head up over the couch. We see in her eyes that Jerry is still inside her and she grabs a hold of Jozeph, putting her hand over his eyes, and pulls him down. Jerry's won. He's gonna get our blood. The pain in my chest and back rocks us sideways on our heels as we reach out to steady ourselves on the fireplace.

It's so close we can smell the flames. But our paw misses the riverbed stone. Our wolf-like razor sharp fingernails can only scrape the mortar as our legs buckle from under. Making us fall deep into the mouth of the fireplace. Instantly the hair on our face and head burst into flames. We wither and thrash around, only feeding it air, heightening the flame around us.

We try to get out but our legs are useless, our spine obviously severed. The flames engulf our clothing now, wrapping around us with a fierce aggression. Our melting butt flesh is feeding the kill. Our Debbie does Dallas heart with arrow through it tattoo withers away into a melted memory. The horrid smell of us sizzling fills what's left of my singed lungs, on my very last gulp of air.

Claire comes running into the kitchen now trying to reach water in the sink. But it's too late. We are fully engulfed in flames now. "Noooooo," she screams, and we can only hear the vibrations that Jerry knows he's lost to the flames what he wanted from us in the end, our morphing blood, our marrow. Jerry's hold over the others burns away from my bones. Our eyes melt away as we sink into our head, knowing in our end, it was all about our blood. Our last moment of evolution is gone, up in smoke, down in flames. The pain is beyond describable. More humanly wretched, mind numbingly tormenting than anything we can imagine. What a horrible way to die in any form or mutation.

Our last thoughts lock onto knowing that we spoiled all their efforts to use the very end of us to change their stranglehold over humans. Our mouth melts open to laugh but the flames only tear through the insides of us. Knowing that this last thought is somehow worth every pin prick of marshmallow me. They had plenty of time to test my blood when they had me but they didn't have what they needed from me yet. Mooky confirmed this. This last bit of us we are taking with us. Screw you, Jerry, and all the bodies you inhabit. I'm not helping you Alien bastards live like humans on this Earth. You're not from here, and you never will be. Suck on those balls, you Alien pricks! Our Tourette syndrome is running wild in our mind to the very end, as the last of us goes.

The moment it ends the pinnacle of pain inside us is so immense we explode apart from each other as we pass away. We're splitting chromosomes as though each is destined to our own final destination.

It's not right away, but what was left inside my mind of me, the part of Jozeph stuck deep inside, leaps out of this brain, leaving this dimension, traveling through neurons of light-filled energy and penetrates its way to its new host. Hitting my clone with such a sudden force Jozeph twists around and falls to the floor, completely out cold from the mental blast. But he's brought back around by the blunt force of his forehead striking the floor.

And then I'm all me again. Man that hurts!

42

It's like coming to from being knocked out cold from a hammer, my head hurts so badly. "What the...?" I find myself sitting there watching the fireplace and Mike and MacAroy hold me down. The monster in the fireplace is nearly charred to the bone as his flesh and muscle continues to melt away fast, and boy, putrid stink. Why they don't let us do something about it isn't clear. The stink is so bad I find myself breaking free and running to the sink and vomiting.

"Let the bastard burn. It serves him right," Mike says.

"The son-of-a-bitch is a rotten no-good bastard and deserves this ending after what he's done."

"Who was he really?" I ask.

"He was Bolivar Agustin," Claire says.

"No, he was Javier Sanchez posing as Bolivar Agustin. He was on the run from Federal Protection. He murdered his entire drug cartel family in Ciudad Juarez, Mexico, before coming here. Before that he killed a doctor in Frazer Park over a woman he was in love with. And he's killed countless others over the years. He got away from us at a party where we were drugged and nearly killed."

"When Burnstein told us what had happened, we knew that it was our Javier comin' here. That's why we gave you a gun."

"What the hell is all this about film distribution?"

"As far as we know he was engaged to be married to an Olivia Hamilton of Frazer Park, California," Mac says. "But he was already married in Texas with four kids. How he ties into you or Miss Davis, we don't know yet."

I don't like it. "Why us? Why not Junior or Burn? Those two guys have proved, as you two can vouch, that they know shady characters. I mean, this could go back to Jetty and his brother."

"That is correct, we don't know why he came here," Mike says as honestly as he can. "Could be he was just a fixated fan of Claire's."

I look at them, from one to the other. Bastards are lying to me.

"Not a clue," Mac says.

"You know why you two were fired cops in LA?'

"Come on, Picasso."

"You two can't lie well enough to be working actors in New York."

"Hey, I got my SAG card since the eighties."

"Then tell me why you two bullshitters let him in here."

"He got by us."

"Got by you? He knocked on the friggin' front door, Riding Hood."

"We saw from across the road. By then we had to put ourselves in the right position to take him out without hitting any of you."

Junior comes to the top of the stairs. "What in hell is that smell?"

"Javier Sanchez," I tell him. These two guys just barbequed him.

"We shot him and he fell into the fireplace."

"Well there are three cop cars outside and an ambulance. Who the hell called them? I've got an ounce of pot and four grams of coke."

"Might want to flush it."

"Ah shit. Why the hell did I come here? This is really messed up. What a buzz kill you people are."

The two lesbian PAs stop at the top of the stairs, half undressed. They don't seem worried.

"Don't worry, Claire, we flushed everything."

"You what?" Junior must've wanted more.

"We can't have this in the news and have drugs involved," Debbie says. "Not with Claire and Jozeph here."

"Thank you, thank you both."

"Son-of-friggin' writer!" Junior goes out of sight. "Every time I get around you, Picasso, I'm takin' it up the backside."

"We heard you liked it," Mike says smiling. It's all big cop fun.

"Shut up, Tucker."

"Bite me, Junior, and your old man, too," Mac says.

I turn to Claire. She seems sad, with an odd lost-kitten expression on her face. She looks at me as I hold out my hand. "You okay?"

"I think so."

"I couldn't tell what you were doing. Were you making me or stopping me from killing him?"

"I don't know what I was doing. I'm so confused."

I turn and the very end of my footage is rolling by on the TV. I don't remember watching any of it. I look down at the floor and there in my handwriting is a notepad full of scribbled notes. I pick it up. In dark letters written over and over on the same spot, carved into the page, is: "Kill the bloodsucker!" I look closely at it. I read the notes. None of them are about the film. They are all about the behavior of Claire and who we thought was Boli. At the top of the page is written, "No reflection, and halfway down the page are written the words, "He's a Vampire." I look over at Mac.

"Somethin' the matter, Picasso?"

"What? No, just notes on the film." I don't remember writing them. I take the page and rip it out of the notepad and crumble it up. Vampire? What the hell is that about? Did this have something to do with the weird Gray McGuiness? I toss it into the fireplace.

"Jesus, Picasso, have some respect."

"What? Oh, shit wasn't thinking. Sorry."

Pounding comes on the door and Mac moves over to open it. Four policemen and two emergency paramedics crowd into the house, stepping away from the still burning body of Javier Sanchez. Two of them run back outside.

"What the hell?"

"Javier Sanchez?"

"That's him."

The two policemen, who went back outside, run back in with fire extinguishers and spray down Javier with foam.

Claire comes out of the kitchen and looks up at the two PAs. "Pack our things, we can't stay here."

"Give us five minutes."

"But, we... where's Bubba? Bubba?" Bubba comes out from behind the lazy boy he'd been hiding behind. He looks at me, and suddenly he's back to himself and he runs to me, jumping up on me, and I meet him half way, "You're back, Dogman!" I give him a hug, picking him up, swinging him around and kissing him. He licks my face over and over. I look around the room hoping everyone sees how loving I am so they won't try to pin any of this murdering nonsense on me.

"Jozeph Picasso?"

"Yes."

"We'd like to have a word with you."

"Why?"

"Come, please." The officer reaches out for my arm. I pull back.

"Go with them, Jozeph. They probably just have some questions for you. We'll all meet up at the airport. Call us when you're done."

"What? Hell no."

"It's just procedure. We want to get you all separated for statements before you have a chance to talk it over. One of us needs to get back to the station. That's us, so please, let's keep this simple."

"It'll be okay, Jozeph," Mike tells me.

Why isn't that comforting. "It's not okay. I'm not going anywhere. If you have questions you can ask me right here in front of everyone."

"Mr. Picasso, please, we've got to get back to the station."

"Get your hands off me."

Debbie and the other production assistant come down the stairs with luggage. "I'll get my coat and boots. Hang on," Claire says. We all watch Claire get her coat, she's that beautiful. She stops at the door and turns, slight uncertain smile. "I guess we'll see you later."

I look at the clock and it's ten minutes after the New Year. Shit, we missed it with all this calamity. "Claire, where are you going?"

"Junior has a private plane here. If you think Bubba would fly with us, be there in an hour. We'll give him a sedative." The two assistants go outside and the police take their baggage. "You can ask me anything you want on the way to the airport."

"Yes ma'am."

"This is crazy. Why am I the only one being taken away like this?"

"Mr. Picasso, we are questioning everyone."

"Wait, why do you even know my name? What is going on here?"

"Come on, Jozeph. Don't make this anymore of an ordeal."

"Ordeal? There's a body from a madman burning in the fireplace and all of a sudden I'm the one making it an ordeal."

"I think he may be in shock?"

"Kiss off, Mike. I'm not in anymore shock than anyone else. I want to know what the hell is going on."

"Nothing is going on that isn't going on to all of us. A man was shot and fell into the fireplace. He's dead and these men need to take our statements to make it all official."

"Fine, then I'll make it right here. I don't know dick."

"We have to leave the house, Jozeph. It's procedure. This is a crime scene and they will want to do things the way it's supposed to be done. Or they'll catch hell for it."

"Mr. Picasso, if you don't settle down, we will be forced to put you under arrest and take you down to the station in handcuffs."

Just then, Junior appears at the top of the stairs. All three of the police officers pull their guns and point them at him. "Don't move," the one speaking to me yells.

"Hold on, hold on, I'm just the producer. I was up here with two production assistants the whole time having a meeting."

"It's okay, guys, he's with us," Mike tells them.

"I'm leaving. Catching my flight out in an hour and taking Claire. Picasso, I've got your stuff packed. Come on let's get back to LA."

"I can't. Bubba freaks on the plane when his ears start popping. He had a tough enough trip out here on the train. You won't get near him with a needle." Bubba's ears prick up at me even saying it.

"Jesus, Picasso, you're gonna pass up a first class jet ride back home because your dog doesn't fly?"

"You think fear of flying is just for humans?"

"No, obviously nuts like you are just as susceptible."

"Now I know something's wrong. You're using big words, Mac."

"Get him out of here. Take his dog out and he'll follow."

"Get away from my dog."

The cop leans down and picks up Bubba who starts to wiggle since he sees that me, Dogman, isn't planning on going with these men. He's seen Mike and MacAroy take me away. So he bites the cop.

"Ouch! That's it get the cuffs out. Mr. Picasso you are under arrest for interfering with a crime scene."

"You're arresting me because my poodle bit you?"

"No, because we had enough of your interfering and we've got a job to do before this scene is tainted."

I stick my hand in my pocket and pull out the gun, as surprised as everyone that I still had it. "Oh, shit!"

"He's got a gun!"

They come after me and I run. "Picasso, just drop the gun."

I drop the gun and start running around the living room. I finally make it to the top of the stairs to the top landing and head for the second floor exit door leading out the deck that overlooks the lake. I'm planning on crossing the frozen lake if I have to. But as I reach for the knob, the door opens and catches me on the forehead, pointblank. Smack, I bounce back and my head hits another doorjamb corner. I roll over watching Bubba weave through the feet of the on-rushing men as my mind begins to swish and sway. Before I know it, werewolves, and vampires are chasing me through a thorn filled thicket, and I'm out cold... again.

43

I thought what I hated most in life was blindfolds and getting shot pointblank with pistols held by beautiful women. But I have a new stack of shit I hate happening to me. Beginning with straitjackets and padded white cells, with barmy me trapped in them, after being knocked unconscious by an opening door.

What the hell did I do to deserve this mini adventure to nutville? This is almost comical. But note the word 'almost' because it's really happening to me and I'm finding very little of any of this outright humorous. They must think I'm a danger to myself, strangers and love ones alike, to lock me up this way. In the past, when I was just a suspected mass murdering landlord – slash – writer/director, I was just cast into a holding cell with twenty-nine murderers and white-collar crime wannabes. I was left to defend for myself. But not this time, I'm now a lone wolf, singular wacko, a dangerous drill dummy.

My face is pushed against the wall as though they actually threw me into the room and that's how I landed. Now that I move and roll halfway over my nose pushes against the padded flooring. I turn my head the best I can to get some air and I can see a small window on the door that for all practical purposes suggest there's a hallway outside leading to my freedom.

"I'm not alone," I say out loud. Someone is there watching me through the door's window. Oddly, he looks naked. He turns to speak to someone who's too short for me to see. I'm sure I've never seen him before but he seems vaguely familiar. Spanish. Wait a minute. Was that Boli? Javier Agustin? No he couldn't be. I watched him roast in the fireplace until he was nothing but charred bones. He's gone now, I think, so whoever this person is he's not coming in here to see me.

I realize now I may have made a mistake by not wanting to go along quietly back at the house. I couldn't help seeing that I was the only one being treated as though I was a person of interest. My life just keeps getting better and better.

I can't help but notice that none of my friends, neighbors, business partners, cast members, agent, lawyer or dog have inquired to my whereabouts. Maybe they are nearby waiting for the moment I open my eyes to get me out of here. Maybe they are, but none of them have visited my cell as far as I know. Considering I just came to, maybe they are waiting and I don't know it.

I do my best to roll over and sit; putting my back against the wall in case anyone is monitoring so they can see I'm awake. My hands are crossed before me but are held very firmly in my sleeves. I guess I should've watched the Houdini movie a little closer. For all practical purposes, I'm screwed and stuck right here. Shit, and I'm hungry, my stomach is singing an ugly tune of disparity and emptiness.

Okay, let's look back at what I just went through. The star of my movie, Claire Davis, invited me and my dog to spend New Year's Eve with her and two of our fellow film personnel, a production assistant and a makeup girl. To do this, Bubba and I had to decline Erin's invitation, leaving her once again a little bit pissed that we weren't spending New Year's with her and her roommate Janet from apartment 104.

In hindsight, it may have ended up being the right choice. There's no way of knowing if Javier would've shown up at Mystery Towers with the same request. Claire sure wouldn't have been there and as it turned out, it seemed that he was at the rental house to see her more than to see her in the film. I may be wrong. I just don't think so.

Everything was going just fine at the house before Junior showed up with the bad news of Javier's demands and pending visit. I was even anticipating spending the night with Claire Davis, naked, sweaty, and alone. I was until I found out from Junior Burnstein that this lunatic Boli Agustin, aka Javier Sanchez, dirt bag drug cartel boss, was showing up at Claire's Connecticut rental house to view our movie, Crazy Kind Of Love.

I admit I told him on the train to talk to Burnstein first but I sure as hell didn't expect the Burn to sell me and the film out to this guy if he did. The thought that the Burn was protecting me is touching, if not comforting. Was it my safety or my inability to finish the film he was worrying about? Are they one and the same thing in Hollywood?

Regardless, he was insisting on seeing the film first. He was willing to pay cash to the Burn, the same amount of the shooting budget of our film, for just the world-wide Spanish market. The offer was a total fantasy come true for the money guys like the Burn. So Javier must have had some kind of showbiz knowledge coming in because his people made probably the one offer he knew the Burn couldn't turn down, all his money back on one distribution deal.

That's just swell for the money guys. But it opens doors to be a complete nightmare in the making for us, the unprotected creative guys, who don't have our films firmly in the can, fully edited, printed and ready for market.

Now this in itself is nuts enough. However, I know for a fact that this same man murdered two men on the very train I rode there in. And I'm not just saying murdered in the normal name of the game. I'm talking mutilating, ripping off one of their heads type of things, and flinging one of their bodies off the train after ripping out his heart. I didn't see this, but it's what was presented to me by the officials who interviewed me. So yes, I'm upset that this person came to spend New Year's Eve with Claire, Bubba, and I. This also put the distraction of having Junior there too with his smoking pot and snorting coke, along with the two lesbian coworkers.

Poor Bubba dog wasn't feeling well. I'm not sure if it was just the cold or motion sickness from the train. Regardless the air in the room was a little smoky and uneasy to begin with. Then this guy shows up. How he got to the house, I don't know. There were no other cars out front other than the ones Junior and Claire came in. Bubba and I took a limo from the train station. When this guy came in, he was six foot four or five and I don't recall him being so tall.

There was something else about him. I'm not just saying he was creepy because I knew he was a possible real-life mass murderer. Not just a Hollywood faux suspect like me. There was something oddly familiar about him that I still can't put my fingers on. Kind of like that feeling about the guy in this padded cell's door window. That is weird. I must be getting paranoid and people are starting to all look alike or seem as though I've met them before. Crap, I hope I haven't gone schizoid and don't know it yet, and that's why I'm here.

But who wouldn't feel put upon, out of sorts or even a bit schizoid about what I saw happening. From the moment this creep enters the house I'm the third wheel with muck on it. I'm the missing dented hubcap, ruining a perfect ride down memory lane. Claire was on this creepy guy as though he was her long lost lover from another failed TV series. I'm not so sure that Claire wasn't just relieved that there was another available man in the house. Maybe she felt she had made a big mistake to invite me there. Maybe she was regretting setting me up to think that this New Year's Eve would end up New Years Day with me and her under the sheets.

I'm not sure, but it felt that way. The flirting, the popcorn sharing, the smiling and laughing while they watched the cuts, as if almost he was the one who made the film and not me. I mean, not once did she turn to me and smile knowingly because we were both there on the set making this film work. Not once did she reach out and touch me or acknowledge that I was still in the room. Not once, until I pulled that gun out of my pocket to make that bastard leave the house did she acknowledge my presence.

What was even weirder than that is, the whole time that Claire fought me not to use the gun, it sure felt like she was really doing her best to point the damn thing at him and pull the trigger. Now that's probably just me. But it's just weird to be left with these feelings.

Maybe I felt I was being setup, and that's why I argued about being taken anywhere. I know that sounds ridicules to think of Claire's actions this way. Why would Claire do that to me? We're in the middle of shooting our first film together. Why would she set me up, and what did it matter if I had shot this unarmed guy. I mean, Mac and Mike did, and no one was saying anything about that.

Regardless, I don't think things between Claire and I will ever be the same after this. How will I ever be able to close my eyes around her? It's actresses again. Back to my golden rule for good this time. Claire's off my menu, no matter how hungry I get for attention. I'll just pet my poodle.

Wait. Was this all for the publicity? Taking advantage of my past, even though they were potentially setting us up to all die? Would the Burn be so dastardly to think this film needed that kind of press to make his money back? I admit, it's cleaver. Is that why I'm here?

Which brings me to why isn't anyone saying anything about the two ex cops, those dirty dicks, MacAroy and Tucker, appearing all of a sudden in Connecticut to give me a gun. Then blowing that son-of-a-bitch away themselves? Four shots right into the heart of the chest. When he spun around, two more into the heart area from the back.

Now I use guns, I had one. But lost my LA permit to own one. Thanks to all the bullshit I've been through. Still, I've been to target practice enough to know. Shooting that accurate from the distance these two guys shot from, and at that angle from up on the second floor landing, and then both hitting within inches again in the back while he was moving, well shit, that's unnatural. I couldn't do it. I consider myself a good shot. So I question how both of those out of shape cops could shoot like that.

I don't know. I don't. Things were all a little strange. Maybe Claire and Junior are in here somewhere too and they are getting questioned about all of this without the needed jacket and padding. I'm thinking that this is some more of the unexplainable bullshit that has happened to me in the past three years.

I don't claim to know everything about the goings on in the world, but of late, at least since I bought Mystery Towers, strange shit has been happening to me that I just can't put a face of reality on. If this is more of it, then well, hurry up let's get this over with already because I want to get back home to my dog and movie deal. Damn, my movie. I don't even know what day it is. I could've been in here for weeks already as far as I know.

Okay good, we're getting somewhere, because the door with the window suddenly opens and a nicely dressed black man enters. He looks at me, with strangely yellowish eyes like he's known me for my whole life.

"How's it going, Jozeph?"

"Just great. How are you?"

"I'm doing well. So, would you like to go home?"

"Yes, I would, very much, thank you."

"Good. My name is Doctor William Payne Washington, and I'm here to ask you a few questions first."

"Nice to meet you. Do I call you William or Doctor?"

"William is fine if it makes you feel comfortable.

"Can I ask a few?"

"When I'm done."

"Fine. What do you want to know?"

"How old are you?"

"This is the new year?"

"Yes, January first, Happy New Year."

"Thank you. Same to you. I'll be thirty-two in July."

"Very good. Where are you from originally?"

"Michigan."

"And you attended UCLA for two years before dropping out?"

"Two and a half years. I ran out of money, so technically I didn't drop out. I just felt I'd learned what I wanted to learn at that point.

Since I didn't want to get further in debt by accepting any more of their financial aid, they politely asked me to leave."

"We were told there were slight problems with your instructors."

"Not really. They thought my work ethics weren't up to their standards, and I begged to differ."

"It said in your file that you refused to allow members of the class to work on your projects."

"Yes, that's true. Those twits were deliberately trying to sabotage my film. So I fired them."

"Do you often feel this way?"

"That people are messing with me?"

"In general."

"If you know about my school problems then you know what's been going on around me since."

"Yes, we do. How do you view that?"

"A bunch of shit I can't explain. I've had strange stuff happen to me most of my life. Most of it unexplainable, but I never claimed to know every strange thing going on with this planet, and frankly don't want to know."

"Finding dead bodies, watching people get gunned down at work, nearly drowning while fishing, being washed out to sea, waking up and being shot while inside a buried chest. Stuff like that?"

"Yes. It's fodder for the fertile imagination. I might even write it all down someday."

"Make a good sci-fi novel."

"Yes maybe, if I can piece it all together. As long as it stops I'm good though. Water under the Tujunga Bridge at this point."

"And you own Mystery Towers."

"Regrettably at times, but yes."

"Regrettably? Why?"

"Have you ever seen it?"

"I've viewed photos, yes."

"Then you see it's a little strange, spooky looking."

"Not overly, no."

"Okay. It kind of owns me at this point, since I've been feeding it everything I earn thus far. I would've been in less debt if I had stayed in film school.

"But you wouldn't own a home and business."

"True. What else?"

"What do you know about this Mr. Javier Sanchez?"

"Nothing much. Other than what I saw on the train and what happened to him in the house. Oh, and I just saw someone out that window that looked like him."

"When?"

"Just a minute ago."

William looks at the window taking in my angle of view. "Okay. What happened to him in the house?"

"The guy started acting weird. I knew he was dangerous from what I heard."

"What do you mean weird?"

"I don't know, something was off about him. Two officers had given Junior Burnstein a gun to give me for protection, and arranged for a permit for me to conceal it. You know MacAroy and Mike Tucker?"

"Yes, they vouched for you. They delivered the gun to you by giving it to Ernie Burnstein Junior. They did so under signed orders."

"What do you know. Can I go now?"

"There's just a few more questions."

"I'm hungry."

"Lunch time is almost here. So, Jozeph, did you notice anything else peculiar about this Mr. Sanchez?"

"You mean like was he morphing into a werewolf or if he was a vampire or something stupid like that?"

"Well, okay. Let's say yes."

"Doctor Washington, William, I know under the circumstances that I may appear to be a tad insane, even schizoid. I don't believe in werewolves, vampires, zombies, aliens, or anything unnatural like that outside what I make up to put into my fiction stories. I'm not saying they don't really exist beyond my knowledge. I'm just saying in my life, the life I have chosen to believe as to be real, I have never seen any proof that they exist. I prefer it that way. I very much plan to keep it that way."

"Good, smart, simple. So, Mr. Sanchez seemed dangerous under the circumstances of you being warned about him and what you experienced on the train. That was the weird part?"

"Yes. That's why I pulled the gun. I started feeling that there was some other reason why he was there."

"To harm you?"

"And or Claire Davis."

"Yes, Claire Davis. So you felt that he would harm either of you?"

"He was a drug dealer obviously infatuated with Claire Davis and from what I could see was doing his best to seduce her."

"This was threatening to you?"

"Well, in a way, yeah. The others had left us alone, and well things got a little weird."

"How so?"

"I just told you. I got this feeling."

"Describe it. Did he come on to you?"

"What? No. Was that a joke?"

William doesn't answer.

I think for a minute. I'm blank. "You know, I'm drawing a complete blank."

"Okay, I guess that's enough for now."

"Wait a minute. Can I go home?"

"Yes, of course you can. I'll take care of the necessary paperwork right now and we'll get you home."

"Where's my dog?"

"He traveled with Claire Davis, oh and she said she'll see you back on the set when you get home."

"You spoke to her?"

"Of course. Like the officers told you in the house, everyone needed to be separated and interviewed accordingly."

"So, I'm free to go."

He moves to the door. "Yes. In a few minutes. Someone will come get you."

"Okay, I'll be here. Wait. I just have one question."

He turns back to me. I swear I know him, but I don't. I'm sure of it. "Alright. What is it?"

"Do you believe in werewolves, vampires, and aliens?"

"No, those kinds of beliefs can get you a home in a place like this." Doctor William Payne Washington turns around, opens and walks out the door. It shuts behind him, seemingly by itself.

"Don't forget lunch?" I yell after him. Damn, I'm starving. "Shit. Hey, William, hello? Can someone call my friend Erin to tell her I'm okay and coming home today?"No one comes to the door. "Anybody, hey, is anyone there? Is anyone watching me? Hey, am I alone? Hello?"But no one comes back to the door to answer my questions. Crap, I hope Doctor Washington remembers to send someone back with my lunch.

44

I've got to admit when the door reopens and an elderly gentleman enters dressed in prison guard clothing I was a little let down. I was hoping for a familiar face to come rescue me. So when Mac and Mike follow him in, I am almost pleased to see them.

"Come on, Jozeph, this place gives us the creeps. Let's get some fresh air," Mike says.

I just look at them because I can't stand up on my own. They come over and pick me up. The elderly guard helps me out of my jacket, and hands me the shirt and sweater I had on last night. My legs are half asleep, my feet still tingling and nearly numb. A feeling I've had the unfortunate displeasure of experiencing before. Only now for some reason, I'm okay with it, no frustration. I'm somehow at piece with my predicament, only hungry and wanting to go home.

"What's going on?"

"What do you mean? We're here to take you home."

"But, where are we?" Mac helps me with my shirt.

"We're in LA. We all flew in on Junior's jet last night."

"Hell of a ride." Mike hands me back my sweater.

"You missed out. The stews were outstanding. All we could eat and drink. Junior joined the Mile High Club, again."

"But what are you two doing here? Isn't this a police station or some kind of federal facility?"

Mac takes out his badge and flashes it. "We're back on the force."

"With full promotions and benefits reinstated as of today."

"Come on, we'll explain on the way home. We were told you were hungry, so we'll pick something up for the drive."

Losing the jacket felt like a vast burden off my chest. But having these two guys show up here and be so helpful is a bit too much for me to comprehend right now. I turn to the guard, "Is this legit?"

"You're looking at a couple of LA's finest officers. They got awards coming and everything."

"Don't worry, Picasso, you're invited to the ceremony. Come on, how's the head?"

"What? My head? What do you mean?"

"Man, you don't remember, do you?"

"Remember, I ran upstairs and...." Nothing, I remember nothing from that point of hitting the door until I woke up here.

"You took one in the head, full blast, on the corner of the door. You got a nice bump there on your forehead, and one on the back."

"I do?" They lead me to the door as I feel my sore bumps. Damn. I turn to the guard. "Thank you."

The guard just shrugs. "It's cool." Old hat to him I guess.

We go out the door and walk into a long white hall with many doors. Just like the one I walked out of. I look both ways but no one's there. Just us. I stop.

Mac and Mike suddenly realize that I'm not with them. They turn to me, half smiling. "Come on, it's okay. We're takin' you home."

"For real?"

"Come on, don't make us drag your ass again, I'm hungry."

"Check out these new suits. No need to work up a sweat."

I follow them down the hall, and we exit out another door, where Mike flashes his ID in front of a sensor to open it and we find ourselves in that same hall they once walked me down to get me out of jail after pulling strings, three years ago.

"We're downtown LA?"

"We are now."

"What's that supposed to mean?"

"Relax, Picasso. You're okay. We're okay."

"You tell me that again, I'm gonna kick both of you in the ass."

They laugh.

"Come on, guys, you're acting like we're long lost army buddies. What gives? Am I not the same Jozeph Picasso you once set up for murder charges and a long-lost rotting goodbye in a Sun Valley drainage ditch?"

"We're heroes now, Jozeph. You let us be that. By not pulling that trigger last night and letting us take out that scumbag, with the difficult shots we both took, we're back on the force, with promotions and everything."

"Sanchez would've killed you all, and done who knows what to Claire Davis. This town loves us. We made front page. Close ups even."

"My wife slept with me without me begging for it last night."

"My kids listened to me this morning, and hugged me."

"You mean?"

"Who knows what brought him there. He got away from us in Frazer Park, murdered a beloved small town doctor to get away. So we tracked him across the country, thanks to your report of him on the train, and what he did to those guys hunting him."

"Gruesome shit, too."

"The man was sick in the head. We lost him again from there though, and somehow he got across the border where he killed his whole family, horrifically, because they were trying to kill him first for ratting on them in a trial coming up."

"What the hell are you talking about?"

"He was in a witness relocation program. He got loose and went on a murdering rampage over the woman he was in loved with, an Olivia Hamilton."

"He was set to invest millions up there with her father while posing as Bolivar Agustin, a film distributor and property investor that he killed and took his identity. That's how we found him, through the studio when he sent people there to cut the distribution deal. It's complicated, but it's over. Finally."

"We're thankful. You should be, too. You lived. We're all back to who we want to be."

"What are you talking about? I just spent the night in a loony bin, strapped in a protective jacket. Why was that?"

Mike and Mac stop, letting me catch up. They look at me, almost sad for a second. "You want to tell him?"

"Go ahead," Mac says.

"Some strange shit went down with you last night after you took that blow. You were spouting all kinds of mean-crazy stuff, thrashing about, trying to bite everyone who came near you. It was like you were almost possessed or something. Like something was trying to get either in you our out of you. It wasn't too clear. So they had to sedate you as quickly as possible and we had to pull a lot of bullshit strings to get you on that plane and out of Connecticut."

"What kind of crazy shit?"

"You don't recall?"

"Obviously I don't, Mike."

"It was nothing worth repeating. Just some harsh shit you've probably had pent up inside for some time now. Needless to say, you freaked the girls out with all the foul language about them being Jerry's Alien whores, whoever that is. I'm not so sure Junior will be talkin' to you for a while either."

"Why? What did I say to him?"

"You kept referring to his mishap with the Magical Man, that Gray McGuiness character Jetty murdered. Calling him Gray's little butt buddy in front of everyone, including Claire and those other two."

"You were pretty graphic, Picasso. I never heard anything like it outside a loony bin."

"You had some punk things to say about us, before it was over, but we forgive you."

"Once the drugs set in, you were okay, though."

"So, I'm free to go?"

"Yeah, no one knows you're even here. No one talked to the press. Claire, Junior, and the girls all swore to forget you had lost your mind momentarily due to the blow to your head. They got jobs and don't want any of this shit to get in the way of paying their mortgage or car payments."

"Claire's got Bubba? He flew back on the plane?"

"Actually, they had to give him a little pill, so he slept all the way, and Claire took him to a vet just in case. She picked him up about an hour ago and dropped him at your building. He's with a friend of yours, Erin."

"Erin. Does she know any of this?"

"Nobody knows nothing about where you've been. Just the three of us. We kept your name out of it. You're just visiting us as far as anyone here knows."

"There was a Doctor William Payne Washington who came to see me." They look at me blankly as we reach the gate where the same skinny woman sat once before. She's still there. She hands out my belt, wallet, watch, and a ring my father gave me. The five hundred dollars I had with me in hundreds is still there. "Here, you go," she says this time. No animosity, no snarling I hate you looks. "Good luck on your film, Jozeph."

"Thank you." I look back at her and she's actually smiling.

262

Mike opens the door and we step out onto the sidewalk like we had done three years ago. A brand new unmarked white cruiser sits there. Mac hits his key alarm and it chirps open. I can't help but notice they didn't answer me.

"Do you know a Doctor Washington?"I ask again.

"William Payne Washington? Never heard of him."

"But he came to see me."

"Nobody saw you, Jozeph. We made sure of that. But if someone did we know nothing about it."Mike Tucker and Lenard MacAroy walk over to the cruiser and patiently wait for me. They are new found men, rectified cops on the move up. They are as new as you can get in LA. Both are overnight sensations, media fodder darlings, but truly happy as if reborn. Funny, it's good to see them this way, and not threatening to put me somewhere dank and dark forevermore.

"This is yours?"

"Hell, yeah."

"It's brand new, right off the assembly line. Look at that new interior and computer system."

"You guys must have saved some pretty powerful butts catching up with this Javier"

"Let's just say the Governor is glad to have us back."

"From two states."

"Good. It explains the shit-eating grins."

"Happy is my new name."

"Come on, get in the back."

"You want tacos, burgers, sub or what?"

"Ah, you know what? Can you just take me home?"

"Come on, I'm starvin'. There's Lucy's Drive-Thru, a taco joint, not far from here, almost on the way home."

"It's okay, I've been there. But stop and get yourself something. I'm feeling a little off. I think I'll lie down for a while. Maybe I'll have a Coke. I think my sugar level is a little low."

"It's your life."

"Yeah, I hope so."I get in the backseat of the cruiser. I've been in some before. More often than I deserved to. But this time I'm a free man cruising LA in my two buddies' new car. We pull away from the curb as I find my seatbelt and strap myself in, just in case. "So you two guys are all okay with me?"

"What, you talkin' about the wet butts from sodas in our seats?"

"Ah… maybe."

"Suppose you know nothin' about that?"

"Ah… no I suppose I don't know a thing. But if I did… I'd be sorry that it happened to you guys."

"Don't be, Picasso. We tried to ruin your life, left you for dead. We done some bad shit over the years, thanks to Jetty Dazarrio and his brother Leonie having us under their thumbs. Gettin' a little back from you in retro is fair play."

"Okay."

"We ain't those guys anymore."

"Not by a long shot."

"So, we cool?"

"Us, you mean, we're friends?"

"If you accept our apologies?"

"Ah, guess I do. Thanks," I say.

"Then don't worry, Picasso, nobody will be messin' with you on our watch. You have a need, give us a call anytime you want. But everything on the up and up."

"You guys are starting to freak me out."

"We ain't gonna whack you, Jozeph. We're serious. From now on we are two of LA's finest, and though it's been a long road, somehow getting involved with you and all this shit worked out for us. So we're thankful to have gotten a higher perspective and a second chance with our lives."

"Our families will be better for it. Our kids will have us back. And who knows, my wife is talkin' about me coming back home. I'm even thinkin' about it."

"Okay, then."

We turn south on La Brea and into Lucy's Drive-Thru that serves fantastic greasy, authentic Mexican food, and pull up to the order window.

"You sure you don't want anything?"

I almost change my mind. "A Coke."

"Whatever you say."

45

We pull up in front of spooky old Mystery Towers and there on the grass between the sidewalk and the curb is Bubba doing his doody dance in the shade of the pines. He's a sight for suffering eyes if I ever saw one. A smile grows on my face. I'm back, I'm okay, I'm free and I'm home, at last. Oddly, and I don't know why I feel this way, but for some reason I feel as though I've been traveling afar for a long time and somehow this is my triumphal return. Almost as though I've overcome some great horrible feat, and I've gained some perspective from where I've been. Some kind of insight to what will really make me enjoy my life, what will truly make me happy.

Erin looks up as we come to a stop, skeptical at first seeing Mike and Lenard's faces smiling up at her. But when I open the back door her face brightens up with an honest to goodness smile of welcome home. Before I can get out of the back seat Bubba is up wanting to go for a ride. He sees Mike looking back at him and growls.

"It's okay, Bubba. Daddy's home."

"Good morning," Erin greets me, holding the door.

Mike rolls down his window. "Enjoy your day, Jozeph."

"Thanks, guys. See you both around I guess."

MacAroy leans over the seat, "Hey don't forget us when you have the premiere of your film. We want invites."

"You'll get them."

They smile as Mike rolls up his window and Mac drives his new cruiser down Mystery heading toward Ventura Boulevard.

It feels overly good to be home. I still don't know why, but I'm overcome with the feeling that I wasn't so sure I'd ever see this place again. The relief that I am home is heartfelt and makes me smile. I'm smiling. I don't do enough of that. Feels good, too. It's okay to feel good. And I do, admittedly, I do feel good.

Erin looks at me with an inquisitive smile back, thinking maybe I'm being a little strange. "How was New Years?" Erin asks probably knowing full well of the nightmare it turned out to be in Connecticut.

"Pretty weird. How was yours?"

"Okay. I don't have lumps on my head at least. I called your cell. You didn't answer. Do you need to see a doctor?"

"No, I'm good. So, you called?"

"Yes, but only six times."

"I must have lost it. I don't even know where it is."

"It's with your luggage. It showed up a couple hours ago with your computer and Bubba. It keeps ringing, so I'm assuming it must be somewhere inside."

"Oh, good." I pick up Bubba, and Erin moves in close for a quick hug. I hold on to her and squeeze her for I'm sure more than she expected, but enough to let her know I'm glad to see her and that she feels good. She pulls back after letting me have a moment.

"You okay?"

"Yeah, I'm just glad to see you. Glad to be home."

"Well then, welcome home, Jozeph."

"Thank you, Erin, and a very Happy New Year."Bubba starts licking my neck. "Happy New Year to you too, Bubba." Just then I hear Caw up on the veranda to my apartment, "Caw, Caw, Caw!" I look up at Mystery Towers shimmering dimly in the morning light, its sandstone facing seemingly not as stained as I remembered. The pine trees are much less daunting, and somehow the building itself not nearly as menacing. Caw jumps up to the railing looking down at me, and swoops at us as I hold out my arm, landing softly. He gives me that garbled crow banter that sure sounds like he's trying to talk to me. I look at Erin, and she laughs.

"What?"

"That bird has been driving us all crazy, swooping down at people who came to any of the doors."

"That's his job, isn't it Caw?"

"Caw, caw, caw!"

"He didn't hurt anyone?"

"No, but two guys can attest that this bird means real business. They were trying to get in on the Graystone side door, and Caw lit into them. He chased them down the road into traffic, where one of them was struck by a pickup truck and knocked on his butt."

"Who were they?"

"I don't know. I heard a commotion outside my patio doors and looked out as they scaled back over the fence, running for their lives."

"Did you do that, Caw?"

Caw lets out a garbled answer nodding his head, throwing spit into my face. Bubba squirms in my other arm and I hand him over to Erin. He's still not so sure about sharing food, spit, or the limelight with Caw.

"They left some damage on the door, trying to get in. That's how I know they were up to no good."

"Well, thanks for looking after things."

"So you didn't get my message. J.J. got the new series."

"What? It's a done deal?"

"Yes, signed and sealed. After he went in with your agent and pitched it to the networks, a bidding war took place, and next thing I knew he's the star of his own show."

"Consider it Done, Matt Dunn, they bought that old thing?"

"Yes. Wait, you already knew this was happening, remember at Christmas dinner."

I think for a minute. I do know. "Holy crap, I forgot all about it. Are you sure, it's a done deal already?"

"J.J. stopped by last night for Champaign and told us the good news. That's partly what we were calling you about. It's now sci-fi."

"I'll be damned."

"Oh, and your agent, Gerald, dropped off this envelope."

"His Geraldness came by himself?"

"Said it was on his way home, and wanted to save a buck."Erin goes over to the steps and picks up a vanilla envelope. "He also made it clear three times to have you read it by the end of the day with notes, and hand it to him personally, if you wanted your input counted on the pilot."

"Input?"

"And I think he was hitting on me."

"Gerald? Come on, he's about seventy years old."

"He's a lot spryer than you think. Don't worry he was charming in an old fart kind of way. Said his new young wife, Brenda, would love to meet me. Read into that what you want."

"Well thanks. They must have changed a lot to want my input."

"He said the check inside will smooth out whatever your thoughts are on it, if you don't like what they did with it. And that you and a guest are invited for dinner tonight at his place, cocktails at eight."

I open the package and pull out the check minus commission fees. "Take a look at that."

"You get that every week?"

"Created by. I get another for executive producing."

"Every week?"

"According to this, just twelve episodes so far."

"Oh my god, that's crazy."

"Yeah. For doing nothing. Where's J.J.?"

"Shopping."

"You know what? Are you hungry?"

"I've got something we can...."

"No, let's go have brunch somewhere, to celebrate."

"It's New Years Day. We'll have to wait in line."

"Hey, I'm Jozeph Picasso, murdering manager–slash–working writer/director and now slash – producer. I wait in line for no one."

"In that case, Mr. Big Shot," Erin says, "I'll meet you downstairs in half an hour."

"Make it ten minutes, I'm starving. We'll take the Corvair."

"The Corvair? This is a special day. You haven't driven it around town in months."

"I know, bring a scarf or something, I'll put the top down."

"Yes, it's a beautiful day."

"It is."

Erin hands me back Bubba and goes up the front stairs.

"Hey," she turns. "You want to go tonight? Meet Gerald's wife?"

"To your agent's house for dinner?"

"Why not?"

"I, ah, I don't have anything to wear."

"Then let's go shopping, my treat after brunch."

"You're taking me to buy clothing on New Year's Day?"

"A pretty dress and nice shoes. I'm a working stiff now. I don't want to go alone, and well, it will be fun to hang out like grownups away from this place."

"Okay, Janet's got a date. So I'll be right down."

"That'll work." I look at my dungeon of a garage. I don't have keys to get into my own place. So I put down Bubba, and let Caw back into the air as I go to the gate and look inside. Bubba waits there with me. He's such a good dog. Tim from apartment 101 is getting into his truck. I wait for him to pull up. I'm such a good manager. The gate opens and I enter.

"Hey, Jozeph. Happy-Happy. Where you been?"

"Connecticut."

"Really? I love winter back East. How was Claire?"

"She was fine, as was everyone else there. A full house.

"Too bad."

"Hey, are you working on anything on your own right now?"

"You know, always busy trying."

"Look, I'm going to lunch with Erin. Would you have time to look this over? I know it's a holiday, and we're already working on a project together, but it's the pilot for J.J., and I'm Executive Producing." I hand him the package minus the check. "Get me some notes on this and I'll see about getting you on staff after 'Crazy' wraps, either writing or directing, or whatever we can do to find you a paycheck."

"You serious, Jozeph? Directing?"

"Yeah, very. I want someone on staff that can be my eyes and ears. What do you say?"

"I'm there. I'll read it right now at Starbucks."

"Thanks. I'll be back in a couple of hours."

Tim pulls out of the garage and I walk all the way back to view my new F150 Black Ford truck and Corvair. My 1966 Corsa. There she sets waiting for me, red and black and all freshly restored after being shot to shit. I almost let it go, but changed my mind at the last minute when the guy said he was going to change the color for his girlfriend. I look around to see if anyone is watching. I don't know what's come over me, but for some reason I'm overcome with joy that keeps washing over me. Like I'm the luckiest person alive.

My two best friends, Michael and Roger, who followed me out here from Detroit are not alive. I wish they were here right now to see what's going on with my life. To see that I'm doing okay, making my dreams come true. Working with me. I miss them both so much. I pick up Bubba and hug him tight, tears welling up in my eyes.

"Jozeph?"

Holy cow, "Roger?"

I turn around and nearly jump out of my skin. Standing there in the middle of the dungeon are my two lost friends, looking just like they did, last I remembered them. Michael died five years ago now, blondish brown hair down around his shoulders and Roger, thick black wavy hair and beard. Here they are. Ghosts?

I blink my eyes, looking at Bubba to see if he sees them, and he does, because I can feel him trembling in my arms. "Ah...."

"It's okay, Jozeph," Michael says

"Am I actually seeing you guys?"

"Yeah, we're here, Jozeph. For just a moment," Roger answers.

"Why? Have I done something? Am I dead, too?"

"No, Jozeph, you're good. You live a long life as things are now," Roger says.

"They could change?"

"Always. The Earth and all that is on it is in a constant flux."

"You've got to sell this building, Jozeph," Michael tells me.

"Sell it, but I just finished it."

"Trust us on this," Roger says.

"You've got to let us go."

"Go? Go where?"

"Away from here. It's time."

"But..., have you guys been goosing girls in the elevator and moving my pool furniture around?"

"Not us. There's others here."

"A German oil baron who built this place hangs out in there. He's the one."

"And they won't let us go if you don't sell the place."

"But... they? Who's they?"

"Please, Jozeph, let us go where we need to go next."

"But this is my home."

"It's not yours, Jozeph, it never will be. Put it back on the market. Someone by the name of Buckley Jones will come by in a few days and give you a good price."

"Buckley Jones, do I know this guy? I don't understand."

"You don't want to understand. Just do as we say, please." They start to fade.

"I guess I don't want too.... Michael, Roger, I miss you."

"We miss you too, Jozeph, congratulations on everything."

"We like, Erin."

"We're proud of you. Enjoy."

"Thanks. I will."

"Don't make us come back."

"I won't."

"You won't what?"

I turn and Erin is standing there in jeans and a black turtleneck sweater.

"I ah, won't miss this place."

"What do you mean, you're moving out?"

"Selling Mystery Towers. Just made up my mind."

"But why?"

"It told me to." Bubba squirms so I put him down and he goes over and sniffs around the ceiling support where Michael and Roger stood.

"It? Are we getting weird again?"

"It's time, is what I mean. I want a house, and if I sell this place I can get one. I don't need the income from it any longer."

"But we like you being here. As odd as it might sound, you make us feel safe in this weird place."

I smile, because knowing what people have said about me and this place over the past couple years, it's funny to think that I'm considered the protector from any kind of bodily harm by anyone who lives here.

"I know, Erin, and thanks, I appreciate your trust in me. We'll have to work on that part, and see what happens next."

"Okay. Are you sure you're okay? Your eyes are all glassy."

"Yeah, I'm fine. It's just everything that's happening to me. I'm not used to such personal joy. I'm a bit humbled by it all. Plus, I've taken another lump on the head last night. I've got this feeling if I stay here much longer I might end up with matching genius bumps. So, come on, get in. Everything's good."

I open the Corsa's door for her, and she slides onto the leather red and black bucket seats. I reach in and unlatch the top and hit the electric top button and it folds back effortlessly. As always, it's worth every dime putting it in so that I don't have to start the car first. I pull out the boot cover and snap it in place.

Erin pulls on her scarf over her hair and ties it under her chin. "So where do you want to move?"

"I don't know. I just made up my mind to sell, moments ago."

"You're gonna be busy with the movie for awhile. You want me to help you look around?"

"You know, that's a good idea, Erin. Would you?"

"Of course, silly. That way I'll know where to find you."

I get in the front seat and reach up under the dash for my backup keys in a tin. I start up the engine and the carbs fire up, sucking in air. I look at Erin.

"Would you consider moving in with me?"

"You mean, in your house?"

"No, in my boat?"

"Boat?"

"Yes, my house."

"We'll see."

"Good. No pressure, think about it, though."

I put the Corsa in gear and hit the gas. Off we go, hitting the gate remote and into the California sunlight. I take my sunglasses down from the visor and put them on. Erin puts her glasses on, and tightens up her scarf to keep her shoulder length dark brown hair from blinding us both in the wind. We be too hip to fly.

"On to new adventures." I look back in my review mirror as I pull up the street and stop for traffic. Standing there are Michael and Roger, pointing down to the bottom of the gate.

"What's the matter?"

"Nothing. I was just thinking, we'll have to get a pool and take that old furniture with us. It's the one thing I want to keep."

"Why?"

"Memories."

I slam on the Corsa's breaks, suddenly realizing what they were both trying to tell me.

"Jozeph!"

"I forgot Bubba."Bubba scampers up the ramp just before the gate catches his tail, pissed and scared as all hell. I open the door and he jumps on my lap, "I'm driving, Dogman!"Overhead Caw lets out a yell and drops a load of bird poo, splat, just missing the hood, and off we go. "LA and beyond."

I look at Erin as I hang a right onto Mystery Avenue. She turns to me, the sun perfectly illuminating her face, key lighting her happy smile. There's a word that describes the content I'm feeling about what I found without even knowing I was looking for it?

I believe it's called serendipity.

The End

Jozeph Picasso's Alien Trilogy Filmmaking Adventures.

Stay tuned for

ALIEN
DEFECTS

Super Human Powers

Act One
of the next

Jozeph Picasso's Alien Trilogy

Filmmaking Adventures!

ABOUT THE AUTHOR

To invent a life worth writing about, I stuck my thumb out at 19 to explore America and beyond. It's been quite an adventure since and I'm still writing the crest to wherever it's taking me. There are many things I would've done differently if I'd known better. Rides I would've taken advantage of, roads I wouldn't have taken. But I am the writer I am today because I did what I had to do to survive. Looking back, I'm lucky to be alive many times over, and I've witnessed and held in my hands strangers and loved ones who didn't make it on the way. I'm grateful I had the freedom to meet the people I've met, and the nerve to make those choices to create a family while it was happening. I see my life as half full with many goals still to accomplish. And I'm a better man because of the life I've lived thus far. Jozeph Picasso's Alien Adventures are based on those personal stories and though many of the people and adventures in these stories are real and happened to me just as I wrote them, they have been twisted together into a sci-fi tale to fit within these pages. Erin is still with me now as my loving wife, and we have four wonderful children. We are forever beholding for the introduction to each other while taking the Magical Mystery Towers Tour together.

Karl J. Niemiec